just my luck

just my luck

escape to new zealand book five

ROSALIND JAMES

ISBN-10: 0988761947
ISBN-13: 9780988761940

author's note

The Hurricanes, Blues, and All Blacks are actual rugby teams, and there is at least one climbing gym in Wellington, which would not be nearly as successful as it is if its management and practices resembled those of the gym in this book in any way. This is a work of fiction. Names, characters, places, and incidents are products of the author's imagination or are used fictitiously and are not to be construed as real. Any resemblance to actual events or persons, living or dead, is entirely coincidental.

table of contents

new zealand map

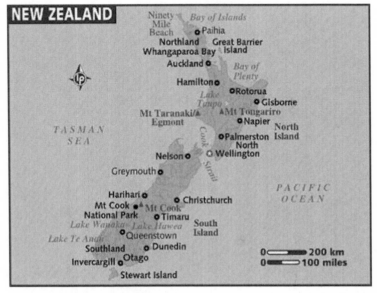

NOTE: A New Zealand glossary appears at the end of this book.

fear and loathing
in the climbing gym

♡

Nate Torrance knew he was going to fall that day. He just didn't realize how far he'd go.

He reminded himself desperately that he was wearing a safety harness. That the harness was clipped into a rope, that the man on the other end was his most trusted friend, and that he, unlike Nate, actually knew what he was doing. But none of those messages seemed to be reaching Nate's sweating hands.

Now he understood the reason for the bags of chalk many of the other climbers in the gym wore clipped to the back of their harnesses. Too bad he didn't have one. He made the mistake of looking down, and actually felt his arms tremble. He was a good fifteen meters up, with another five or so to go to reach the top. And he didn't think he was going to make it.

"Another foothold for your right foot, just up and to the right."

He heard the voice coming from beside him, looked across in surprise. And there she was, the reason he was up here hanging on so hard it hurt, like a baby monkey clutching its mother's fur. The girl who'd got him into this mess. Her slim, graceful body leaning back a bit in her own harness, dark almond-shaped eyes showing concern, the wide mouth smiling encouragingly. *Encouragingly.* At *him.*

"Just move your foot," she suggested again. "Don't make your arms do all the work."

Nate told his foot to move, but it refused to obey. In fact, he realized with disgust, he was frozen to this wall, terrified at the thought of the endless space beneath him. All because he'd seen a pretty girl and had had to follow her.

"Lean back in your harness like I am," she instructed now. "Take a rest. The rope will hold you, and your friend will too. You can't fall."

He obeyed the instruction, only because his hands were desperately slippery with sweat by now, his fingers cramping in their unaccustomed position, gripping the ridiculously tiny knobs.

"That's good," she said as he put all his weight on his harness. The relief was immense, and he had to force himself not to sigh with it.

"I'll stay with you," she said. "If you're ready to go down, or if you want to try climbing again."

"I'm good," he said brusquely. "You go on."

She glanced at him in surprise, then something in her expression shifted. She shrugged, grabbed for a handhold, and resumed her swarm up the wall like a...like a cat. If cats climbed walls. Her sleek, dark brown ponytail swayed against the crossed straps of her deep yellow tank top, and her bum looked every bit as choice framed by that harness as it had when he'd first seen it. When he'd followed it up this bloody thing like some kind of hormone-crazed teenager.

"Try something easier first," Mako had cautioned. But oh, no, Nate thought bitterly. He hadn't listened. Mako had been coming to the climbing gym for a month or so now, ever since they'd come back from the World Cup. Had kept talking about his lessons, until Nate had become curious to see what all the fuss was about.

"Mental fitness," Mako had called it when Nate had expressed his surprise. Climbing didn't seem like an obvious choice for his best mate. Mako didn't exactly possess the lean, streamlined body type that predominated in the gym. Not so much of a race-car, Mako. More of a tank.

But when Nate had seen the two women preparing to tackle the toughest-looking wall in the place, the sport had become a whole lot more attractive.

"That climb's dead hard," Mako had cautioned again as Nate clipped into the rope at the base. "I've only done it a couple times myself, and you've only just finished with the training ones. Try something easier first, mate."

"She's doing it," Nate had argued, jerking his chin toward the rope fixed next to them, where the brunette had already begun her graceful, startlingly rapid ascent, belayed by a truly spectacular blonde who hadn't looked at them, her eyes glued to her climbing partner, her hands moving steadily to keep the rope taut.

"She's good, though," Mako had attempted to explain. "Right," he'd sighed in resignation at Nate's scowl, clipping into the rope himself. "Belay on."

Now, Nate got the point. This was a lot harder than it looked. He glanced down at Mako again, still patiently holding the rope, his broad brown face upturned, and could read the concern there.

"All right?" Mako called, his voice booming in order to be heard in the cavernous space. "Coming down?"

"Nah," Nate answered. "Climbing."

The brunette was already being lowered down as he progressed on with grim determination. Her slim legs were out-stretched, the toes of her climbing shoes bouncing lightly off the wall as she passed him on her descent. She glanced across at him, and he tried to feel less like a sullen fool as he pinched his fingers around tiny protrusions, wedged his toes against bits of rock that were surely much too small to hold his weight. But she didn't say anything, which was good. Because Nate knew that he would only have snapped at her again.

"I'm actually driving men away now," Ally told Kristen wryly. She clipped into the top rope with a few quick motions so her friend could attempt the challenging climb, then looked across the gym to watch the two men leaving. "I knew I was out of practice, but this is ridiculous."

"What happened?" Kristen asked. "I'm always so nervous about belaying you right, especially on something that high, I didn't realize what was going on."

"He froze. Tried something too hard for him, got scared. And he's one of those guys who can't handle screwing up, or a woman making a suggestion."

"He was brave, though, to try this climb," Kristen said.

"Or just trying to impress you," Ally said with a smile, determined not to let one encounter with a jerk ruin her day. Too bad. He'd been pretty attractive until he'd opened his mouth and spoiled it. Not handsome, maybe, but he was working the tough, intense thing for all it was worth. And that was one terrific body he had there, muscular and hard. Not overly tall, six foot or so, but wow, was he fit.

He'd tried to pull himself up by his arms, that was all. Like so many men, he was used to being able to rely on his upper-body strength, and hadn't followed through with his legs enough. And when you coupled sweaty, nervous hands with the strain of all your body weight hanging from your fingertips, a mind could get out of control fast. She'd seen it often enough.

"I'm not the one he was looking at," Kristen protested. "That was you, all the way."

"Really?" Ally couldn't help feeling a little cheered by that, until she remembered his scowl when she'd tried to help him. "He must not have seen you, then. That's a first. Put that one on your calendar."

"Don't say it like you're jealous," Kristen said. "It isn't really that much of a compliment."

"Right," Ally said dubiously. "Having guys walk into doors and fall down stairs because they're looking at you isn't a compliment."

"They don't want to know me," Kristen explained. "They don't think, gee, I'd sure like to talk to her, she looks so smart and interesting, like they probably do with you. They just want to have sex with me."

She finished clipping in, looked up at the wall assessingly. "I'm not sure I can make it all the way up this one," she said, reaching back for her chalk bag and rubbing her hands together. "But I'll give it a shot."

Ally smiled at her encouragingly. "As soon as you've had enough, just let me know and I'll lower you down," she promised.

"Right." Kristen took another deep breath, let it out with a *whoosh*. "Face the fear," she muttered. "The only failure is the failure to try."

She grabbed for a handhold and readied herself. "OK," she said with determination. "Climbing."

sharing a beer with nate

♡

"I'm not wearing anything with a bondage collar," Ally protested that evening, handing the sandals back to Kristen. "Including shoes."

Kristen sighed. "They do not have bondage collars. Ankle straps are in."

"Don't you have anything that doesn't say, "Tie me up and spank me?" Ally complained.

"You just don't get fashion," Kristen argued.

"I get this," Ally said. "I'm pretty sure I get the influence there."

She watched as Kristen set the brown leather sandals, with their thick buckled ankle straps ("bondage collars," Ally muttered under her breath) gently back into their spot in her neatly organized closet.

Ally looked at the lineup appraisingly, pulled out a pair of pointed-toe pumps with heels that weren't as stratospherically high or as precariously thin as the rest of Kristen's collection. "How about these? I can't believe your most conservative shoes are red, but these would work, right?"

"Perfect with your jeans," Kristen confirmed. "Well, not as perfect as the ones I picked for you, but pretty good." She flipped expertly through her hangers of color-coded clothing, came up with a short-sleeved, finely woven ivory sweater with an asymmetrical hem and a wide neckline designed to slip off one shoulder.

"This'll be good with the flowered jeans and those shoes," she decided. "Keep it simple, since you have all that going on with the color and print. And since the jeans are so skinny, you want a little more drape on top."

"I'll take your word for it," Ally said. "Good thing I had the jeans, since pants are the one thing I can't borrow from you. Are you sure I can't just wear my own shoes, though?"

"No." As always, Kristen sounded much more sure of herself when she talked about fashion. "You cannot wear your ugly, boring, *flat* shoes to a party. You're as bad as my sister."

"Who doesn't seem to have done so badly for herself," Ally pointed out. "Something worked for her, and it's still working, judging by the way Drew looks at her. And I haven't seen her in a pair of do-me-now shoes yet."

"Hannah's…I don't know. Extra-lucky. Extra-good at making her life work out. And it's not about attracting men," Kristen explained patiently. "I'm not trying to do that either, remember? It's about looking your best, so you feel confident."

"All right," Ally grumbled. "I'm confident. But I'm not sure I want to go to a party with a bunch of rugby players."

"It won't only be rugby players, Hannah said," Kristen reminded her. "There'll be women there, too. And we both need to meet some people. Having Hannah and Drew in Wellington to introduce us to everyone is our perfect opportunity. Unless you *want* to sit in our flat with me, night after night. We could get a bunch of cats, I guess, and watch game shows on TV. Or we could go to this party, meet some people, and who knows? Maybe even have fun."

♡

It started out well enough. Ally was glad that she and Kristen didn't have to show up alone, or even navigate their own way through the winding, steep streets of Kelburn, the glamorous inner suburb that bordered the sprawling green space of the Wellington Botanic Garden. Ally had a good sense of direction, but she wasn't familiar enough yet with the city to feel confident getting around. She was just as happy that Drew was driving, and that, as always, he seemed to know exactly what he was doing.

She and Kristen had stayed with Kristen's sister and brother-in-law during their first few nights in New Zealand, before driving down the North Island from Auckland to Wellington to start their new lives, and Ally had to admit that Drew was nothing like her preconceived notion of a star athlete in one of the roughest sports going. The retired captain of the All Blacks might be the best-known—and undeniably the most popular—person in the country, but there was no celebrity attitude there. Pretty quiet and unassuming, in fact. If big. She shifted her feet again. There wasn't that much room for them, not with his seat pushed all the way back. Which was why long-legged Kristen was sitting behind her sister.

"Kristen told me you'd found a job, Ally," Hannah said now, turning around in her seat to smile at her. "That didn't take too long."

Hannah's dress was simple, Ally had already noticed, her heels decidedly low. Nothing like Kristen's flirty, deep purple— Oh, whoops, amethyst, Kristen had corrected her—lace skirt and top, accented by a funky black metal-studded belt and stiletto-heeled ankle boots. Ally would have been more comfortable if she'd left her dress choices up to the older sister. At least her feet would have been.

"I got it sorted out within a week or so," Ally agreed. "Which was good, because my savings won't last long. I'm not scheduled for too many hours yet, but I'm supposed to start for real on

Monday, though things won't really heat up till after the New Year, they said. I was afraid I was going to have to work in a café all year, but turns out they were glad to have a woman at the climbing gym. They don't have any now, and women tend to like female instructors better, find them less intimidating when they're learning. Although male clients can sometimes be a different story."

"The boys don't like you to know more than they do, eh," Drew put in with amusement, negotiating another tight corner.

"No," Ally answered with a secret grin at Kristen. "Some of them can be downright rude about it."

"I'll have to come down and have a go while we're here," Drew decided. "I don't mind being instructed by a woman. Maybe I can get you to do it with me," he suggested to Hannah. "I'm sure the three of you girls could outclass me pretty thoroughly. Good for me to struggle a bit, I'm sure."

"You never struggle at all," Hannah said fondly.

"I've struggled heaps," he protested, reaching out to give her hand a quick squeeze. "Struggled to get you, didn't I. And it was well worth it."

He pulled into a parking space on a street overlooking the lights of the Harbour below. "Bit of a climb up the hill here to the house," he told the women. "Hope everyone's shoes are OK with that."

"Who is this person whose party we're going to?" Ally asked as she slammed the car door. "This Toro guy? I guess with a name like that, he's a rugby player. Good thing, because carrying groceries up here must be a major challenge."

"The new All Black captain," Hannah explained. "Captain of the Hurricanes too, Wellington's Super 15 team. You'll be hearing more about them pretty soon, once the season starts. It's been an extra-long offseason, since they played the World Cup in October. Are they training already, Drew?"

"Preseason training for most of the boys will have started already," Drew said. "Mid-December now. But the All Blacks don't have to turn up to their teams till the first of February this year, though some of them'll start sooner. So, yeh. Long break. Gives them time to take a real holiday, let all the niggles settle, get fired up to go again."

"It must feel strange not going back," Kristen put in. She still sounded a little shy with her brother-in-law, Ally thought, even after all these years.

"It does, a bit," Drew admitted. "I keep having to remind myself that I'm not doing this anymore. It's all good, but it's a bit odd. I won't be turning up at many of these things. Need to back off, let the new skipper take the reins. And the spotlight. He's welcome to that. But as we're down here, I thought it'd be a chance to have a chat with a few of the boys, introduce you two around."

That had been Hannah's idea, Ally suspected. The visit to Wellington, and the party tonight too. Making sure her beloved sister was settled, even if it meant leaving their two-year-old with his grandparents up north for the week.

She felt another flutter of nerves as they made it to the top of the steep walkway, went through a gate and up a flight of steps to the front door of the brightly lit house.

It's this or the cats and game shows, she reminded herself, taking a deep breath and putting on her Party Face.

Which was wiped clean away as soon as they walked through the door and she recognized the man coming forward through the chatting knots of people to greet them, shaking Drew's hand and giving Hannah a kiss on the cheek as Ally and Kristen stood behind the pair. The jerk from the climbing gym.

She saw the moment when he recognized her in his turn, the blink of surprise, the expression of discomfort almost immediately replaced by a polite smile. "Kristen and Ally," Hannah said, turning to them, "this is Nate Torrance. Nate's the Hurricanes captain, and even though this is a hard thing for me to say," she added with a laugh, "he's the captain of the All Blacks too. How does that sound, Nate? Pretty good, I'll bet."

"Pretty good," he admitted with a sheepish grin. "Bit intimidating, following a legend like you-know-who. Got some big boots to fill."

"You're all right," Drew said confidently. "They wouldn't have chosen you if they hadn't thought you were the right man for the job. It'll be your team in no time."

"You'll be getting a knighthood soon, I hear," Nate said, obviously turning the conversation. "Figured it'd be happening, of course, but congrats on that."

This time Drew was the one who looked sheepish, merely muttering a quick "Cheers" in response.

"You're kidding," Kristen said. "You're going to be a knight? Sir Drew? Sir Andrew, I guess. What does that make you, Hannah? And why didn't you *tell* me?"

"A Lady," Hannah said with a happy smile. "Lady Callahan. Doesn't it sound funny? Not that anybody will ever call me that. And, oh," she realized. "Sorry. I got all carried away with my elevation to the...whatever it is. Well, Drew's elevation, and my being along for the ride. But let me finish my introduction. Nate, this is my sister Kristen Montgomery, and her friend Allison Villiers."

"Ally," Allison said, putting out her hand to shake Nate's, unable to keep the mischievous smile off her face. "So your nickname's Toro, I guess. The bull. Hmm. And we've already met."

"We have," he said, looking embarrassed. "Today," he explained to Drew and Hannah. "Mako took me to the climbing gym to show me what it was all about, and I met...I had a... er...I had an encounter with Ally here."

"That sounds like a story," Drew said. "Let me guess. You have a problem with women instructing you."

Nate looked thoroughly discomfited now, Ally saw. "Never mind," she told him with another smile. "I'm sure you're much better at playing rugby than you are at climbing."

"I'd better be, hadn't I," he said, clearly rallying his forces. "Because I was rubbish."

"Most people wouldn't even have tried that climb," she said more seriously, deciding to let him off the hook. "It takes some getting used to, trusting your harness and your climbing partner."

He nodded briefly, and she realized with another inward sigh that he felt patronized. He obviously had to be the best at everything. Oh, well. There had to be fifty people here. Surely there was somebody amongst them who would actually want to talk to her.

But to her surprise, Nate stayed with her when Drew and Hannah were inevitably swept up in the crowd of guests, Kristen moving with them.

"I wanted to tell you," he said determinedly, "thanks for trying to put me right on the climb today. I was in a bit over my head. I didn't realize it'd feel so...high. Used to having my feet on the ground."

"It's different," she agreed, warming to him a little. "That's one of the few instinctual behaviors babies are born with, actually. The grasping reflex, where they grab hold. It comes from our distant ancestors hanging onto their mothers as infants, being afraid to fall. So you could say that fear of falling is ingrained. Which automatically makes climbing scarier than other things."

"Sounds like you've told people that more than once. Reassuring the timid. And I didn't know that. I don't know much about babies' instinctual behaviors."

"Yeah, except for the suckling reflex, grasping is supposed to be the strongest," she assured him.

"Well, I do know a bit about that one," he said with a smile. "If it means what I think it means."

Oh, great. She'd barely met the guy, she still wasn't sure she liked him, and he already thought she was talking dirty. This was so not the signal she wanted to send him.

He cleared his throat at her silence. "Can I get you something to drink?"

"Please," she said with relief.

"Beer? Wine? Something fizzy?"

"Beer would be great."

He turned to leave her, and Ally took the opportunity to look around. The house might be traditional in style, but the décor was most definitely modern, much like Drew and Hannah's fairly dazzling Auckland home. She was beginning to realize that New Zealanders favored up-to-date styles. Maybe because it was such a young country, but she was still surprised. If she'd thought about New Zealand at all before coming down here with Kristen, she'd considered it a backwater, a quiet, traditional place. Instead, Wellington seemed almost resolutely trendy. And this house was no exception, with its stark white walls, the leather and glass furnishings relieved by the warmth of the polished hardwood floors, the huge wooden beams across the ceiling. A lot of house for one person, and she hadn't heard any mention of a partner.

She wandered further into the spacious lounge, seeing Kristen still standing near Drew and Hannah, in the middle of several men who must have been rugby players, from the look of them. She moved closer, feeling self-conscious standing on her own, and caught the eye of the man who'd been with Nate at the gym, just entering the room now. That one *had* to be a rugby player. Not overly tall either, but almost square with muscle. He smiled in recognition, moved to approach her as Nate reappeared with a couple glasses of beer.

"Nate!" A young blonde on heels even higher than Kristen's whirled at the sight of him, pink lips stretching in a delighted smile, eyes avid. She rushed forward, and Nate turned to greet her. The blonde reached up to kiss him, and he turned his body to avoid spilling the beer just as his friend was arriving at Ally's side.

Ally watched the glass in Nate's right hand making contact with his friend's swinging arm, the beer flying from the glass, as if it were happening in slow motion. Saw the golden arc landing in a sudden, drenching shower across the front of her thin sweater, and a moment later, felt it too.

She gasped at the shock of the cold liquid, looked down at herself, and immediately wished she hadn't. And that she hadn't worn the nearly transparent bra. She'd always scorned any kind of padding. She might not be huge on top, but she thought her breasts were kind of...cute. Well, they were sure putting themselves on display now as the frigid beer soaked through the layers of clothes and reached her skin.

She stared at Nate, and saw him staring back. And not at her face.

The girl was babbling an apology, and Nate was handing both glasses to his friend, who was shaking his head and trying to hide a smile.

"Sorry," Nate said. "Let me..." He reached his hand out as if, Ally thought wildly, he was going to wipe her off. Yeah, that was happening.

He pulled his hand back again, looking completely rattled. "A towel," he decided. "A tea towel. I'll get you one."

"Never mind," she said, fighting the urge to giggle at the ridiculousness of it. "Just tell me where the bathroom is, and I'll go dry myself off."

She doubted she'd find a hairdryer, alas. She was fairly sure this guy was single. And no matter what she did, she was going to spend the rest of this party smelling like a brewery.

anxiety attacks

♡

"Good one, mate," Liam congratulated Nate as Ally took herself off and the blonde retreated in confusion. "Talk about your bull in a china shop. Here." He handed his friend both glasses again. "You could probably use these." He watched as Nate set them down and wiped his wet hand absently on his slacks.

"Geez," Nate sighed. "Could I have mucked that up any more?"

"Maybe if you hadn't stared at her tits as well," Liam said helpfully.

Nate groaned. "Go on. Rub it in."

"She doesn't seem impressed with your smooth technique so far," Liam said. "Maybe try spilling food on her next."

He was still chuckling as he turned away. Toro might be his skipper and his best mate, but no question, he took things much too seriously these days. It was good for him to get shaken up a bit. And Liam had a feeling that girl had started the job already. If Toro wasn't careful, she was going to turn him right around. Chew him up and spit him out.

He stopped thinking about his friend, though, when he saw the other one. The blonde he'd stood next to at the gym this afternoon. The one who had barely noticed him beside her, so fiercely had she been concentrating on belaying her friend, on getting it right.

He'd thought she was gorgeous then, without any makeup, her golden hair pulled into a high ponytail, her tall showgirl figure rocking the simple T-shirt and climbing pants, not to mention the harness. Yeh. The harness. And now, in those lace clothes that made him think immediately of lingerie, the high heels making her endless legs appear even longer, the waves of golden hair falling around her face, down her back, she was nothing short of spectacular. The skirt was long enough, at least it would have been on somebody without all that leg. And nothing was all that tight. It was just...her.

But something was wrong, he realized. She stood a couple meters away, facing him, several of Liam's Hurricanes teammates surrounding her, doing their best to chat her up. It couldn't have been a new situation for her, somebody who looked like that. She had a glass in her hand, a smile on the beautiful lips. But the smile was frozen, and the sapphire-blue eyes had a desperate look to them that he recognized. She was doing her best to maintain, but for some reason, she was overwhelmed.

♥

Kristen tried to overcome the feelings of panic. *Breathe through it,* she told herself desperately. *Ride the wave.* But nothing was working. She felt trapped, and she was going under.

She'd tried to find some women to talk to, but somehow had never been able to join the group, hovering at the edge until she'd given up. She wasn't sure where Ally was, and Hannah and Drew were in the midst of a group of people in the far corner of the room. So here she was, standing in a group of men, all too big, too tall, too avid, while the familiar coils twisted in her belly, rose through her body.

She started at a touch on her arm. It was the man from the gym, she realized. The one who'd stood next to her, belaying his friend while she had been doing the same for Ally. She'd noticed him because he hadn't tried to talk to her. He'd just smiled at her, and she'd thought at the time that he had the kindest eyes she'd ever seen. Now those eyes held a look of concern, and the smile was missing.

"All right?" he asked her quietly, his deep voice still audible over the hum of voices, the pulsing background music.

"I'm…" She started to say she was fine, changed her mind as the anxiety spiraled higher. "Is there a quiet place?"

"Yeh. Come with me."

She cast an automatic smile around the group, then followed the solid, thick figure leading the way. He stepped through the lounge doorway into a passage, and she worried for a moment that he'd misinterpreted her question. But he was walking into a big, modern kitchen now, where he stopped at the breakfast bar and turned to her.

"Sit down," he told her. "Glass of water?"

"Please," she said, her breath still feeling too shallow. She hopped up onto a stool and hooked her high heels over a rung, pressed her hands between her knees for warmth.

He nodded, turned to a cupboard, seeming to know his way around perfectly, pulled out a couple glasses and filled them from a bottle in the fridge, handed one to her.

"Cheers," he said, a smile lightening the effect of the much-broken nose, the misshapen ears and close-cropped, wavy black hair over a neck that was so thick, it was almost a continuation of the head above. Then he looked at her more closely.

"Breathe," he told her, taking the glass back from her and setting it on the bar again. "Deep breaths."

Tears came to her eyes as she obeyed.

"You need a paper bag?" he asked. "Hyperventilating?"

She shook her head wordlessly.

"Cup your hands over your mouth," he directed, demonstrating for her. "Deep breaths, in and out." He kept his intent gaze on her, his scrutiny oddly comforting, as she followed his instructions.

"Thanks," she said shakily when she was feeling more herself again. She reached for the glass of water, took a drink. "How did you know?"

"Anxiety attack, eh," he answered. "I know the look of it."

"Did you know somebody who had them?" she asked, wanting to hear him talk some more, the rumble of his voice soothing the remaining jitters.

"Yeh. Me."

"*You?*"

"I guess you know by now that anxiety doesn't discriminate," he said, taking a seat on the stool one over from hers. Not getting too close, not crowding her. "Or that how you look on the outside isn't always how you're feeling on the inside."

"You're right," she said, still shivering a little with nerves. "I should know that. I'm sorry."

He got up again, opened a door leading to a back porch, came back with a flannel shirt that he draped over her shoulders without touching her, before going back to sit on his stool. "There. Warm up a bit."

She pulled the heavy thing around her gratefully. "Thanks. I'll be all right in a minute. I thought this was going to be fine. I thought it might be fun. A chance to get back out into the world a little." She felt herself choking up again, blinked the tears back. "But I don't really want to be back out there after all, I guess," she said, hating how forlorn she sounded.

"Bad breakup?"

"Divorce," she sighed. "It's been final about four months. That's why I'm here. A change."

"The New World," he agreed. "The *new* New World."

"That's right. New job, new name…Well, the old name back. New me."

"I don't know the new name," he said. "But I'd like to. I'm Liam Mahaka."

"Ma…Sorry. I didn't quite get it."

"Mahaka," he repeated, putting the accent strongly on the first syllable, the second one almost disappearing.

"Kristen Montgomery," she said. "And I'd better let you get back to your party, and get back myself before Hannah gets worried and comes looking for me."

"Hannah," he said slowly, speculation dawning in the brown eyes.

"My sister."

"Then you have nothing whatever to worry about out there," he told her with a rueful grin. "I'm going to take a guess here that those boys don't know yet that you're Hannah's sister. Do I take it you're not interested? That you didn't come here tonight looking for…love?"

"Not love, not an imitation either," she sighed. "I was thinking, maybe meet some people, start making some friends. Women too, I hoped. But I don't know. That's always hard. I haven't found any friends here yet, not at my job either. I'm sure glad I have Ally. And I'm sorry." She brought herself up short with a little laugh. "Why am I telling you all this?"

He ignored the question, focused on what she'd revealed. "Because you intimidate them," he guessed. "Because they make assumptions about the kind of person you are."

"How do you know so much?" she wondered. "I wouldn't think…"

"That I'd care about people, because of how I look," he finished for her with a gentle smile completely at odds with his appearance. "See how easy it is to do?"

She laughed, feeling a whole lot more cheerful than when she'd come in here. "Guilty." She slid to her feet, took off the flannel shirt with regret and handed it back to him. "And thanks. I'm going to go back out there again now, and soldier on."

chance encounters

♡

" I need to stop going for coffee," Ally said the following Friday afternoon. "It's just way too tempting a habit."

She was sitting across from Kristen at one of the little triangular tables of Espressoholic, the explosion of funky art and color around them a perfect backdrop, she thought, for Kristen in her simple work outfit of cream silk shirt and fawn trousers. Kristen was always so accessorized, too. Belt, bag, earrings, the works, all looking like she'd just happened to throw them on and they just happened to look perfect. Whereas Ally felt like she was doing well if her socks matched. She sneaked a peek down beneath her climbing pants. Yep. Match. Score.

"I'd be happy to pay for you next time," Kristen assured her. "I needed some company tonight. I wish you didn't have to work. We could have gone out. Or even," she said with a little smile, "found another party to go to. Since the last one was so successful."

Ally groaned. "Skulking around in a wet sweater until Hannah realized what was up and insisted on our leaving early. I couldn't have done a much better job of spoiling the party for all of us. Yeah, that worked. Anyway, you can't spend money on me. You can't afford that either."

Kristen had got little enough, Ally knew, after the divorce, considering her ex-husband's wealth. Had walked away without very much more than the wardrobe her rat bastard ex had bought to show off his trophy wife. Before he'd found a new trophy.

"And yeah, split shifts are the worst," she said, changing the subject, knowing Kristen didn't want to talk about money. Or the past. She took another sip of the large trim flat white that was going to get her through until nine, and then however long it took to close. "At least there'll be an evening crowd. It's always easier when it's busy, although it won't be as busy as it should be. I wish Mac's outlook wasn't quite so blokey. He doesn't realize what he's got there. A climbing gym should be a meat market on Friday night. A *healthy* meat market," she added at Kristen's startled look.

"Maybe you could suggest some things," her friend offered.

"After two weeks...I don't think that would go over too well," Ally said wryly. "Probably not ever."

"You have such good ideas, though," Kristen said loyally. "It's too bad you're not running things."

"Yeah," Ally sighed. "But nobody's clamoring to put me in charge."

She glanced over as a young man leaned across from the next table. She'd noticed him as soon as she and Kristen had sat down. Dark, straight hair in a carelessly tousled style that had probably taken some effort to achieve, a startlingly handsome face over an open-necked white shirt and stylish slim-cut gray suit, he was the male equivalent of Kristen. Now, he spoke to them for the first time.

"Sorry," he said. "Horribly rude of me to eavesdrop, I know. But do you work at Mac's climbing gym, by any chance?"

"I do," Ally said cautiously.

He smiled with satisfaction, revealing noticeably long canine teeth. Ooh, a vampire. And that's exactly what he looked like. Suave and dark, a bit like a young George Clooney.

"I just had the most brilliant idea," he said. "They don't come along that often, so I have to grab them when I can. I'm a publicist for the Heat—the Wellington netball team," he explained at her blank look. "And I was thinking, maybe there's some way we can get the girls filmed doing some climbing. What d'you think?"

"I think it's a great idea," Ally said at once. "Climbing always looks so impressive, even the easiest walls, if you're not used to seeing people doing it. And it would be a great team-building activity, because you're literally supporting your partner."

"Good point. And, of course, they'd look dead sexy doing it," he said with another of those wolfish smiles. "Men would watch that, I know. But what about women? As a woman, what would be your reaction if you saw a segment like that on TV?"

"I'd like it," Ally said. "It's a really empowering image for women. Overcoming obstacles. But I've been a climber for a long time, so I'm probably not the best judge. What do you think, Kristen?"

"I'd like it too," Kristen decided. "It's…powerful, like you say, but fun too. And I'm just a beginner, so I'm not prejudiced like Ally here."

"Think your boss would be keen, if there were publicity for the gym in it for him?" the man asked Ally.

"Absolutely," Ally said, her excitement growing. "Not just appealing to women, but showing men what women look like when they're climbing. Fitness and sex appeal, like you said. It'd be a great marketing idea." This would be the perfect way to get her ideas across without seeming pushy. If she brought Mac this opportunity, dropped it into his lap.

The man nodded his dark head in satisfaction, his smile reaching the bright blue eyes. "Let me work on the idea a bit, run it by the team," he decided. "I'd like to pick your brain as well, if I could."

He pulled out his wallet, extracted a white business card and handed it to Ally. "Devon O'Neill," he said unnecessarily. "If you'll give me your name and mobile number, we could talk some more, coordinate our approach so it works for both of us."

Ally gave both to him, then introduced Kristen. To her gratification, Devon remained focused on her even after the introduction to her more beautiful friend. Maybe she actually had something that appealed to New Zealand men, Ally thought in surprise. First Nate, and now this guy. Although Devon was a long way more appealing.

And just like that, here Nate was, she realized with disgust. She just didn't seem to be able to escape him. Walking behind his friend Liam into the café with a wary, closed expression that was at odds with Liam's broad smile, all for Kristen. Who looked cautiously pleased herself to see him again. Unusual, for Kristen.

"What luck finding you in here," Liam told Kristen after a brief hello to Ally. "I've been at the gym three times this week, missed you every time."

"I'm working," Kristen began to explain. But Ally had stopped listening, her attention caught by the silent drama playing out in front of her.

Devon had turned at the approach of the other men, and Ally had seen the moment when his eyes met Nate's. The mutual recognition, the instant antagonism on Nate's face, the way his hands tightened, Devon staring back at him defiantly until Nate turned around and walked out.

Liam glanced in surprise at his friend's retreating back, then said hurriedly to Kristen, "You'll be there tomorrow, then? Could you use a climbing partner?"

"Yes," she said, her cheeks faintly tinted with what looked like pleasure. "Ally's going to be working, so I could definitely use a partner."

"Ten? Meet you there?"

"OK," she agreed. "See you then."

Liam nodded again, said a quick goodbye, and hurried out. Ally could see Nate standing across the street, hands shoved into the pockets of his jeans. His quick shake of the head at Liam before he strode away, the other man caught off guard again, having to hustle to keep up.

Ally looked at Devon with speculation.

"You noticed, eh," he said. "We don't like each other much."

"That was obvious," she admitted. "And I'm curious, but not too surprised. He's not my favorite person either."

"Really." That had *him* looking surprised. "That's not the general opinion."

Ally thought about her two disastrous Nate-encounters. "I guess I'm a maverick, then. Because he sure hasn't impressed me. And I have to get to work." She pushed her chair back to stand.

"I'll walk you," Devon suggested, standing up in his turn.

"I'd like that." It was flattering to have such a good-looking guy interested. Unless it really *was* just the work angle, but she didn't think so.

"So. Not the best of friends with Nate?" she asked as they set out for the waterfront amidst the crowds of young people on the busy pedestrian mall that was Cuba Street, already starting their Friday evening revels.

"Not exactly," Devon said. "Although we were good mates once. Flatted together at Uni, in fact."

"Really. I didn't realize rugby players went to University."

"He did, anyway. Right here in Wellington."

She was longing to ask him what had happened. Looked the question at him, and was gratified when he obliged.

"Yeh," he said. "Best of mates, like I said. Then he got important, and he was too busy for me. He knew how much I wanted to do sport publicity, and you've probably realized that rugby is the ultimate Kiwi sport. You're American?"

"Canadian. And yes, I've noticed."

"Well, he could've had a word in someone's ear, anytime these past five or six years," Devon said. "Specially after he was made captain, selected for the All Blacks. But he can't be bothered."

"It seemed like more than that, though," she said hesitatingly.

"Because I asked him for the favor, a few years back, and he flat refused. He doesn't do favors unless he's dead sure it's in his interest, that he'll be getting something back. Too ambitious for that. We had a few words about it at the time, got a bit heated, I'm afraid. I said some things I probably shouldn't've, knowing how self-important he can be. Not too clever of me at all, considering how much pull he had in En Zed sport, not to mention how much more he has now. Never been good at hiding my true feelings, I'm afraid. I tried to make it up later, but he's had a down on me ever since. So, now…" He shrugged. "Now, it's what you see. Oh, well, can't be helped. I've done all right without him, haven't I. Making my way up on my own merits, which means more anyway, doesn't it?"

"It does," she said. "I hadn't realized he was quite that arrogant. But I can't say I'm entirely surprised."

They'd reached the gym now, its imposing height rising above the pedestrian pavement that lined the wharf. "Thanks for walking me," Ally said.

"That's all right." He smiled back easily, and she thought again how very handsome he was. "I'll ring you tomorrow, shall I? And maybe we can go for a drink, talk over that project."

"Sounds good." She went in to start her evening shift buoyed by the prospect. It wasn't going to be the cats and game shows after all, not this weekend. Wellington was looking better and better.

♡

To Ally's surprise, though, Kristen wasn't entirely convinced by Devon's denunciation of Nate when they discussed it late Saturday night.

"I don't know," Kristen said, sipping her herbal tea at one end of the couch, her long legs in the striped leggings she wore as pajama bottoms curled beneath her. "You only have Devon's word for what happened. Are you sure Nate's as bad as that?"

"He hasn't exactly been impressive," Ally said.

"No," Kristen agreed with a smile. "He hasn't. But he hasn't been...bad. And they're careful, you know, who they choose for the All Blacks captaincy. It's not just about being a good player, or even a good leader. It's kind of like being an ambassador. And Liam says..." Ally could see the color rising again as Kristen resumed. "He says he doesn't think that's the reason for the bad blood."

"Did Nate give him some other reason?" Ally pressed.

"Well, no," Kristen admitted. "I don't think so. But Liam's so kind, I can't believe he'd have a good friend who was...the way Devon says."

"Of course he thinks the best of his friend," Ally said impatiently. Honestly, Kristen could be so naïve at times. It was like she still didn't want to believe there were bad people in the world, even with all the evidence she'd collected to the contrary. "But I believed Devon. Why would he lie to me?"

Kristen shrugged. "I don't know. Your date was good, then? You liked him?"

"Lots of fun. That is, I guess it was a date. We *did* start out talking about the netball team thing, and I think it could really work. But then we just talked, and he was so interested. Not how men usually are, you know, at least in my experience. How often does a man really listen to you? It was great. And you know," she said thoughtfully, "that was the first date with a new person

I've been on in years, and it was so much fun. I wouldn't have thought that could be true."

Her first date since her senior year of college. Not that you could call most of the hanging out she'd done in college "dating." There hadn't been much dating with Brian either, come to think of it. Mostly climbing together, backpacking, going out for Thai noodles when they could afford it. Being poor together, which had been fine with her. But no romantic gestures. She'd never thought she'd needed them.

Brian had sure never looked like that in his clothes, so elegant and yet so casual. He'd been a whole lot more likely to wear Vibram Five Fingers toe shoes that had Ally cringing in embarrassment than an open-necked shirt under a slim, European-cut suit. He'd never looked at her meaningfully across a glass of wine in an elegant restaurant, had never touched her hand lightly, smiled at her like that, leaving her tingling, wondering what he was thinking. Wanting more, and then ending the evening with a quick kiss, another smile. And no mention of whether she would see him again, whether it was more than just business. Leaving her off-balance, which was actually kind of fun, too, in a bizarre way. Exciting. New.

"But how was the climbing today?" she asked guiltily. She hadn't even asked Kristen, had been too wrapped up in her own affairs, too excited by the prospects. *All* the prospects. "You'd left by the time I got to work."

"It was good," Kristen said. "He's so *nice*. And when he's holding the rope...It's like I know he'll never, ever let me fall."

"Well, thanks very much," Ally said tartly.

"Oh, I don't mean you'd drop me," Kristen hurried to say.

"Did you guys go out afterwards?"

"Just for a quick coffee." Kristen actually sounded happy about that. "I was nervous that he'd ask for more of a date, and I'd have to tell him no. But he didn't even ask. He just said he'd really enjoyed climbing with me, and did I want to go again after the New Year, as he's leaving town for the holiday in a few days just like we are. And when I said yes, he gave me his email and phone number, and asked me to let him know whenever I needed a belay partner. He said he'd probably only need a half hour's notice, and he could be at the gym whenever I was ready."

"So he asked you to ask him out. And that was a bonus?"

"Guys always ask me out," Kristen said simply. "Nobody's ever let me make the move like that. Now I get to choose, even if I want to climb with him. And I do."

tea with a hooker

♡

"Is that all right with you, Ally?" Hannah asked again. "To have company on our outing?"

"What?" Ally looked up from her cozy spot, her back against the wall, legs stretched out on the padded window seat, and put down the hiking guidebook she'd been studying.

She and Kristen had spent Christmas in Auckland with Hannah and Drew, and she'd been persuaded—without too much difficulty, despite feeling like a bit of an interloper—to come with them on their beach holiday until after the New Year as well. Mac's gym, like most Wellington businesses, was closed throughout the holiday period, so it wasn't as if she were giving up hours. And there were worse things than staying in a gorgeous beach house along a beautiful stretch of coastline in the height of a New Zealand summer, doing some of her favorite things.

"Sorry," she told Hannah now. "I wasn't paying attention. What did you ask me?"

"Are you still good with going kayaking if Nate and Liam come with us?" Hannah repeated. "Or would you rather stay home and go another time? Because I'm not sure Nate's your favorite person, but he and Liam are up here too for a few days, and Drew's invited them to go out with us today."

"Didn't realize you really didn't like him, or I wouldn't have done it," Drew apologized. "And..." He rubbed his nose and looked a bit embarrassed. "I forgot, Hannah, we lent the single kayak out. So we only have four spots. Should've thought of that sooner, I know."

"I'll stay home, then," Hannah said at once. "You go on, take Ally and the boys out. Probably better anyway. That way you guys can make a real day of it, since I'm not up to that much."

Drew smiled. "Whatever it is we do to get this sorted, it's not going to be that. Tell you what, we'll both stay home, send Kristen and Ally out with the fellas. You can look after them, Ally," he said with a grin at her. "Keep them out of trouble, eh."

"Of course you should both go," Ally said hastily. "I'll stay here. I don't mind a bit."

She'd been looking forward to kayaking, she thought with a pang of disappointment. She hadn't had much chance to do it in recent years, not since the college summers she'd spent working at the kayaking company in Santa Cruz. Now it was just another expensive hobby she couldn't afford anymore.

But Hannah and Drew had been putting her up for a week now. Babysitting for a few hours was the least she could do. And going kayaking with Nate? She needed more time with him like a hole in her head.

But when it came down to it, that was exactly what she got.

"If it's all the same to you," Liam said when they were all sitting on the deck listening to Drew's plan for the day, "I'll stay here, give Kristen a hand minding Jack. I'm not too keen on kayaking anyway, tell you the truth. Terrible thing for a Maori to admit, but I get seasick. I'm better with babies than boats."

The way Kristen's face had lit up when the men had pulled into the driveway and she'd seen Liam emerge had been too obvious for Ally to make any further objection. She knew how wary

Kristen was about men, but Liam seemed to have made it past her barriers.

"Cheers," Drew said. "That makes it easy. Though it's not going to be too challenging today. We'll be keeping it pretty short and simple." He reached an arm out to pull his wife gently against his side on the wooden porch swing. "Have to keep Hannah's stomach happy."

"We're expecting another baby," Hannah told the men, a faint blush rising to her cheeks. "We're not announcing yet, because it's still early, so don't say anything, if you don't mind."

"No worries," Liam said with a smile. "That's great news. Congrats."

"Benefits of retirement," Drew said. "I'll get to be here for this one. Change a few more nappies, eh."

"You'd better plan to change all of them, if you're going to make up for all the ones you've missed," Hannah teased. "I notice you didn't retire until I got Jack toilet-trained. Very sneaky. And you'll be here for all my morning sickness, too. Sure you don't want to rethink the retirement?"

Drew laughed. "I'm sure. I'm ready to put in the hard yards."

Nate glanced at Ally where she had swung herself up to perch on the railing. "I can see you over there, imagining yourself being capsized. No worries. I'll stay a safe distance away from you, keep you out of danger."

"Well, no, you won't, mate," Drew said. "It's a double. Which means you'll be in the back doing the steering, because even though Ally did eat a fair bit of pavlova at Christmas," he said with a wink at her, "I think you're still heavier. See if you can keep from killing her, will you? We'd have a hell of a time covering that up."

Ally had to laugh at that. "Thank goodness for life jackets. And I did not eat that much pavlova."

"Oi. I have kayaked a bit," Nate protested. "I kayak almost as well as I climb."

"Oh, boy. Maybe I should just assume the worst and wear my swimsuit," Ally decided.

"Maybe you should," Nate said.

She saw the way he looked at her, and got a little thrill despite herself. He wanted to see her in her swimsuit? Well, maybe he should wear his, too. She didn't have to like him to enjoy looking at him. Because he was so worth looking at, in a T-shirt, shorts, and jandals today, the Kiwi summer uniform. He wasn't as tall or as heavily built as Drew, but he had an awful lot of chest, shoulder, and arm going on, was working that light-gray T-shirt pretty hard. Those were some powerful legs too, she thought, sneaking a quick peek. She'd never thought much about men's thighs before, but wow, did he ever have some.

And his face. The short light-brown hair over the rough-cut planes of forehead, cheekbone, and chin, the square jaw stubbled with a couple days' growth of beard. The nearly ice-blue eyes, the way they had of focusing so intensely on whatever he was looking at. Whatever he was interested in.

No, not exactly good-looking, she thought again, but all man. So, yeah, she had to admit it. She'd like to see him in his trunks.

♡

Kristen watched as Drew hefted the solid form of his two-year-old son into his arms. "Mind you listen to your Auntie Kristen, now," he told Jack. "Do what she says." He held the boy for Hannah to kiss as well, then set him down again. "Right, then. If everyone's ready, we'll be off."

"I fixed Jack a lunchbox, in the fridge." Hannah turned back on her way to the car. "He likes eating from his box. And there's plenty for you and Liam too. Quiche, sandwich stuff. Or you could fix a salad. Help yourself to anything."

"I think they've got it, sweetheart," Drew said. "I'm guessing Kristen's been making her own lunch for a good couple years now. And Mako definitely knows his way around the inside of a fridge."

"Go on," Kristen urged, laughing. "Have a good time." She picked Jack up herself, loving the weight of him in her arms, and saw Hannah cast a last anxious glance back before Drew shut the door of the ute behind her.

Liam chuckled beside her as she and the boy waved goodbye. "Not sure who she's looking out for more, you or Jack."

"I know," Kristen sighed, setting the little boy on his feet again and seeing him squat down immediately to play with his trucks. Jack was always busy. "It's kind of nice to come stay with her and be taken care of, even though I can't let her do it too long, or I find myself backsliding."

Liam looked at her, but didn't say anything.

"Auntie Kristen," Jack said, looking up from his truck. "Want to go to the beach."

"Please," Kristen reminded him.

"Pease." Jack looked up at her with a frown of determination. "Want to go to the beach *pease.*"

"Looks just like his dad when he does that," Liam said.

"Doesn't he?" Kristen agreed. "And the resemblance doesn't stop there."

"Do it *myself,*" they heard more than once as they gathered up towels and toys, got Jack ready for the short walk. Which wasn't quite as short as intended, since Jack insisted on walking rather than being carried by her or Liam.

Kristen watched with surprise as Liam helped the little boy build a sand castle, took him paddling at the edge of the gentle sea. She was used to seeing Drew with his son, so it wasn't that she didn't think rugby players could be kind, or good with children. But Jack wasn't anything to Liam, was he?

She sat on a towel in the sand and watched the unlikely pair. Liam hadn't taken off his T-shirt, to her relief. She could tell he was heavily built and powerful, she didn't need to be reminded of it. And she wasn't about to wear her own swimsuit in front of him, either.

He kept his attention focused on the little boy, though, and she found herself relaxing to an extent that surprised her. He even gave Jack a bath to wash off the sand while she fixed lunch, then did the washing-up while she put her nephew down for his nap.

"I'm going to have a cup of tea," she announced, coming back into the sunny kitchen where Liam stood looking out the French doors onto the deck and the sea beyond. "And drink it out on the deck," she decided. "Would you like one? But you'd probably prefer a beer. There are some different kinds in here, looks like." She opened the door of the fridge and peered inside. "Mac's Black, Monteith's Original."

"Tea's good," he said. "I don't drink."

"Not at all?" she asked, then recollected herself. "Sorry. I always thought beer and rugby went together."

"Three years sober," he said, but didn't elaborate, just turned to lean against the edge of the kitchen bench, watching her make the tea.

They carried their cups out onto the deck that wrapped around three sides of the house, settled into two comfortable wooden chairs that overlooked the patch of level green lawn with its edging of native bush, dropping to the golden crescent of sand, the placid blue sea.

"So," he said after a pause. "You've been having a holiday, eh, letting Hannah take care of you a bit. Because you're on your own there in Welly."

"I am. Well, alone except for Ally. And the new job's pretty challenging, so it's been nice to have the break. Thank goodness everything shuts down like this."

"Do you do modeling? Is that it?"

"No, though people always assume that. Kind of like when you're a really tall man, and people assume you play basketball."

"Well, tall and looking the way you do," he said with a little smile. "You look more like a model than a basketball player, I have to say. *Are* you a basketball player? Have I got it all wrong?"

She laughed. He was so easy to talk to. Why was that? "No. Of course not. I'm a clothing buyer for Lambert & Heath. The department store, you know?"

"Course. Sounds glamorous, specially at a flash place like that. D'you go around to fashion shows, then? See all the beautiful people?"

She smiled again. "Not too much. More like looking at spreadsheets. Not that glamorous at all. I spend most of the day sitting in a cubicle. But it's serious," she said, hoping he understood. "It's moving up."

"I see that. It's important to make progress, eh. Specially when you're climbing back up out of that hole."

"Exactly," she said with relief. "You get it."

"I ought to. Spent a fair bit of time down in that hole myself. Good to have family around while you're starting over, too. I'm a bit surprised you didn't move to Auckland, though."

She wanted to ask what he meant, but she didn't really know him yet, did she? How did you say, 'So, tell me about your alcohol problem?' You didn't.

"I needed to stand on my own feet, do it myself," she said instead. "Just like Jack," she added with a smile of remembrance.

He nodded, took another sip of tea, not pressing any further.

"You know," she told him, "I realize I don't even know what position you play." And that was unusual. Normally, men talked to her about themselves. Boy, did they ever. Nobody had ever thought *she* might be fascinating.

"You didn't—" he began, then cut himself off.

"I didn't what?"

He gave a little laugh. "I was going to say, you didn't check me out online. Makes me sound like I have a big head, eh."

"People usually do," she guessed. "Because of the rugby thing. Sorry. It's not that I don't think you're interesting." She stopped, then. She didn't want him to think she was interested. "I mean…"

"No worries. I'm a hooker."

"What?"

He chuckled. "Nah, not that kind. Don't think I'd get too far with that. It's a position. A rugby forward."

"Like Drew. He's a forward," she said with relief. She'd had an interesting mental image for a minute there.

"Right. Doing the hard yards up front, and down in the dark places. The hooker's in the center of the front row in the scrum, so he can hook the ball with his foot, send it to the back for the halfback to pick up. Well, for *Nate* to pick up, in my case. But anyway. Bit of bashing going on up there, how I got all these trophies." He touched his ear and nose lightly. "Nothing flash about it. A worker bee."

"Well, some flash in being a professional rugby player, not to mention an All Black," she pointed out. "I do know that much, without looking anything up. I'm Drew's sister-in-law, you know, and I do realize that that's why you two are friends, because you've played together. For quite a long time, right? How long?"

"When was I first selected, you mean? Four seasons ago, when I was twenty-three. But not consistently on the squad, not until the last couple years. Had some ups and downs."

She wasn't really listening, though. "You're twenty-seven," she said slowly.

"Yeh, I am. What, I seem older? I know it. It can be a bit aging, footy."

She shook her head. So she was older than he was. What did it matter? It wasn't like they were going out. "Never mind." She looked at his cup, empty now. "You want another one?"

"Nah. I'm good." He was looking at her, his gaze steady on her face, and she suddenly felt awkward again.

"Thanks for helping me with Jack today," she said, trying to make some kind of conversation.

"I think you know why I volunteered for that," he said with a smile that extended all the way to his eyes. His best feature, she thought, large and liquid, the irises a beautiful dark brown against the clear whites. Maori eyes.

"Though I wasn't lying," he added. "I really do get seasick."

"I should tell you." She was going to take the bull by the horns for once. She was trying to be honest these days, and he'd been so nice, she owed it to him. "I'm not dating right now. It's not you," she hurried on as he continued to look at her calmly. "I was divorced recently, like I said, and it was pretty ugly. So I'm taking a break."

"How long were you married?"

"Two years. Not too good, which is my track record anyway. I thought I had my issues worked out, but turns out I blew it again, so I'm abstaining until I'm sure I can do better. I've taken a vow of celibacy, in fact, for the time being," she said with a nervous laugh. And that had all come out much too fast. She took a couple deep breaths, trying to calm herself down, rubbed her hands up and down against her thighs, saw him watch her do it. Boy, this was hard.

"Because you think the failure of your marriage was your fault," he said after a moment.

"Well, not that so much. It's hard for a marriage to succeed when one person's cheating, and has decided he doesn't really like the other person anyway." Since she was baring her soul here, she might as well go all the way. "But marrying him was my...not my fault, maybe, but my bad judgment. Before I get involved with anyone again, I want to make sure my judgment is a whole lot better."

"Right. You don't need a lover just now. Message received and understood."

"That's it," she said with relief. "I don't. And I don't want to lead you on. Besides, I'm three years older than you."

She stopped in confusion. Why had she told him that? Because she was attracted to him, she realized with some surprise, even though he was nothing like the relatively handsome, slim man she'd married, or all the cute guys she'd dated in a romantic career that had begun well before she was fifteen. His harsh looks, the bulk and strength of him, instead of putting her off, made her want to move into his arms, feel them wrap around her, hold her close. Hold her safe.

But it wouldn't be safe, she reminded herself. It would be just the opposite. If she looked for her safety in yet another man, how had she learned anything at all?

He nodded. "Fair enough. But could you use a climbing partner, and a friend?"

"A friend," she repeated slowly. "You want to be my friend? And that's all?"

"I won't lie," he said. "I try not to do that anymore. I want to be your lover. But I accept that that may never happen. And whether it does or not, I'd like—I'd really like—to be your friend."

thrills and honesty

♡

Hannah looked back at the house as they pulled out of the driveway, waving to Jack, who was waving hard back at her from Kristen's arms.

"Are you sure?" she asked Drew. "That Liam's...OK? To stay with them?"

Drew glanced at her with amusement. "I'd trust Mako with my life. Or, more importantly, my son's life. Most reliable bloke I know, eh, Toro."

"He is," Nate agreed from the back seat. "Nobody better."

"But didn't he have some trouble in the past?" Hannah persisted.

"He did," Drew said. "And got himself sorted, too."

Ally glanced across at Nate, but he was silent. Whatever the story was, she wasn't going to get it from him.

♡

"How are you finding Wellington so far?" Nate asked when they were out on the water. He'd managed to launch them from the beach with a shove, and even climb in again behind her without any mishaps. Ally was actually a little sorry. She'd been half-anticipating going over, and enjoying the prospect of teasing him about it. He definitely needed it.

"I love it," she said, keeping up a steady stroke and feeling the calm that always came over her when she was surrounded by sea and sky, enjoying the effort, the rhythmic motion. She was going to be out here with him for a while, so she might as well keep this pleasant. She didn't even have to look at him, after all. You couldn't really turn around in a double kayak without tipping the thing, which was probably for the best in this case. "I've been wandering around getting happily lost, and finding my way home again. It's a lively place, isn't it? Lots of outdoor stuff to do too, which is my favorite thing."

"It can get a bit wet and windy," he cautioned.

"I've heard," she said, unable to keep the amusement from her voice. "I've had a few discussions about the weather already, you see."

She heard him groan. "I'm rubbish at chatting girls up," he admitted, surprising a laugh from her. "I never know what to say. Everything's either dull, or it sounds like a pickup line. I generally end up opting for dull."

"Honesty works, though," she told him. "That was pretty good right there."

"Really." He sounded surprised. "I should throw myself on your mercy, you think?"

"Definitely. A strong man being endearingly awkward…I like it. It's an approach, anyway."

"Better than spilling a beer on her, I reckon."

"Much better." She realized that she was paddling along with a smile on her face. Why hadn't she met *this* guy before? She liked *him*.

"I'll try again, then," he said. "Did you spend Christmas here as well, on the Coromandel?"

"No, in Auckland. And it rained one day, but otherwise the weather was good. Just to anticipate you."

He laughed. "Do anything special?"

"I did, actually. I bungy jumped off the Sky Tower. Kristen's Christmas present."

"Damn. This is me shuddering back here."

"No, really?" she asked in surprise. "It was amazing. You should try it."

"I'll take your word for it," he decided.

"You don't like thrills?"

"I love thrills. Know how to get them, too. And it's not by jumping off buildings."

Wow. She didn't think she'd pursue that one. Maybe he meant rugby. Yeah, right. He hadn't meant rugby.

They were silent for a few minutes. Ally could tell from the speed of their progress that Nate was, in fact, paddling strongly in sync with her. So he actually did know how to kayak. And he hadn't felt the need to let her know that, which impressed her even more. He was steering them into a bit of chop now, around the big rock that stood well offshore and into an area of churning waves on the back side.

"The Washing Machine, they call this," he told her as they went through it, to her delight. "I thought you'd want to experience it."

"You were right. I love waves. This is fun." Drew and Hannah were staying well out of the chop, she noticed. Drew keeping Hannah's stomach happy, of course.

"I've got a question for you," Ally said as they left the area behind, headed further up the coastline. "My own conversational topic. Those nicknames you guys have. You always call Liam 'Mako,' don't you?"

"Yeh. Rugby nicknames. We like nicknaming things anyway in En Zed, and with rugby, it's a bit of a tradition. A bonding thing, I guess."

"All right. So what's Mako mean? Isn't it a fish?"

"Yeh. It's a play on his surname, of course, Mahaka. But mako's Maori for a type of shark. Fastest shark there is. Aggressive, too. Hook a mako, and it can jump straight into your boat and fight you. Hard as hell to bring in, no quit in them at all. And that's Mako, too. Takes two or three blokes to bring him down, and he'll be fighting all the way to the end, every time. He's the man you want beside you in the tough spots. He's a warrior."

"He didn't seem like that," Ally said in alarm. "What Hannah said...does he have anger issues? Should I be concerned for Kristen?"

"What I said, that's just on the paddock," he assured her. "It's a rugby nickname, eh. With women...nah. No worries."

"OK," Ally said dubiously. "I guess you'd know. And your nickname is Toro. For Torrance, I figured that out. But if Mako's about the shark, Toro probably *does* have to do with the bull thing, right?"

"So they say."

Oh-kay. That was all she was going to get out of him. Which made her wonder just what that nickname really *was* all about. *Don't go there, Ally.*

"So what's Drew's nickname?" she asked instead, turning her mind hastily from the danger zone. "Everyone seems to just call him 'Drew.'"

"Well, his name's Andrew," Nate pointed out.

"Yes, and your name's probably Nathan. Why isn't he... Callie, or something? Callo. Drewie." A laugh escaped her at the idea.

"You'd never call him that," Nate said immediately. "Specially not Drewie. Geez. I'd like to see somebody try. He's always just been Drew. Because he's one of the boys, but he's...not."

"That thing about him. That stature he's got."

"Yeh. His mana. Greatest All Black ever, you'll hear people say. The best captain, too, and that's saying something. There's never been a man on any of his teams who wouldn't walk through fire for him. Because he'd be walking right in front of them, leading the way."

"So what's that like?" she asked impulsively. "Following somebody like that into the captaincy? Trying to become that person for the team? That kind of leader?"

She heard the silence from behind her, and regretted the question. This was clearly sensitive territory.

"Sorry," she said quickly. "You don't have to answer that."

"Nah, that's OK. You're not the first to ask, believe me. The answer is, I've learnt heaps about what it takes, doing all my playing beside him on the ABs. So for that, it's good. And for the rest…I'll just have to see how I go, hope that I've learnt a bit being the Hurricanes skipper."

Not a very satisfactory answer, but she'd pushed enough, so she closed her mouth on the questions she still wanted to ask, concentrated on the day around her, on keeping her stroke smooth and even through the slight chop.

"And here's my final conversational topic," Nate said after a minute. "How're you going with your own job? Drew said you were working at the gym."

"Pretty good," she said with relief. "Nothing too exciting. I've done this for a long time, and it isn't much different in New Zealand."

"Not too many boofheads rejecting your sound advice?"

"Well, the occasional one," she admitted. He was sounding so human, she decided to test him a little. "I'm working on something pretty exciting right now, actually. A publicity deal with the netball team. When you saw me last, I was just discussing the possibility."

She could almost hear the door slamming shut. "You'll want to be careful there," he said stiffly. "Out for himself, Devon. Not too scrupulous when it comes to getting what he wants."

"Funny. That's pretty much what he said about you."

"About me." He sounded genuinely surprised.

"You haven't been all that helpful to him yourself, have you?"

"No," he said shortly. "I haven't. And I never will be."

Well, that was that. He was such a puzzle. One minute he was so pleasant, even able to laugh at himself, and the next he was cold and stiff again. She didn't understand him at all. Oh, well. She didn't need to, did she?

♡

"How long are you and Kristen staying?" he asked after they'd all gone for a lunch during which he'd shown the pleasant side again, and were back at the bach. Nate had helped Drew clean and store the boats and gear, though Ally had offered to help, of course. And had had her offer rejected, of course. There were advantages to going kayaking with macho guys, she'd decided. And now, Nate had come to join her on the deck while he waited for his friend to return from the walk he was taking with Kristen, their babysitting duties done.

"We're just here a few more days," Ally said. "Although I've been thinking I should give them all some family time. They've been so nice about including me, but you know what they say about guests and fish. After a few days, they start to stink. And I've been with them a whole week already. That's a long time, especially with Hannah pregnant and not feeling well."

Nate laughed. He was sitting forward on the wooden chair, legs apart, elbows on his knees and hands clasped, grinning at her. And looking more attractive than ever, which only confused her more.

"Not so long by Kiwi hospitality standards," he said. "I doubt they're whispering to each other at night that they wish you'd take yourself off. But what did you have planned to keep yourself from stinking?"

"I was thinking about hiking tomorrow, anyway, get myself out of their hair."

"Want some company? I'm here a bit longer myself, and I know a few good tracks."

"Why?"

"*Why?*" He sounded completely flabbergasted, and the grin was gone. "What d'you mean, why?"

"I mean, do you actually like me?" she heard herself asking. "Or is it just that you can't stand to fail? Because I can't decide."

"Geez, you're blunt."

"Well, I haven't dated for years," she tried to explain. "I don't know the rules anymore, if I ever did. So I figure that means I get to make up my own."

"Not for years, eh."

"Nope." She thought about explaining that, abandoned the idea.

"Conversational topic for tomorrow, then?"

"Maybe," she smiled. "If my life history's really of any interest. And if you tell me why you're asking me out."

"Right. You said honesty was good, so I'll have a crack at it. Because I like how you look. A lot. Because you keep surprising me. And because," he said with another grin, "I really, really hate to lose."

"And honesty wins the day," she decided. "All good answers. Sure, I'll go hiking with you. Hiking's pretty safe."

hidden dangers

♡

"Careful here," Nate said the next day. Damn. He hadn't been on this track in a couple years. He hadn't realized how over-grown it had become with gorse. The nasty stuff was everywhere, its bright yellow flowers looking mockingly cheerful in the sun-shine, belying the vicious thorns. "I should've told you to wear long pants."

"It's all right," Ally said. "It's worth it for the view." They were at the edge of the headland now, the coastal vista spreading before them. The indentations of rugged cliffs creating hidden bays, the foaming lines of white surf and endless corrugated blue of the sea beyond.

It *was* fairly nice. He'd got that bit right, anyway. And she actually sounded pleased, to his relief. He couldn't imag-ine another woman who would've got her legs scratched up like this without whingeing. And she wasn't even a Kiwi. Maybe Canadians were tough too, though. He hadn't known enough to tell.

He turned now as he crossed a stile into a paddock, reached for her hand.

"Nate," she sighed, "I appreciate your gentlemanly concern, but you don't have to help me. I can do the uphills, and I can do the downhills, too. I can cross a stile without falling. I'm sorry if you'd like me to be more helpless, but I can't fake it."

"Yeh. Right." He was thoroughly rattled now. He kept forgetting that she was a professional, kept automatically reaching back for her. This wasn't going well at all. He'd thought it'd be a chance to make up some ground. Instead, he was on the back foot once again. Right, then. Conversation. He'd try that.

"This is some more of the honesty thing," he said, embarking on a steep uphill section of track and making a conscious effort not to help her. "Making up your own rules for dating, because you haven't done it in years."

"That's it," she said cheerfully, sounding not in the least winded as she came along behind him. For somebody with such a pretty body, she was in fantastic shape. Or maybe that was why she had such a pretty body.

Geez. He was losing his train of thought again. Back to the topic.

"So why is that? Scare them all away?" She'd teased him enough. He'd try a bit of it on her.

She laughed. OK. Teasing was working. "No. I had somebody. Well, sort of. I've been with the same guy since college. I mean," she corrected herself, "I *had* been. Until I came here."

"You left him to move here with Kristen?" If she was a lesbian, he was going to have to get his signal-reading sorted. And have a chat with Mako. On the other hand, that would be pretty hot. Hmm.

"Well, not exactly." She sounded a bit more serious now. "Kristen was planning to come down here, and she was nervous about it, about being by herself. And I thought, maybe I'll come with her for a few months, get a job, share a place. If you're into adventure sports, you want to come to New Zealand, you probably know that. So I mentioned it to Brian."

"And he didn't like the idea," Nate guessed. OK, then. Not a lesbian. He was startled by the depth of his relief. Even though he still thought it would've been hot.

"No. That wasn't it. He said it sounded fun, and I should go ahead."

"And that was bad?" He was completely confused now. "It was a test, and he didn't know it, cocked it up? Poor bugger."

"You think? Say it's you. You've been with a woman for six years."

"Six years?"

"Yep. Six big, long years, ever since college—sorry, University. So you've been with her all that time. Living with her for years. And she says, I think I'll go live in a new country without you. What's your reaction?"

"Am I meant to be in love with this woman?"

"Well, hopefully, if you've been with her that long."

"Then the answer is, over my dead body," he said immediately. "I mean," he pulled himself up short, "I'm not a Neanderthal. If she had to do a work thing, something like that, that's one thing. But she just wants to go off someplace new? I'd be thinking she was breaking up with me. That she was going to be meeting somebody else."

"You'd be jealous," she said. "You'd be upset."

"Too right I'd be jealous. Like I said, I hate to lose. Course, I can't quite imagine being with somebody for six years anyway. Not without being married, or engaged, or something."

"I guess I assumed that would happen," she admitted. "That we were moving toward something. But it didn't, just stayed the same. And when we had that conversation, the way it went, I realized it was never going to change. That he didn't want any more than what we had, at least not with me. I was just a...convenience. Who wants to be that? So that was pretty much that. We didn't go out with a bang. Definitely a whimper. Not even a dramatic breakup scene. And it hasn't been too bad, being on my own. Different, but not too bad. So I guess I wasn't all that invested either, was I?"

"A bit hard being alone at Christmas."

"Yeah," she admitted. "Not alone, but not with my own family. Or Brian. But most times when I miss him, I think I just miss how much easier it is being part of a couple. And having that central person in your life, that person who knows you. Which isn't exactly the same as being passionately in love, is it?"

"Do you want to be passionately in love, then?"

"Well, yeah. Don't you?"

"Don't think about it much. Too focused on the footy."

"Does one rule out the other?" She sounded startled, and he realized he'd let his honesty run away with him.

"No, wait," he said in confusion. "I didn't mean I *wouldn't*. I just mean I *haven't*." He could almost see his chance slipping away, even from up here. He turned to look at her, and the expression on her face confirmed it. "Oh, bugger. I'm making a hash of it again, aren't I?"

"I don't think either of us is doing too well," she decided. "Telling you about my old boyfriend is pretty much Dating Mistake Number One, I do know that. I'm starting over on the dating thing with no skills, as you see."

"I wouldn't say *no* skills," he protested, starting to walk again, realizing that he had a goofy smile on his face. Geez, she amused him.

"Really? I have skills?" she asked, sounding ridiculously pleased.

"Well," he conceded, "you're not much on the flattery, and your style's a bit unorthodox. But you look good. That's a fairly important skill."

"Look pretty, and shut up. Gotcha," she said gloomily.

He laughed. "Nah. I've decided I like the honesty thing too. Women usually...perform for me. It can be a bit exhausting."

"Perform? Like a stripper pole?"

He smiled again. "Nobody's tried that. That one might actually work. But you know, being a sportsman and all, they...turn it on."

"Being the new captain of the All Blacks," she guessed. "Bet that helps."

"Yeh. But that's not me, is it? It's just what I do. So even though you aren't always flattering, at least you're...real."

"Oh, I'm real all right. OK. Your turn. Tell me something fascinating about yourself."

"You already know it. I'm a rugby player. That's about all I've got, fascination-wise."

"And it usually works, I'll bet."

"Well, yeh. Usually."

"But you went to University too. I know that," she pressed. "So what did you study?"

"Law."

"*Law?*"

"What did you think? Physical education? Basket weaving? Yeh. Law. I'm a rugby player, and I'm a lawyer as well." He knew he sounded a bit defensive, but geez.

"You're a *lawyer?*"

He sighed. "There've been All Blacks who're doctors, lawyers, engineers. All the professions. You do have to have a reasonable brain to do this job at a high level, you know. It isn't easy, and it isn't all physical."

"OK. Sorry," she said hastily. "Reassessing here."

And here they were, at the end of the track. "Careful," he said, putting an arm out across the path, the brush hiding the edge of the hole. No matter how independent she wanted to be, he wasn't going to let her fall in. "Fatal drop if you step too far."

"Oh!" She stood back hastily. "What is it?"

"It's a blowhole. Wait a sec."

Within a minute, he felt the ground shake. Heard the rumble, the *boom,* and felt the spray coming up out of the deep chasm below them. He'd judged the tide right, then.

She laughed. "Wow! It really is! And no guardrail, either. Has anyone ever actually fallen in?"

"Don't think so. Not too many people up here anyway, from the looks of that gorse. And you get the idea pretty quickly round here that you'd better look where you're going. Not too many guardrails in En Zed, other than the big tourist spots."

They stood a few more minutes, watching the spray, feeling the power, the force of water hitting rock through their bodies, then turned to retrace their steps.

"You want to lead this time?" he asked. He'd automatically walked in front of her the entire way out here, he realized. Another point lost.

"Sure." She sounded pleased, and he sighed with relief at getting it right. And this was a much better idea anyway. Because now he got to look at her. And she looked so good. Her snug black shorts were...short, and her slim legs looked just as good in them as they had the day before. Although a bit scratched up from the gorse, which still made him wince. But the way they curved out from her trim waist, and over that round little backside...that was something he could look at all day. Maybe he should have put her in the water yesterday after all. He'd like to see her wet again. He'd like to *get* her wet. All that honesty in bed...that would be a novelty. She was flexible, too. He'd seen that when she'd been climbing. He had a sudden vision of pushing those legs up over her head, and had to pull himself back fast. Getting way ahead of himself here.

"What are you thinking about back there?" she asked.

"Uh..." His mind blanked.

She turned on the track to smile at him. A smile that faltered as she looked at him, read something of his thoughts on his face.

He schooled his face quickly into a neutral expression. "Sorry," he said. "Off someplace else for a moment there."

She nodded and turned back, the silence getting a bit awkward. They reached the steep section again, and she headed uphill at a good clip. He watched her climb, tried without success to keep the image of his hands yanking those shorts down, of a bit of athletic outdoor sex—somewhere with less gorse, obviously—from entering his unruly mind, and followed after her.

"Careful," he couldn't keep from saying, just as she stepped on a loose rock that rolled under her left foot, and he saw her start to fall. He lunged, grabbed for her. And pulled her further off balance. She twisted as she tried to regain her footing, her right foot sliding off another slippery rock, and she toppled. He felt the *thunk* as her face made solid contact with his elbow on the way down. She let out a little yelp, fell to her knees, put her hands out to catch herself, not quite quickly enough.

"Ally." He grabbed her, pulled her upright again. "Are you all right?"

"Yeah," she said with a shaky laugh. "After all that telling you I didn't need help." She put a hand to her eye. "Ow."

He helped her up the track to a level spot. "Let me see." He took her face in his hand. "Bloody hell. I've punched you in the eye." The red bruising was already apparent, her eye starting to swell a bit too. He'd thought he couldn't cock things up with her any worse than he already had, and now this.

She looked up at him and started to laugh, then winced at the motion. "Ow. It really hurts. I hope this is a first. That you've never given a woman a black eye before."

"Bloody hell," he said again, feeling horribly responsible. He looked down at her knees, the cut that had opened up on one of them, the bruising from her fall onto the rocks. "Your leg, too." He pulled his water bottle from his pack, bent to squirt the clean water over the spot. "We'll wash a bit of the dirt out of it, anyway. It's not bleeding too badly. Are you OK to walk back?"

"Well, yeah," she said with another laugh. "What are my options? You going to helicopter me out?"

"I could run back for the ute, drive up the farm track. Get closer, anyway."

"No. It's less than an hour, isn't it? I'm fine. I can do that."

Still, by the time they were back at the ute, she was limping pretty badly, and that eye was puffing up even more. He was going to have some interesting questions to answer from Drew, Nate thought suddenly. He knew the other man wasn't his skipper anymore, but he couldn't help thinking of him that way. And punching his houseguest in the face...that probably wasn't on.

"We'll go sit in the café for a bit, get some ice on your face and your knee," he decided as he put the ute in gear and pulled off the verge.

"You don't want to do that," she objected. "You don't want everyone to see me with you like this. They'll take your picture, you know they will. And then there you'll be, sitting with a woman with a black eye. I've spent enough time with Drew and Hannah to know how interesting that'll be to your eager public."

"What? That doesn't matter." He brushed the objection aside. "It's a good twenty-minute drive back to Drew's place. We need to get ice on that straight away, and get a sticking plaster for that knee."

♡

He really hadn't seemed bothered by the obviously raised eyebrows, the not-so-discreet cell phone cameras, when he'd been sitting in the café with her, her injured leg propped on a chair, a bag of ice on her bandaged knee, another bag pressed to her eye. And that had impressed her. It certainly wasn't the worst injury she'd ever suffered. A bit ridiculous, really, that somebody who'd climbed so much would have hurt herself falling on a perfectly easy trail. But no more ridiculous than climbers she knew who'd slipped on the bathroom floor, or banged themselves in the knee with the car door on the way to a climb. When you were climbing, you were paying attention, looking out for the dangers. And when you weren't...Well, she'd been paying attention to Nate, all right. That's how she'd got distracted in the first place. By the look she'd seen on his face when she'd turned around, especially. That look still had her steamed up, two hours and a couple of pretty good bruises later.

She was lying on her bed now, another pair of icepacks having been hauled out of Hannah and Drew's freezer, which, not surprisingly, held a pretty good supply. Hannah had made a comforting fuss over her for somebody who, Ally knew, had seen more than her fair share of bruises, most of them a whole lot more spectacular than her own. Drew, meanwhile, hadn't looked pleased at all, had given Nate a long, frowning look, as if it had been his fault that she'd fallen. Drew was a throwback, no doubt about it.

Her attention was gradually pulled from the book she was reading by the sound of voices outside her window. Nate and Liam, she realized, standing in the driveway. Liam had come by to help Kristen take Jack to the playground and for a picnic lunch while she and Nate had gone on their hike. Giving Drew and Hannah some time, he'd said. But he'd really come to see Kristen, Ally knew. He was going about it the right way, too, allowing Kristen the safety of their pint-sized chaperone, not rushing her or asking too much. Maybe the shark thing really *was* just about rugby.

She didn't mean to eavesdrop. Really, she didn't. But what could you do when people insisted on talking outside your open window? They must not have realized her room was back here.

Everyone else was in the lounge at the other side of the house, she knew.

She started off amused at their conversation. And then it changed to something much less comfortable.

"I'm just saying, be careful," the voice she recognized as Nate's was saying now.

"I wouldn't do anything else," Liam growled. "I need to be careful, don't I. Because she's fragile."

"That's what I mean," Nate said with obvious exasperation. "That's one high-maintenance woman. And an expensive one, too. She's already got one failed marriage behind her, from what I hear. How d'you know she's not over here hoping to bag Number Two? And finding an All Black, first time out of the gate, ready to get soft about her?"

"You're dead wrong about her. And there are two of us over here today," Liam pointed out. "I could say the same to you."

"Yeh, but I'm not the one flirting with career suicide, looking to mess with Drew's sister-in-law," Nate said, keeping his voice low, but not low enough. "And I'm not about to get trapped, either, or get myself off track. I know how to keep them from expecting too much. Look, it's one thing to have a bit on with a pretty girl when you see something you want. Have some fun, no strings attached. That's what *I'm* doing here. But it's another thing entirely to strap that dynamite around your neck and light the fuse."

"We've been mates a long time." That was Liam, the edge in his normally soft voice evident even to Ally. "And I control my temper these days. That's why I'm giving you fair warning. Shut up about Kristen. You're wrong, and you're out of line. And as for you...Well, I'm sorry for you, Toro. That's all I'll say. One of these days, you'll find out what it's like to care about something besides footy. When you do fall, you're going to fall hard. And I reckon it's going to take a lot for you to bounce back."

Silence, then, followed by the sound of car doors slamming, the ute reversing out of the driveway. And Ally, her book forgotten in her hands, doing a complete reassessment of her big day out. And taking a good, hard look at her spectacular lack of judgment, out here in Dating World.

something more special

♡

Nate pulled into Drew's driveway again the next morning, stepped out of the car. His program for the day had begun as planned, with a visit to the gym. But afterwards, he'd found the car seeming to steer itself here. Well, of course he was popping by, checking on Ally after yesterday's disaster.

He didn't have to explain his presence to everyone, he found to his relief. Ally was sitting out on the deck reading a book, an icepack on her knee again, sporting a pretty fair black eye. And looking at him without any enthusiasm at all, to his surprise. Had she decided to blame him after all, then?

"Hi," he said, taking the seat beside her. "Came to see how you were feeling today. Thought you might like to go for a coffee."

"No," she said. "Thank you," she added after a noticeable pause, then turned her attention ostentatiously back to her book.

"Uh…" He scratched at the stubble on his cheek. "I was thinking, you said you wanted to give Drew and Hannah some space. Maybe I could help you do that."

"I don't need your help." She actually looked angry now. "I wouldn't want to *trap* you, after all."

"Huh?" What was she talking about?

"Go on down to the beach, is my advice." She was closing her book at last. And glaring at him. "I'm sure you can find a girl to *perform* for you. And hey, she might already be half-naked. That'll save you some time. You can get right into it, have a bit on, no strings attached."

"Oh, bugger," he breathed. This was all sounding much too familiar.

"Oh, and another word of advice?" she continued, her color high, her breath coming hard now. "Next time you're talking about a potential conquest, not to mention belittling her best friend, maybe make sure she's not *six feet away.* Because it tends to put a little damper on the romance, if you see what I mean."

"Look, I'm sorry," he said, knowing how lame it sounded. "Bloody stupid of me. I didn't mean you to hear that."

"Well, obviously. But I should really be saying thanks, shouldn't I? Because as you know, I'm out of practice. And my dating radar's obviously completely off. I was actually liking you. How stupid is that? I thought you were being honest with me. I thought you *liked* me. I clearly don't know how to recognize somebody who's just out for his own gratification, and doesn't care about anybody else. Even though Devon told me. Even though he warned me about you."

"Devon." He was getting angry himself now. "Yeh, that's a good idea. Take his bloody word for it."

"And why not?" she flashed back at him. "He knows you. He knows how stuck on yourself you are. You think you're a hero, because you're a great big fish in this little tiny pond. But nobody else in this world even *cares.* So go on down to the beach. But make sure you only talk to the New Zealand girls, because nobody else thinks you're special."

He got up, feeling as if he were the one who'd been smashed in the face. "Are you done?"

He saw the sheen of tears in her eyes, the tremble of her mouth. "Yeah," she said, and he could see her losing the battle, the tear that had welled over the lid of the black eye, was making its way down her cheek. And, despite the anger he felt, hated that he'd made her cry. Was disgusted with himself, and didn't know what to do about it. So he just turned on his heel and left her. Got back in the car and drove himself on out of there.

♡

"Was that Nate?" Kristen asked, coming outside.

"Yeah." Ally blinked the tears back, surreptitiously wiped away the one that had escaped. "Come and gone."

"What happened?" Kristen asked.

Ally had shared the story with her the night before. Well, some of it. She hadn't seen any point in passing along what Nate had said about Kristen. That would only hurt her, and Kristen didn't need to be hurt any more.

"I told him I'd heard him," she said shortly.

"Oh, man," Kristen sympathized. "That must have been awkward. And so uncomfortable for him, too. I can't imagine how embarrassing it would be to find out you'd been overheard like that, caught saying something so wrong."

Ally snorted. "I don't think he's suffering. I might've hurt his pride, but he seems to have enough of that to spare. Looks like you and Hannah have the inside track on attracting rugby players who are...worth attracting. I could have got laid, I'm pretty sure. I could have had casual sex with the captain of the All Blacks. Lucky me. But I think I'll hold out for something a little more special."

new opportunities

♡

They said the hair of the dog was the best remedy. If that were true, Ally thought, opening the door to Devon a few days after she and Kristen had returned to Wellington, she should be cured any time now. Being asked out by a handsome, charming guy, after her recent disastrous almost-dating experience, was good. Being asked out by a handsome, charming guy who disliked Nate Torrance as much as she did was *great*.

Devon greeted her with a flashing smile and a quick kiss that did nothing to depress her fizzing spirits.

"You're ready, I see," he said approvingly, casting a glance down her body. Not enough to be sleazy, just enough to make her feel appreciated.

"I am," she agreed with a laugh. She'd been pretty excited when he'd called, at the prospect of having a real, grown-up date. No pretext of consulting about the event this time, he'd simply asked her out for dinner because he liked her, because he wanted to be with her. And wasn't that something?

"I'll have to give it some thought," he'd said when she'd asked how she should dress, where they were going. "Find someplace good enough for you. Someplace special."

Which had given her some pretty good warm fuzzies, but left her still confused about what to wear. After a serious consultation with Kristen, she'd settled on a not-too-short skirt, a not-too-low-cut V-neck sweater with tiny buttons down the front, and some not-too-high heels.

"A little sexy," Kristen had approved when she'd had Ally outfitted to her satisfaction, "but not over the top. Second-date appropriate wherever he takes you, unless it's a bowling alley. And just enough to make him wish he could see more."

"You're the expert," Ally had agreed. And judging by Devon's expression, Kristen had come through again.

Devon held up the plastic bag he was carrying. "Can I interest you girls in a glass of wine before we go out? We've got time."

Ally exchanged a quick glance with Kristen, settled on the couch for the evening.

"I was just going to my room." Kristen uncurled her long legs and stood quickly. "You two go ahead."

"Nah, please stay," Devon urged. "I've hardly had a chance to chat with you yet, and you know what they say. The best friend's important."

Kristen smiled again, sank back down as Ally went for glasses.

"Just sorry it's taken so long," Devon said when the wine was poured, "to see you again, Ally. Hazards of meeting somebody you like in mid-December. Did you have a good holiday, though?"

"You did pretty well," Ally said with a smile. "We've only been back a couple days. And yes, we did. We spent it with Kristen's sister and brother-in-law. The very best part was that they have a great bach on the Coromandel, near Hahei. That was quite the bonus."

"Really," Devon said. "Your sister's married to a Kiwi, is she?" he asked Kristen. "Or did they emigrate?"

"A Kiwi and then some," Ally laughed. "Her sister's married to Drew Callahan."

"Really," Devon said again, taking another sip and sitting back in their single good chair. "That would explain how you know Nasty Nate."

Ally choked on her wine, which made him laugh. "Yeah," she managed to say at last, getting up for a paper towel and laughing at herself in her turn. "And he doesn't improve upon further acquaintance. You were absolutely right about that. We saw *him* over Christmas, too."

"Bet you did," Devon said. "He takes care to cement his friendship with Drew, I'm sure. Quite the ambitious fella, our mate Nate. But I've never heard anything but good things about Drew," he hastened to assure Kristen. "I expect you could tell me, though. You must know him well."

"Pretty well," Kristen said. "As well as you could expect, considering that they've been here all these years, and I've been in the States. But you're right, he's a great guy."

"Pity you aren't able to be closer to your sister, now that you *are* here," he sympathized. "Must be hard, being so far from home, and not even in the same city with what family you do have. D'you get to see much of her? They ever come down here to visit you?" He reached out to refill Kristen's glass, but paused as she hastily put a palm over the top.

"Once," Kristen answered. She smiled briefly at Ally, then stood. "And now I really am going to my room. I've got some homework to do. Have a nice time."

"You were a little standoffish with Devon tonight," Ally said when she was back in the flat again a couple hours later, after a romantic dinner complete with candlelight and wine, some good-night kissing that had been pretty nice, too, had started a lovely little fire inside that was still glowing. "Don't you like him? It's not the first time I've seen your touch-me-not thing, but I was surprised that you used it on him. Did you think he was coming on to you, maybe?"

"No, of course not," Kristen said. "And maybe I'm overly cautious these days. I probably just don't trust that handsome, smooth type anymore."

"You're going for the ugly, awkward ones now?" Ally asked with a smile.

Kristen flushed. "Looks aren't everything," she said, a rare edge to her tone.

"Sorry," Ally said hastily. "Of course they aren't."

"What I care about most these days," Kristen said, "is sincerity. I like people who are open, where I can tell they mean what they say, even if I don't always like what they say. People like you," she added with a smile. "And Devon...he seems perfectly nice. Perfectly friendly and interested. There's nothing exactly wrong with him. He sure never says anything that isn't flattering, does he? That's it, I guess. And if I can't tell, I tend to assume the worst, I suppose. But don't go by me, because I'm probably over-sensitive to that. Listen to your own instincts, what they're telling you."

What Ally's instincts were telling her was that she could really use a flirtation—or more—with an attractive, interested man. And that she couldn't wait to see him again.

She'd assumed she'd hear from him within a day or two. Once again, he'd said, "I'll call you," but nothing more specific than that. She found herself on edge, as excited as a teenager hoping for an invitation to the prom. Checking her mobile too often at work, keeping it near her at home. Well, no wonder. The last experience she'd had with this kind of dating practically *had* been the prom.

Devon was a whole lot better-looking than any boy she'd known in high school, though, and her body was letting her know fairly insistently that she hadn't had sex for months. Some fun times, maybe even a real relationship with a handsome Kiwi, she'd already decided, would be the perfect addition to her year abroad.

She told herself the first day that it was too soon for him to call. That he wouldn't want to seem that eager. And when that day had passed, she told herself that, well, it was still only Thursday. But when Friday came and he still hadn't called, she looped back through their evening together, wondering if she'd misread his signals. Especially when he'd flattered her by asking her opinion of the PR he was doing for the Heat.

"We're just not getting the traction we should," he'd sighed. "The games are televised on Sky Sport, right enough, but we aren't getting the viewership numbers from women *or* men that we'd projected. The time should be right for women's sport, but somehow we aren't quite where we'd like to be. What d'you think? Any bright ideas?"

"I did look the team up online," she admitted, "and saw the news stories and so forth. It could be this is just me, but it seems like a lot of what you've done is more...soft news. Fluffy, you know?"

"Fluffy," he said slowly.

"I'm not being critical," she went on quickly. "Just giving you my impressions."

"No, please," he insisted. "Tell me."

"Well, I didn't see a lot of emphasis on them as athletes," she said. "It all seemed to be almost glamour pieces. And I thought you said that you were trying to get the sport taken more seriously."

"We are," he said immediately.

"Well, first thing I'd say, maybe stop having them play in little dresses," she said with a laugh. "Because that just screams 'girly non-sport,' doesn't it? But you probably can't do anything about that. So maybe show them in the gym, training, taking part in clinics with schoolgirls, things like that. Emphasizing their skills, even their personalities, as long as it's their drive, their athleticism you're talking about. Focusing less on their looks and their personal lives. Because even though netball's so resolutely non-contact," she added, "which, along with those dresses, does make it seem a little girly to me, I can tell they do have skills. But it's almost like you're scared to show that."

Now, she wondered. Had that been too blunt? Nate had commented on that aspect of her personality, after all. Even Kristen had, and Kristen rarely said an unkind word about anybody. Ally knew she was pretty direct by North American standards, and in polite New Zealand, she was beginning to realize, she might well qualify as downright abrasive. Had Devon resented her criticism? He hadn't seemed to at the time, but even though it had seemed like he'd enjoyed himself too, and he'd appeared even more interested than before, the week turned into the weekend without another word, not even a text. So she snatched at her mobile when she saw his name come up on it as she sat eating a late breakfast with Kristen on Saturday.

"Hi," she said happily, seeing Kristen's eyes sharpen on her across the table. Too bad she was working late tonight, Ally thought quickly. She'd have liked to have dinner with him, and that was probably what he was calling to ask about.

To her surprise, though, it wasn't. "I was wondering," he said instead, "if you and Kristen would like to go to the City Market with me tomorrow morning. Do some food shopping, have a look around, a bit of breakfast. It's a nice outing, and I'd love to talk to both of you before the event next week, get any last-minute thoughts."

"Hang on." Ally felt the disappointment rise. Did he really want to go out with Kristen, then? Was he thinking he could somehow switch roommates? Good luck with that. Kristen wouldn't do it even if she liked him. Or maybe Ally actually *had* offended him. No, that couldn't be it, or why would he be asking her out again at all?

She gave up on the speculation, pressed the phone against her chest. "Want to go to breakfast with Devon and me tomorrow?" she asked Kristen. "He's invited both of us."

Kristen was shaking her head vehemently. "You're busy," she hissed. "Say, 'Sorry, I'm busy.'"

"What? I'm not, though," Ally whispered back. "I want to go. Do you?"

Kristen shook her head again. Ally shrugged, put the phone back to her ear. "Kristen's busy," she told Devon. "But I'd love to go."

"Why?" she asked Kristen when she'd hung up after making plans to meet Devon near the Market the following morning.

"He's calling you Saturday, for Sunday morning," Kristen pointed out. "After not calling for days."

"So?"

"So he's telling you you're not important," Kristen insisted. "Giving himself the upper hand, because he knows you've been waiting to hear from him. Now he knows he doesn't have to bother to call in advance, or to hide the fact that you're not the one he's taking out on Saturday night. He's not even coming to pick you up."

"Maybe he's broke, like me," Ally protested. "Maybe breakfast is all he can afford."

"Then why couldn't he have called you a couple days ago to schedule it?"

Ally shrugged. "I don't know. Maybe he's been busy. Or maybe he's more spontaneous, also like me. Anyway, I can't play those kinds of dating games."

"OK," Kristen sighed. "But I have a feeling he can."

♡

"So. Sport," Devon said when the two of them were perched on tall stools in a seating alcove behind the City Market on Sunday, drinking coffee and eating an assortment of delicious items, from tiny dumplings filled with chopped prawns and fresh ginger to an almond croissant from the French Bakery table that had Ally's eyes almost crossing with food lust on her first bite.

"So," she said, smiling back at him and taking another bite of croissant. Oh, yeah. Just as good the second time. "Sport."

He laughed. "You've had a good dose of it, sounds like, since you moved to En Zed. Not only everything you've done, but all the rugby exposure. Most visitors seem to manage to discover, eventually, that Kiwis are keen on rugby, but not many of them spend their Christmas with the captain of the All Blacks."

"Retired captain," Ally pointed out over another sip of her trim flat white. Boy, Wellington had some good coffee, she thought appreciatively. And this was one of the best yet.

"You're able to see, though," Devon persisted, "how much more important rugby is here than any other sport. Oh, people love it when we do well in basketball," he admitted, "or when we send the All Whites to the soccer World Cup, win the sailing and rowing medals at the Olympics, but nothing really compares to rugby."

"I'm gathering that. It must get a little frustrating, trying to drum up interest in something else."

"Exactly! You've got it exactly." He smiled at her with an appreciation, a warmth that made Ally feel just a little bit smarter, a little bit more appealing. "Which is why," he said, "though I'd never presume, I do hope you'll tell me if Drew and Hannah pop down again to visit Kristen."

"How do you know her name?"

"You told me."

"No," she said slowly. "I don't think I did."

He shrugged. "Must have read it somewhere. But, yeh. If they do, I'd love an intro. That'd help. Having Nate so dead set against me—it makes it tough to break in. And now that he's captain, it's even harder. But Drew still has heaps of clout."

"Mana," Ally remembered. "Right?"

"Yeh. You know about that? You keep impressing me, the way you pick up on things. The way you get straight to the essence. That thing you said about athleticism, last time we were out, that we'd focused too much on glamour...that was brilliant. I took that straight back to the office. Made us all think a good bit."

"Really? That's great. I'm glad I could help."

"Yeh. So, much as I hate to ask..." He smiled ruefully. "I'd love the intro, if the chance ever comes up."

She looked down at her coffee cup, rearranged her croissant on its paper napkin, then met his eyes again.

"I'm sorry," she said, "but I don't think I'd be comfortable doing that. Drew gets so much of that, I know. And they've both done a lot for me," she hurried on. "I just can't..."

"No worries." He smiled easily. "I'll get my chance someday, one way or another. Keep working hard, doing my best, and the opportunities will come, I'm dead sure of it."

"I'm sure they will. And I'm sorry I can't help," she said again.

"Nah." He waved her apology away. "Forget it. Now, let's put our heads together about this event. I'm getting quite nervous, tell you the truth. Only a couple days away. Just glad you'll be there to hold my hand."

partners

♡

Kristen jumped a bit when she heard the knock, even though she'd been anticipating it since she'd buzzed Liam in. They'd made this climbing date after their picnic with Jack, and he'd called her a few days ago to confirm. And to ask if she wanted to have lunch afterwards, to which she'd found herself, surprisingly, saying yes. But she'd been thinking Ally would be here when he came by, and Ally was out with Devon.

She ran her hands down her pant legs, because she could tell that her palms were sweating, took a deep breath, let it out, and went to open the door to him.

"Morning," he said, and he didn't look scary at all, just stood there quietly and looked big, and strong, and solid, and…good, like he always did to her. Even the broken nose merely seemed like another badge of strength, an essential part of him. Just like the Maori tattoo that extended down from his T-shirt sleeve to well below his elbow, the intricate whorls and twists a dark pattern against the background of smooth brown skin. She knew it continued up to cover his shoulder, one entire solid slab of pectoral muscle, because she'd checked online. And she'd thought that looked good, too.

He stood patiently where he was, and she realized she'd been standing there like an idiot, staring at him. "Oh. Sorry. Come in. I'm ready to go, I just need my bag." She stepped back so he could enter the living room.

"You look pretty," he said, and she glanced down at the skinny deep-blue pants with their suggestion of a zebra stripe, the drapey silk top tucked loosely into the waistband around which she'd slung a black leather belt with copper accents.

"I know we're climbing," she apologized, picking up her gym bag. He was already in shorts, she saw, would only have to change his jandals for climbing shoes. "But I thought, if we're going to lunch, I'd change at the gym, then change back afterwards, you know, so I could look a little nicer, walking around." She snapped her mouth shut. "Sorry. I'm babbling. I'm a little nervous."

"You're allowed to be nervous, inviting me round and all. Even," he said with a smile, "as a friend. Still a big step. And dressing up's good. I'd be the last to complain about that, wouldn't I, since I'm the one who gets to look at you. But—" He looked down at her feet. "Why are you wearing those shoes?"

She looked at the low-heeled sandals with surprise. "Because...uh..."

"Because if you wore the shoes you'd normally wear, you'd be taller than me," he guessed.

"Well...uh..."

"How about showing me what you would've worn, if I weren't such a stumpy fella?" he suggested.

He smiled in satisfaction when she came back from her bedroom holding the high black suede heels. "Much better," he pronounced.

"But you don't mind?" she asked, sitting on the couch to slip off her sandals and slide her feet into the heels. When she stood up, she topped him by a good half-inch or more, she realized with a flash of worry. "Because I can change back. When you're five-ten, you get used to adjusting your shoes to the...the occasion."

"The minute my masculinity feels threatened," he promised, "I'll let you know. And don't you feel better now?" he asked, taking her bag from her and holding the door as they left the flat, seeming not in the least bothered by their height difference. "Now that you like how you look?"

"I do," she admitted. "But that's shallow of me, I know."

"Why? If I like looking at you too?" He was holding the car door this time.

"So that *is* why you want to be with me," she said as he slid into the driver's seat of the substantial, if unflashy, sedan.

"Nah," he said, turning the key and starting the car, heading down the hill to the CBD. "I want to be with you because I like you. I like how hard you're trying even though you're scared. I like the way you love your family and your friends, how sweet you are with Jack. But I'll admit, the way you look is a pretty good bonus."

♡

At the gym, he waited without complaint for her to change, then took turns climbing and belaying her, and Kristen found herself gradually relaxing.

"You know what the bonus of you is?" she asked him as he stepped down, lightly as always for such a big man, from one of the intermediate climbs.

"Nah, what? That you know you'd have a big target to land on, even if I let you fall?"

She laughed, saw a man belaying nearby turn to check her out at the sound. A man who'd been eyeing her for the last five minutes, until right now, when he caught Liam's eye and turned hastily away again.

"That," she said. "That exact thing."

"What?"

"That nobody bothers me," she said simply. "At least not when you get back down to the bottom again and they see you, they don't."

He laughed himself, a low rumble that seemed to slide right inside her, come to rest there. "Good to know my face has its uses."

"Oh, I don't think it's just your face. I think the rest of you has a little bit to do with it, too. Not to mention that they all know who you are."

"Some advantages to bashing other blokes for a living," he agreed. "Let's get you up on this one, then. I can't promise that I'll be the only one who looks at you up there, but I'll be the only one talking to you down here, if that's what you want."

"That's what I want," she said. "Exactly."

♡

Afterwards, he waited again while she changed out of her climbing gear, then took her to a nearby waterfront café where he insisted on paying for lunch.

"If it's friends," she argued, "I should pay my own way."

"I said you could be taller," he said, sliding his EFTPOS card through the reader. "I never said you could pay."

"You're such a great climbing partner," she said impulsively after their meals had arrived. "I love climbing with Ally, but she's so good."

She stopped, appalled by what she'd said. "I don't mean you're not good," she stammered. "Just…"

He just smiled. "No worries. I don't have to be taller than you, or older than you, or a better climber than you. If I have to be better than you at everything, I'm not much of a man. Long as you let me pay, I'm happy. That one's non-negotiable."

She looked down at her plate, poked at a lettuce leaf with her fork. "I wasn't just trying to let you down easy, you know. I'm really not ready for dating yet. I'm not sure I'm even ready to be friends, if I even knew how to be friends with a man. Climbing was nice, but trying to talk feels hard. Lunch probably wasn't a good idea. I'm not *good* at this anymore. I'm just this…pulpy mess inside. Everything's all so raw. And I can't be…" She looked up at him, felt the tears in her eyes, threatening to fall. "I can't be charming," she said, hearing her voice break a little, and hating it. "I can't be fun. I used to be *fun.*"

He laid a big brown hand over her own where it lay clenched on the tabletop. "I don't need you to be charming," he promised. "I just need you to be you. Not to try to hide how you're feeling from me. Can't you tell that I want to get to know you?"

"I don't see why," she said with the honesty he'd asked for. "When what you've seen so far has been so unimpressive."

"D'you want to know what I see?"

"Do I?"

He laughed gently. "It's all good, no worries. I see a woman who's had some hard knocks, had her faith in herself shaken, who's determined to start over and do things differently. You could've gone to live near Hannah, couldn't you? Bet that would've made your life a lot easier, and that she wanted that. But you came here instead, so you could do it on your own. To a new city where you don't know anyone except your one friend, and a job that's a big challenge for you. You could be trying to show me all that charm right now, too. I'll bet you still know how to do it. Instead, you're being honest with me, and that's a challenge too, I know. That takes real courage."

"I don't feel like I have courage," she said. "I don't feel brave. Exactly the opposite. All this, even talking to you. Even going out with you. It's terrifying."

"That's what being brave is, though," he told her. "Being scared to do something, and doing it anyway. If it were easy, they wouldn't call it courage."

75

"So," he said after a pause, "what d'you think? My face scare you off too much, or are we OK here?"

"We're OK," she decided. "As long as you're all right with this being all there is. I meant what I said about the celibacy thing, and I still have a long way to go. I said a year," she added in another burst of honesty, "and it's only been about five months. And anyway, I'm not *ready*."

"I'll tell you what," he said. "We can be celibate together. You can be my climbing partner, and I'll be your celibacy partner."

"I would never ask that," she said with shock. "That wouldn't be fair to you. It's not my business what you do."

"I'd like it to be your business, though. And I'm not proud to say this, but I've had more meaningless sex in my life than is good for any man. I reckon it's time to hold out for something that's going to matter. For both of us."

"I can't promise," she warned him.

"And neither can I. We'll just spend some time together. Some celibate time. And see how we go."

a bad boy

♡

"It's going well, don't you think?" Devon asked, coming over to stand beside Ally at the training wall.

"Just a second." She stepped forward to speak to the blonde coming down now after her first climb. "Legs out," she called up. "Bounce your feet off the wall, and you won't spin."

She supervised the two women as they unclipped and switched places, watched a minute more as the second woman began to climb.

"Sorry," she said to Devon, keeping her eyes on the climbers. "What were you saying?"

He laughed, an easy sound, and she cast him a quick smile.

"I meant to talk to you about how it was going," he said. "But I can see that this isn't the time and place."

"Probably not. Sorry."

"No worries. We'll have to find another time and place, that's all. How about Friday?"

"How about Friday what?" She decided to tease a little. "You want a climbing lesson?"

"Nah," he said with that flashing smile. "Too hard on the ego. I'd like dinner, though. And maybe a chance to...talk to you. A chance to get to know each other better, because you're someone I really want to know better."

She shot him another quick glance, and the heat she saw in his eyes left no doubt of the exact way he wanted to get to know her. Which was just fine with her.

"I'd like that," she contented herself with saying, trying to stay cool, to channel Kristen a little.

"Collect you at seven-thirty, then?"

"Seven-thirty would be good," she said, then remembered that she was supposed to be closing Friday. Well, she'd get somebody to switch with her, because she wanted to do this.

The thought crossed her mind that she could ask Devon to switch to Saturday instead, but she dismissed it. She wanted to see him sooner. And she wasn't ready to channel Kristen *that* much.

Devon moved a bit closer, put his hand to the back of her neck, under the ponytail, and gave it a brief caress that had all Ally's erogenous zones springing to attention.

"See you then," he murmured in her ear. "Can't wait."

And then he was off to talk to a cameraman, and Ally was watching him go. Until she remembered what she was supposed to be doing, brought her attention back with a jerk.

"That was good," she told the two women hastily. The brunette who'd just done her climb was on the ground again, and both women were unclipping. "You're ready for one of the real climbs now. Come on over and I'll get you started."

"I see you've got to know our Delicious Devon," the brunette said as they walked across the gym. "Lucky you. He's fit, eh, Theresa?"

The blonde sighed. "Yeh. Pretty much defines the word, I'd say. I don't know anyone who's had a go with him, though I've heard rumors."

"Rumors of what?" Ally couldn't resist asking.

"That he can be a bit of a bad boy," the blonde laughed. "And bad can be so good now and then, can't it?"

Ally wouldn't know, because she'd never been with a bad boy. But she was more than ready to find out.

♡

Devon didn't look bad when he showed up on Friday night, though. He looked *good.* The same gray suit, an open-necked shirt, the shiny sable-dark hair a bit mussed. Casual elegance, that was Devon. But all the same, Ally was glad that Kristen was here, and that Liam was with her. The two of them had gone climbing after Kristen had finished work, had come back so Kristen could change before they went to dinner.

"I'm not sure you two know each other," Ally said as Liam stood up from the couch to greet the other man.

Liam nodded at her introduction. "Devon," he said briefly, and Ally heaved an inward sigh. Obviously taking his cue from Nate.

Devon wasn't deterred, though. "Good to meet you," he said. "Been an admirer for some time now, of course. I'm restraining myself from asking for your autograph, because I'm trying to seem a bit sophisticated to Ally here, but it's an effort."

Liam only nodded again. "Ally was just telling me how well the Heat event went. When can we look forward to seeing it on the telly?"

"Next week sometime, I think," Devon said. "If you'll give me an email address, I can let you know for sure. No trouble. I'd be interested to know what you think of it."

"No need for that," Liam said. "Kristen will let me know, I'm sure."

Ally jumped in to fill the pause that ensued. "What did the players think of the event, Devon?"

He didn't seem flustered by Liam's rebuff. "Went down a treat," he said with a smile. "You may see some business out of it. Some of the girls said they'd be back. D'you do lessons, Ally? They were asking."

"I do," she told him, just as Kristen came out of her bedroom, looking beautiful in a simple sleeveless yellow sheath dress that showed off her long, shapely arms and legs. And the bondage shoes, which, Ally had to admit, looked great on her.

Ally watched Devon's reaction, but he passed this test too, greeting her with friendly courtesy, nothing more. Of course, that could have had something to do with Liam's subtle shift of posture, the way he seemed to square off to the other man, his gaze steady on him.

"That's how I met Kristen, in fact," Ally went on, filling yet another conversational gap. "Climbing lessons, right, Kristen?"

"Right," Kristen said. "Ally's a wonderful teacher. She was so patient with me, and believe me, I was a challenge, wasn't I, Ally? Pretty nervous at first."

"But you wanted to learn, eh," Devon said. "And sounds like you did. Good on you."

"Eventually," Kristen said. "Though I'm still nowhere near Ally's level, of course. Luckily, I have a partner to get better with now, and we're pretty well matched, I think." She glanced at Liam with a smile.

"We are." Liam smiled back at her with all the warmth he hadn't shown Devon.

"Well, looks like that climbing partnership worked out pretty well for you and Ally too, Kristen," Devon said. "Brought you all the way across the world together."

"It did," Kristen agreed. "It was a good day for me when I took that first lesson, in more ways than one."

"And it's been good to chat," Liam put in, "but Kristen and I have a booking, so we'll say goodbye."

"I just had a thought," Devon said. "Here we all are—maybe we should just have dinner together, what do you think? We could ring up and get a table for four. Could be fun."

Ally exchanged a glance with Kristen. *What?* She'd thought this was going to be a romantic evening. Now, once again, Devon wanted to include other people?

"Sorry," Liam said. "I'm a bit selfish. Don't want to share Kristen's company, I'm afraid. But you two have a good time."

He put out a big hand for Devon to shake. Ally could see from the expression that appeared momentarily on Devon's face that Liam was squeezing hard, which surprised her. Nate again, she supposed, and felt a flash of anger on Devon's behalf.

"Sorry I suggested that," Devon said when they were seated in the intimate little café on Willis Street. "It was a bit of an impulse. Thought it might be nice for you to have friends with you. I know it's not easy to go out with somebody new. But afterwards I wondered what I'd been thinking, because here I've been wanting to be with you all week, looking forward to seeing you across the table from me, just like this." He took her hand briefly in his own. "I was looking forward to seeing you in a skirt again, too," he said with a warm smile that made him look even better. "And I have to say, my memory wasn't nearly good enough. Because you're so much more beautiful even than I remembered."

Thanks to Kristen, Ally thought, and sent another gratitude-wave her friend's way. She was wearing a deep brown skirt that was showing plenty of leg even on her shorter figure, and a caramel sweater with a wrap neckline that offered a hint of cleavage too. All of which, she could tell, Devon was appreciating.

His focus was all for her, and as they lingered until the candles on the table had burned low, the other tables gradually emptying along with the bottle of wine, the warm glow had grown to something more. Devon was holding her hand openly now, his thumb brushing against her sensitive skin in a slow, steady rhythm that was somehow being picked up in her breasts, tingling all the way down to her center. And when he suggested stopping at his flat for another drink, that didn't sound like a bad idea at all. It had been months, and that was long enough. And she wanted, she really wanted, to find out just how bad a bad boy could be.

a good man is hard to find

♡

"I heard you come in," Kristen said the next morning at the kitchen table. "But it was late."

"Yeah," Ally said glumly, stirring milk into her tea and looking at it without enthusiasm. "After one."

"So...what happened?"

"We had dinner," Ally said. "Which was good. And then we went back to his place and had sex, which wasn't, particularly. I'd say Devon's all hat, no cattle."

"Ouch," Kristen said sympathetically. "How bad?"

"Not horrible," Ally shrugged. "But pretty...selfish. Not worth it. I was with Brian a long time, and OK, it wasn't always the most exciting, but I always got there, unless something really wasn't working. Because he *cared* that I did."

"You did?" Kristen asked in surprise.

"Well, yeah." It was Ally's turn to look surprised now. "Don't you?"

Kristen laughed, but she didn't sound all that amused. "No. Not always. Not usually. I usually just fake it."

"That's awful. That you feel like you have to, I mean. But you *can,* right?" Ally asked hesitantly. "Sorry. Is this OK to ask? You don't have to tell me if you don't want to."

"Yes, I can. When I'm...alone. But a lot of guys don't know how, or they don't care enough to try. Or I don't feel like I can ask them to do what I need. Even Marshall. *Especially* Marshall."

Ally sighed and nodded. "I guess when you look like Devon does—or you have as much money as Marshall did—you're used to being the sought-after one. To the woman putting in the effort, having it be all about you. But that wasn't the worst of it," she went on, determined to tell Kristen, to be honest with herself about what had really hurt. "It was how he was afterwards. Like, OK, we're done. He didn't *say* I had to leave, but it was pretty clear that he didn't want me waking up with him. I said, well, I'd better get home. And he popped right up and said, 'Let me call you a taxi.' Romantic, huh? Couldn't even be bothered to drive me home."

"You know what they call that," Kristen said. "Get in, get off, get out. Except he was making *you* get out, which is even worse."

"So what was the point of taking me out? If he didn't want any more than that?"

"That he could," Kristen explained. "Guys like that, they think the first time's the best. Because they got you. Because they won. And then they get to throw you away, and that's even more of a win."

"But the first time—it's not even that great!" Ally protested. "Like I said!"

"Bet it was for him, though," Kristen said. "I'll bet *he* had an orgasm. And that'll be all he cared about."

♥

So that was her love life, crashing and burning. And her big career move had been just about that successful too.

Oh, she'd worked hard enough on the Heat event. But Mac hadn't ever acknowledged her part in making it happen, the fact that so much of it had been her idea in the first place, not to mention everything she had contributed to make it a success. And when she'd suggested holding a women's climbing clinic to build on the publicity they'd be receiving, bring more women into the gym, Mac had brushed her off.

With all that, Ally's normal cheerful spirits were dampened over the next few days. Her suspicion had been correct. Devon hadn't called her again. Well, she didn't want him to, did she? It wasn't him she was regretting, anyway. It was having to face the fact that she'd been a fool, that everyone had been right. Kristen, whom she'd always, she had to admit, felt a bit superior to. And, worst of all, Nate. Whatever the true story was between the two of them, she suspected she hadn't heard it yet. Because, she realized, Nate had never told her. Devon had been quick enough to trash Nate to her, but other than letting her know that he didn't like the other man, Nate had never reciprocated.

Eventually, though, she got tired of beating herself up. "I've decided to let this go," she told Kristen briskly on Friday night when she got home from work. Another late closing, and she had to open the next morning at eight. Well, good thing she didn't have a hot date, then. She'd get plenty of sleep. Wow, she was really clutching at straws here.

But right now, it wasn't too bad. She'd plopped down on the couch beside Kristen to watch the end of *The Proposal* and help her friend finish off a big bowl of air-popped popcorn.

"Let what go?" Kristen asked absently. "Oh, this is the part where he comes back. I love this."

Ally smiled. Kristen was such a romantic, still secretly hoping, Ally knew, that there was a Prince Charming out there for her somewhere, despite all the frogs she'd kissed.

Ally waited patiently until the movie was over and Kristen had sat back with a sigh of satisfaction, then said again, "I've decided to let this go."

"Oh, I'm sorry." Kristen turned to her. So cute in her striped leggings and T-shirt, Ally thought fondly. "I forgot you were telling me something. What?"

"This thing with Devon," Ally explained. "I mean, what did I do? I slept with the wrong guy. How many wrong guys do most single women sleep with in their twenties?"

"Way too many," Kristen said. "Enough that you don't want to count anymore, because it's just depressing."

"Exactly!" Ally pounced. "And I've slept with *one.* I'd say I've made one mistake, except that I think spending the better part of a decade in a relationship that isn't going anywhere is a mistake too. But never mind. Do you want to know how many men I've slept with?"

"Well…" Kristen said doubtfully. "Do you want to tell me?"

"Five," Ally said with disgust. "My high-school boyfriend. Two guys I dated in college. Brian. And now Mr. Wrong. My only one-night stand, too, which hardly counts as a one-night stand, does it? Because I didn't even know it was going to be one night."

"That's how they usually are, though," Kristen explained. "Guys don't say, 'Let's have sex and then I'll never call you again, all right?' They say, 'Oh, baby, you're so beautiful. I think I'm in love.'"

"They lie, you mean?"

"Oh, yeah," Kristen assured her. "They lie."

"Why do they do that, though?" Ally asked wonderingly. "Don't they feel guilty?"

"I don't know," Kristen admitted. "If they do, they seem to be able to live with themselves. But if anyone ever says, 'I'm not ready for a serious relationship right now,' just so you know? That doesn't mean, 'I haven't met the right woman yet, but maybe you're the one who can change my mind.' It's man-speak for 'This is a one-night stand.' That's a guy's version of being honest. And they wait to say it until you're right about to do it, when you're totally into it. That's when you get up, put on your clothes, and leave, unless you *want* a one-night stand. I learned that one the hard way."

"All right, then," Ally decided, swiping the last of the popcorn. She was going to have to rethink her image of Kristen as naïve. Kristen might be the Last of the True Romantics, but she was a whole lot smarter about this stuff than Ally was, it was clear. "So now I've learned what every other woman in Dating World already knew. OK, it took me two times around, one close-but-no-cigar with Nate, and one cigar-but-who-cares with Devon. And I got a valuable life lesson, right? I didn't have unprotected sex, I'm not pregnant, and I don't have an STD. And I'm a whole lot smarter than I was a week ago. It's all good. Yay, me."

"Yay, you," Kristen agreed with a smile. "And they were both idiots. Because you're beautiful, and you're awesome."

photo opportunity

♡

Ally took her renewed good mood into work the next morning, and had it put to the test immediately, when Mac called the four staff members on duty over for a quick meeting.

"Got something on I need to tell you all about," he said smugly. "The Hurricanes backs are going to be coming in for a preseason team-building event next Friday. I'm going to need everybody to be available. Don't be planning anything for that day, because you're going to be working."

"What are hurricane backs when they're at home?" Lachlan, an Irish kid who'd started at the gym only a few days earlier, asked.

"The rugby squad," Mac said impatiently. "Just the backs, not the whole team."

"The Wellington rugby team," Ally muttered near Lachlan's ear. "Forwards and backs. Different positions." Funny how Mac assumed that even his overseas staff would know something about rugby, that it was on everyone else's radar even during the offseason, just because it was so important here. No wonder Nate was so full of himself.

"Does this have to do with the Heat promotion?" she asked Mac. "How did it happen? Who set it up?"

"What?" Mac glared. "You think you're the only one who can talk to somebody? I set it up, and I'm telling you about it."

"How did they hear about us, though?" she persisted.

"That doesn't matter." Mac brushed the question aside. "What matters is, they'll be here, and we need to have the place looking sharp. Plan to spend some extra time tidying up this week."

"What kind of thing do you have planned for them?" she asked.

Mac waved a hand. "Usual stuff. The easy routes. I don't think any of them have climbed before."

"If it's going to be filmed, though," she suggested, "how about setting some new, easier routes on the high wall for it? That's an opportunity we didn't take, last time around. It only occurred to me later. But those guys are fit. If we make the climbs easy enough, they'd be able to get up high, even the first time. Well, unless they were scared of heights," she amended, thinking of Nate. "And that'd look much more impressive on TV, for the team and for us."

Mac didn't say anything, just grunted, and Ally heaved an inward sigh.

"Still beating your head against that brick wall, I see," her coworker Robbo said after the meeting broke up and they were doing their safety checks of ropes and carabiners in preparation for the lunch crowd. A climber snatching a few months of casual employment during the busy season, Robbo had started at the gym a couple weeks earlier. He was a cheeky young Australian with more attitude than height who'd asked Ally out his first day, shrugged good-naturedly at her refusal, and moved smack into the Friend Zone.

"It was a good idea," she protested.

"It was bloody brilliant," Robbo corrected her. "And that's why Mac'll be doing it next week. Or I should say, having you come in early or stay late to do it. And pretending he thought of it."

Which, of course, turned out to be the case. Ally did work late Thursday night to help set the new routes, and was back again Friday morning at seven. She saw the sign outside the gym: "Closed till noon today for private event: Hurricanes Training," and tried not to think about Nate.

She'd bet the whole thing had been Liam's idea anyway. She saw him at the gym once or twice a week, sometimes with Kristen and sometimes on his own, and he always had a smile and a word for her. But he was a forward, she knew, so that didn't make sense, because Mac had said it was the backs who were coming.

Nate was a back, she thought for the hundredth time. And, for the hundredth time, shoved the thought aside. He wouldn't even be there. Drew had said the All Blacks didn't have to report to their teams until the first of February, and that was still a week away. And she'd be in the background, anyway. Mac would want the limelight today, she knew. He might even let her leave once she'd finished with the routes, she thought hopefully.

But he didn't. Of course he didn't. Which meant she was right there when the fifteen or twenty fit young men in bright yellow warmup suits sauntered into the gym, preceded by a camera crew who filmed their entrance and followed by several handlers. Ally wasn't entirely surprised, after all, to see Nate in the group. Somehow, she'd known he would be here.

She got busy distributing shoes and harnesses, trying not to stare as the guys stripped down to short shorts and shirts that stretched tight over muscular torsos. No hulking behemoths here. Backs, she'd read during a bout of Internet research she wasn't especially proud of, were primarily kickers and ball runners, lean and fast, and they looked it.

"Ally," Mac called from where he was standing with a young man who'd been introduced to the group as Simon, a member of the Hurricanes' PR team. And with Nate. Of course. With Nate.

She squared her shoulders, took a deep breath, and walked over to the little group. Acknowledged Nate with a nod, then tried not to look at him.

"Simon thinks you should do the demo of how to put on the harness," Mac told her. "For the cameras, eh."

"You put yours on first," Simon suggested, "do a bit of adjusting, much as you can manage. The more the better. Then have Nate put his on, and adjust it for him. A bit of sex appeal never hurt anything."

Ally's eyes flew to Nate's. He was looking a little uncomfortable, too, which definitely made her feel better.

"I am so not adjusting your harness for you," she muttered to him when the two of them were standing in front of the group, each man holding his own contraption of black webbing, buckles, and carabiners.

"No worries," he said, his voice equally low. "Not asking you to."

She demonstrated stepping into the harness, pulling it into place as the men followed along.

"You'll want to tighten it around your waist and thighs," she instructed, demonstrating as she'd been told to, turning around, running her fingers under the leg loops to show them how snugly the thing should fit, and trying to forget that she was being filmed, wishing that she'd worn something less form-fitting than her usual tank top and capri-length tights.

"Or, for some of you," she added, looking around with a smile, "you'll actually need to loosen those buckles on the leg openings in order to get them on." Because, wow, there were some seriously muscular thighs out there.

"Check Nate's, Ally," Simon called from his spot next to the cameraman.

You can do this, she told herself. She turned to Nate, put her fingers gingerly underneath his waist strap at the side, and tugged.

"That's good," she told him. "Nice and tight, just like that." She didn't care what Simon said, she wasn't touching his thighs.

"Now, you may want a chalk bag," she decided to add. "In case your hands start sweating." Ha. That should even things out a little.

His eyes flew to hers, then a slow smile appeared. "Good idea," he said. "I may get nervous up there. May even need rescuing, you never know." The others laughed, and Ally had to smile in spite of herself. He got a point for that one.

"We'll clip it on back here." She turned him with a touch on his shoulder, then fastened the tubular bag to the back of his harness, trying not to notice what a truly great butt he had, muscular and tight. Well, of course he did. He was an *athlete.* She'd already spent way too much time watching it, she reminded herself, hiking behind him. And look how well *that* had turned out.

"Reach in there," she told him, doing her best to maintain, "rub around a little, then pull your hand out and rub it together with the other one. Get good and chalked up before you even start. And when you're on the climb, if your hands do start to sweat, you just lean back in your harness, let it support you, and do it again. That'll give you a moment to catch your breath, too."

"Cheers," he said with another smile. "I'll do that."

He was the first to start up the wall. Naturally. And she had to admit, his second attempt at climbing was more impressive than his first. Of course, thanks to her resetting of the routes so they only *looked* difficult, he wasn't having to work as hard. But she could see that he was more comfortable now that he knew what to expect, and managed a more credible performance that she somehow ended up watching. It wasn't easy to make yourself try something that had scared you the first time, she knew. It was probably willpower that was forcing him up that high wall, but willpower, she suspected, was something he had plenty of.

"Good to go," she told another pair a few minutes later, then stood back and watched another fit young male body make its way up the wall.

"Keep that rope a bit tighter," she told the man belaying. "You want it pretty taut."

"Sorry about that, earlier." She heard the voice behind her shoulder, didn't turn from her supervisory post. "I know you'd rather not have done that."

She stepped a pace away from the belayer and spoke quietly, still without looking at him. "You can't always get what you want, I guess."

She could hear his sigh. "I said I was sorry. Not sure what else to say."

"Nothing else to say. It's done. No big deal."

"It is, though. I wanted to say, today...I wanted to..."

"What?" she asked in exasperation. She shot a quick glance at him. Why did his hair have to be so messy? Why did he have to have stubble again, and look like he'd just got out of bed? It was so totally unfair.

She turned hastily back to her climber again. "Good job," she called up. "Move your left leg up a little, to the left."

She kept watching, made sure he was all right. "Why are you here, anyway?" she couldn't resist asking Nate. "I didn't think you were training yet."

"Ready to get back into it, that's all," he said. "And I wanted to come today."

"Nate," came the welcome interruption from behind them, just when Ally was softening. The PR, Simon, again. "Could we get you holding the rope for somebody?"

"Belaying," Nate said. "Yeh. Half a mo."

Ally glanced at him again, could see him hesitating. Then he shrugged, went to where his teammate stood waiting, and clipped in. And that was the last time she spoke to him.

a lesson for nate

♡

"Oh, no," Ally exclaimed involuntarily a week after the Hurricanes event, looking over the day's schedule when she got into work. Right there in the last block under her name. "Lesson: N. Torrance." At five o'clock, the last hour of her shift.

Robbo was there, looking over her shoulder. "You may not like Captain Fantastic," he said with a grin, "but I think he likes you. Dunno why, you're so bloody standoffish. Must be a case of treat him mean, keep him keen."

"I do not treat him mean," she muttered. "No meaner than he deserves. He's a jerk."

"Didn't seem like one to me," Robbo said. "Typical Kiwi, I thought. Polite, humble, modest, all those boring Kiwi things."

"Trust me. I know him a lot better than you do. And he's a jerk."

♡

"Why?" she was asking Nate the moment he got close enough. She was standing near the front desk, body language spelling "tension" at the sight of him.

He sighed inwardly. He hadn't made any progress the other day after all. And he'd have his work cut out for him today.

"Because I want to learn to climb," he said. "And you're a good teacher."

She continued to stare at him, a hint of temper in the dark eyes. "All right," he admitted. "Because I wanted to see you again, and this was the only way I could think of to do it."

"But you're in the middle of training. You're getting plenty of workouts. It isn't good for you," she said, then snapped her mouth shut as if she didn't want to be caught being concerned about him.

He shrugged. "This is stretching, and something different for my body. I've had a long break, and I'm fit. And," he added, glancing pointedly at the clock on the wall, "I've paid for my hour. So come on. Teach me."

"And that isn't going to bother you," she challenged. "My telling you what to do."

"Did I seem bothered last week?"

"I don't know. I was trying not to look at you," she admitted, and he was startled into a laugh.

"All right, then," she finally said. "Let's get you a harness and shoes."

He lifted the black Adidas bag he was carrying. "Bought them already. And a chalk bag, and chalk. Got it all right here."

"You're really serious about this, then," she said in surprise.

He was serious about something, all right. Even if it wasn't climbing. But he wasn't sharing that, not while she was this wary.

He did his best during the lesson that followed to listen to her, to do exactly what she said.

"Use your legs more," she instructed from beneath him. Where she was belaying him, he reminded his monkey mind, which insisted on telling him that he was in danger. "Right arm, left leg. Left arm, right leg. Don't let your arms get way up above you, so you wear yourself out pulling yourself up." And even though he didn't like this much more than he had the first time, he held on grimly and obeyed.

"Damn," he said after half an hour, on the ground again to his everlasting relief and flexing his fingers. "My hands are cramping up."

"That can be one of the tougher things," she agreed, "especially for someone as strong as you. It won't be your arms and legs, or even your core, in your case, that limit you. It'll be the tendons and the small muscles in your hands, the things you probably don't use as much in rugby. You may not want to overdo it today. You don't want to strain something in there."

"You're right," he decided. "My hands are pretty important to me. But d'you have some exercises I could do, maybe? A way to get my fingers stronger? Wouldn't be a bad thing in any case."

She looked at him in surprise. "Well, climbing's probably the best thing, if you're serious about this. But I could loan you a little contraption I have, where you squeeze with one finger at a time. If you really want to. If you're coming back again."

"I'm coming back again. If you have a look, you'll see that I bought six lessons from you. But maybe we could use our extra..." He looked at the clock again. "Twenty-five minutes, and have a coffee, or even a beer, as you're done for the day."

"Which you knew," she said slowly.

"Well, yeh," he admitted. "I checked. So, a coffee?"

She seemed to be searching for an excuse, finally shrugged. "We're on your time, you're right. Let me grab my stuff, change my shoes, and we'll go."

♡

"So," she said when their coffees had been delivered to the table at the little café ten minutes later. She'd vetoed a beer, no surprise. "This would be when you tell me why you're doing this."

"Because I wanted to see you, like I said." He sighed as she said nothing, her gaze steady on his face. "Look. I know I did everything wrong, that I got offside with you in the worst possible way. But ever since then, I've been regretting it. I've been thinking about you. I thought we could start again, that you might give me another chance to get it right."

She looked at him warily, still not speaking. But she wasn't actually telling him to shove off, so he decided to have a go.

"My name's Nate Torrance. I'm a rugby player, and I'm a clumsy boofhead who spills things on girls, and hits them in the face—accidentally," he hurried to add. "And says all the wrong things. But I like you, and I want to get to know you better, and I'm prepared to take as many climbing lessons and buy as many coffees as it takes to do that."

"And that's it?" she asked, looking at him with a searching intensity that had him squirming a bit.

"Well, no," he said reluctantly. "But if I were forced to be dead honest, I'd have to admit that I'm desperately attracted to you. That I've been imagining you naked since the first time I saw you, and that I want to get you alone, take off all your clothes, and make love to you for hours, every way there is, until neither of us is able to move. And I reckon that would just about spoil my chances for good."

"Maybe not, though," she said after a long pause. He'd seen the flush moving up her cheeks, the look of shock dawning on her face. Had heard himself saying those things, half of him wanting to slap a hand over his mouth to stop himself, and the other half wanting to go on. To tell her more, everything he'd imagined doing to her. To reach across the table, take her head in his hands and kiss her until her mouth was swollen with it, until she felt the way he did. And then to take her home, put her on his bed, and do it all.

"You think?" was all he said. All he could manage to say.

"Well, not about the...hours deal," she said, that flush rising a bit higher. "I'm not interested in being another...bump in your road. An obstacle that defeated you temporarily, until you won again. I'd have to be sure that isn't all that's driving you, and I'm not sure you can even tell the difference yourself. I don't trust my own judgment that much these days either, to tell you the truth. So you're going to have to convince me that it's more than that. More than some conquest."

"Whatever it takes," he promised.

"All right, then," she decided, and he felt a surge of relief. Who knew that honesty could actually work?

"Climbing lessons," she said, "and coffee. And for the rest of it—we'll just have to take it slow. And...see."

♡

"You're from Canada, eh," he said over their next coffee together. Another late Friday afternoon, the little café crowded with tourists and locals enjoying the summer weather. Nate in T-shirt and shorts once again, bare arms and legs showing way too much tanned skin and lean, defined muscle for Ally's peace of mind. He'd offered a beer, but she'd decided they were safer sticking to coffee.

"Another conversational topic?" she asked with her best sassy tone.

He laughed. "Too right. I'm trying to stay on safe ground here. And at least 'where are you from?' is a bit more personal than the weather."

She had to smile at that. "Much better than talking about taking off my clothes, too." Which had given her some sleepless minutes over the nights since he'd said it. And made for some very naughty thoughts.

He cleared his throat. "So. Canada."

"Yep. Calgary. Cowboy country."

"How d'you know Kristen, then? Because she and Hannah are from the States, I know that."

"I was born in the U.S. My dad's American, my mom's Canadian." All right, getting-to-know-you stuff. That was good, right? Starting over, like they'd said. "We moved to Canada when I was little, and I think of myself as Canadian. But I actually have dual citizenship. I went to college in California and stayed on in the San Francisco Bay Area afterwards, working. I met Kristen when she came in to take climbing lessons last year, and we got to be friends."

"Never known anyone from Canada," he said. "Well, apart from the rugby teams they've fielded for the World Cup. Pretty good blokes."

"I never even knew we went to the World Cup. How did we do?"

"Had a good whack at it."

"Uh-huh. In other words, we stunk."

"Well..." He grinned back at her. "Reckon we wouldn't do too well at hockey either. Couple of those boys had the biggest beards I've ever seen, though. If it'd been the World Cup of Beards, now, you'd have taken it."

"Sounds like Canada," she said. "A little of that frontier mentality."

"Not so different from En Zed, then."

"You're right. That's occurred to me more than once since I've been here. Lots of open space, lots of outdoor activities. But more ocean here, and you have better weather." She smiled at him. "And now you've got me doing it."

He smiled back, but persisted. "Surprised you didn't stay there, then. Since outdoor activities are what you do."

"There seemed like more opportunities in the U.S.," she explained. "My parents thought so too. And, of course, the relationship I was in, that's another reason I stayed in the Bay Area.

Besides, I didn't think at the time that I was going to do this kind of thing, the outdoor stuff, as a career. I just thought it was fun, and it turns out that I've never wanted to do anything else. And I want—" She stopped herself. "I thought it was fun," she repeated.

"What? What do you want to do?" he pressed.

"Never mind. You don't want to hear about my hopes and dreams."

"I do, though. But we can save it for next time, if you'd rather. Conversational topic, eh."

Yeah, right. She was going to confide her ridiculous career ambitions to somebody who'd achieved the pinnacle of his by the time he was in his late twenties.

"So," he prompted. "Calgary."

She shrugged. "It has a huge statue of a bull in the middle of it. That's about all you need to know. That pretty much sums it up. How about if we talk about you instead?" He had to be a more interesting topic than her unexciting childhood. She might not know much about dating, but she had a feeling it was better not to actually bore the guy to tears. Besides, you were supposed to ask them about themselves, weren't you?

"Hannah told me that lots of New Zealand rugby players play their whole careers for the team closest to where they're from," she went on. "Drew's only played for the Blues, I know, which surprised me, because U.S. athletes move around a lot. Every year or two sometimes, I think. There's usually no local connection at all. Which makes it a little harder, I think," she mused, "for fans to feel that sense of loyalty to a team, when the guys come and go so much. Anyway." She'd drifted away from the original topic, she realized. "Did you grow up in Wellington? Or someplace close by?"

"Nah. Pretty far away, in fact. In Gore. Well, outside Gore. Which is in Southland," he added at her blank look. And when she still looked lost, elaborated further. "The bottom bit of the Mainland." He sighed. "The South Island. Of New Zealand. Which is where you are now. I could draw you a map, if you like."

"The *Mainland?*" she asked, trying hard not to laugh. "The South Island's the Mainland? I thought hardly anyone lived there."

"Oi," he protested with a straight face. "It's heaps bigger than the North Island. And we have twenty percent of En Zed's population. Not to mention half the sheep, and almost all the mountains. And don't get me started on our sandfly advantage."

"Oh, excuse me," she said with exaggerated politeness. "I stand corrected. I'm sure that…Gore…is quite the metropolitan center."

"Oh, yeh. I'll see your bull statue and raise you a sheep."

"You have a statue of a *sheep?*" She lost the battle and started to laugh. "Where?"

"At the entrance to town," he admitted, beginning to chuckle himself. "And that's not the only decorative object. There's a trout sculpture down the other end, not to mention a pretty massive chainsaw on top of the farm equipment shop. All the Kiwi essentials, and all on the one street . It's a regular cultural wonderland, Gore. Actually, that's not true," he corrected himself. "It's also the country music capital of New Zealand. So there you go."

"Sounding more and more like Calgary all the time. And I still think my bull wins," she said sternly. "It's a very *big* bull. A rodeo bull."

"Nah," he said. "My sheep and trout win. Because a bull's actually exciting. Not too many sheep rodeos around. Sheep riding, now, that'd be a boring event. And there you go again. You have rodeos, and we have Farm Days. I win right there, even without the sheep statue."

"Well, mutton-busting," she pointed out.

"Huh?"

"Riding sheep. In rodeos. Kids do it. Never mind," she said as he continued to look puzzled. "I guess you don't do that. But what about sheepdog competitions? Those are *fun*. I saw *Babe,* and I know."

"One event. *One.* Everything else? Dead bore. Besides," he went on when she would have argued further, "I've actually heard of Calgary. I could even have told you it was in Canada. How many people does it have?"

"Not that many. Maybe a million."

He pointed a triumphant finger at her. "Ten thousand. I win."

motorcycle boots

♡

"D'you want to stop and look?" Liam asked, the third time he saw Kristen's eyes stray to a shop window. They'd finished their climbing already on this sunny Saturday, their fifth time together. They'd already knocked another few weeks off her seven months. Pity there were still six long months to go. He'd suggested they take a stroll up Lambton Quay, have lunch there for a change. He'd had a hunch she'd enjoy window-shopping, and he'd been right, he saw with satisfaction.

"Oh, no," she said hastily. "No, that's fine."

"Because I don't mind," he insisted. "Come on. Show me what you like."

"Do you really want to know?" she asked doubtfully.

"I really want to know." He stopped on the busy pavement, forcing the passing pedestrian traffic to veer around the pair of them. "That shop back there. That was the most interesting one, eh."

"Well, yes, it was," Kristen admitted, looking back. "I shouldn't want to look at clothes so much, I suppose, since I do it all day for work."

"Why not? Just means you've found the right job for you. How much rugby d'you think I watch? Heaps."

"But you probably have to do that," she said, moving back toward the windows of that shoe shop all the same, as if irresistibly drawn there.

"I'd do it anyway. Because I love footy, just like you love fashion. It's work, and it's fun. Neither of us is performing brain surgery here, but that doesn't mean there's anything wrong with what we do, or what we love."

They were in front of the shop now. Mi Piaci, he saw. Shoes.

"Which d'you like best? Those purple ones," he suggested, pointing to a pair of high suede heels, "they'd go with those lace things you were wearing at Toro's party, eh."

"Mmm," she said dubiously. "I probably wouldn't do that. Too matchy-matchy."

"Really. I thought matching was the point."

"It makes an outfit a little boring," she explained. "It's a lot more fun to have a little surprise, a little contrast. A little... funk."

"So which of these would be a better choice? What would be funky?"

"Hmm," she considered, studying the colorful array in the window, then nodding with decision and pointing. "Those. Yeah, those would be super fun."

"Right. Let's go, then," he said, indicating the shop door.

"What?" she laughed. "You mean, try them on?"

"Well, not *me*," he said with a grin of his own. "I was thinking you. Why not? You have something better to do today?"

"No," she said slowly. "If you're sure you want to."

"I'm sure."

Watching Kristen put shoes on and take them off, he thought a few minutes later as she slipped the studded, buckled motorcycle-inspired black boots on, stood and walked to the mirror with that unconscious sway that came from a body put together absolutely perfectly—well, it wasn't the very best thing he could imagine. But it wasn't too far off.

"So fun," she said wistfully, turning and posing, looking back over her shoulder at herself in the mirror, lifting one foot to stand on a toe, smoothing both hands over her hips. And making Liam seriously doubt, all of a sudden, that this celibacy thing was going to work after all.

"What do you think? Cute, huh?" She pivoted, peered over her other shoulder at him with a smile, then turned again, struck a pose, and did a model-glide across the floor to him. Just having fun, he knew, and he was glad of it, though it had steam all but coming out of his ears.

"Yeh," he said, smiling up at her from his spot in the chair. "Cute."

She laughed. "I meant the *boots.*"

"Yeh, those are cute, too."

"Lovely on you," the saleswoman put in. "They go a treat with those skinny jeans, but they'd be awesome with a short skirt too, for a fun look."

"Exactly what I was thinking!" Kristen said with delight, giving the woman a warm smile. "*So* funky and fun. But," she sighed, sitting down to take them off again, "not in my budget, I'm afraid. Not today."

"Nah," Liam said. "We'll take them."

Kristen looked up at him sharply, arrested in the act of pulling a boot off her foot. "What? Liam…"

"We'll take them," he said firmly, bending to scoop up the box, motioning the woman toward the counter. "Leave them on if you like, Kristen."

♡

"You really can't buy me clothes," she was still objecting when they were on the street again. "Lunch is one thing, but those boots were *expensive.*"

"Good thing you wore them then, isn't it? Letting me see them on you, giving me my money's worth. And talking of lunch," he added, "this is a pretty good spot." Not too noisy, he knew, and comfortable. Homey.

"You don't have a—" she started to say, then broke off as they entered the little café.

"A what?" he asked. "A purple dinosaur? A vestigial tail?"

She laughed in surprise, then sobered. "A...you know. A foot fetish," she whispered.

He laughed himself, which caused a few heads to turn, a few eyes to sharpen in recognition. "Nah," he said with a smile. "No vestigial tail, and no foot fetish, either. At least, your feet wouldn't be the first thing I'd kiss. Put it that way."

He regretted saying it when he saw the almost imperceptible drawing back, her hasty turn toward the counter.

"Sorry," he said penitently. "I can do the celibacy. Can't always do the celibate thoughts, though. That gets away from me, I'll admit. Let's order. Then we can talk about it more, if you like. Or not."

She didn't like, it was clear. So he concentrated, instead, on chatting, once they'd placed their order and sat down at a table near the window to await their lunches.

"What are you buying now, at work?" he asked. "Motorcycle boots?"

"No," she said, but she smiled again, at least. "Though it's not a bad thought, because we're looking at autumn clothes right now. You're always two seasons ahead. But unfortunately, our shoe selection is really limited. It always has been, I guess, which I don't understand, because shoes are *great*. Shoes are a big draw. At least they are for me," she said with another smile. "As you saw."

He'd asked a couple more questions, could see her starting to relax again when they were interrupted by the appearance of a young Maori woman carrying a baby.

"Can I just ask," she said apologetically, "can I get a snap of you with her? Her dad would love that."

"Course." He reached for the little girl with her halo of dark curls, her bright eyes and perfect rosebud of a mouth.

"Eh, sweetheart," he crooned, settling her into his arm and bouncing her a bit so she laughed, then turning to face the mum, holding her camera phone now. He waited while she took the snap, then asked, "What is she, eight months or so?"

"Seven," the mother confirmed.

"Got a tooth coming in, too." He peered into the little mouth while the baby favored him with a beaming smile featuring one tiny dot of ivory on the bottom.

"I've got a niece a bit older than this," he told the mum, handing the little girl back. "She's been dead slow on the teething, though. Still got a mouth full of gum."

"I'm almost wishing Eva didn't have any either," the mum sighed. "Been making her right fussy, these past couple days."

"Have you tried a frozen bagel?" he asked. "One of those little ones? The taste keeps them sucking it longer than those rings, and the freezing helps. Gets a bit messy, but well worth it."

"I'll try that. And I'll let you get back to your lunch. Cheers for the photo."

"That's all right."

"What?" he asked Kristen in surprise. She was sitting over there *laughing* at him. Better than the withdrawal he'd sensed earlier, he supposed. "What's funny?"

"Let's see," she said, still smiling. "You go shoe shopping with me. You hold babies and talk about teething. If you suggest we watch *The Notebook* together because it's your favorite movie and you need a good cry, I'm going to *know* you're just trying to impress me."

"Oi." He did his best to sound pained. "I'm actually a pretty sentimental fella. I'm Maori. We're romantic, haven't you heard? That's our specialty."

"I thought that was war. Or maybe rugby."

"All of the above. Or, you know, could be I'm a secret cross-dresser. Using you as a decoy, eh. Could be popping back into that shop later on the sly, asking if they've got those shoes in a thirteen. Though I'd probably go for the purple ones, myself."

"I guess I'll worry when you encourage me to shop for lingerie," she said.

"When I encourage you to shop for lingerie," he couldn't help saying, "it won't be because I want to wear it. That's a promise."

sharing another
beer with nate

♡

Pretty good, Nate thought on Monday. He'd even talked Ally into a beer at the brewpub this time. And she'd smiled, looked happy to see him instead of nervous when he'd arrived at the gym tonight, the last thing on her schedule as always. Getting better every time, and it was only Lesson Three.

"I've got a question for you," she said, smiling her thanks at the server who'd just set down her glass. "I got so distracted last time by the sheep and bulls—"

"Not to mention the trout," he put in. "Don't forget the trout."

"*And* the trout," she agreed, "that I didn't think to ask you the obvious question. Why are you in Wellington? I looked it up, and there's a rugby team down there, near where you're from. Not in Southland, but in O—however you pronounce it. Why don't you play for them?"

"Otago. Yeh, the Highlanders, in Dunedin. Which is a lovely city. No, really," he protested at her skeptical look. "I'm not just saying that because I realized, belatedly, that I'm not meant to be slagging off the sheep of my homeland. Let alone the farmers," he said with a shudder. "Got a bit too relaxed there, I'm afraid."

"You don't have to watch yourself," she said. "I'm not going to tell anybody that you weren't the Perfect New Zealand

Ambassador. You can be honest with me. Heaven knows I have been with you."

"Cheers for that," he said with real relief. She seemed to understand, to his surprise. Well, she did know Drew and Hannah. But Drew never put a foot wrong, he thought glumly. You'd never catch Drew making a disparaging remark about Farm Days. More likely to see him riding the tractor to open the show. And looking as if life could offer nothing finer.

"Anyway," she persisted, "why Wellington? *Was* it too much of the sheep and cows? Because I have to say, you don't strike me as that much of an urban animal."

"Nah. I'm not, really. I like being out in the bush as much as any other Kiwi joker. But I do like Welly," he said hastily. "Being in the capital, the excitement of the place. That it's lively, like you said."

She sighed. "Quit worrying about what I'd be writing if I were a journalist, and just tell me what you think."

"Right." She had him confused again, this time because she was being thoughtful. Understanding. Why was he always so off-balance with her?

"I came here for the footy," he began, actually wanting to explain. And wasn't that a novel feeling. "Well, for everything, really. Though none of it was my idea. I was fifteen, starting to get pretty good at it, at rugby. And Gore's small, like I said. So I needed to go somewhere else, someplace I could play in the First Fifteen. The schoolboy competition," he explained at her blank look. "And my mum wanted me to go to a better school too, one that would challenge me more. She never really took to me being a rugby player. Not her dream for me, and all the injuries as well. But anyway. I had an uncle in Wellington, so…" He shrugged. "This is where I came."

"And lived with your uncle," she said slowly. "It must have been hard to leave your family, though, wasn't it?"

"Cried every night for weeks, in bed," he found himself admitting. "Missed my mum. My dad, my uncle...they're pretty...tough. Typical Kiwi blokes. All the softness came from my mum. I missed my big brother, too. Tagged around after him my whole life, and when he wasn't there, geez, I missed him. And Wellington was so big, and I kept getting lost. New school, no mates...it was a bit rough."

"More than a bit," she guessed. "It must have been brutal."

"Yeh. At first. But I wanted to play, and my mum was right, the school was better. It all worked out in the end. Made some good mates, most on the team, of course, but some not. And we came third in the First Fifteen, eventually. Then I made the En Zed Under-19s squad, went to Uni, played in the Under-20s..." He stopped, feeling self-conscious despite the many times he'd shared this story with interviewers. "And, eventually, the Hurricanes, then the All Blacks. There you go. My life story."

"Condensed," she said slowly. "Because to do all that...everything you've done, and to do it so well. The captaincy, too, of both teams. How old were you when you became captain of the Hurricanes?"

"Twenty-four. Which isn't that unusual," he said hurriedly. "The skipper got injured, they popped me in there. Then he went overseas to play, and I hadn't done too badly, so they kept me on."

"Because you're so...serious. So focused. All that's taken a *lot* of effort. A lot of strength and determination. Which is the Toro nickname, I'm getting it now. The bull."

He shrugged, fully embarrassed now, even as he felt the glow of knowing that he'd finally managed to impress her. Because he'd cried when he was fifteen, and got over it. He didn't understand women, and that was the truth. "It's like I said. A lot of this game, specially at test level, at international level, the All Blacks. A lot of it's mental. Of course you have to be fit, and in form. Not injured. Be the best at your position every year. More than that, every series. Have a rough patch, turn up for the season out of shape, and you'll be on the bench for your squad, and not selected for the ABs at all. And you have to have the instincts, be able to lift your game to the pace, because everything happens so much faster at test level. But some of it's just how much you're willing to flog yourself. How consistent you are. How much it… burns."

"And it burns pretty hot in you," she guessed.

"Well, yeh. It does. It always has."

enjoying it heaps

♡

"Maybe we could just try it for a month, see how it goes," Ally suggested to Mac, trying not to show her frustration. She was standing behind the counter with him, late on a Friday afternoon. An afternoon that should have been a lot busier than it was. She shouldn't have time for this conversation, but she did, so she'd taken another shot at changing Mac's mind. With, as usual, no results.

Mac sighed with exasperation. "I told you already. No. No bloody kids' birthday parties. This isn't a playground, it's a climbing gym. What bloke wants to climb with a bunch of kids running around? Probably why they're coming to the gym anyway, get away from them."

"Sunday mornings, maybe," she persisted. "That's always a quiet time. And it'd get women to see that climbing isn't intimidating too. We could offer some women's classes during that same time slot. Early, when there aren't so many people around. Women like to get up early anyway on the weekend and do their exercise. Fit it into their day, get their partners to watch the kids, for the mothers. We could even do a two-for-one special, or just a discount," she went on, caught up in the idea. "Women like to try new things with a friend, make it not so scary."

"Why the hell would I focus my energies on getting more women in?" he asked. "You don't go after your worst customers. You focus on your target market. We don't get that many women in because women aren't *interested*."

"You're right. You only have twenty-nine percent women right now. I did a quick survey, this past week," she explained at Mac's sharp look, his frown. "And that figure's well below industry standard. I checked. It should be higher. It *could* be higher."

"Do us all a favor," he growled. "Don't waste the bloody time that *I'm* paying you for to do something I never asked you to do. You've got a job to do. Do that."

"But…" she began.

"You've got Nate Torrance coming in today for another lesson, haven't you?" he demanded. "That's the market I'm interested in going after. That's the kind of thing that'll get the boys into the gym. See if he'll bring in some more of his mates. That's who I'll give a bloody discount to. Meanwhile, you can go check harnesses. That's your job. Not marketing. Not promotions. And not running the bloody gym."

♡

"You're a bit quiet today," Nate said when he'd had his lesson and they were sitting over a beer that had been all too easy for Ally to agree to. "Did I stuff up that badly? Are you trying to think of a tactful way to tell me to give it up?"

"What? No," she said with a hurried smile. "You're doing great. You know you are. No, just a conversation I had with Mac before you came in. Still on my mind, I guess."

"You having trouble at work?" he asked with surprise. "Should I have a word, tell him what a good instructor you are?"

She was touched. "Well, I wouldn't say no, if you wanted to do that. That wouldn't hurt. But it's not really trouble. It's just that…" She stopped.

"What?" he pressed.

"I feel stupid telling you," she admitted. "Telling you about how I'm not getting ahead at work...well, it makes me feel like a little bit of a loser, you know?"

"You're not a loser. You just haven't found your focus yet, maybe. Tell me what happened."

She sighed and repeated the gist of the conversation to him.

"We ought to be doing everything we can to get more women in," she finished, "but Mac's too fixated on men. He doesn't realize that women climbers are what really put a gym over the top. Couples climbing together, men coming in to meet women."

"Hmm," he said thoughtfully.

"Because I know you don't have any problem meeting women," she went on. "I'm sure all you have to do is show up. But for the average guy, his chances in a bar? Not that good. And who wants to meet their next partner in a bar anyway? People say the grocery store, but really, what are the chances of picking up a woman there? When they ask you how to tell if the cantaloupe's ripe...How often do you think that works?"

He laughed, and she realized all at once how much she'd come to enjoy being with him. That sitting across from him at an umbrella-shaded table in the pub's busy outdoor seating area, the cold beer sliding down her throat, the relaxed crowd around them in a festive summer Friday-afternoon mood, the blue sea sparkling just a few meters away, was so very much the best thing about today. When had that happened?

And looking at him...The way he was sitting back, one arm hooked over the back of the chair, showing off all that bicep, the vertical ridges of muscle down his forearm. The other sinewy, oversized hand caressing his beer glass in a way that had riveted her when she'd first noticed it, then made her look hastily elsewhere. His amused gaze on her, the smile that cocked up at one side of his mouth.

"No idea," he said, and she had to wrench her mind back to recall what they were talking about. "Never thought of that one."

"Yeah," she said, smiling at him in her turn, seeing his gaze sharpen, watching him sit up a little straighter. "Because you don't have to."

"Well, not so far," he admitted. "Never done much lurking round the vegie aisle, anyway."

"I'll bet you haven't." Even if he hadn't been a rugby player. But since he was...No. He wouldn't have been resorting to the grocery store.

"But for normal men, men who aren't you," she went on, forcing herself to keep to the topic, "a climbing gym—that's just tailor-made as a place to meet women. Or for women to meet men, for that matter, since you need a partner to do anything but bouldering. What better way to get to know somebody? She gets used to seeing you around, you offer to belay her? Start a little chat, ask if she wants to meet you there again tomorrow?"

"That'd work," he agreed. "Least, I'm hoping it does."

"And people look more attractive doing athletic things, right?" she asked, deciding to pretend she hadn't understood his meaning.

"So they say," he said with a crinkle around his eyes that she could tell meant he was trying not to smile.

"All right," she said with a laugh of her own. "I get that women think *you're* attractive doing athletic things." She sure thought so, anyway. Or *not* doing athletic things. He was looking pretty good just sitting there.

"Nah, that isn't what I was thinking of," he protested. "I was thinking about how attractive *you* looked doing them."

"Oh." She stopped, took another sip from the tall glass just to buy a little time. "Well. OK. So we agree, right?"

"Yeh. I'd agree with you, all good ideas. Don't think anybody ever went broke overestimating men's desire to get sex."

"I wouldn't have put it quite like that." She could tell she was smiling like a fool, but couldn't seem to help herself. She forced herself to continue the conversation. Pretended they were talking in the abstract, even as the tingles she was feeling in all the right places were letting her know that this conversation was happening on a whole different level. "But that's the basic idea. And women want to meet men, too, or to do something fun with their boyfriends. It's a great couple activity, don't you think?"

"I do," he said solemnly.

She cast a sharp look at him.

"Oi. Why d'you think I'm doing it?" he asked plaintively, that grin showing up again, showing her that he knew exactly what they were talking about. "I told you."

"OK, but admit, you're enjoying it."

"Oh, I'm enjoying it," he assured her. "I'm enjoying it heaps."

♡

It was true, Nate thought, although every time he'd seen her, his body had urged him to speed things up, was fairly shouting at him by now. The season was starting, and soon he'd be spending half his time on the road. And there were plenty of blokes in Wellington better-looking than him. Blokes who'd be here while he was gone. Who'd never spilt a beer on her, or given her a black eye, or been caught discussing their plans to have a quick fling with her. He'd never worried about competition before, had always known, much as he hated to admit it, that he was a desirable commodity, that most women would queue up for the chance. But Ally wasn't one of them, and that worried him.

He couldn't rush it, he reminded himself, or he'd lose the one chance he had. All he'd be doing then was proving to her that what she'd heard had been a true statement of his intentions. Which, to be fair, it pretty much had been at the time, but there was something else there now.

He still wanted to take her to bed, wanted it more than ever, in fact. Was spending far too much time imagining it, time he should've spent thinking about the team, the season ahead. But it was more than that. He was actually looking forward to the climbing, even getting a bit better at it now that some of his fear had left him. And enjoying the time afterward, talking to her, more than he'd ever enjoyed being with a woman he wasn't sleeping with.

And she was relaxing with him too, he could tell. He was making progress, he was sure of it. The way she was looking at him right now...He was sure of it.

ally takes the plunge

♡

Ally shifted her balance a fraction, stretched again for the next handhold. And once again, came up short.

She sighed in annoyance. She'd started working on resetting the route as soon as she'd come in this morning, but clearly hadn't been focusing hard enough, had placed this hold a few critical centimeters too high. The worst part was, she couldn't say whether it was the conversation with Mac, her frustrated career ambitions that had been distracting her, or yesterday's outing with Nate.

Well, yes, she could. It was Nate. It was all Nate. He was the reason she hadn't slept well the night before, too. The incident with Devon might have shut her down for a while, but oh, boy, was her body ever awake now. Awake, and clamoring for something she couldn't even quite define, because she'd never had it. But she had a feeling that Nate could provide it.

Quit thinking about sex. Quit thinking about Nate and FOCUS, damn it!

There was no hope for it. She'd put the handhold too high. She looked to the side, her hands cramping a bit now, stretched as far as she could to get her right foot onto the adjacent climb so she could reach the offending handhold, reset it. Felt her left hand slip on the tiny protrusion, tried to adjust, and lost her hold entirely.

A frantic millisecond where she continued to grip with her right hand, her left foot, and then she was off, falling awkwardly to her right, all three meters down, swinging below her final anchor point. Unable to avoid the crash into the vertical wall, even as she blindly thrust a hand, a leg out to cushion herself. She felt her right forearm and shin knock against the rough concrete, the impact yanking her body to the left again, her forehead making jarring contact with a fair-sized handhold as the rope jerked and held.

She lay against the wall for a moment, stunned and limp. Heard the commotion around her, struggled to focus against the pain in her head.

"Ally!" It was Robbo, underneath her, his voice sharp with fear. "You OK? Ally!"

"OK," she got out. "Just a knock."

"Lowering you," Robbo said.

She reached shaking legs out automatically to avoid twisting on the rope, and was down within seconds. On her feet, reaching for the wall to steady herself. Fumbling to unclip the carabiners attaching her harness to the rope, her rope to the harness. Robbo's hands pushing hers aside, doing it for her. Pulling her to sit on the mat at the base of the climb as the others crowded around.

"Bloody hell." That was Mac, sounding, if anything, angry.

Ally reached a shaking hand up and felt her forehead, the lump rising already, glanced down at her shin, exposed in her capris. Exposed, bruised, and abraded. She lifted her arm, saw that the underside of her forearm was in even worse shape.

"I'm OK," she said again. "Just a little banged up, that's all. No big deal." Except for her head. That really did hurt. She put her hands down, tried to push herself to stand, but Robbo was there again, shoving her back down. And Mac was crouching next to her now, looking at her injuries in his turn, his expression holding annoyance, but also concern. Whether for her or the gym—or just his Saturday staffing—Ally couldn't tell.

"Need to get that head checked out," he said gruffly. "I've rung 111. Stay there, Ally. Robbo, stay with her till the ambos get here. Lachlan, get her a blanket from the back. And a bottled water, sharpish."

He stood up. "That's it," he told the interested onlookers. "She's all right. Back to what you were doing."

♡

"Goodness," Nate heard his mother exclaim. "You wouldn't think she should be out and about, would you, Lil?"

Nate looked up from where he'd been ostensibly studying the roses, and really thinking about the Captain's Run yesterday. He was a bit concerned about the clearances. The backline wasn't everything it should be, and the Bulls would be onto that straight away. He'd have another go at getting that sorted during the walk-through this afternoon, he decided.

But all that went straight out of his head when he saw what his mother and aunt were looking at. *Who* they were looking at. Because it was Ally, walking—limping, really—round the circular rose garden, and looking like she belonged in the casualty ward.

He was at her side in a moment. "What happened?" he asked in alarm. "Here, let me help."

"What?" she asked, startled, then laughed, though the laugh didn't sound any too steady. "No, I'm fine. All this was yesterday. I'm in recovery mode now. And hey, you should see the other guy."

"What? Somebody did this to you?" he exploded. The left side of her forehead sported a truly nasty bruise in glorious black and purple, and her right shin, exposed beneath her usual short shorts, looked just as bad.

"No, of course not. Just a joke. Just a saying." She brushed the explanation away. "I'm fine, really." She glanced at the two women who, Nate saw, were watching the two of them with

frank curiosity, moving to join them now. "Don't let me inter-
rupt your day out. I got sick of sitting on the couch, decided I
needed to walk, try to loosen this leg up."

"You didn't walk from your flat," Nate said, his frustration
building by the moment.

"Well, yeah," she admitted. "Which was maybe a little ambitious. I'll get the bus back."

"Nah, you won't," he said. He could help with that, at least.
And she looked pretty shaky to him, no matter what she said.
"I'll drive you home. But come sit first. We were just going to
have a coffee, eh, Mum."

"Is this your mom?" Ally asked, looking interested. "No,
really, Nate. Go do your family stuff. I'm good."

"Like hell you are," he growled. "Quit being so bloody
stubborn."

"Nate!" his mother exclaimed. "What a way to talk!"

"You don't know her, Mum," he tried to explain.

"Well, no, I don't, do I?" she responded tartly. "I'm Georgia
Torrance," she said to Ally, putting out her hand. "And I know
it's hard to believe, but I actually *did* try to teach this shockingly
rude young man some manners, once upon a time. Oh, and this
is my sister Lillian," she added. "But you poor thing, come sit
down over here." She indicated the nearby café with its plentiful
array of outdoor tables. "Nate can make up for his shortcomings
by buying us all a nice coffee. And get some scones as well, darling," she decided. "Go on, now."

Nate looked at Ally, saw her laughing back at him. Shrugged,
grinned, and turned to obey.

♡

"At least I didn't do it this time," he told Ally when he'd returned
from placing their order inside the café. "And here." He shifted
the umbrella overhead. "Give you a bit of shade."

"Thanks," she said, smiling at him. It *was* gratifying, she had to admit, to have him make a fuss over her. That was the worst of getting injured in a foreign country. There were so few people around who cared what happened to you. Kristen had been suitably horrified, of course, but Ally had forced her to go ahead and go to breakfast with Liam, and then, finding it too boring and depressing to hang around the flat by herself, had embarked on this admittedly overlong outing.

"What d'you mean, this time?" Nate's mother asked. She didn't miss a trick, Ally was already beginning to realize.

Nate rubbed his nose, looking sheepish, and it was suddenly possible to see the six-year-old boy he had been. "I, ah, caused Ally a bit of damage myself once. Not too different from this."

Georgia looked between the two of them, exchanged a speaking glance with her sister. "Well, you're going to have to explain *that,*" she decided, then looked up at the server with a smile of thanks as their order was delivered.

"He didn't really do it," Ally protested, taking a sip of her large trim flat white. Nate had remembered exactly what kind of coffee she liked, she realized with pleasure. And much as she hated to admit it, he was right. Her head hurt, and she *had* needed to sit. "We were hiking, and my, ah, eye just reached out and smacked Nate in the elbow, didn't it, Nate?"

"Yeh," he grinned back at her. "Told you not to hit me so hard, but did you listen? Nah, that temper gets the best of you every time. Who'd you forehead-butt this time around?"

"That would be the climbing wall," she said wryly. "I tried reasonable persuasion, but when that didn't work, sterner measures were called for. So I took a few whacks at it. It's learned its lesson now, I can assure you."

"You fell," he said, no smile now, his gaze hard on her. And the six-year-old boy was gone, the leader of men in his place. "How?"

"Setting a new route," she admitted. "Lead-climbing to test it out, and I'd made a mistake, couldn't reach the hand-hold. Slipped and fell a few meters. But the rope caught me," she assured the women at their identical gasps. "That's why you clip in. This is just a bit of superficial damage. I'm really not that accident-prone, I promise. New Zealand seems to be getting the better of me, that's all. And the plus side," she said, trying to get rid of that look of frowning intensity on Nate's face, "is that I get an unexpected couple days' holiday. I'll get paid for it, they tell me, and the embarrassing ambulance ride and everything are covered too. I guess your version of workers' comp is the ACC. Though I don't think Mac's too thrilled with me right now. I hope I still have a job when I do go back in."

Nate glanced sharply at her, then nodded. "Time for me to have that chat with him about how much I appreciate your skill as an instructor," he decided. "Ask him about another session with the team, maybe, for a recovery day."

"If you don't mind," she said, a little glow filling her at his concern. "It would sure help."

"Can't do it today," he apologized. "Not with the match tonight. I'll ring him tomorrow, though."

"That's right," she realized. "The first game is tonight, huh?"

"Yeh. It's what Mum and Auntie Lil've come up for, to see that I get off to a good start," he said with a smile at the women.

"I didn't even think about it yesterday, that you had a game today," she said, feeling guilty. Why hadn't she asked him more about his own work, his own preparations for the rugby season? Because he always seemed to have it so together, that was why. Because, in that aspect of himself, he was so…formidable. Easier to tease him about climbing, enjoy flirting with him, watching his eyes on her. Thinking about having sex with him. Which she was doing again right now, in front of his *mother.*

"So you two are up here for the game?" She turned hastily to the women, catching another meaningful glance being exchanged. "From…from Gore? Did you just get in?"

"Last night," Georgia explained. "I came from Gore, but Lil's in Dunedin."

"The metropolis," Nate put in.

"Nate told me that Dunedin was beautiful," Ally said. She wouldn't share what he'd said about Gore. Or ask how the sheep statue was doing. "How long are you staying?"

"Oh, just the weekend," Georgia said. "We'll be off again Monday. Frank can't do without me much longer than that, not with the calves and all."

"My family are dairy farmers," Nate explained. "Dad and Ned, my brother. That's why I became a rugby player. Get out of working so hard, eh."

"Oh." That required a bit of mental readjustment. "Then coming up here really *is* a treat," Ally said to Georgia. "If it's a busy time at home."

"Oh, yes, it is," Georgia agreed. "You know, until Nate moved here, I'd only been away from the Mainland a handful of times in my life. And now I've been all over the world, haven't I, darling? Thanks to you."

"Well, a bit of it anyway," Nate said with a smile. "Mostly the European bit. Seen more of it than me, anyway. If anyone wants a guidebook written about airports and rugby stadiums, though, I reckon I'm the man to do it."

"He does have to travel so much," Georgia confided to Ally. "I'm always so knackered after just one flight, I don't know how he does it. But what am I saying? I'm sure you know what his schedule's like."

"No, not…not really." Ally looked at Nate in mute appeal. How did you say, 'I'm not sleeping with your son?'

"Ally's not as fascinated by me as you're imagining, Mum," Nate said. "Hasn't quite got the fixtures memorized, I'm afraid. But she knows a bit about rugby players all the same. Her flat-mate is Hannah Callahan's sister. That's how we met."

"Well, not exactly," Ally said.

"Shh," he said, his eyes laughing at her. "Don't tell. Let my poor mum preserve her last few tattered illusions about her baby boy. And I'm sorry to cut this short," he said, "but I do need to get cracking. We walked here from my house," he explained to Ally, "as it's not far. But I'll just have a wee jog back for the car, come collect all of you. Meanwhile, have another coffee if you like."

He reached for his wallet, handed his debit card to his mother. "You know the code," he said. "Maybe a juice or something for Ally, keep her hydrated."

And, paying no attention to Ally's protests, he was off.

♡

It was clear enough to Ally that Nate's mum and aunt weren't in any danger of losing their high opinion of him.

"Oh, yes," Georgia was telling her now, having duly trotted in for an orange juice that she'd insisted on Ally drinking, "he gives his dad and me a lovely holiday every year. Anywhere we want to go. We've done a cruise in the Mediterranean, toured all round Britain and Ireland, done Italy...so many places. And when his dad can't get away, he sends Lil and me."

"Everything first class, too," Lil put in. "He's got us both quite spoilt."

"That's nice," Ally said lamely. All right, so he was kind to his mother. Most people could manage that, couldn't they? "Especially since I'm sure you don't see as much of him as you'd like."

"Well, no," Georgia said. "Though we get up here as often as we can to watch him. He always takes us to breakfast, the morning of a game. That's our little ritual. Flew us all the way to England for the World Cup final last year. And he does come home as much as he can manage. We had him for Christmas, of course."

"And after the World Cup," Lillian reminded her. "The day out in Gore. That was lovely."

"Oh, yes," Georgia agreed. "He did a community day," she explained to Ally, "when he was home for a wee visit after England. Speeches, of course, games for the kids, a lolly scramble, signing autographs. He gave a beautiful speech thanking everyone for their support. And he rode into the Domain on the back of the fire engine," she added with a laugh. "That was quite the sight."

Nate showed up again before his mother and aunt could relate the story of the time he'd walked on water. Well, your mother was supposed to be your Number One Fan. All the same, Ally was afraid she was going to have to break down pretty soon and admit that he was a good guy. Boy, she hated being wrong.

♡

Nate dropped his mum and aunt back at the house, knowing that they were going to have a few questions for him when he got home. Pity he wouldn't have any answers.

"Will your game tonight be on TV?" Ally asked when he'd pulled out again, headed toward Aro Valley and her flat.

"On Sky Sport," he confirmed.

"Oh. Too bad. We don't have any premium channels. Will the other games be on regular TV?"

"Nah. You'd need Sky."

"I guess I just assumed," she said, actually sounding a bit upset about it, "that since rugby matters so much here, it'd be easy to see it."

"You could always find a pub that's showing it, if you're interested," he suggested. He found himself holding his breath a bit, waiting for her answer.

"Good idea. I'll try that, because I really would like to watch. Maybe Kristen will come along, keep me from having to go alone. Pubs aren't quite like bars back home, but I'd still rather have company."

He'd rather she did, too. *Female* company. "No walking, though," he told her. "Stay off that leg, and give your head a chance to get right, too. Bet it's hurting right now, isn't it? Have a rest when you get home."

"Yes, Daddy," she laughed.

He glanced across at her sharply, then turned hastily back to the road.

"What?" she asked.

"Nothing," he muttered. When had he got so pervy? Or maybe it was just that she had him so twisted round by now, everything she said turned him on.

"Take a right here," she instructed. "This is me, two drive-ways up on the left. Don't get out." She reached for her bag as he pulled to the curb.

He ignored that, moved around to open her door, gave her a hand out, getting another nasty jolt at the sight of the raw abrasion on her forearm. He'd thought it was bad seeing her injuries the first time around. That was nothing, though, to how much it was bothering him now.

He walked her to the door leading to the block of flats. Not flash, pretty boxy and ugly in fact, but not as shonky as he'd expected either. Well, maybe Kristen had a bit of money.

"Thanks for the ride," she said, fishing for her keys and look-ing a bit self-conscious. "And good luck tonight. I'll find a place to watch you."

"You can let me know what you thought when I see you on Monday," he said with a smile.

She laughed at that. "I'm sure my opinion will be enlightening."

"And, Ally," he went on, putting a gentle hand on her cheek, smoothing her hair back. He felt her lean into his hand for just a moment, her eyes going soft. It felt so good to touch her, he'd like to have stayed there, kept doing it. Instead, he leaned forward and brushed the other cheek with his lips.

"Take care of yourself," he said. He wanted to add something about looking after herself at the pub, but forced himself to stop. That'd put the final nail in his coffin, acting like a jealous fool. Instead, he gave her cheek a final caress, stepped back and watched her open the door and go inside before he turned back for the car. And the interested inquiries that, he knew, would be waiting for him at home.

diving in

♡

"When are you off work?" Nate asked, standing on the gym floor again two days later, taking off his harness and watching Ally take off hers, which gave him the same ridiculous thrill it always did. It was a climbing harness, he reminded himself with exasperation, not a skirt. But it didn't seem to matter. He still liked watching her wriggle out of it.

He'd lasted the full hour today for the first time, thanks to some pretty determined practice on her little finger-exercise contraption. Well, one thing he knew how to do was train. He hoped he'd impressed her at least a little bit with that. And that was new, too. He hadn't had to worry about impressing a woman in a long time.

"I'm off now, actually," she said. "You were my last duty today. Which you probably arranged, so don't pretend it's a surprise."

"Have time for a beer?" he asked, trying to sound more casual than he felt. Remembering to ask her, not to assume.

"Sounds good," she said, "but I was planning on a swim."

"You've been climbing all day, and now you want to swim? Your head OK for that? Those scrapes?"

"I'm fine," she said impatiently. "I'll bet you play entire rugby games with injuries a whole lot worse than this. For that matter, you played two days ago and are out here climbing today, when any normal person would be in the hospital after what I saw you do. I had no idea it was quite so rough. And I'll just point out that you've got a few scrapes and bruises too."

"Yeh, but that's me. That's different." Her arm and leg, he'd noticed, were healing over, but that bruise on her forehead was still pretty noticeable, even faded to yellow and green, though she insisted it didn't hurt anymore.

She sighed in obvious exasperation. "It's been more than four days. I'm not that delicate, Nate. Sorry if that disappoints you. Anyway, I've been instructing today, not climbing. Nothing aerobic about it. And it's not just swimming. Something a whole lot more fun than that. Want to come?"

Anything she classed as "fun" automatically had him dubious. On the other hand, seeing her in her togs—that sounded pretty good. And it was the first time she'd suggested extending their time together. That had to be a good sign.

"Yeh," he decided. "Don't have my togs with me, though."

"Not a problem, as long as you've got something dry to change into. Where we're going, there's no dress code."

"I'm parked just across the bridge," he offered when he met her outside the changing rooms. She was wearing a short, simple cotton dress that showed off her toned arms, her slim legs. And, he devoutly hoped, was covering up not very much at all.

"We don't need to drive. It's close by," she said.

The trepidation he'd felt all along increased at that. The beach wasn't that close. And she hadn't sounded like they were going to the pool. That only left...

"Oh, no," he groaned as they approached Te Papa, the massive bulk of the museum set just back from the waterfront. And in front of it, on the wharf, the ladders of the jump spot, crowded on this sunny day with young blokes eager to impress each other and get an adrenaline rush. "How did I know."

"I've wanted to do this for ages." Ally's eyes were sparkling with excitement as she dropped her gym bag on the pavement and pulled off the dress, oblivious of the interested glances she was attracting from the dripping young men, and every other fella passing by, too. "As soon as I realized what this was. I couldn't believe this would be here, that they'd actually set up a spot where people could jump from way above the wharf into the sea."

"Only because they were jumping off the roof of the Free Ambulance building before," he grumbled. "Because they're bloody fools. So the council decided it was safer to have a dedicated spot, and a reasonable way to get up there."

He sighed in resignation and pulled off his T-shirt. Looked at the iron ladders, all the steps and rungs. *All* the steps. "That high platform has to be ten meters up from the water," he protested.

"You can go off the lower one if you'd rather," she assured him. "I promise not to laugh."

She turned on him, then, climbed to the top. Of course she did. And he followed her. Of course *he* did. Acknowledging the greetings of the other fellas with a nod, but never losing his focus. Following that absolutely fantastic bum once again like the fool he was.

Not a tiny bikini, alas. An athletic two-piece in an orange pattern that still managed to show off a fair bit of her pretty body, though he'd rather have seen more skin. But it had him climbing that ladder behind her all the same. And thinking about where he'd be putting his hands right now, if he could.

She didn't hesitate, jumped straight off, dropping much too far to the sea below, bobbing up after long seconds with a gasp and a laugh, her arm sweeping a bit of errant hair from her face.

"Great!" she shouted up to him, breast-stroking out of the way, over to the pilings holding up the wooden wharf. "Try it!"

He followed her down. He really had no choice. His stomach dropped as he looked down, and when he was plummeting toward the water, he honestly thought he might be sick. But by the fifth time, he could almost say he was enjoying it.

He was certainly enjoying looking at her. Seeing her wet, the water sliding down her arms and legs, down her midriff, into the top of that bit of orange covering her. And she was looking at him, too, he could tell. So all in all, this was working out for him.

"Let's swim out around the piers, to the end of the wharf," she finally suggested. "I need to stretch out."

"You're not meant to," he protested. "Meant to go over by the rowing club. Or to the swim beaches."

"I thought Kiwis weren't that big on following the rules," she said. "But if you're scared…"

"Right," he said grimly. Swimming wasn't his best thing anyway. Not enough body fat, and too much dense muscle and bone. He didn't float in a pool, he sank. But the water here would be salty enough to keep him afloat. He hoped.

"OK," he gasped, pulling himself up the ladder and onto the wharf when, to his eternal gratitude, she had finally had enough. "Is that it? Or is there some cliff diving you wanted to do?"

"*Is* there cliff diving?"

"No," he said firmly. "Joke." He reminded himself never to go anywhere with her that had cliffs and water. He wasn't doing that. Or bungy jumping, or skydiving. No matter how pretty her bum was.

"All right, then," she decided, running to her bag and bending over to pull out her towel, wrapping it around herself to the obvious disappointment of the blokes who were still jumping. Nate shot them a glare that she didn't even notice, but that had them turning hastily away all the same.

"Let's go find a place to change, and have a beer," she said. "Since you're buying."

♡

"I'm hungry," he said when he met her in front of the changing rooms again. He tried to make it sound spur-of-the-moment. "Can I take you to dinner instead?"

"Dinner," she said speculatively, feeling her wet hair, pulled back in a ponytail. Which was still sticky with salt, he knew, because his was the same. "I'm not exactly dressed for it."

"Doesn't matter. I'll take you to a flash place another time, when we're both prepared for it. But for right now..." He nodded at the pub across the way. "We could go warm up inside, get something hot to eat."

She was shivering, he'd noticed. He wished he had something to wrap around her. He thought about those old movies where some fella took off his jacket and put it around the woman's shoulders. A bit corny, he'd always thought. Now, he wished he could do it.

"OK, but...Dinner and what else?" she persisted.

"Well, dinner and head-banging sex, if I get my choice," he said, trying out a grin. "Or just dinner. Or anything in between. I'll take what I can get."

"Dinner," she decided, giving him a smile of her own.

♡

"Can I give you a lift home?" he asked when they'd eaten. After he'd watched her laughing across the table at him, teasing him, flirting with him. "Now that you've revealed where you live and all."

"Sure," she said with a quick smile that made his heart pound just a little harder. "That'd be nice."

They were walking up the broad expanse of bridge and plaza that spanned the busy streets, connecting the wharf with the main body of the CBD, when they heard the music. A few more steps, and the source came into view.

"What *are* those things?" he asked as they approached the two large xylophone-shaped instruments, metal sound tubes of graduated lengths hanging beneath the wooden slats.

"Vibraphones!" she said with delight, moving to join the crowd that had gathered to watch the two women behind the table-like instruments, each beating out her share of the complicated tune with a pair of mallets. A young man with long blond dreadlocks provided a percussion accompaniment on bongo drums, and the result was a joyous, irresistibly infectious melody that had the Friday-evening tourists and locals clapping along and even dancing a little in place.

Nate looked down at Ally, at the wide smile that had spread across her face, her rapt expression. He had a feeling they were going to be here for a while, which suited him. Listening to this, watching her—yeh, that suited him down to the ground.

And then it got even better, because a pair of young blondes, Scandinavians maybe, broke out of the group and began to dance in the center of the semicircle that had formed around the musicians. And Ally was laughing, dropping her bag by his feet, and moving to join them. Of course she was. Whirling and prancing in that little patterned dress with the straps crossed over the back, her bare, tanned arms and legs moving with joyful grace, the sparkle in her eyes, her flying ponytail, her smile radiating pure pleasure in the music, in the moment.

"Come on, sweet thing," she beckoned him with a laugh, a seductive crook of her finger that he could tell she meant as a joke, but that had his temperature rising all the same. "Dance with me."

He smiled back and shook his head. Because that photo would be sure to turn up in the *Dominion Post*, and wouldn't he feel like a fool then. And he wouldn't have done it anyway, because he wanted to watch.

She came back to him, still laughing, after the song ended, while the crowd was still applauding. Nate finished signing autographs for a few excited kids who had spotted him, then turned back to Ally where she crouched over her bag.

"Just a sec," she smiled up at him. "I just need to find my wallet so I can give them something."

"No worries." He dug out his own wallet, stepped forward and dropped a bill into the musicians' basket.

"Cheers, Nate," the bongo player said with a grin, never missing a beat in the new tune the group had struck up.

"Sure you want to leave?" Nate asked Ally as they headed down the ramp on the other side of the wide bridge. "Don't want to listen some more? Or dance?"

"Not if you aren't going to dance with me," she said saucily. "Chicken."

"I wouldn't have had such a good view, then, would I," he teased back.

"Ha. Probably looking at those blonde girls. I know your kind." She gave a little toss of her ponytail that had him smiling again.

"Nah," he told her. "That was all you. Nobody but you."

♡

He still didn't get head-banging sex. But taking her home was pretty good all the same.

"Well," she said, unfastening her shoulder belt after he'd pulled up. "Thanks for dinner."

He clicked the release on his own belt. "I'll walk you to your door."

"No, that's OK," she protested. "You don't have to." But she wasn't moving to collect her bag from the back seat, he realized.

"Yeh, I do." He reached across the console for her. "But I have to kiss you first."

She didn't pull back. Came to meet him halfway, in fact. And now he was able to do exactly what he'd imagined doing, so many times. To put a hand on either side of her head, pull her towards him, and brush that soft, wide mouth with his own. To feel her lips part with a sigh, to settle his mouth over hers to kiss her properly. To revel in the sensation of her arms coming around him, her fingers at his nape, stroking the sensitive skin there.

He dropped one hand to her side, reached his arm around her waist, leaned over a little further, and pulled her as close as he could in their awkward, constrained surroundings. Held her by the back of the neck with the other hand, and felt her excitement increase when he did it, which only made him hotter. Heard her whimper as he licked his way over her lips, into her mouth, feasted on her, and thought he was going to explode. From a *kiss.*

He sat back at last, his breath coming hard, so aroused he hurt. She stayed where she was, staring at him in the fading evening light, her eyes wide.

"Wow," she said on an exhalation of breath. "You really know how to kiss."

He had to laugh a bit at that. "I'd say you did a pretty good job there too. What d'you reckon? Should we go a little further? Want to invite me in?"

"No," she sighed. "Kristen will be home. And...no."

"Right. That's what I figured." He opened his door, hopped out, went around to the passenger side and opened hers, took her bag from her and gave her a hand out.

"Hope this is OK," he said with a smile. "Opening doors, I mean. I know you could do it yourself, but I like to do it for you."

"You can do it for me." She was settling down, he saw, feeling more comfortable again. Which was a good thing, he reminded himself sternly.

He walked her to the door, gave her another kiss there that he'd meant to be a quick goodbye, not pressuring her. And somehow ended up with her sweet body pulled tight against him, and feeling so good there, feeling even better than he'd imagined. Had her hanging onto his shoulders, kissing him with all the passion she showed for everything she did, not holding anything back. Guaranteeing that he'd be having some dreams tonight.

"Goodnight," she sighed, reaching for her key and opening the door with fingers that, he saw, shook a little. And he didn't think she was still cold.

"Goodnight," he said. "Till next time."

bridal fantasies

♡

Kristen took a final look at herself in one of the many mirrors set up in the crowded, makeshift dressing area through which excited half-dressed women rushed, attended by busy Lambert & Heath salespeople who buttoned, zipped, and tweaked.

Everyone else was thrilled to be doing this, she could tell, so why wasn't she? Maybe because they were going out there fully clothed. But it was for a good cause, she reminded herself, and it wasn't a porno movie. Just a fashion show, and, like all fashion shows the world over, being attended by an overwhelmingly female audience, who were obviously thoroughly enjoying it.

Her mind whispered that there were TV cameras out there too, but she pushed the thought aside, because it was too late now. She'd had her chance to refuse, and she'd blown it.

It had been a rare full staff meeting at the store that Friday in January when Anna, the Merchandising Manager, had taken the floor to discuss the benefit for the Care for Kids charity. The fashions would all be provided by Lambert & Heath, Anna had already explained, while the models would be a mixture of store employees and women from the community.

"Thanks to all of you who have already volunteered," she said. The store had been abuzz with the news for the past week, ever since the signup sheets had appeared. "And if you aren't chosen as a model, be assured that there will be opportunities for everyone to participate. Those helping behind the scenes are equally important to this project's success."

Well, that was good, because that was where Kristen planned to be. When the meeting had adjourned, however, Anna approached the row of chairs where Kristen was filing out, together with two of her colleagues.

"Ladies," Anna said. "I wanted to say thanks to Laura and Ashton for offering their help. I've got you girls down for sports-wear. And Kristen," she added, turning to her. "I didn't see your name, but you'll want to help out, of course."

"Well," Kristen faltered, "I was planning to do what you said, help behind the scenes. I'm pretty good at dressing, and I'd be happy to do that."

"Oh, now," Anna said playfully, "we're not letting you off that easily, not when we have a resource like you. We don't have anyone who's right for the finale. Hard enough to manage the swimwear. Not everybody wants to show their jiggly bits, you know."

"I don't want to, either," Kristen said. "I mean," she went on, seeing Anna draw back with a frown, "I don't really want to model, if that's OK."

"You're not trying to say that you *have* jiggly bits, are you?" Anna laughed. "Because we won't believe it, eh, girls?"

"No. We wouldn't." That was Ashton, her fellow assistant buyer, who'd never seemed to warm to Kristen despite her friendly overtures. "And we're doing it, aren't we. It may not be what you're used to," she told Kristen with patently false sincerity. "Nothing flash, just a wee fashion show down here in the Antipodes, but the rest of us are managing it."

"You've done it before, I'm thinking," Laura, the Assistant Merchandising Manager, put in, her voice kinder. "And we *are* all doing it. Come on. It'll be fun."

Kristen smiled at her gratefully. Maybe she was going to find a friend here after all. And maybe it *would* be fun, if they all did it together.

"Well..." she wavered. "If it's nothing too risqué, I guess."

"Wonderful," Anna said briskly. "And no worries. You'll be beautiful, and perfect for it. You won't even have to do a change, because you'll only have one bit, and it'll come at the end."

♡

The final model appeared at the edge of the curtains now, and Anna nodded to Kristen, who had moved to stand in her starting position. Anna held up a hand, counted silently to five, finger by finger. Up went her pinkie, and she pointed at the stage. And Kristen went.

"And finally...doesn't everybody love a beautiful bride?" the announcer asked with a flourish. Applause rang out as she went on, describing the designer gown in loving detail.

Kristen looked straight ahead, placed each high-heeled foot down with precision, and glided to the end of the runway. Since she was here, she'd do her best. She *had* done this before, it was a beautiful dress, and she looked good in it. It was hard not to get a little thrill from the attention, too, from knowing she was performing well. She got to the end of the raised platform, looked down and swept the crowd with her best smile as she pivoted, showed her stuff.

And that was when she saw them. Four big, solid figures, incongruous in the crowd of women, seated in the front row near the end of the runway in their sober suits, white dress shirts, and ties. Of course. It was a charity event in Wellington, and the Hurricanes were here.

But not just any Hurricanes, because one of them was Liam.

♡

Liam saw the moment when she noticed him. He smiled back at her, and wondered why her own smile wobbled. Because she was absolutely gorgeous. Fully made up, the golden hair pulled straight back from her forehead and confined in a severe knot that only emphasized the perfection of her bone structure.

And then there was the dress. An elegantly strapless, form-fitting ivory gown of some kind of textured material that followed her curves from the tops of her breasts to the strongly defined indentation of her waist, caressed the swell of her hips, then frothed out below her knees.

Why hadn't she told him she was doing this? Had she thought he'd think she was vain? She ought to know him better than that by now. She couldn't help being beautiful, any more than she could stop breathing. Any more than he could stop looking at her.

She turned once more, then walked away, her hips swaying, her smooth shoulders rising out of the white material. Even her back was gorgeous. The indentation of her spine, the curve of a shoulder blade, it was all…perfect.

"Shit," Teddy breathed next to him, and Liam couldn't have agreed more.

But Kristen didn't leave the stage as all the other models had. She was taking another slow turn in the center now, and then, when she'd faced front again, reaching behind her, pulling down her zip, all the way to her bum. Her gaze far away as the gown fell to the floor and she stepped out of it, like a mermaid rising from the sea foam.

"But what's a wedding," the announcer said now to the accompaniment of more murmuring, some laughter and applause, "without a wedding night? At Lambert & Heath, we know that the dress is only half of the story. You'll find a full range of the very finest bridal lingerie in all sizes, to make every bit of your wedding day truly memorable."

"Bloody hell," Teddy said on an explosion of breath, and Liam wanted to jump up onto the stage and hustle Kristen straight off it. She was still doing her best, doing that model strut she'd first showed him in the shoe store when she'd tried on her motorcycle boots. But she'd been doing that because she was happy. And she'd been doing it for him.

It wasn't that he didn't look. He couldn't help it. The strapless lace corset with mesh inserts that were even sexier than seeing her bare skin, the garters that held up her stockings, the smooth perfection of her upper thighs, he had a good long look at all of it. And then she got to the end of the runway, straight above him. No smile for him this time, but he was close enough to see the bright dots of color on her cheeks, visible even through the heavy makeup. And, when she turned, her backside as well, thankfully covered, but not any too thoroughly. He had a good view of that, and so did everybody else here, and every TV camera too.

"I'll have that," Teddy sighed. "Yes, please." And it took every bit of Liam's self-control not to grab him by the throat and choke the words straight out of him.

Kristen hadn't been sure he'd turn up. She'd arranged to meet him at the gym today, had wanted the comfort and release of climbing with him after what she'd suspected would be a stressful day. And she hadn't known the half of it. She hadn't dared to look at him when she'd walked down the runway for the second time, but she'd seen the rigidity of his posture out of the corner of her eye, and it hadn't taken much imagination to guess what his reaction would have been.

She'd taken her time changing into her climbing clothes, wiping off the heavy makeup. Delaying the moment when she'd have to see him again until, now, she was ten minutes late.

She spotted him the moment she stepped inside the gym. Standing near the front desk, waiting for her, his expression hard and forbidding in a way she'd only seen, until now, on TV, on the rugby field. And suddenly, something shifted inside her, and she wasn't dreading this. Suddenly, she was mad.

"What?" she challenged, walking right up to him. "What's wrong?"

"You know what's wrong," he growled, and she quailed for a moment, then gathered her courage again.

"It was for *charity*," she told him, feeling the anger rise, drowning the embarrassment. "I didn't want to do it, but I did it anyway. And you didn't get up and excuse yourself because you didn't want to see girls in their swimsuits, did you, when they did the beachwear? They were wearing a whole lot less than I was! You're just upset that it was *me*. Well, every one of those women today was somebody's daughter, you know. Not just me. Every one of them! And you didn't mind looking at *them*. You didn't mind that *they* were showing their bodies."

"That's not it," he protested.

"Then what?" she challenged. Her voice was rising. She never yelled, but she was yelling now, a little bit, and she didn't care. "And I don't believe you anyway. It's that you don't want anyone to see me like that. Anybody but you. And that I haven't even let *you* see me like that. You feel like everyone's looking at what belongs to you. But I *don't*," she said, and there were tears in her eyes now. "I *don't* belong to you. I belong to myself!"

He'd lost the stone face, anyway, was just looking thoroughly upset as he reached for her arm. "Kristen. No. Let's go outside." He cast a look around the interested faces turned their way. "Come on," he urged.

She walked out with him, not wanting to do this part either, but knowing she had to. She was still trembling with anger and disappointment. Liam was just the same as everyone else after all, and that *hurt*.

He seated himself on a low concrete wall at the edge of the wharf. "Come on," he said again, indicating the spot beside him. "Sit down. Let's talk."

She sat, because she didn't know what else to do. Glanced at him once, then looked away.

"It's not just that," he said after a moment. "Well, yeh, it's partly that. I didn't like everyone looking at you that way. Every man there thinking…what they were all thinking. I didn't like that at all."

"Well, only the straight ones," she couldn't help pointing out. "Which cut it down a fair amount. It was a *fashion* show, Liam."

He smiled a bit at that, although she could tell the smile was offered reluctantly. "I didn't like my teammates seeing it," he admitted. "But that wasn't all. It was that you did it at all. Because you can't tell me you wanted to."

She looked down, then. Picked up her gym bag and set it on her lap, wrapped her arms around it and hugged it to her, just for something to hold on to.

"I didn't," she admitted, still not looking at him. "I wouldn't have minded doing the regular clothes. Well, I didn't even want to do those, not really. And I *really* didn't want to do that."

"Then why did you?" he pressed.

"Because…" She sighed. "Because when I said no, at first, everyone thought it was just me being a snotty American again, I could tell. That I didn't want to help. That I thought I was too good for them. Too…You know."

"Too good-looking," he suggested. "Entitled."

"Yeah. That I was stuck on myself. So I had to say yes, don't you see?"

He was silent for a few moments, and she waited for him to speak, hating that she cared so much, that she was letting him judge her. And at the same time, wanted him to understand.

"So," he said at last, "your choice was, do something that made you uncomfortable, but that other people wanted you to do. Or say no and make them angry."

"Yes," she said with relief. "That was it."

"You decided," he said, "that you'd rather disappoint yourself than disappoint anyone else. That making yourself uncomfortable is OK, but making anyone else feel that way is wrong."

She looked at him in surprise. "Yes," she said slowly. "I did."

"D'you see why I was narked, then?" he pressed. "Watching you do something I *knew* was making you feel so bad? And something that made me feel bad too," he admitted. "Because I did feel bad. Wanted to jump straight up there with you, cover you up, and take you out of there."

"I wish you had," she said, beginning to smile, but feeling her mouth trembling a little as she did it. "When I saw you sitting there with your teammates, I wanted to turn around and run. Except that when I turned around," she added with a shaky laugh, "I was giving you all a pretty good view, too."

"Yes, you were," he said with a smile of his own. "And I'd just like to say for the record here, I'd love to see every bit of that again. As long as you were only showing it to me."

His expression grew serious again. "You're a beautiful woman, Kristen," he said. "That doesn't give anyone any rights to you. Just because they want a piece of you, it doesn't mean you have to give it to them. Because that's what it feels like, doesn't it?"

"Yes," she sighed. "That's it. That I'm always having to prove I'm a regular person. To go out of my way to do it, or they'll assume that I think I'm, what you said. Entitled."

He nodded. "I know, because I get that too. Not so much for my pretty face, oddly enough," he said, making her smile this time, "but being a footy player, being recognized."

"Being a celebrity."

"Yeh. Means you have to draw your boundaries. And if something feels wrong to do, don't do it. That line's different for everyone. I don't talk about my private life, but some of the boys have Twitter accounts, and heaps of followers, too. Tell everyone when they went to the dentist, what they ate for dinner. Course, could be I don't do it because I'd be embarrassed that nobody'd want to follow me."

"No," she said. "I suspect you don't do it because you value your privacy."

"Well, that's what I tell myself, anyway."

"You said you'd made some bad choices too, though," she said. "Which I have to tell you, was such a *relief.*"

He laughed at that. "A relief? Glad to help, but how d'you mean?"

"I mean," she tried to explain, "take Ally, for one. She's so confident, isn't she? The first time I met her, she was teaching me to climb. I was such a mess, right after my divorce. I was only doing it because my therapist suggested it, and I was *scared.* And Ally...she just seemed so strong. I thought, why can't I be like that? I still think so, all the time. And then, of course, Hannah."

"Hannah. Does she climb too, then?"

"No," Kristen said with a smile. "That's about the only thing I do better than her. Well, that and dress. She's still a *terrible* dresser, a lot of the time."

Liam laughed. "Can't say I've noticed, but I'll take your word for it."

"She's great," Kristen assured him, "and I love her more than anybody, but she does everything so *right,* you know? It's so hard not to compare myself to her, especially when she's right there in front of me, living her perfect life with her perfect husband and her perfect baby and her perfect job. She doesn't have any idea of what it's like to get it all so wrong and have to start over, knowing that everybody *knows* how wrong you got it."

"Everybody's made some mistakes," he said. "I'm sure, if you asked her, Hannah'd tell you about all the ones she's made. May not have been as spectacular as yours, but I imagine they're there all the same. All you can do, all anyone can do, is stop making the same ones over and over. And that's exactly what you're doing."

She sat for a minute, absorbing what he'd said, realizing that he was right.

"And d'you want to climb now," he asked with a smile that went straight to her wounded heart, "or would you rather go straight on to dinner?"

"Climb," she said with decision. "Please. And then go to dinner with you."

She reached out impulsively for him, felt him stiffen for a moment before he wrapped those big arms around her, pulled her close. And being held by him, resting against the solidity and the strength of him, felt just as good as she'd always known it would.

She relaxed into him for a few comforting seconds, his cheek warm against hers, then released him and sat back again.

"Sorry," she said, feeling the prick of tears. "I just needed a hug."

"No worries," he said. "Though I'm beginning to think you were put on this earth to test my self-control. It's been a hell of a struggle to get it. But that's nothing to how hard it is to hold onto it when I'm with you."

a timid man

♡

"Here we are," Nate announced, arriving at the gym's front desk on Saturday afternoon and finding Ally, as always, waiting for him. Ready for him. "My final lesson. Do I get a bit of a ceremony here? A lovely wee certificate naming me 'Most Improved?' Which means, as we all know, that I was rubbish at the start, and yet I'm still here, but maybe not quite such rubbish."

She laughed. Lately, she'd been looking more than pleased to see him. And today, she also looked...excited. And a bit nervous, too. Which was fairly cheering, wasn't it?

"You *are* the most improved, and you know it," she said. "I've never seen anyone work so hard."

He shrugged, but felt a glow of pleasure at her words. "Training's what I do. And learning. If you're not trying to get better, it's time to hang up the boots. Reckon climbing isn't much different."

"Not much different at all," she said. "But you're good to do it today? You sure? After playing last night?"

"Yeh. I'm good." Truth was, he was sore. But a bit of climbing wouldn't hurt him. And he wouldn't have canceled this for anything. "Let's go for it."

"All right, then," she decided. "As it *is* your last lesson, we'll get you on that overhang that we haven't done yet, last thing today. That'll be your ceremony, because then you'll have accomplished everything."

Well, not everything, he thought, getting himself kitted up. But he was getting closer.

When he stepped lightly down from the final climb, the overhang that he'd never managed to get all the way up before, he had a huge grin on his face. She smiled back at him, put up her hand, and smacked his palm in a high-five.

"Congratulations," she told him. "Mr. Most Improved."

"Thanks to my awesome teacher. And you're done for the day, eh. Now that you've accomplished the impossible here, taught me to climb."

"I am. Done for the day, I mean," she said, still smiling. Looking happy to hear what she had to know he'd be asking next.

"So what can we do to celebrate?" he asked. "I brought my togs today. I'm even prepared to jump off high places with you again if I have to."

She laughed again, and he thought that a man would give a lot to be able to bring that look of pleasure to her face. "I didn't miss that swimming wasn't your favorite thing. You were a great sport, though."

"Also my job," he pointed out. "So what, then? Want to have dinner with me?" He waited for her answer, still surprised at how much it mattered to him. In fact, he'd rung Logan Brown already, booked a table. Perfect for her, he'd thought. Wellington's finest restaurant. A beautiful spot, beautiful food, but not too formal. She'd be able to relax, he hoped, be comfortable.

They'd managed to squeeze him in, accommodate his request for a quiet corner, as he'd known they would. He tried not to ask for special treatment, but he needed this. Now all he had to do was get her there. He didn't think she'd be impressed just because he spent money on her, but he wanted to show her that he was making an effort. That this mattered to him. That *she* mattered to him.

"I'd like that," she said, and he could tell from the serious look she gave him that she knew what he was doing, that this was a big step. "But a bit later, do you think?"

"Yeh," he agreed. "As it's only five now. And I wasn't thinking about popping out for fish and chips. I thought we could get togged up a bit, go on a—what do they call those things? Oh, yeh. A date."

"That sounds fun," she said, and her expression looked to him like anticipation, mixed with a bit of nerves. A bit of adrenaline. "And if it's going to be a while, maybe you wouldn't mind belaying me for a few routes first. I'm off the clock now, and I haven't had a chance to do any real climbing for days. Would you be willing?"

She'd taught him to belay, of course, but had always kept her routes short, saying that he wasn't paying to watch her climb. Even though he would've, and gladly. He realized that this might be the biggest step of all. She was trusting him with her safety, asking him for help, asking him to do something just because it would give her pleasure.

All he said, though, was, "Course. Long as you want."

She started with the route he'd just done, the hardest in the gym. And went up it the same way she'd climbed the first time he'd seen her. Like a cat, so sure and so fast that he, who'd just struggled up the thing, could hardly believe it.

"Thanks for doing that," she said at the end of forty minutes or so, during which he'd lost count of the number of climbs she'd done. She was sweating just a bit, her cheeks pink with effort. "It was great. You're very patient."

He had to smile at that. "Don't you know how much I like watching you? Thought that would be pretty obvious by now."

"You do?" she asked, the flush deepening a bit more. "Even climbing?"

"Definitely climbing. It's not just that you're so good at it, though that's hot too. It's the climbing harness. How it looks, what it draws attention to. Why d'you think I was up on that thing, the first day? When I got stuck?"

"Why?" she asked with fascination. "You mean…me? You weren't just climbing that because you assumed you could do the hard stuff?"

"That too, probably," he admitted. "Because I was a boof-head, as I may have mentioned. But the real reason?" He looked straight at her, not smiling now. "It was you. I thought you were sexy as hell. I still do, in case you were wondering."

"Wow," she said, lifting her hands to pull the elastic out of her ponytail, shaking her hair out, which was a sexual signal if he'd ever seen one. And his own climbing harness was going to be showcasing too much itself if he kept up this line of chat. He turned away, loosened the straps and pulled it off. Looked back and saw her doing the same, but looking a bit self-conscious about it. He had a feeling that dinner with her was going to be good.

♡

Ally walked to Nate's car with him, feeling as if her head were spinning. She'd hoped that today would go something like this, but now that it was happening, she was definitely nervous.

A feeling that wasn't helped at all at the sight of the man approaching on the busy Saturday-evening pavement. Devon.

It wasn't the first time she'd seen him. Wellington was too small, too centralized, too pedestrian-friendly to avoid him. All good things, except when you really didn't want to run into somebody. She normally either pretended she didn't see him, if that was feasible, or gave him a curt nod. While he, on the other hand, always looked perfectly comfortable at seeing her. Well, he was probably used to seeing his one-night-stands on the street. She'd bet there had been a lot of them. But seeing him when she was with Nate—

She felt Nate stiffen beside her, and knew he'd seen Devon too. And, to her surprise, Devon *didn't* look comfortable, not this time. He glanced between the two of them, his expression hardening. And Ally was glad to see it. She hoped it made him sweat, thinking about her with Nate. She looked straight back at him, sent the message as hard as she could. *He's bigger and better than you. In every...single...way.* She'd bet it was true, too.

Nate glanced down at her, but she kept walking. Speeded up, if anything. Averted her gaze now, with her best look of contempt, and walked right on by.

Nate didn't say anything until he'd opened the car door for her, put her bag, which he'd insisted on carrying, into the backseat with his own, and climbed in on his side. Until they were driving over the hill to Aro Valley.

At last, though, he spoke, seeming to choose his words carefully.

"You don't have to ignore him for my sake," he said. "I don't like him, that's no secret. But I know you do, and that you did that Heat thing with him. I can be civil if I have to be."

"I don't, though," she said. "You were right. He's a...He's not a good person."

He looked across at her, arrested, then turned his attention back to his driving.

"What did he do?" he asked, and she could see that his hands were gripping the wheel a bit too tightly. "Something with the shoot? He's ambitious, I told you that. He'll use people to get what he wants."

"Yeah," she said bitterly. "I figured that out."

They were outside the block of flats now. Nate pulled into a parking spot, but didn't move to get out of the car.

"What happened?" he asked again, turning to her. "I should've told you more about what he was like. I don't like to talk about him, but I should've warned you."

"I'm not sure I would have believed you," she said honestly. "He comes across so well, doesn't he? Seems so…interested."

Realization began to dawn on his face. "Ally. What did he do?"

She shrugged, tried to pass it off. "It wasn't any big deal. Happens to women all the time, I know. It's just that it had never happened to me before. He acted interested, like I said. And turns out he wasn't. I think, looking back at it, that he wanted to get some kind of introduction to Drew, once he realized who Kristen was. Or he could have even known about that before. I wouldn't put it past him. Anyway, he tried with her, and when that didn't work, he tried with me. And when *that* didn't work…"

She sighed, not wanting to admit how stupid she'd been. Wished she didn't have to tell him, but she'd asked him to be honest with her, hadn't she? And that went both ways. With the way he felt about Devon, she didn't want him to find out later and think she'd lied to him.

"He decided he might as well get the consolation prize," she said at last. "Because I think he was…mad at me about that, somehow. And he wanted to win."

"So he slept with you," Nate said slowly. "Gave you the full treatment to get there, I'm sure. Made you think it meant something. And once he got it, made it clear that he didn't want it anymore. Went out of his way to make you feel cheap."

"That's about it." She hated that he knew this, but tried to keep her tone light. "Which should maybe make you reconsider. Could be I'm just not good in bed."

He didn't answer her directly. His face, his tone were grim. "This is my fault. I should've told you, so you'd have been warned about what kind of scungy dickhead he is."

"How can it be your fault that I slept with the wrong guy?" she protested. "I'm a big girl. I made a mistake. I don't go around sleeping with random guys, though." She knew she shouldn't have to defend herself, but she couldn't bear to have him think of her that way. "I really thought he…"

"You thought he was serious," he finished for her. "Because he took care that you thought so."

"But how do you know?" she asked. "Is that why you don't like him? Because you saw what he was like, when you were flatmates?"

"Yeh, nah, not exactly," he sighed. "That is, I saw what he was like. How he is with women, I mean. At least how he was then, and I doubt he's changed much. I don't think he likes women at all, really. Seems to enjoy…hurting them. Not physically," he hurried to explain. "But making them fall in love, or at least sleeping with them, and then dropping them. He likes that, I think."

She winced a bit, hating to remember how gullible she'd been. She really had been nothing but prey, and that hurt.

"But I let it go," he went on, "just like I did with you, which is on me. I told myself it wasn't my business, until it was."

She waited to hear more, though she already had a glimmer. And his next words confirmed it.

"Because I had a girlfriend back then," he said. "During Uni, a couple years there. I was mad for her. When I said I'd never been passionately in love…that was a lie, or something I'd rather forget. And Devon…"

"He slept with your girlfriend," Ally said. "He turned that charm on her. And she cheated on you with him."

"Yeh," he admitted. "Tore me up at the time. Her, too, when he dropped her. Just did it to see if he could, I think, and to score on me. Because he was jealous of me, of what I had. What I'd done, I guess. Even though…"

"Even though you'd earned it," she finished for him. "Since you had it and he didn't, it was unfair. Is that about it?"

"Yeh. I never could understand that, but that's how it was. So that's what he did. And he was right, it worked. It hurt. And it broke us up, of course. Afterwards, she wanted to come back to me. Told me she still loved me, that she was sorry. But I couldn't look at her the same way again, not after she'd been with him."

Ally felt sick inside as the full realization of what he'd said hit her. Of what it meant.

"OK," she said, wishing her voice sounded stronger. "I see why you don't like him. And..." She made a helpless gesture. "Thanks for the coffees, and the beer, and everything. I'll see you."

She reached back for her bag, got out of the car, walked hurriedly to the front door, pulling out her keys with eyes that were blurred by tears. It wasn't enough that Devon had...had seduced her, she thought, the old-fashioned word seeming like the only appropriate one. Now he'd wrecked things with Nate, too. And she *liked* Nate. She liked him so much.

"Ally." He was beside her, his hand on her arm. "Wait."

"It's OK." She shook his hand off, got the key into the door. "I know it seems awkward, but it doesn't matter. Better that you found out now."

"It *does* matter," he insisted. "And I'm not going to let you go. Not till we talk this over."

"Then come upstairs," she sighed. She didn't have to worry that he'd jump her, after all, not any more. All her caution seemed ridiculous now, anyway. There was only one good guy in this scenario, and it was pretty obvious which one he was. How could she have got it so backwards?

He didn't try to talk to her until they were in her flat. Kristen wasn't home, Ally registered briefly. Out with Liam, she supposed. *Kristen* wasn't reading guys wrong. She'd been right about both Nate and Devon all along.

"Sit down," she told Nate now, gesturing to the couch. "Do you want a beer or something? I think we have some."

He waved a hand. "Nah."

He waited until she was seated beside him, then began to speak. Sitting forward in his typical pose, legs apart, elbows on his knees, hands clasped, head turned to look at her. "I should've told you about Devon at Drew's. When you...mentioned him."

She winced. "When I told you what he'd said about you."

"Yeh." He didn't look any happier than she felt, was looking down between his feet now. "And I didn't, because it's not something I like to think about. It sure as hell isn't something I like to talk about, or that I wanted to tell you about. But if I had, you'd have known, wouldn't you. You'd have known what kind of man he is, and he couldn't have done that to you."

She shrugged helplessly, surprised at how miserable she felt. She'd told herself she wasn't sure if she wanted Nate. Who had she been kidding? "It's not your fault. I guess I needed to have that experience. I haven't dated much, like I said. Turns out there's a type of man that I didn't recognize. Kristen did, but I didn't listen to her."

"I suspect Kristen's met her share of Devons," Nate said with a little smile, the first he'd shown since they'd started talking about this. "Who want to score off her, be able to tell their mates they've had a woman that gorgeous. Happens the other way round, too, you know. Get a bit of fame, and a man gets that same thing. Course, men seem to be able to live with it."

"I'll bet. And you're right, Kristen's a lot smarter than I am in some ways. And I didn't know what I didn't know. Now I do, and I can be more careful. So like I said," she went on more briskly. "No harm done." Except, of course, that their almost-romance wasn't going to happen.

He looked at her searchingly. "Hope that's true. That he didn't hurt you too much."

"Yeah, well," she said wryly. "Kinda hard to get your heart broken after a few dates. I was embarrassed, but that was about it. He wasn't exactly memorable, or all that regrettable either, if you know what I mean. I think I have a pretty good idea of why your girlfriend wanted to come back to you."

He smiled again. "Good to know, I guess."

"But I'm wondering," she said, "if that's the case, if he did that to you, why does he seem to hate *you?* It's like it was the other way around, that you did something to him. Is that just the jealousy? Or did something else happen?"

"Just one thing. Hard for me to see how he can resent me for it, but who knows how he thinks. A couple years ago, he asked me for an intro to our head of PR. I couldn't believe it. Said no, of course, and he wasn't too happy."

"He did say something about that. But seriously? He thought you'd help him?"

"That's what I thought! He seemed to think it shouldn't matter anymore. That I'd somehow have forgotten it, or forgiven it, or something. Couldn't believe it."

"Because women don't matter to him, like you said," she guessed. "And he didn't understand why you'd still care yourself."

"Yeh. Reckon you're right. So anyway, I told him what I thought of him, and that I'd be doing my best to see that he never did get anywhere, not in rugby. And he hasn't, and I'm guessing he knows why. That it's been because of me. And somehow, he doesn't see that that's because of what he did. It's something I did to him. So," he finished, "sorry again that I didn't say more, and I think you're letting me off the hook too easily, but I appreciate it. And now that we've got that sorted at last, we can put him out of both our minds. Forever, I hope. And go to dinner, because I'd much rather think about you."

"You don't want to go to dinner with me, though, not now."

"Now what?" He looked genuinely surprised.

"You don't want to take out somebody who was with him. I know you don't. I know how much that would bother you. You broke up with your girlfriend over it."

"Ally." He took her hand. "She cheated on me. And your past is over and done, just like mine is. D'you think I only date virgins? It's been a long, long time since I was a woman's first. And it doesn't make me think less of them. Because I'm none too clean in that area myself, I'm sorry to say. We could compare notes, but I don't really want to share my history."

"Really?" she asked, searching his face.

"Really. I really don't want to share. Because you'd think I was a slut, and wouldn't want anything to do with me."

She laughed for the first time, and felt the relief of it. "As long as you're only dating one woman at a time these days. And as long as you're not about to tell me that you're not ready for a relationship right now."

"I'm not going to say that," he said with a smile of his own, giving her hand a squeeze. "That means it's casual. That it's likely to be...short."

"Ha! Kristen was right again!" She pulled her hand out of his to clap hers together.

"What?" He looked confused.

"She told me that was man-speak for 'This is a one-night stand.' And she was right!"

He sank against the cushions, put his head back, and groaned. "Am I ever going to get used to you saying exactly what's on your mind? Or stop getting sucked into answering? Short doesn't necessarily mean one night. Just means what I said. When I'm not looking for a relationship, I don't like to lead women on. I don't want them to...hope, if that's not what it is."

"So when were you planning to say that to me?" she demanded. "Earlier, I mean?"

He looked uncomfortable. "Before we went too far. So you could choose."

"Uh-huh. Once you'd got me all hot and bothered."

"No worries," he grumbled. "Looks like I'm never going to get you hot and bothered. Every time I get close, I stuff up."

"Oh, I wouldn't say that. You've had me hot and bothered for a while now, and you've only kissed me...twice, haven't you? Kind of slow, aren't you?"

"Slow?" he demanded. *"Slow?"*

"Oh, yeah." Her spirits were fizzing now with the relief of having passed through the crisis, the laughter bubbling down deep. "I'd say you're being pretty slow, wouldn't you? I mean, even if we were in high school, if you took me out over and over and never even tried to hold my hand, I'm afraid I'd have to dump you. I've been giving you a pass, because I know you're a little scared of me, but..." She sighed. "Well, I guess you can't help your lack of confidence. I can see I'm going to have to take the lead here."

He actually sat there with his mouth open for a second, then shut it again. "You're going to have to take the lead, eh," he said, his eyes beginning to gleam. Starting to look a little bit dangerous. And dangerous was a really good look on him.

"Afraid so." She sighed again. "It's not really my preference, but what are you going to do? With a timid man..."

♡

Timid. Nobody had ever, *ever* called him timid. And even though he knew she was teasing him...

He reached for her and pulled her to him. She came willingly, laughing at him. Then he put his mouth over hers and kissed her the way he'd imagined doing it. Hungrily. Aggressively, his mouth and tongue claiming her own, his hand fisting in her hair, and she wasn't laughing anymore. She was making some noise beneath him, though, urgent little sounds that he smothered with his mouth as she grabbed at his shoulders, hung on. And she wasn't trying to take the lead one little bit.

He had her down on the couch, her upper body underneath his, his hand under her tank top, when they heard the door open, the voices.

"Oh!" Kristen said from behind them. "Excuse me! We'll just..."

"No, we won't." Mako's voice, then, as Nate sat up hastily, pulled Ally with him, and folded his hands over his lap. "Toro's got a house of his own, doesn't he. He wants to kiss somebody on the couch, he can do it there."

Nate cleared his throat, wished he could stand up, but that would be a very bad idea just now. "We stopped by so Ally could get changed," he said. "As we're going to dinner."

"And you were helping her," Mako said, then remembered himself. "Sorry, Ally. Nice to see you. Sorry we barged in on you."

"That's OK," Ally said, jumping up and pulling her tank top down self-consciously. "Nate's right. I'll just...I'll go get changed, so we can go out. Is there time for me to take a shower?" she asked Nate.

"Course," he said, thankfully able to stand at last. "I'll go home, get my own gear on, and come back for you, shall I? Seven forty-five OK? Enough time?"

"Sure," she agreed, looking adorably rumpled and flustered. "Perfect."

leather and lace

♡

She didn't look rumpled and flustered the next time he saw her, after Kristen had opened the door to his knock. She looked hot. And like nothing he'd ever seen from her before.

She saw the look on his face, faltered to a stop halfway across the lounge. "What? Wrong?" she asked in confusion. She looked at his open-neck white dress shirt, black jacket and dark jeans with the black shoes. "Should I be wearing jeans? I thought you said dress up some. I thought, a skirt."

"Ally. Wait," he said with a laugh. He went to meet her, gave her a gentle kiss, not wanting to spoil her makeup. Which was also something new from her. Smoky eyeshadow and liner that accentuated those exotic, almond-shaped eyes. But she'd kept her lipstick more natural, which pleased him. He loved her mouth exactly as it was. And her dark, shiny hair was down, tumbling around her shoulders, a bit messy. On purpose, he could tell, meant to look like she'd just climbed out of bed. With him.

"You look perfect," he assured her, taking both her hands in his and standing back to get a good look. "Leather, eh."

"Kristen said…" She still sounded doubtful, cast a glance at her friend, who smiled back at both of them.

"Bye, kids," Kristen said, turning for her bedroom. "Have a nice time."

Nate remembered to say goodbye to her before shifting his focus back to Ally. "Do me a favor," he said, dropping one of her hands. "Twirl for me."

She smiled slowly back at him, confidence returning to her expression, then did a pirouette with the aid of his hand, giving him the full view.

"Oh, yeh," he sighed, seeing the zip running down the entire back of the slim black leather skirt that hugged that gorgeous bum, ended several inches above her knees. The short-sleeved lace top she wore with it was wonderfully tight and stretchy, hugging her pretty breasts, a sort of...beige color that gave her that almost-naked look.

Eyes on her face during dinner, mate, he reminded himself. The color of the top was matched in her high heels—with no stockings, he saw with pleasure. He did love a woman with bare legs, and hers were the best. But he knew he'd be walking behind her tonight, looking at that zip. It was just a few centimeters undone, there at the bottom. Which was going to kill him.

"It's all Kristen's," she said happily. "I don't know where we're going, but she thought...this."

"And she was right," he assured her. "It's perfect. Come on. Let me take you out. Because I can't wait."

♡

Down on the street, he held the car door for her, waited until she was settled inside, then slammed it shut again, went around the car and got in himself.

"I really love it when you do that, by the way," she said impulsively.

"What?" he asked, startled. "Start the car?"

"Carry things for me. Open my door. It makes me feel... special. Like a woman."

When he didn't answer immediately, she hurried on. "Never mind. I'm not a very sophisticated date. I'm sure I should be acting like it's the least you could do for somebody as fabulous as me, and like I dress up all the time and get taken to nice places by desirable rugby stars. But this is actually all pretty new to me, and I'm not too good at pretending."

He smiled across at her, pulled out of the space, and headed back down to the CBD. "Which is a bonus, trust me. Women are usually—" Now he was the one who was cutting himself off.

"What?" she asked. "Usually what?"

"Never mind. I was about to sound like an arrogant prat again. And I'm trying hard here, in case you can't tell, not to spoil my chances with you."

He didn't have to worry too much about spoiling his chances. His chances were looking pretty darned good. When he'd kissed her like that tonight...Wow. She'd *never* been kissed like that. Like he wanted to eat her up. She shivered a little at the memory. And the way he'd looked at her when he'd showed up to take her out...Yeah. Not to mention the way *he* looked. That was pretty good, too. This whole thing might be another giant mistake. She might be headed straight down the road to ruin, but what a way to go.

She didn't tell him that, though, just enjoyed pulling up to the elegant building with him, having the valet come forward to open her car door, doing her best to step out with some grace and dignity in the tight skirt. And finding Nate there again, taking her hand to walk inside.

"I always thought this was a bank," she said as he held one of the huge double wooden doors for her and they stepped into the marble-lined entryway. "There's no sign on it that I've seen."

"It was." He nodded a greeting to the smiling man who came forward to welcome them. "The Bank of New Zealand. And now it's a restaurant. I thought you might enjoy it."

He really seemed to care whether she did, focused on her despite the attention he was garnering from the wait staff and many of the other diners. Nobody exactly fawned over him. New Zealand was too egalitarian for that, she'd figured that out a while ago. But they definitely knew who he was, although everyone was leaving him alone tonight, to her relief. She guessed that the staff at a restaurant like this, in the nation's capital, too, would see their fair share of celebrities. And that probably went for the patrons as well.

His smiling attention was all for her throughout the evening as he kept up a joking discussion about his climbing prowess, asked her about the outdoor climbing she'd done back in the States. She tried to focus, tried to answer him as best as she could, although the look in his eyes was making her shiver. She could tell where his attention really was, because hers was there, too.

"Something the matter?" he asked. She realized she'd become distracted again by his smile, the look on his face. How had she ever thought those eyes were cold? They were warm enough now. They were heating her up. And her hand, she realized, was holding the fork that rested on her plate, but wasn't moving.

"Not enjoying that lamb, eh," he said. "Should've told me. I'd've had them change it out for you."

"What? No," she said, starting a little. "I'm fine. I'm just... I'm looking at you, and...Nate. I want to go home with you. Please, take me home now."

She felt the shudder running through her as he looked at her, startled, and set his own fork slowly down. Those eyes were burning with intensity now, and she was burning too.

He lifted a hand for the waiter, pulled his credit card from his wallet and handed it to the man with a few words, then stood and led Ally out of the elegant room, collecting the card along the way, signing the receipt. And outside, there was his car, already waiting.

Nate collected the keys with a brief "cheers," then stepped around the man who would have opened the door for her to do it himself. She saw his eyes on her legs as she swung them in, the leather skirt riding up a bit. And then he was inside, and driving fast.

♡

He hadn't thought he'd make it out of the restaurant. Had thought for one wild moment, when she'd said that, when she'd looked at him like that, that he was going to pull her into some back room. And by the time he steered into the garage set into the hillside, he wasn't sure they were going to make it out of there, either.

He was out of the car, around to her side, pulling her out within seconds of turning the engine off. And then had slammed her door shut and backed her up against it, one hand hard against the back of her head, holding her for him, the other one firm at her waist. His mouth demanding that she open hers, then taking everything she had. And feeling her kissing him back just as desperately, making those little noises again, grabbing for his shoulders to pull him even closer.

He let go of her head at last and reached around, his hands finally going to that round little bum that he'd been craving for so long, and it felt every bit as good in his palms as he'd known it would. He was pulling her up higher, off her feet, holding her hard against him while he kissed her, and he knew that he needed everything. Needed her naked, underneath him, and that he couldn't wait any longer.

"Inside." He pulled back from her, set her on her feet again. "Let's go."

Up the stairs, then. Into the house, letting go of her long enough to pull off his jacket, his shoes and socks. Watching her kick off the heels, sorry to see them go. Pulling her up the stairs to his bedroom, slapping the rocker switch that turned on the bedside lights. Seeing her, eyes huge and smoky, staring at him. Her mouth open, breath coming hard with effort and desire. He could see the nipples pebbling under that lace top as he'd watched them do all evening, just like that first night when he'd spilt the beer on her. And now he was going to have them under his hands, under his mouth. He was going to have all of her.

He reached for her, got his hands under that top, pulled it off her and tossed it, and realized why he'd been able to see her nipples so well. Because her bra was nearly sheer, a light mesh of flesh-colored material over the thin bands holding it in place. He pushed her down across the big bed, came down over her, and was there. His hands on her. His mouth, kissing, biting, pulling her inside. Feasting on her.

Her hands were in his hair, grabbing him, and she was making those sounds again, incoherent cries that pushed him even higher. He reached a hand down, over the leather skirt, beyond to the warm flesh of her thigh, could feel the way her legs were straining against the heavy material, trying to open for him, and felt himself losing another bit of control. She jerked against him as he ran his hand up one of those smooth, slim thighs, under the leather, then settled it over the center of her. He rubbed the seam of the tiny, triangular front of the thong into her, felt what it did to her, how she was squirming against his hand, crying out as he continued. She was ready to come right now, but he wasn't ready for her to do it yet.

He put his hands on her hips, flipped her over. Found the fastening for the bra, undid it, lifted her upper body with one hand while he pulled it off her with the other. Then had both hands under her, cupping her breasts, as he straddled her. He rubbed her, pinched her, heard her sobbing breaths. Saw her head turned to the side, the one eye he could see open and glazed with passion.

He moved off her, then, stood behind her where she lay on the bed, ran his hand down her back. And then over the black leather, all the way down to the hem.

"When I saw this zip tonight," he said, his voice sounding rough in his ears, "I knew I'd be doing this." He reached for the little tab that had taunted him all night, partly undone already and begging him to finish the job. Pulled it slowly up, all the way to the top. The black leather parting to reveal her thighs, then parting more, falling all the way open. Showing him all of her, the thin strip of thong barely visible. Looking like a delicious fantasy come true.

He pulled her back towards him so her hips were at the edge of the bed, and his hands were parting her thighs, exploring those smooth cheeks, then delving between them, over her, rubbing the silky material into her. And she was writhing against the bed, against his fingers, crying out.

"Nate," she said, her voice muffled against the duvet. "Nate. Turn me over. I want to see you. I want to touch you. Oh, God. Nate."

He was aching to take her this way, to have her like this. But he needed to do more to her first. He needed to do it all. He grabbed the thong in both hands, yanked it down her legs and off her. Flipped her over again and pulled her up so her head was on the pillow. Moved down her body, put a hand on either thigh. Spread her legs for him, and thought he'd lose it right then from the sense of power it gave him. And then put his mouth to her. Tasted the excitement flooding her, filling her. Her hands were in his hair, her hips were moving against him, and she was crying out. And then she was coming so hard, for so long, he could tell it almost hurt.

♡

Ally was whirling. Spinning. From the time she'd climbed into his car, she'd felt it, that exhilarating sensation of standing at the edge of the very steepest black diamond slope, pushing herself off. The moment when she knew she was caught, that she had to take this ride all the way to the end. The rush of being at the screaming knife-edge of control, fighting to keep herself inside that thin line. Excitement at the edge of panic. Pleasure at the edge of pain. And she knew she was almost all the way there now, that she was losing herself in his touch, in the pleasure he was making her feel, in the thrill of being overtaken.

She realized, opening her eyes at last, shuddering with the trailing jolts of pleasure from one of the most intense orgasms she'd ever experienced, that he was still dressed. That she hadn't even touched him. He came up over her, and she reached for his shirt, jerked it out of the waistband of his jeans, began to fumble at the buttons, her fingers trembling and clumsy.

"Nate. Now. Please," she got out, hearing the strain in her voice. He finished the unbuttoning job for her, pulled the shirt off. Her hand was already on his belt buckle, yanking it open. And then she was unzipping him, reaching beneath the waistband of his briefs, greedy for the feeling of him filling her hand, the smoothness and the size of him. And no, the nickname wasn't just about determination and strength. Not at all.

He swore viciously, rolled to one side, pulled everything off in one quick series of movements. Grabbed for the drawer of the bedside table and pulled out the packet as she finally, blissfully, ran her hands over him from behind. His back, then around it, stroking the defined muscles of his abdomen. But only for a moment, because he was over her again, pulling her arms up over her head.

"Reach behind you and grab hold," he ordered, moving over her.

"I want to touch you," she protested.

He was straddling her, and his hands were over hers, placing them over the edge of the low headboard. "Grab hold," he told her again. "Hang on. Because you're going to get it hard."

And she did. She was rocketing down that slope, almost too fast, almost gone. She could hear herself, as if from a distance, making sounds she'd never heard come from her mouth before. She had her knees all the way up by her shoulders, the wind rushing in her ears, telling her that she'd gone almost too far, was all the way out on that razor edge.

And then he took hold of her legs, shoved them all the way up, and the tension in her was off the charts, every muscle in her body gripping as he held her tight, stretched her out, his hands hard on the backs of her thighs. He was driving into her, every stroke pushing her higher, further out, to the limit.

And finally, with an agonized cry, she was all the way over. Tumbling and rolling, again and again, her eyes squeezed shut, mouth open, wailing with the intensity of it. And feeling, hearing him going right along with her, straight over into the dark.

♥

"Bloody hell," he groaned when he could speak again. When he'd let her go and she was lying next to him, her breath even more labored than his own. "Bloody *hell.* I think you killed me."

"*Me?*" she gasped. "*I* killed *you?* I may never have the use of my legs again."

He laughed, heard the shakiness of it, reached out for her and pulled her against him, bent to kiss her. "And I never did let you touch me, did I? No worries, we'll get to that. We'll take it slowly next time, I promise. I just...I had to get that done first."

"Mmm," she agreed, stroking her hand over his chest, leaning over to kiss him there, which felt pretty bloody good, too. "Next time, you can hold the headboard and let me explore. But first—" She rolled to one side of the big bed. "I need a shower."

He saw her hesitate, look back at him. "If you're OK with me staying, I mean."

"You're joking." He pulled himself up so he could watch her. "If you think I'm letting you out of here for the next forty-eight hours, you're dreaming. I've got two days off, and a fair few frustrated weeks to make up for. And all sorts of wonderful things I need to try, as well as whatever you come up with."

"Well, sadly," she said, getting up and moving toward the ensuite bath, giving him the chance to take a good long look at the sight of her walking away, "I don't have two days off. I have to work tomorrow afternoon, and close, too. Which means I'll be there till nine."

"Then we'll have to make the hours count, won't we," he decided. "And I've just realized that I need another climbing lesson after all. Last thing tomorrow."

men's valentine's day

♡

"Now I know what your mom meant," Ally sighed the next evening, just before taking another enthusiastic bite of Thai takeaway. She wriggled back against the headboard a little more, lifted her plate from her lap so she could cross her bare legs. At least she was wearing underwear and a camisole now. Dressed for dinner.

That shocked a laugh out of Nate, sitting back himself in nothing but a pair of warmup pants, making short work of his beef and vegetables. "I'm almost scared to ask. This scene isn't really something I'd associate with my mum."

"When she—or was that your aunt?—was talking about how much you spoil them," she explained.

"Oh, yeh. Buying you Thai food, that's a major. I'd better watch myself here, setting this kind of standard."

"OK, but giving me a ride home this morning, then waiting while I packed so you could drive me to work—that's a lot of spoiling, admit it. And then coming to get me again tonight."

"Because I needed my lesson, is what that was. Needed to give you a bit of a lesson, too. Even things out a little."

"Mmm," she said happily. It had been awfully nice to see him come through the door tonight. To see him smile at her. To smile back at him, and to think, *That's mine. He's here for me.* To want him so much, and know that he wanted her just as badly. To spend the hour climbing with him, teasing him, laughing with him, all the while knowing that they were going to end up here.

And then what had happened when they actually *had* ended up here. They'd had to reheat their takeaway after what she'd intended as a quick shower had turned much soapier than anticipated. They'd started in there, continued out here, in bed. And on the floor. The floor had been especially…special.

"You know what's extra nice?" she went on. "I was feeling kinda bad a couple weeks ago that I wasn't going to have a boyfriend for Valentine's Day. Not that anybody's ever done much for me on Valentine's Day, but at least I didn't have that feeling that I was the only leprous, unloved person on the planet, know what I mean?"

"Don't think men get that feeling," he said with a smile. "We're a bit late here, but I could nip down to the shop and buy you a card. Half price, even, which would mean I could probably do the choccies too. They'll still have them up in that bargain bin."

She laughed. "No, thanks." She leaned over and kissed the top of his shoulder, loving the fact that she could do it. "I was just thinking that I sort of got a Valentine after all, and that it's nice. But maybe you want a card, since you missed it too. And, as you've pointed out, they're cheap now."

"Well, you know what they say about Valentine's Day and men."

"No, what?"

"It's a woman's holiday. We don't really care. I read online somewhere that some bloke proposed they have one just for men, maybe the next month. *This* month, in case you want to do a bit of planning."

"Uh-huh," she said skeptically. "I can't wait. What do men want for Valentine's Day? Not candy and flowers, I take it."

"Nah. What this bloke was saying was, beer, steak, and a… and oral sex. Men's Valentine's Day. Easy as."

"Wow. That's so romantic," she breathed, eyes wide in mock admiration. "I'll just point out here that you're drinking a beer right now, and you had a steak last night. And that you got the other part tonight, too. I'm pretty much three for three."

"Yeh," he grinned. "Every day's Valentine's Day, far as I'm concerned. You're keeping me pretty happy so far."

"I'll keep you happy as long as you keep me happy. I really like what you do. I haven't done very much before," she added in a burst of endorphin-induced honesty. "Not that much variety, I mean. I'm really liking trying some new things, and I can't wait to do even more."

He stopped with his fork halfway to his mouth, then finished off his dinner in a couple bites, set the plate aside.

"What kinds of things, exactly, can't you wait to do?" he asked. "Should I be taking notes?"

"You know," she faltered. She looked down at her plate, toyed with a piece of broccoli. Had she really said that? "I like how it's fun, with you. Different positions, different places. I haven't done that before. And I just figured, maybe you had some other ideas, too."

"So what we have here," he said, a smile beginning to form, "is your basic male fantasy. A woman without much experience who wants to be…instructed."

"Well…" She hesitated, could feel the red creeping all the way up from her chest, betraying her. "When you say it like that, it sounds so…dirty."

"Oh, it's going to be dirty," he promised. "How dirty, that's up to you. You can tell me how far you want to go. Because I'm ready to go all the way."

"I'm not sure," she admitted. She'd said this, she might as well keep going. Nobody had ever accused *her* of being timid. She took a defiant stab at that broccoli, raised it to her mouth, and chewed.

"I'm guessing there are things that work in a fantasy," she finally went on, "but wouldn't be that great to actually do. I'm pretty sure I'm not into pain. Giving or receiving it, either one. Or actual coercion, if I really don't want to, you know." She hoped it wasn't necessary to spell that out, but who knew what he thought "all the way" meant? "Oh, and no multiple partners," she said as it suddenly occurred to her. "Beyond that...not sure. I'd have to try it and see. But if you're thinking about pulling out your riding crop and those clamps," she added, trying to get on top of the situation again, "that's a no."

"So many restrictions. I guess that means choking's out too. Bugger," he sighed.

"Joke," he added quickly at the look on her face. "No worries. I never understood how it's hot to force a woman, or to hurt her. I get enough pain out on the paddock, giving *and* receiving. Don't think I could do that anyway. That black eye was the last time I'm going to be hurting you. But introducing you to some new...ideas, a bit of experimentation, a little role-playing, now...that's something else."

Role-playing. Wow. She could feel the heat pooling inside, the throb that had begun again as soon as they'd started talking about this, was so strong now that she could feel each pulsing beat. She was sure he could read it on her face.

"OK," she said, wishing her voice hadn't dropped to a whisper. "I can do that."

"Oh, I know you can," he assured her. "And that you will, just as soon as I tell you to."

"Oh, boy," she breathed. What had she let herself in for? And why wasn't she worried about it? Because she wanted to do it, that was why. And she wanted to do it with him.

priorities

♡

"We should get our schedule sorted," Nate said the next morning, pushing his plate aside and pulling his mobile out of his pocket.

"Uh...OK." Ally took another bite of eggs on toast. They'd got up pretty early. Nate was an early riser, no surprise, and there were only a few other people in the café. After this, it was sea kayaking in the Harbour. A day off was good. A day off with Nate, sex, and kayaking was *great.*

"I have training tomorrow, and then a photo shoot in Auckland," he went on. "What about the rest of the week? What's your work schedule look like?"

"I can't remember, off the top of my head. Wait, though. You're going to Auckland tomorrow? And coming back again?"

"Yeh," he said, brushing it aside. "The flight's less than an hour. Some days I do it twice, if I've got something in the morning, something else in the evening."

"Wow" she said blankly.

"Your schedule, though," he prompted. "Don't you have it on your phone?"

"Oh." She recalled herself from the contemplation of a life that included four trips to the airport—and four flights, however short—in a single day. "No, strangely enough, I don't. I don't have to be that organized. I have Saturday evening off, I know that, because I was checking to see whether I'd be able to watch your game. I ought to see that, don't you think?"

"Yeh," he said with a smile, "if you're asking me, I'd say that'd be good. I could get you a ticket if you like. You and Kristen both."

"Kristen has a buying trip in Australia, so it'll just be me. But I'd love to watch you play in person. Do you think you'll win this time?"

He laughed. "Do our best. Why, you don't want to come unless we're going to win?"

"Of course not," she said hastily. "I want to come watch you either way."

"Right, then." He typed in a quick note. "I'll get the ticket emailed to you, find some company for you if I can." He looked up. "Well, I would if I had your email. Better give me that, and your mobile number as well."

"Wow. This is kind of like the first day at a new job. I'm wondering when I fill out my enrollment form for the benefits."

He smiled. "Sorry. I tend to get a bit efficient at times."

"Yes, you do," she agreed. "But OK. Here you go." She recited her information, was startled again when he raised his phone and snapped a picture of her.

"What?" he asked at her frown.

"You can't remember who 'Ally' is unless you have my picture to remind you?"

"Nah. Just want to be able to look at you, that's all." And his smile was so sweet, she melted a little.

"You'd better give me yours too," she realized. "I don't have a camera, but I think I can remember who you are without a picture. I'm pretty sure I can, anyway. If you remind me again."

"I'll remind you again," he promised. "Whose idea was this kayaking anyway?"

"Mine, but you agreed. You said it'd be fun. And I need a rest anyway. I thought I was in shape, but I'm clearly going to have to do some more working out to keep up with you."

He laughed, then looked back at his phone again. "You don't know what other days you're working?"

"Uh…" She wracked her brain. "I think I have tomorrow off, or maybe it's Thursday. And I know I'm opening on Wednesday, which means I'll be done at five."

"How about Sunday?" he prompted. "Next Monday?"

"Sorry. Can't remember."

"Text me your schedule," he decided. "We'll see if we can work something out during my time off, because I'll be off to Perth on Monday afternoon. As far as this week…Tuesday's my toughest training day. Got some meetings, too. And Thursday," he added, pushing a couple buttons, "we're doing a school visit after training, then I'll be having dinner with Mako and a couple of the other senior boys, talk about what we want to focus on during the Captain's Run on Friday. Wednesday'd be all right, though, wouldn't get too late if you'll be done by five. I could collect you after work and we could make dinner at my house, maybe, and you could stay over, though I'll have to drop you back at home fairly early Thursday morning. Good for you?"

"Yeah. I think so," she said, feeling like she'd just been engulfed by a sea of detail.

She was about to say something else when they were interrupted by a trio of young women requesting autographs. Ally waited as patiently as he could while Nate signed with a quick smile and a "Cheers" before turning back to her.

"Sorry," he said. "That's why I thought, dinner at my house. What were you saying?"

"I didn't realize dating you was going to be such a logistical challenge. Are you sure you can fit me in?"

"Course." He looked up in surprise from his typing, then shoved the phone back into his pocket. "Gets pretty busy during the season, that's all. Makes you wish we hadn't wasted so much time, doesn't it?" he added with a grin.

"Yeah, right," she scoffed. "If we'd started this when *you* wanted to, you'd have been done with your preseason fling weeks ago, and you'd be doing all this pesky scheduling with somebody else."

He actually choked on his final sip of coffee, had to cough a bit, reach for the napkin she handed him.

"I'll never get used to the things you say," he got out at last. "But come on." He stood up and pulled her to her feet. "We've got some kayaking to do. I need some thinking time. Need to see if I can come up with another new experience for you. I'm planning to get everything I can out of this day. Make the most of it while I can, because I've got a pretty tough week ahead of me."

"What d'you think?"

Nate turned to see the backs coach, Nigel Henderson, coming up to join him, his eye, like Nate's, on the group of players running lines opposite. The sun was shining, but the winds were swirling on this Wednesday afternoon as they so often did in Wellington, making long passes more difficult and causing more than one ball to drop to the ground uncaught.

"Russell looks OK," Nate said, referring to the new young outside centre who'd been introduced into the squad this season to take the place of a player leaving, as so many of them were now, for the brighter lights and bigger paychecks to be had in the Northern Hemisphere. "Thought he did a good job of creating space against the Chiefs. Not easy to do against them. Good in support, too. Got good instincts, fast to react. He'll do all right."

"Agreed," Nigel said. "But?"

"Well, you know what it is," Nate said. "It's how dodgy the backline is, still. Specially Manny turning up unfit. We'll have to make sure we don't commit too many to the breakdown, so we've got a bit more flexibility on defense. Need to keep the pressure off at the back, because they're not up to it."

They both looked gloomily at the big left wing. Nate closed his mouth on any further expression of disgust at the extra five or six kilos Manny was still carrying, so obviously slowing him down, depriving him of the explosive burst that was the essence of a quality winger.

Nate had never understood how a player could let himself slide like that during his time off, jeopardize his—and the team's—season. All right, he knew it was harder for the Samoan and Maori boys. Time spent with big, loving families, family gatherings centered around food, frames that packed on fat as easily as they added muscle. But they knew it, too, and it was part of the discipline of playing this sport at its highest level. You turned up fit, and that was that. If you weren't willing to do what needed to be done—*everything* that needed to be done, everything the game asked of you—you didn't deserve to be out here.

He could have added a comment about the patchy form of their starting fullback, his lack so far of the flashes of brilliance he'd shown the previous season, the fact that the stretches of mediocrity in between seemed to be increasing. The tackles he'd missed the previous week, the kick that had been charged down and returned for the Chiefs try that had won the other team the game.

Yeh, he could have said all that. But instead, he trotted out to join the drill, to take the opportunity the wind provided to get some practice in under adverse conditions, make sure his own passes didn't go awry on the night. He wasn't here to whinge from the sidelines. He was here to play.

♡

Ally looked up when he arrived at the gym that afternoon, seeming almost surprised to see him. She was sitting on the mat next to the wall, long legs crossed in front of her, stuffing her climbing shoes and harness into her gym bag. Looking pretty, as always. Slim and sleek and a bit exotic, those dark eyes framed by slanting brows, the high cheekbones and wide mouth. Giving him a mental flash of some of the expressions he'd seen on that face last weekend, a quick tug of anticipation for the night ahead.

Yeh, she was looking pretty. But not happy, he realized. "What?" he asked.

"I wasn't sure you were coming." She stood up in one fluid motion, reminding him again of how much he liked the way she moved, the grace and flexibility of her. Just now, though, she was still looking a bit narky.

"Why?" he asked in confusion. "I'm on time, aren't I? It's five. And we scheduled it. You watched me type it in. If I'd had to cancel, I'd have texted. Did you forget which day it was? Didn't you put it down on your own calendar?"

"I don't have so many dates that I have to put them on my calendar." She was still looking upset. "Come on, let's go."

She waved a goodbye to the young Irish bloke behind the desk, then led the way out of the gym, leaving him to follow, still confused.

"What?" he asked again when they were on the wharf.

"Nothing. Where's your car?"

"Ally." He stopped where he stood, waited until she was, seemingly reluctantly, looking at him. "Something's wrong. Tell me."

"It feels stupid, though," she muttered. She put her bag down, reached for her ponytail with both hands and pulled it tight. Uh-oh.

"Tell me," he commanded, fixing her with his best captain's stare. "We're not going anywhere till you do."

"It's just…" She shrugged, looked out at the Harbour. "I thought you'd text me or something, about the plan. Call me, maybe. Something. Since it's only our second time together. It's like you did it, you got there, and now you're…done."

"Done," he repeated. "What d'you mean, done? I'm not done. Here I am, waiting to take you home with me. Not a bit done."

"Done courting me, I guess," she said, and he could see how uncomfortable this was making her. "I didn't expect, you know, flowers or anything. But maybe…" She trailed off. "Maybe a text. Saying, I don't know. 'See you tonight.' Like that."

"We calendared it, though," he repeated in confusion. "We agreed."

"Well, I need more than that, OK?" She was showing some exasperation now. "I'm not high-maintenance. At least, I've never thought of myself that way. But you started sleeping with me, what, five days ago? It'd be nice if I still felt a little bit special, you know? Like you were looking forward to seeing me."

"Special," he said slowly.

"Yeah," she muttered. "Special. I'm a girl. Sue me."

"Right," he said, the light dawning. "Right."

He took her hand, turned her to face him, waited until she was looking at him. "I've been looking forward to tonight," he told her. "The past couple days have been pretty stressful, and I've been thinking how good it'll be to be with you again. I thought we could do a bit of food shopping together, buy a couple steaks, a nice bottle of wine, and then go to my house, and you could take a shower, because I know you like to do that, first thing after work. Though I may have to join you in there," he added, trying out a smile and seeing her beginning to smile back. "Which may make dinner happen a bit later. But, yeh. I've been thinking about that, and looking forward to it. Because you're special, and I've missed you, and I want to be with you tonight."

He waited, tried to think what else he could say, but couldn't come up with anything. Saw her lift her hands to that ponytail again, pull out the elastic, then pause, seemingly unsure what to do with it. She was wearing that strappy yellow tank top again, with stretchy black tights that ended just below the knee. No pockets, he guessed.

"Here." He reached out a hand for it, took it from her and shoved it into his own pocket. He smiled at her as she ran her fingers through her hair, shook it out, and saw her smile back, beginning to shine for him with that warmth, that glow that was Ally, and sighed with relief.

"All right?" he asked quietly.

"Yeah," she said. "All right."

out on the paddock

♡

Nate was the first out onto the field as always, the Cake Tin still a sea of yellow, most of the brightly colored seats not yet filled. People tended to think that he was setting some kind of example by going out there before the rest of the squad to warm up, but Nate knew the truth. He was just the most eager to get started. Once he'd laced his boots up, he wanted to be on the paddock.

He went through the usual warm-ups and stretches, the rest of the boys gradually coming out to join him. Mako was running through scrum drills with the rest of the pack, he saw. Well, their forwards were all right. And the Blues were minus their two most experienced loosies, now that Drew had retired and Finn was off to Japan. Yeh, they could win the battle up front. It was going to be down to the backs. Nate traded kicks with Aaron Cooper, the fullback, tried to send confidence his way. If Coops showed some form tonight, they were in with a good chance.

And then, finally, they'd done all they could, and were trotting back into the tunnel to get ready to come out for the kickoff. Another game underway, and he was fizzing. He couldn't wait.

♡

"Do they always come out beforehand like that?" Ally asked Marika. She'd been gratified to find that Nate had arranged for her to sit with Liam's parents, and that they'd been so friendly. At least they'd probably know something about the game, and hopefully would share some of that with her. Ally suspected that her grand total of two games watched in the pub, barely able to hear the commentary, wasn't going to help her much, not without a TV camera to focus on where the action was happening.

"Like what?" Marika asked absently, her eyes, Ally saw, tracing her son's path into the tunnel.

"Do they always warm up first, right in front of everyone?" Ally tried to explain. "Or is that just something special tonight?"

Marika turned to her in surprise. "Course they do. Have to get warm, don't they. They'll have been sitting, getting taped up and all."

Ally considered explaining that watching the players do their groin stretches wasn't something North American audiences would have been treated to, but decided not to bother. She'd certainly enjoyed watching Nate do his, and everything else, too. She was pretty keyed up for this, in fact.

She actually caught her breath when Nate led the team out of the tunnel again and onto the field, and couldn't resist looking at the big screen at the end of the field just to see his face as he trotted out, holding the ball.

If he'd ever looked tough to her before, that was nothing to how he looked now. His set jaw rough with stubble, his eyes hard, he looked like he could win the game all by himself, or at least give it his very best shot.

He was her Nate, but he...wasn't. He was so much more. The gulf between them suddenly yawned wide, and she saw it with a sudden clarity, a shock of recognition that sent a cold shiver down her spine. She'd thought it would feel good to watch him like this, and it did. But it also felt strange, and a little uncomfortable, too.

And then the teams took up their positions for the kickoff, and the Hurricanes had sent the ball sailing to the back of the Blues' half, where a player caught it in sure hands and immediately sent it straight back again. Back and forth twice more, and then once again, without much running in between.

"Are they just going to kick it?" she asked, her momentary discomfort forgotten.

Marika laughed. "Playing for territory, bit of a chess match. Just wait a sec, and something will happen."

Something did. The Blues got the ball this time closer to midfield, and the player began to run with it, passed it to another man, who passed it to another, and was brought down by two Hurricanes players who plowed into him ruthlessly, the bodies piling up.

And after that, it was...fast. Played without a single break except a brief pause at halftime, and only a few substitutions, none of whom was Nate. Played even with an injured man lying on the field, being tended to by a doctor. The whole thing even rougher and more intense than it had looked on TV.

Ally could tell that, but that was about all she could tell. Except that the Blues seemed to be playing a little better, much of the action taking place in the Hurricanes' half, the Hurricanes forced onto defense that did seem to hold up, because late in the game, the score was only 13 to 6 in favor of the Blues. The margin would have been a single point, except that the Hurricanes kicker had missed two penalties that had had the crowd groaning, so Ally guessed that he should have made them.

But then the teams squared off in another scrum—at least Ally knew what that was—and Nate fed the ball into it, ran around to the back to pick it up when it squirted out, and handed it off. And the Hurricanes were advancing down the field, Nate somehow there instantly after every tackle to collect the ball from the tackled player and distribute it again. Which must have been according to some plan. He certainly seemed to know who he wanted to give it to, and what should happen after that, because as soon as he handed it off, he was running with the ball carrier. Well, he'd said you had to have some brains to play this game, and obviously, he was right. Because the speed of the decision-making out there was impressive. And his reaction time...that was just crazy.

The Hurricanes advance was short-lived, though, because suddenly, after another tackle tantalizingly near the Blues' try-line, there was some scrambling on the ground, and the crowd was groaning again.

"What happened?" Ally asked in confusion.

"Another turnover," Marika explained.

"Too bloody many turnovers," her husband Vernon, an older and even broader version of Liam, growled. "Not to mention the knock-ons and the spilled passes and the missed tackles. And," he sighed a moment after the Blues player kicked the ball long, getting it out of the danger zone, "that dodginess under the high ball."

Because, indeed, the player standing alone back there had missed catching the long, high kick, was having to scramble for it now, and then had his returning kick charged down by a fast-arriving Blues player. Which resulted in another turnover, which resulted in another flurry of passes, and, finally, a Blues player sliding across the line for an all-too-easy try that put the game away.

♡

Ally stepped out of the lift the next day and saw Nate leaning against the doorjamb. He stood up straight as she approached, and she realized she was smiling like a fool. She pulled the door open, surrendered the fabric bag of groceries, the duffel that held tomorrow's clothes to his demanding hands, then gave in to her emotions, pulled his head down for a kiss.

"Hi," she smiled up at him, her arms still wrapped around his neck. "Big shot."

He laughed. "What does that mean?"

She let go, followed him to the car and hopped in while he stowed her bags in the boot and jumped in beside her. "It means that I was impressed," she said.

"Should've known my brilliant personality wouldn't do the business, that I'd have to get you out to the park," he sighed.

"Oh, you impressed me before this too," she assured him. "OK, maybe not at first," she admitted at his laughing glance. "But fairly quickly. By the time you were climbing with me, I was definitely impressed."

"But somehow," he said, winding through the hills now, nearing his house, "you're more impressed now, even though we lost."

"Because you're so good at it. And being the best at that, at something that hard...that really means something. I finally got it, why you're such a big deal. And it was close, too. Right up until the end."

He grimaced, punched the button for the garage door, and pulled in. "Doesn't matter how close it was. It was a loss, and I'd rather have shown you a win."

"I don't care about that. I was impressed. I was more than impressed." She followed him up the steep flight of concrete steps that led from the back of the garage to the villa.

"Yeah," she sighed from behind him, watching him climb the steps in his shorts, remembering how he'd looked the night before. "Something about watching that...it's pretty effective, as a woman-attracting device."

He laughed. "I met you at the wrong time, that what you're saying? The offseason?"

"Maybe," she admitted. "But no, not really. I'm glad I got to know you first as a...as a person. I'd have been way too intimidated otherwise, if I'd watched you play like that and then met you."

He frowned down at her as he held the door. "You'd have worried that I'd hurt you, you mean, that I'd be too rough. I meant what I said. I don't do that."

"Of course not," she hastened to say, following him through to the big, modern kitchen at the back of the house, with its view out to a patch of manicured lawn and native plantings of agapanthus, flax plants, and tree ferns, a wooden deck with comfortable, cushioned furniture. They should have dinner out there tonight, she thought fleetingly.

"I didn't mean, physically intimidated," she tried to explain. "Just that I've never dated anyone famous before, anyone with a stadium full of people cheering just because he showed up. It was an odd feeling, but a good feeling. Watching you run out there, especially. That was a *really* good feeling. But I didn't like watching you fall down so much," she continued, watching him ease onto a bar stool with a sigh of his own. "Getting hit so hard. How're you feeling? You look pretty sore."

"A bit sore," he admitted. "A bit tired, too. I was glad when you said you wanted to have dinner in, tell you the truth. Though you didn't have to cook."

"I wanted to, though." She began pulling the perishables out of her grocery bag and stashing them in the stainless-steel fridge. "And don't get your hopes up. It's nothing all that fabulous. I only make things that I can do in a half hour or less."

What she'd really wanted had been to do something for him. And now that she'd seen the stiff way he was moving, the fatigue that was still evident, she was glad she'd thought of this.

"So what are we doing this afternoon?" she asked. "How'd you spend your morning?"

"Bit of stretching, got a massage, put ice on various things. Same boring morning-after as always. But now that you're here, I thought I'd show you something special about my house."

"Something special about your house," she repeated slowly. "If you've got some kind of sex room, I'm pretty sure I don't want to see it."

He smiled at her, and she thought how much she loved being able to make Nate smile. Watching his normally intense expression lighten, and knowing it was for her.

"Much more pleasant, I promise," he said. "Come on." He picked up her duffel. "Upstairs." He led her up the steps and through the doorway, dropping her bag next to the bed in the spacious master bedroom, its many windows offering a panoramic view out over rooftops and trees, the Harbour below. "You do have to take off your clothes, I'm afraid, to see this special thing."

"Uh-huh," she said, watching as he stripped down. "Sounding more ominous all the time."

She didn't much care for looking at the bruises and scrapes that covered his arms and legs, but she was definitely enjoying the sight of his defined abdomen, the muscles flexing in his broad chest as he lifted the T-shirt over his head and tossed it on the floor. And then he took off his shorts and underwear, and she took a good long look at that too. Oh, yeah. Thighs. And... everything.

"You're not keeping up," he pointed out.

"You're distracting me," she complained. "I haven't seen you enough times yet to be used to it. And I'm just going to say here, it's pretty interesting that you made such a big deal of my banging myself up one time on the climbing wall, with the way you look every week."

"Told you, though. That's me. I'm meant to get banged up, you aren't. That's how it is." He sank onto the end of the bed with another sigh. "And now," he said, "time for you to get that gear off. Come on, give me a show."

"What?" She started to laugh. "I'm supposed to do some kind of strip tease for you? I wouldn't even have an idea how."

"Oh, I think you could manage if you really tried," he said, leaning back on his elbows now and smiling at her, so completely comfortable in his nudity. And no wonder. Naked was a really good look on him.

Well, she'd wanted to make him happy today. That had been the whole plan. She might as well start now. He wanted this? He was going to get it. She gave it a moment's thought, then kicked off her low sandals.

"Strippers do it in high heels," he pointed out.

"I guess you'd better go on down to Calendar Girls and watch one of them, then," she tossed back, making him smile again. "Or you could stay here and watch me. Your choice."

She reached for the elastic holding her ponytail in place, pulled it out, dropped it onto her sandals, and ran her hands through her hair.

"That's probably my favorite," he said. "That thing you do with your hair."

"Oh, I'm done? Good. I'll stop."

"Nah. You're not done," he assured her. "Keep going."

She closed her eyes, tried to think sexy thoughts. To imagine that she wasn't Allison Villiers, tomboy, climber, and adrenaline junkie, and was some kind of sex goddess instead. The kind who turned men on. The kind who moved slowly and seductively, as aware of their bodies as the men who watched them.

She turned her back to him, crossed her arms over her chest so her hands reached down over her upper back, and caressed herself. Looked back over her shoulder at him, and saw him sitting up again, starting to look pretty interested. Which was fairly encouraging, wasn't it?

She was glad she'd worn a dress today, wanting to look pretty for him. And that it had buttons down the front. She turned around again, stared straight into his eyes, no smile at all for him. Thought about how it had felt, that first night, when he'd flipped her over, unzipped her skirt, and tried to project the desire, the ache she'd felt then. Tried to show him what he did to her, with her eyes. With her body.

She reached for her buttons and began to unfasten them, starting at the deep V-neck and moving on down. Slowly. Patiently. Pretending it was his hands that were doing it, that were caressing the skin they uncovered with each leisurely release of a button, and sent that message to him with everything in her.

One thing about doing a strip tease for a naked man, she thought, her hands below her waist now, continuing their slow work, you got a pretty good idea of how well you were doing. And she was doing great so far. The realization gave her confidence, inspired her. She kept her eyes locked on his, lifted the skirt to her hips so she could reach the last buttons, saw his eyes drop to the expanse of thigh exposed beneath the flare of yellow cotton.

She held the dress together with her hands a moment more, swiveled her hips a little. She'd have felt stupid doing it, except that it was working, for her as well as for him. Oh, boy, was it working for her. She slowly opened her arms, pulling the two sides of the dress apart, showing herself to him. Turned again, dancing a bit, and let the fabric slide down her arms, drop from her outstretched hands, flutter to the floor.

Her bra had a front clasp, she remembered. All right, then. Still dancing, she turned to face him again, reached a hand up, ran it through her hair. A little cheesy, but he'd said he liked it, and he was definitely liking it again now.

She kept her hand there, her fingertips at the back of her neck, elbow over her head, staring him down, her hips moving to the music, the insistent beat that had begun playing in her head, was throbbing now, a drumbeat straight to her core, and put her other hand to that front clasp.

And, as soon as she popped it, turned so her back was to him again. Gyrated, did her best bump and grind, and let the bra fall down her arms as the dress had, until it had joined the other garment on the floor. Crossed her arms over her breasts, turned again for him and, slowly, caressing every inch of the way, moved them down, down, until her breasts were revealed to him. Danced a little more for him, swaying to the beat that was so loud now inside her, she could have sworn he could hear it too. And then put a thumb on either side of her underwear, grateful that she'd worn a thong again, determined to make the most of it. To give him everything she had.

Time for him to get another look at what she was beginning to suspect was his favorite part of her body. She kept dancing, turned her back on him one final time. Inched the tiny strip of fabric down her hips, bent forward a little to let him see it all, pulled the thong down a little bit more. Lowered it one slow inch at a time until she finally, slowly, dropped it.

She stepped out of it, kicked it aside. Spread her legs a bit, still leaning forward, and ran her hands slowly, lovingly over her hips, down her thighs, and back up again. Over the curves of her bottom, up her sides, over her breasts. Imagined those hands were his, and tried to show him how good he made her feel when he touched her. When he held her there. She put one hand down to cover herself, the other arm across her breasts, kept her hands moving as she turned.

She shook out her hair again, looked him straight in the eye, let her hands drift slowly down her sides, stood and showed herself to him. And waited.

♡

Bloody hell. Nate felt as if his tongue were several sizes too big. He'd started out amused, had tossed out the challenge as a joke. He should have known that you didn't challenge Ally, not if you didn't want your challenge answered. And had she ever answered it. Without music, without wine, without sexy lingerie or dim lights, she'd given him one hell of a show, had made him forget all about his aching body, the nagging disappointment of the loss.

"Come over here," he got out, and saw the way she tossed her head, the way she walked toward him, proud and fierce as a catwalk model.

He spread his legs, pulled her by the hips to stand between them. Then looked into her eyes, scooted back on the bed, and lay down on his back.

And she followed right along, as he'd known she would. Slid herself over him, reached for him, stroked him. Then bent down to kiss him, her hands on either side of his head, her tongue in his mouth. She took her time with him, moving to kiss his neck, his shoulders. Her hands over his chest, down to his thighs. All over him, her touch firm enough not to tickle, soft enough to let him know she was a woman. And making him burn.

Then she'd swung a leg over him, was leaving him, and he felt the loss of it through his entire body.

"Ally," he protested. "Come back."

But she was back over him now, ripping the packet open. Kissing her way down again, rolling the condom onto him. Moving up, then, taking hold so she could slide herself onto him. He groaned as she did it, his hands reaching for her hips.

But that was all he had to do, because she did it all. She drove herself over him, bent down to kiss him, to rub her pretty breasts against him. Which gave him the chance to put both hands on that gorgeous arse, handle her there, hold her tight, the way he'd wanted to do the entire time she'd been showing it to him, teasing him with it, flaunting it at him.

And then, finally, as she began to move faster, to take him deeper, he was reaching for her, rubbing her. Pulling her down with the other arm so he could reach her breast with his mouth, hold her there, too, so that she was caught over him, squirming against his hand, gasping above his head, lost in her pleasure. And he could feel himself getting lost right along with her.

He felt the first racking spasms taking her, heard her begin to cry out. Then he was there, too, emptying into her with a release that was all the sweeter for the fatigue, the ache in the rest of him. Feeling her surrender to it, and riding that beautiful wave with her, all the way down.

♡

"What was it you wanted to show me?" she asked. She curled herself against him, kissed his chest. "Here I got all naked for you, and I still haven't seen it."

"If you're going to get naked like that," he groaned, "you're going to make me lose my train of thought every time. We'll never get anywhere."

"No productivity whatsoever," she agreed. "Not a single constructive thing accomplished. What a pity."

He laughed, and she smiled back at him, leaned over to give him a soft kiss. "Still waiting," she prompted.

He gave her a slap on the bottom that made her jump and laugh, then sat up, pulling her with him. "I was thinking this would feel good, be a bit sexy too. Didn't realize we wouldn't even get in there before you had me going." He took her hand, led her into the bathroom.

"We're taking a shower?" she asked doubtfully. "Well, that's nice, but we already did that."

"Nah." He reached for the open shelves that held rolled white towels, grabbed two of them, then opened a door that she'd assumed led to a closet, to be met by a cloud of steam. "This is my special room. Sorry that it isn't some sex torture dungeon. I know how disappointed you must be, but I actually prefer this, and maybe, if you give it a chance, you will too."

She walked through ahead of him, stopped for a moment to let her eyes adjust to the dim light. "A sauna," she said, turning to him. "I've never known anyone with a sauna in their house before."

"Just a small one. But I don't have big parties in here. Works for me."

The tiny room was completely paneled in wood, she saw, with an upper and a lower bench running the entire length of one wall, and filled with the most wonderful steam.

"Up or down?" he asked.

"Uh...down," she decided. That was going to be plenty hot for her.

He spread her towel on the lower shelf, then climbed to the upper one himself, spread out his own towel and lay down on his back. She followed suit, felt the delicious warmth, the moist steam enveloping her, soothing her, felt her body melting into the wooden slats of the bench, her heart rate slowing, her breath deepening as her lungs filled with warm, moist air, and could only imagine how good it must feel on his abused body.

He made her get out after ten minutes or so. Pulled her into the big shower, turned the water on, gradually twisted the handle until she was yelping under a stream of cold water, then led her back into the sauna again for another session, back for a second shower, warm this time, where they scrubbed each other down, blissfully limp and spent. They barely managed to stagger back to the big white bed, crawl beneath crisp, cool sheets. And slept the afternoon away.

♡

197

Nate came back out onto the deck the next morning, smiled at the sight of Ally, her back to him, legs stretched out in front of her, sipping from her mug of tea. So obviously relaxed, so clearly enjoying herself, as happy to be here with him as he was to have her here. The tui were running through their impressive repertoire in the branches of the big trees at the back of the garden, and in a few minutes, the two of them were heading out on a walk to Kelburn Village for breakfast, followed by a stroll through the Botanic Garden. Which sounded, to him, like the very best way in the world to spend the morning. Like exactly what he wanted to do before getting on the plane this afternoon.

They hadn't woken the day before until after five, had cooked the simple dinner of salmon, greens, and roasted kumara and agria potatoes she'd bought from the Sunday market, eaten it out here to the accompaniment of a pretty nice Sauvignon Blanc he'd had in the fridge, and then had snuggled on the couch to watch a movie.

"Can't believe action movies are your favorite," he'd said. "You're like the perfect woman."

And afterwards, he'd taken her back to bed and done his best to repay the favor she'd done him, with interest. She'd seemed to appreciate the effort, and his body was feeling a whole lot better just now than it had this time yesterday. It was feeling good. *He* was feeling good.

He slid back into his chair, set his laptop down and opened it. "Right. Schedule for week after next, as I'll be gone all this week. D'you know yours this time?"

She hopped up herself, went into the kitchen and came back pulling the piece of paper out of her purse, held it out to him between finger and thumb. "Behold," she told him, "how well I prepared for this meeting."

He smiled. "Still don't have it on your phone, I see."

"Hey. I remembered, didn't I?"

He set the printed staffing schedule down next to his computer. "Pen?"

She fossicked about in her purse for long enough that he was just about to go into the kitchen to get one from the tub, then, finally, extracted one and handed it to him.

He went through the printout, circled all her shifts. "If you do this," he pointed out, "you'll be able to see them more easily. Probably remember them better, too."

"Hey," she objected. "I always make it in. My way works for me."

He shrugged, then began to click through his calendar, compare it to her list. "I'll be back from Brissy at two on Sunday, En Zed time," he began. "How about Sunday evening? We can go out to dinner. Not that that wasn't awesome last night," he broke off to assure her. "Every bit of it. But, yeh. I'll take you out. Bring your stuff for work Monday, and I can collect you around seven-thirty, drop you back at the gym the next morning in time for your shift, and I'll still have time to watch some film in the afternoon."

"OK," she said agreeably.

"Other than that..." A bit more clicking and looking. "Thursday night. I can't do dinner, but d'you want to spend the night? And come to the game Saturday? You and Kristen?"

"Sure," she said. "I'll check with Kristen, but I'm pretty sure she'll want to come."

"Two tickets, then." He typed it in. "And I'll collect you from your flat at eight-thirty Thursday, on my way back from dinner with the boys. We can have an early brekkie, then I'll drop you at your flat again Friday morning."

"OK," she said again. "I'll take that."

He finished typing, sat back. "What does it look like on there?" she asked. "Just how hard is it to squeeze me in?"

He swiveled the laptop, showed her the spaces, most of them filled.

"What are these Auckland trips?" she asked. "Something to do with the All Blacks?"

"Sponsorship things, media things," he explained. "One for the All Blacks, one personal one this week."

"So next Wednesday," she said slowly, "you've got training until noon, then an autograph-signing session with the team, and then you fly to Auckland for a couple hours for—a TV interview?" She looked up, got the confirming nod. "And then you're back here again in the evening, and training again Thursday morning. Wow. You *are* busy."

She clicked again. Glanced at him, startled. Clicked some more, and looked at him again.

"What?" he asked. "What is it?" What had her looking like that? He tried to remember if she could be seeing anything dodgy on his calendar. No. Not possible. Because there wasn't anything.

"Ally-D," she read. "Sunday night. And I'm on there for the next day too, until one. All nicely filled in. And down here," she clicked again, "on Thursday, we have Ally-S."

She looked at him, the dark brows drawing down a little over the brown eyes, and he could almost feel himself squirm.

"I'm guessing," she said slowly, "that Ally-D means you're having dinner with me."

"Yeh," he said with relief. "That'd be it."

"No Ally-B in either place," she pointed out. "Presumably you think you can remember that we'll have breakfast."

"Yeh," he said again with a smile.

"And," she went on inexorably. "Ally-S? Don't tell me, please don't tell me that you're calendaring sex with me."

"When you put it like that," he protested, "it sounds bad."

"Well, yeah, it does." She shoved the laptop back towards him. "What is it, a haircut? Are you telling me that unless it's on your calendar, you wouldn't remember? That you can't hold that thought in your brain?"

"Nah, it's not that," he tried to explain. "Just that there's a lot to do, and I can't afford to forget. So I put down as much as possible. It's just a habit."

"Well, unless you take that *S* away," she informed him, "you aren't going to have to calendar it, because it's not going to be happening."

"Geez," he muttered, grabbing the laptop from her and pressing "delete" over the offending character. "I'd like to play the 'Ally being quiet and obedient' roleplaying game. When am I getting that one?"

He'd meant it as a joke, but found himself getting a little jolt at the thought. Looked at her, saw the shudder, her surefire sign of arousal. That had got her going too, had it?

"Hmm," she said with a sigh, clearly reading his mind as he continued to look at her. "You probably *could* get that one. I seem to be pretty easy, sorry to say. I'm guessing that all you'd need to do would be to play the 'Nate being an attentive boyfriend' game, and I'd go for it. What are you doing?" she asked as he began to type furiously again.

"Calendaring the texts I'm going to be sending you this week. And reminding myself to make another Logan Brown booking for Sunday. We didn't finish dinner last time, eh."

"And you want to make sure you get to eat all your steak? Nate…"

"Nah," he said. "I want to tell you to leave your dinner this time. So we can play that game."

riding the roller coaster

♡

"You really did book us in here again," Ally said with pleasure as Nate pulled the car to the curb outside Logan Brown a week later, where the valet came forward to meet them.

"What?" Nate asked in surprise. "You saw me calendar it."

She waited until they were inside, seated at another intimate corner table, to continue the conversation. "So let's see. If you calendar something, it happens? And if you don't, it doesn't?"

"That's about it. Well," he amended, "not quite, or I'd've calendared a win in Brissy yesterday."

"Mmm. I have a question about that, if you don't mind answering it. Well, two questions."

"If it's two," he decided, "we'd better order first."

Which they did. "Right," he said a few minutes later. "Two questions."

"Gosh, you're efficient," she marveled. "Do we have an agenda for this meeting?"

"Oh, yeh," he said, and his eyes were warm on hers. "I've got an agenda. Think you know about that already, but I'll be glad to run through the points for you later."

She cleared her throat, shifted a little on the leather banquette. "One of my questions, actually. But it's Question Two, so

I'll start with Question One. Since I know how orderly you like to be."

"Question One, then," he prompted.

"You may not want to answer it," she cautioned.

He looked at her in mock alarm. "If you're actually having second thoughts about sharing, maybe I should be concerned. But I'm pretty tough. Go ahead."

"Just about your team, and the All Blacks," she began. "I mean, I know the All Blacks get selected from all five of the New Zealand Super 15 teams, right?"

"Right."

"So does how well your team is doing, your Super 15 team I mean, how much impact does that have on whether you're selected for the All Blacks?"

"*That's* your sensitive question?"

"Yeah. What? That's not sensitive? I mean, the fact that you've…" She couldn't help her voice dropping a bit at the word, "lost a few games?"

He laughed. "You can say it. If it's too much for my delicate feelings to hear that we've lost, I'd better not read the papers, eh."

"*Do* you read the papers?"

"Nah," he said, still smiling. "Never read your press. That's pretty much Rule Number One when you're a sportsman. You'll either become a tall poppy, or slink away into a corner in shame. I know how I'm going, what I need to work on, what the team needs to work on. And anything I've missed, well, that's why you have coaches. But I'm going to take a guess here that the newsies have pointed out that we've lost, and have explained exactly why, too. That they've wondered why we haven't got those obvious things put right yet, and that the general public's weighed in as well."

"Yes, they have," she said. "All of the above, and it makes me so *mad.* And you care, too, even if you don't want to read about it. I know you do."

"Course I care." He was serious now. "I told you, I really, really hate to lose. And that's why I do everything I can to win. You can't always, though, doesn't matter what team you play for. Even," he said with a smile, "the All Blacks. It's never fun, you're always gutted, but that's sport. Flush the dunny and move on."

"Nice metaphor," she said wryly. All right, he didn't want to talk about it. "So, OK. If your team isn't winning—and not every New Zealand team does well every year, right?"

"Right. Sadly."

"So my question is," she pressed, "what does that mean for the All Blacks, if your team isn't very successful?"

"If the squad were selected by the public, or even some of the press, it'd mean a hell of a lot. Most of the journos know better, but there are a few . . . But anyway, since the selectors are looking at individual form, and they know what they're doing, it doesn't matter so much. Course you look better if you're on a winning side, but they know that doesn't always happen. They're looking at who's in form, wherever he's playing."

"OK. Good," she said with relief.

"Were you worried?" he asked with another smile.

"Well…I'm glad to know, let's just put it that way."

"So that's Question One sorted. What was Question Two, then?"

"You still remember that there was a Question Two?"

"I'm organized," he pointed out. "As you've noted."

He was interrupted by the arrival of their dinners, and they paused for a few minutes.

"Thanks for your email Friday night, by the way. Made me laugh," he said at last, cutting another bite of steak. She'd teased him about ordering the same thing both times, to which he'd just answered, "I know what I like, and I get it." Which had been followed by a look that she'd had not the least difficulty interpreting.

"Oh!" She brought her mind back with a start. "I thought you might appreciate that." She smiled at him. "That you weren't the only one."

I tried to show a guy how to climb today, she'd written. *I thought he was actually going to ask to have the person in charge—you know, a MAN—help him instead. He thought about it, I know he did. So I did what I usually do, got really matter-of-fact, really impersonal. And after he left, Robbo told me that he asked if I was a lesbian! He really did!*

He'd emailed back,

Interesting. Glad I know better. And by the way, in case I haven't mentioned it, I'm one hell of a lucky man.

Which had sure been nice to hear.

"Hope I wasn't as bad as that," he said now. "But I'm thinking maybe I was."

"Well, maybe. But at least you didn't ask that. Of course, that was probably because you ran away so fast."

He laughed. "You're probably right."

"I have another question for you, though," she said, taking another bite of her own dinner. Fish, this time. Much easier to eat than lamb, when your mind was elsewhere.

"Would this be Question Two?"

"Nope. Question...One and a half. How do you know what to say, when the announcer interviews you right after the game? Do you practice that?"

That got another smile from him. "Nah. But I've done it a fair few times now, you know. Pretty simple. Just tell the truth, win or lose. Say what you did well, what you'll be working on. What the other side did well. That's about it."

"You're so honest, though. That surprises me."

"Not going to deceive anybody by trying to sugarcoat things," he shrugged. "Everyone saw the match. If the kicking was rubbish, if you need to get the scrum sorted...they can all see that."

"The crowd seemed pretty hostile over there," she said next. "I heard some boos when you guys came out."

"That's Aussie. Specially Queensland. A bit more excitable than Kiwis, that's all. And that wasn't Question Two either," he prompted. "Where are we now? One and Seven-Eighths? Anything else?"

"Well, I did want to know why you kick the ball so much. I mean, why do you give it right back to the other team? And then they give it back to you, so what's the point?"

"What?" she asked as he started to laugh, unable to resist laughing herself in response.

"If I read this in the *Dominion Post* tomorrow," he said, "I'm going to know you've been on a stealth mission all along. Sleeping with me to get access to my innermost thoughts, do an exposé. Not that anybody'd pay for that. I'm a pretty boring fella."

"You are not," she protested.

"Yeh. I am. But you're just stalling now, Ally. Come on. Question Two."

"I'm embarrassed," she admitted.

He fixed her with those ice-blue eyes. "Question Two," he commanded.

She looked down at her plate. She'd got through a pretty good amount of her dinner tonight, unlike last time. And she supposed it had tasted good.

"It's kind of a shame, really, that you keep bringing me here," she said. "Since I can't remember anything about eating either meal, and I noticed that it's really expensive."

He ignored that. "Question Two."

She cleared her throat. "Umm...when we talked last week. When you calendared that you were going to bring me here, you said..."

"Yeh? What did I say?"

"Well, when I made you take off the *S*," she clarified. "You asked me when we were going to..." She looked around, leaned closer. "Play that game," she whispered.

"I told you," he said, looking surprised, though she could tell it was an act. "We're going to do it tonight. What, did you think I'd forget? I decided it was like breakfast. That I could manage to hold it in my head. And what d'you reckon, I've done it."

He raised a hand, signaled for the check. "And I said that I was going to make you leave your dinner this time," he said. "You'll notice I was efficient, as usual. Finished mine. But you're done."

♡

And that was the last thing he'd said to her. They were in the car, nearly at his house, and he still hadn't spoken, and the tension was too much for her to bear.

"All right," she burst out when he'd turned the corner into his street, was slowing and punching the button for the garage door. "I give up. I lose. You win."

"I know I do," he said equably, pulling the car in, punching the door closed. "You don't have to tell me. That's the point of tonight, eh. I win."

With that, the tingle she'd felt during dinner, long since grown to an insistent pulse of arousal, gave another thrum, and she felt herself actually squirming a little. They were sitting in the dim light of the garage, and he wasn't touching her. But she'd never been more aware of him, and she knew he could tell exactly how she was feeling, too.

"Nate..." she began.

"No," he said. "No. That's what this game is. You don't get to talk. You don't get to say anything. You're just doing what I tell you tonight. Everything I tell you. Unless you want to stop," he added as an afterthought. "If you want to stop, say so, and we'll stop. Otherwise…we're playing."

"When do we start?" she managed to ask.

He smiled a bit at that. "Haven't you noticed? We started about an hour ago. And that's it. No more talking. Unless I hear 'stop,' you're not talking till I tell you we're done. And that's not happening for a good long time yet."

She looked at him, opened her mouth to speak, saw the look in his eyes, and closed it again. Oh, yeah. She'd play this game. He needed a win? Well, he was going to get one, because she wanted it, too.

"First thing, get out of the car," he said. "And follow me up to the house."

She did it. Of course she did it. She was inching up the biggest hill on the tallest roller coaster there was. Knowing that the drop was coming, knowing it would be almost too much, knowing that she'd be screaming when she got there. Half of her wishing she could stop the ride and get off, and the other half anticipating the thrill of the fall.

She walked up the steps behind him. Waited silently while he unlocked the door and motioned her inside. Then she stood there and waited for that drop.

He hung his keys on their hook. Of course he did. Leaned back against the solid wood and looked at her, standing in the middle of the entryway.

"Take off your clothes," he told her. "Everything but the shoes. Leave those on."

She did as he told her, dropping one piece at a time at her feet, until she was standing before him, naked.

"Yeh," he said. "That's good. That's what I want. Now walk upstairs to my bedroom."

He wasn't taking off his clothes? They were still moving up the hill, and she wasn't sure she could stand the anticipation.

She turned and obeyed his instruction, could feel his gaze on her as they began to climb. Then jumped with surprise, came to a halt when his hand closed around one cheek, began to rub.

"Keep walking," he told her. "While I feel this."

She shuddered a little. He had the other hand over a breast now, was caressing her in both places, pressed against her, climbing right behind her. And then they were at the top of the stairs, and she came to a stop, every part of her quivering.

"Keep going. My bedroom," he prompted.

She shivered again, walked into the center of the room, and stopped again. Because he was right behind her, and he had both hands on her, one in front, the other moving in from behind. And those hands were merciless. Her breath was coming hard, and she was rocking in the high heels. She could feel him behind her, pressed into her, and she wanted him so much it hurt.

He didn't stop until she was nearly there. Then he took both hands from her abruptly, forcing a little gasp from her at the loss. He was turning her around, bending to kiss her, his hands gripping her behind, pulling her up on tiptoe, rubbing her over him, creating a delicious friction as her sensitive center slid over the woolen fabric of his trousers, and she could feel herself opening for him. Needing him so much. Needing him right now.

He set her down, took a step back. He was breathing hard, too, not nearly as firmly in control as he wanted her to think.

"Take off my shirt," he said. "Slowly."

When she was on her knees, removing his shoes and socks, she could tell the roller coaster was almost at the top. And when she was unfastening his belt, it was teetering at the rim. And after that, it was all the way over, and she was falling.

But it wasn't the big hill yet after all, because he was still in control, and he wasn't letting her go yet. He was talking to her, telling her what he wanted, moving her at last from the floor to his bed. And every time she got close, every time the cries rose in her throat, threatened to escape, he was moving her, shifting positions, dropping her down a bit, making her climb that next hill.

There was nothing extreme, nothing rough, nothing they hadn't done before. Nothing but her silence to make this different, but that was enough. And at last, she was on her back, holding onto the headboard again. One hard hand was pressed against a thigh, holding her open, his fingers were inside her, his mouth was on her, and he was finally allowing her to let go, to surrender to the pleasure he'd given her, and she couldn't hold back anymore. And before she'd finished, before the last cries had left her mouth, he was inside her again, and they were racketing down the big hill together, their arms in the air, their mouths open, their screams left behind in the wind.

"Right," he sighed when he was holding her again. "You can talk now."

"Mmm," she managed. "Too bad I can't form a coherent thought anymore."

"You liked that game, eh," he said, and she could see the smile.

She leaned over to kiss him. "I wouldn't want to play it every day, but, yeah, I did. I liked that game a lot."

spike through my heart

♡

"How's your shoulder?" Kristen asked Liam as soon as she saw him in the gym on a breezy late-March Sunday. He stood waiting for her like always. She was beginning to suspect that he got there early, just so she would never have to stand and wait by herself.

"Pretty niggly still," he admitted. "I've had the MRI, nothing torn, thank goodness. But I'll be out for next week's game, at least, if not the one after that. And now that the medical report's out of the way," he added with a smile, "time for you to tell me what you thought of your first footy match. Well, the first one you watched live."

"Exciting," she said promptly, "even though both Ally and I were confused, I have to say. Thanks for getting your first win for me. That was awfully nice of you, wasn't it?"

"Wasn't me. Not with me getting my shoulder buggered in the first half, it wasn't. That was all Toro, in the sheds at half-time. Fair blistered the paint, telling the boys to...to go back out there and play with some intensity, would be the polite way of putting it."

"Well, it worked," she said. "They did. It was like a different game in the second half, even I could tell that."

"Good. But just now, we're here, so let's get you up on this wall."

"You can't climb, though," she protested. "Let's just go for coffee or something."

"Why? I can still belay you."

"With one arm?"

"No worries. I'll just do the work with the left."

"Well," she said doubtfully, "maybe a couple climbs. If you're sure you can."

He'd been right. He could. Well, one of Liam's arms was definitely equal to two of a normal man's, so that probably made sense. She kept it short, though. She wasn't going to aggravate his injury.

"We've got a bit of extra time," he said when she'd finished, changed, and joined him again. "We could take a walk, do a bit of window-shopping before lunch, maybe."

"You know I'm never going to say no to that," she laughed.

"Want to look in here?" he asked hopefully when they were on Lambton Quay again, walking past Bendon.

"Mmm...no." She cast him a sideways look, unable to avoid a smile. "You just keep walking. You've already seen me in my underwear."

"Yeh. And once was enough, eh. Heaven forbid I'd have to look at *that* every day. Bloody nightmare."

Her smile turned to a laugh. "Shoes. Moving right along next door here. Much safer."

"Found the funkiest ones for you," he said after a minute. "Inside, there," he pointed. "You'd look a treat in those."

"Wow," she breathed. "Those are amazing."

"Let's go, then," he urged. "If I can't look at you in your undies again, this'd be the next best thing."

She laughed in delight when she had them on, posing in front of the mirror and twisting so the light caught the conical spikes sticking out from the sides of the high-heeled pumps in fiery, glittering red.

"Shoes as weaponry," she turned to tell a grinning Liam. "Amazing."

"Pretty accurate," he said. "Specially with that short skirt. Telling all the boys not to get too close, or you'll stomp all over their hearts. Dead fierce."

"Really? That's how I look?" she asked with pleasure. "Fierce?"

"Yeh," he assured her. "That's exactly how you look."

♡

"We need to stop doing this," she sighed when they were in another cafe, one Liam had scouted out specially last week for her, but he wasn't telling her that. He caught her sneaking a peek down at her new shoes. The spikes still made her smile, he saw. And seeing her put them on, strut around in them hadn't been too bad from his point of view, either. He had a quick image of her wearing them with red lingerie to match that he had to shove out of his mind fast. That one, he'd save for tonight.

"Nah." He did his best to keep his thoughts from showing on his face. "Makes me happy, makes you happy. What could be bad about that? I hope you have some more room in your closet, because I can tell we're going to be doing this again. Oi," he protested as she shot him a look. "A man can live without sex. He can't live without romance. Buying you shoes is as close as I'm coming to romance just now, and I'm doing it."

"Well, buying me shoes and sending me flowers when you were in Brisbane. I loved that, but you didn't have to do that, either."

"Nah, I didn't. And what d'you reckon, I did it anyway, because I wanted to."

"I'm glad you were playing at home this week, though," she said. "I'd rather have tickets than flowers. And I loved watching you play in person, seeing you be so strong."

Here was the chance he'd been waiting for. "If I impressed you, you know I want to keep doing that as often as possible. And I was thinking, it might be better if you had Sky Sport. MySky, too. That way you could see every game. If you wanted to, that is. Could record the ones coming up in Safa, watch them at a reasonable hour. Watch those movies you like, too, at night. Not too many movies on, otherwise. I know it can be a bit spendy," he hurried to say, "but maybe that's one thing I could do. That and the shoes, since they're both actually for me."

"Well…" She looked down at her salad, poked at it a bit with her fork. "Actually…I already signed up for it." She met his gaze again, laughed a little. "I'm just waiting for them to install it. Although now I'm having second thoughts. If you're going to keep getting hurt, I'm going to stop watching. I love watching you play, but I hate watching you bleed. I *hate* it."

"Now you know how I felt last month, then," he said, looking into those sapphire eyes, "watching you strip down to your undies. I loved seeing it, and at the same time, I hated it, too, because I could see how much it hurt you to do it. We're even now, that's all."

"Except that I'm going to be watching you get hurt a whole lot more times," she pointed out. "And you're never going to see me doing that again. No more walking around in my underwear for me, because you were right. I've been working on my boundaries, like you said, for a while now, but I didn't even recognize that that was what was making me so uncomfortable. It's so hard to know, isn't it, at the time?"

He was about to answer her, but stopped at the sight of the woman walking through the door.

"What is it?" Kristen asked in alarm. She turned to see what had arrested his attention. But Liam was already standing, because Anahera had noticed him now. He saw the hesitation, then the decision on her face, the lift of her chin as she came to meet him.

"Liam," she said, stopping next to the table.

"Anahera." He thought about kissing her cheek, settled for taking the hand she offered, giving it a gentle press, and dropping it again. "This is my friend Kristen. Kristen, this is Anahera."

Kristen looked confused, he saw.

"His ex," Anahera explained briefly, then turned back to Liam again. "How are you?" she asked.

"I'm good. You? How's Joseph? And your mum and dad?" He cast another quick glance downward, quickly looked back at her face again.

"All good as well. And yeh, we're expecting." She put a protective hand over the swell of her belly and smiled for the first time. He could see how happy she was, and was happy for her sake, because she deserved it.

"Congrats," he said, tried to put all the sincerity he had into it. "And to Joseph, too."

She nodded. "Good to meet you," she said to Kristen. "See ya, Liam."

"You don't have to..." he began.

"Nah. I'll go. But..." She hesitated. "I'm glad to see you doing well. I really am."

"Thanks," he said over the lump that rose in his throat. "Thanks."

And then she was gone.

♡

"Talking of choices," he sighed, sitting down again and watching Anahera walk away, walk out the door. "And wrong ones."

"Your ex," Kristen said slowly. "Your ex what?"

"My ex-wife. Married to somebody else now, having a baby. Having the life she wanted to have with me."

He paused a moment, but she didn't answer, just looked at him, waiting for him.

"So, yeh," he said. "When you keep telling me how many mistakes you've made...I think you're giving yourself too much credit."

He saw her jerk of surprise at that. "Yeh," he continued, "I'd say you're an amateur. What've you done? Married the wrong bloke? Pssh." He made a dismissive gesture. "One bloody thing. Amateur."

"You mean," she said hesitantly, "your marriage. Was it to do with...the drinking?"

"No secret about it. My marriage, and everything else. You haven't looked up the story yet, eh. Because it's still there for everyone to see, and it'll never go away."

"No. It never occurred to me, actually. But, no. I wouldn't do that, invade your privacy like that. If you want to tell me, though, I want to hear. I want to understand."

"Right," he said. "Right. I should do that, then. Before you *do* see it online."

He paused a moment to think about it while she sat quietly opposite him, her gentle gaze on him, waiting.

"Rugby's a funny old thing," he said at last, sitting back, looking down at his clasped hands. "There you are, a young fella, not nearly as clever, not nearly as strong as you think you are. Some of the boys seem to do all right. Some of them learn quicker than others, maybe, because they never put a foot wrong. But I wasn't one of them. Too much money," he went on, looking up at her now. "Too many people who think you're special. Girls paying attention to you like they never did before. And you're gone half the time, away from your family. Feeling the pressure of it, too. So you tell yourself you need to relax, cut loose a bit. That you deserve it."

Going out after the games at first, he remembered, getting pissed. Getting angry. One confrontation after another, some of them coming to blows before a teammate, usually Toro, pulled him away. The coach finding out about it, putting him on the bench for a game or two, which had only made him angrier at the time, but had made him more careful, too. For a while. And then being selected for the All Blacks, the thrill of it. More money, more pressure, more weeks away. And more drinking.

And then the day he'd awoken in a cell in an Aussie jail, barely able to remember what had happened the night before. That he'd got in a fight outside a bar, had thrown some punches that had done some real damage. Had gone that one step too far, and there was no taking it back.

Appearing in court had been bad enough. But the press conference—that had been the worst. That had been the bottom.

"Knew I had to front up," he told Kristen when he'd finished the long, sad story. "Not that everyone didn't already know what had happened, because trust me, they all knew it. It was big news, specially because I was an All Black, and it wasn't the first time I'd been in trouble. And that I was being sent down from the Super 15 for half a season, that I was going to be playing club rugby for a good long while. Maybe forever, if I didn't get myself sorted. So, no. It wasn't news to my teammates, or my family. Or my wife. It wasn't any kind of news to Anahera."

"Is that what broke up your marriage?" she asked. "Being arrested, and…the rest of it?"

"Nah," he said bluntly. "It wasn't being sent down. It wasn't the drinking, or even the fighting. It was the lying. And the cheating."

He could see her wince, but went on. If he wanted her, and he did want her, she needed to know who he was. Who he'd been then, and the man he was now.

"Told myself I wasn't hurting her," he said. "That what I did when I was away from home...that it was separate from us, from how I felt about her. And that I never touched her, even when I'd been drinking. More ways to hurt a woman than hitting her, though, and I reckon I did every one of those."

"So what happened?" Kristen asked. "What changed?"

He shrugged. "Stopped drinking. Easy to say, hard to do. The NZRFU helped. The football union," he explained. "Therapy, all that. Helped me see what I'd been trying to hide from with the drink, helped me find ways to deal with the pressure that wouldn't destroy my life. And my family helped, too, my mum and dad. Fronting up helped, and my dad was there with me for that. Told me I had to do it, in fact. That I'd got myself into this, that I'd let down my whanau, my wife, my mates, my team. Let my country down, too. And that it was down to me now to front up, and to be a man. He went with me to the press conference, stood by me that day and every day since. The rest of it, though, that took a while. Learning how to be the kind of man my dad is, the kind of man I wanted to be, one step at a time. Working my way back onto the team, the ABs. Getting my confidence back, in my game and in myself. Working my way back into some self-respect, so other people could respect me as well. Which took a good long while, I can tell you that."

"But you didn't get your marriage back," she said, her eyes full of compassion.

"Some things you can't fix," he said, and felt the familiar stab of regret. "Some things, when you break them badly enough, they stay broken."

He gave a little shrug, shook it off. "So. When I say I know what it's like to be at the bottom, I mean it. And what it's like to make hard choices that leave you with your self-respect, too."

"Like not wearing your underwear in front of the general public," she said with a little smile.

"Not if it makes you feel bad. Not if it makes you feel cheap."

"Can I just say," she told him, and she had a hand on his arm now, tears in her eyes, too. Had clearly forgotten, in the intensity of her emotion, all about the careful distance she normally kept from him.

"Can I just say," she repeated, "that the man you are now is amazing? That you've never done anything less than impress me, since the first day I met you? Maybe it's been a hard road. Maybe I'm just seeing what you are now, at the end of it. But what you are now," she said, and he could read the sincerity in her face, in the press of her hand, "is something so...so special. Something so strong."

He swung his chair over, put an arm around her. He couldn't help it. He held her against his side for a moment, right there in the little café.

"Well, you know what they say," he told her, and his eyes weren't any too dry themselves.

"What's that?"

"That when you mend something, sometimes the mended bits are stronger than the original. And I have heaps of mended bits."

"Well," she said with an unsteady laugh, "I guess that's better than still having the cracks there."

"Which is you," he guessed.

"Yeah. Which is me. But I'm working on mending them. And knowing that you did it...that helps. That helps a lot."

nate's birthday present

♡

" Is that guy going to be in trouble?" Ally asked. "Because he should be."

"Could be." She could hear the smile in Nate's voice all the way from Johannesburg. "He got red-carded for it, and they lost the game, neither of which will look good to his coach, or his skipper, either. Probably be fined as well. But he's not a bad bloke, really. Just one of those things that happens sometimes in the heat of battle. I decided not to pass your text along to him. Didn't want to scare him, add to his woes."

She had to laugh at that despite her outrage. She'd been furious to see Nate upended in the dangerous tip-tackle, and had jumped off the couch shouting in the wee hours of the morning. Which had resulted in a not-very-pleasant visit from her downstairs neighbor, but oh, well. And a text to Nate, too.

Tell him to watch out for me. Going to turn HIM upside down next time he's here.

"It really seemed that he went after you, though." She pressed a bit more. "And that isn't the first time I've seen it happen. It seems to me like you're a special target."

"Sometimes," he admitted. "When you're the skipper, or when they see you as a threat. You could see it as flattery."

"Or you could see it as thuggery. Or that they're just *nasty,*" she said, which made *him* laugh.

"Sorry I play such a nasty sport," he said soothingly. "Take up badminton instead, d'you reckon?"

"Does New Zealand *have* badminton?"

"Course. The Black Cocks."

"They do not!" She was laughing now. "That isn't true."

"Nah. Not anymore. They made them change the name. Pity, really. I thought it was brilliant. Anyway," he went on, "I wanted to ask you, d'you want to go somewhere with me? I've got a bye coming up, two weeks from now."

"I remember." This was the moment she'd been waiting for. Because she could hear the weariness in Nate's voice already, and he'd have played eight games in a row by that point, the beginning of the season a distant memory. And the final game was likely to be as brutal as the one he'd just endured. The previous night's match had been intense from beginning to end, both teams sinking to the ground at the referee's final whistle in complete exhaustion. The much-needed win would help, but it wouldn't make up for the bruising and battering he'd taken.

And the next game, the final one before the bye, would be played in South Africa as well, enemy territory. Another harsh physical contest, she was sure, then the long flight back. And after all that, once the brief break was over, three days of training with the All Blacks. Away from home again in Mount Maunganui on the Bay of Plenty, then straight to Canberra to catch up with the rest of the team in Australia. A mere two days there before he would be facing a Brumbies squad currently sitting at the top of the table. And then the season interrupted by the three weeks of the June Tests, when Nate would be leading the All Blacks out against France, his first time as the official captain, only the final one of those games played in Wellington.

It was all so much, and he was going to need a break before it began. A *total* break. A *fun* break. And she was pretty sure she knew how to provide it.

"I actually thought of something," she said now, trying to sound casual. "If you have a few days to spend with me. Friday afternoon through Monday?"

"Sounds good to me," he said with a sigh she could hear even over the phone. "Where d'you want to go? I should make some bookings."

"How would you feel about my surprising you? Because your birthday's next week, right? I looked it up. Maybe I don't get to spend that day with you, but I thought I could take you away to celebrate anyway."

"You want to take *me* away." He sounded a little stunned.

"That's right," she said brightly. "I want to take you on holiday for your birthday. What, nobody's ever done that for you?"

"No. Definitely not."

"What? Definitely not, you won't go with me?" She felt her heart sink under the weight of her disappointment. She'd figured it might be something new for him, but really? He had to be in charge that much? She couldn't even plan a trip for them? This wasn't a good sign.

"No!" he said hurriedly. "I just meant, definitely not, nobody's ever done it. Course I want to go with you. I'm just surprised, that's all. And..." He hesitated. "It's awesome that you've got something planned, but I'd like to pay for it."

"That'd be some birthday present, wouldn't it? One that you paid for?"

"But you can't afford it."

"You don't even know what it is. Maybe we're camping, did you think of that?"

"Nah," he admitted, and she could hear the smile now. "But I wouldn't be surprised. Is that it, then? Are we camping?"

"I'm not telling. It's a surprise. Put me on that calendar of yours, and wait and see."

♡

Ally checked the boot of the little car yet again, making extra-sure she'd packed everything. She'd been alternately excited and nervous about this idea for the past two weeks, ever since he'd agreed to it and she'd begun planning in earnest. She wasn't sure, by now, which emotion was stronger. She'd always been a risk-taker, but this was something new. And it was a lot harder to contemplate than a bungy jump. This was either going to be a disaster, or…Well, she hoped it was going to be "or."

She took a deep breath, got in, and slammed the door. Time to go. Sink or swim.

Nate was ready, of course. He had to be the most punctual person she'd ever met. Part of the job again, probably. Punctuality, self-discipline, focus. Hopefully she could help him let go of all three this weekend.

He met her at the door holding his duffel, dressed in jeans and a T-shirt, a parka pulled over them against the rain that was coming down harder now.

"Hope this isn't actually camping," he said. "Because that doesn't sound too comfortable in this weather."

"You don't want to spend three nights in a sleeping bag with me?" she asked, trying to sound hurt.

He laughed. "Come to think of it, camping may not be too bad. But if it really is that, I should probably add a couple things here."

"I've got everything we need," she promised. "Come on."

She took his bag from him at the car. "Go on and get in," she instructed. "I'll pack this."

"You're really serious about this, aren't you," he said wonder-ingly. "You really do mean to surprise me. I'm going to suss out where we're going, though, you know. I do know my geography, and there aren't that many possible destinations. Unless we're flying somewhere, or taking the ferry across to the Mainland. And if that's it, you need to let me pay for it, because whatever you say, you can't afford it."

"Would you be quiet and get in the car?" she asked in exasperation. "We're both getting wet."

He opened his mouth to argue, then shrugged, turned, and got in.

Ally stowed his bag in the tiny boot, then pulled out the item she'd stashed there earlier, wadded it up in her hand. She pulled off her own parka and jumped into the driver's seat, tossing her coat into the back with his.

"Just one more thing," she told him as she put the key into the ignition. "Across the street there," she pointed.

He turned to look, and she moved fast, reached around him with the folded silk scarf, pulled it over his eyes.

"Hold still," she said sternly when he exclaimed, reached a hand up. "This is part of your surprise." She tied the thing behind his head, then had to laugh. It might have been better if it hadn't been pastel pink, with flowers. But she'd had to borrow the scarves from Kristen, and she'd asked if her friend had any she didn't like too much, just in case they didn't come back in pristine condition. Or come back at all. She had plans for those scarves.

He reached his hands up to feel the blindfold. "Very mysterious. Right, I'm surprised. How long does this last?"

"Not too long. Not much more than an hour and a half."

"An hour and a *half?*" he complained. "Going to be a bit boring, isn't it?"

"Don't worry. I'm going to entertain you." She hoped. If she kept her nerve.

"Hmm." He sounded a bit more interested. "You singing to me, or what?"

"Nope. Not me." She started the car and pulled out of her parking space, headed for the motorway, then turned on the radio and pressed "play" on her iPod. And heard Marvin Gaye starting them off on the playlist that she'd named "Doing It," for lack of a more clever title.

"Let's get it on, eh," Nate said. "I'm liking this more and more."

"There's more entertainment," she told him. "We get to have a conversation, too. All about this weekend. You ready to hear about your surprise?"

"Oh, yeh." He was smiling beneath his blindfold now. "I'm ready. I'm thinking it's not camping."

"Nope. It's some more of that experimentation you told me about. Here's the plan. First I get..." She looked at the clock on the dash. "Twelve hours or so, to do whatever I want to you. You're basically my sex slave tonight."

"I am, am I? And what happens after that? This is getting more and more interesting."

"Well, it's really your idea," she conceded. "Your Men's Valentine's Day idea, I mean. I kept thinking, what could I give you for your birthday that was special? And I kept coming up blank. And then I thought...Me."

"You."

"Yeah. Me. Tomorrow," she took a deep breath, then said it. "Tomorrow, I'm *your* sex slave."

"Now that's what I call a birthday present," he said, and the smile was all the way there now. "And I almost hate to ask, but what happens Sunday? Is that when you invite the neighbors round? How far are we going here?"

She laughed. "Nope. Sunday's...free play. If either of us has any energy left."

"Should've told me, so I could've been taking my vitamins," he complained. But he was still smiling beneath his ridiculous pink blindfold. "And packed supplies. That riding crop and all."

"Hey," she protested. "My rules still apply."

"Just joking," he assured her. "I can think of heaps of things for my sex slave to do that don't involve pain or…What was the other thing?"

"Coercion. Or maybe, for the purposes of this weekend, I should say 'force' instead."

"Hmm. Well, not that either. But oh, yeh. I can think of some things."

"Well, you have about an hour and a half here to do it. I'd say you have tonight, too, but…" She heaved a gusty sigh. "I'm afraid you're going to be busy tonight."

♡

She pulled up outside the little house, turned the car off. Reached across and pulled the scarf off his eyes just as the front door opened, an older woman appearing on the porch.

"Stay there," Ally instructed. "I have to get the key."

"I hear and obey," he said. "See how well I'm doing? You may want to take notes, make sure you're ready when it's your turn."

She laughed and got out of the car, spent an endless ten minutes as the woman introduced herself as Joanne and explained— in detail—that she managed rental properties for various owners in the area. Then showed her through the little bach, including the bathroom and bedroom, as if Ally might not have been able to find them on her own.

The bed, to Ally's relief, looked just like the photos on the website, satisfactory headboard and all. She tried to be patient while Joanne showed her how the cooker worked, pointed out the path to the beach, and cast the occasional curious glance at the car where Nate waited. But Ally wasn't about to satisfy this gossipy woman's curiosity about her passenger. This was Nate's getaway. His *private* getaway.

Joanne left at last, though, getting into her own car in the driveway and pulling out. Ally ran back to the Yaris, hopped in beside Nate without speaking, and pulled into the spot the other woman had vacated.

"OK," she was finally able to tell him. "Here we are."

"Where? Not that I care, because I don't think we're going to be taking any tours this weekend. But I may as well know. For my memoirs, eh."

"Himatangi Beach. And it's not raining."

"I see it's a beach, and I see it's not raining," he agreed gravely. "And I'm waiting for my next order," he pointed out.

"Oh." She laughed. "We'd better wait to start until we unload the car and have dinner. We'll never manage the logistics of this otherwise. I'm not that good at giving orders, I'm afraid."

"Interesting," he said thoughtfully. "As it happens, I'm very, very good at giving orders. Maybe I should save you the trouble, take over right now."

"Nope," she said, popping the latch on the boot. "My holiday, my rules. And me first."

♡

They'd managed dinner, only because she'd kept it simple. Steaks, pre-roasted vegies, and salad. But she was so nervous, she dropped her fork twice. Kept starting conversations, then finding herself trailing off again. It was looking at him that was doing it. Eating calmly, looking at her knowingly. The look of speculation in his blue eyes might have been for tonight. Or maybe he was making plans for tomorrow. Either way, it was making her jumpy.

"Finish my steak for me," she sighed at last. "I'm going to take a shower."

"OK. I'll do the washing-up, then, shall I?"

"Good idea," she said. "I'm liking this sex slave idea."

227

He laughed. "That isn't the sex slave talking. That's me wanting to get to the sex slave bit."

She came back into the kitchen wrapped in her dressing gown. "OK. I'm done. Your turn."

"I need to get clean, eh," he said, wiping down the table. Everything else, she saw, was already tidied.

"You do," she agreed cordially. "Because I have big plans for you."

When he came out of the bathroom, she had the duvet pulled back on the bed, the candles placed on either side and lit, the lights off, the music playing softly. He'd seemed to enjoy it in the car, and it was sure working for her. She'd cranked the portable heater in the bedroom up to maximum when they'd first arrived, and the room was cozy. Which was good, because neither of them was going to be under the covers for quite a while, if her part of the entertainment went as well as she hoped.

"We're starting then, are we," he said. He was wearing only a towel, wrapped around his waist. And as always, she was enjoying the sight of him. Shoulders, arms, chest, he had it all. And oh, did she love it.

"That's right," she said. "From now until the morning, you're mine. And right now, I want you to come and lie down on this bed for me. But first, take off the towel."

He obliged. Oh, yeah. He really did have it all.

And then he came over to her. Lifted an eyebrow and gave her his best hard-eyed, ice-cold stare. Which was just as effective on her, she thought with a tingle of anticipation, as it was on rugby opponents. Tomorrow, she had a feeling, was going to be *really* interesting.

And then he lay down smack in the middle of the big bed and just looked at her, waiting.

She reminded herself that this was *her* turn, and took off her dressing gown. Slowly. And revealed the only true lingerie set she'd ever owned, her other big splurge on this holiday.

She'd thought about black or red, but in the end, had stuck with ivory. She'd liked the virginal look, the innocence of the color combined with the sensuality of the thigh-high stockings with their lace tops, the minuscule lace G-string and low-cut, push-up lace bra. And judging from his expression, he liked it too.

"Thought this was your night," he murmured. "And here you are, already giving me my birthday present."

"Take a good look," she ordered him. "Because you aren't going to get another chance for a while."

She knelt beside him, then lay across his lap, presenting him with a close-up view of her backside as she reached across him for the bedside table drawer. She pulled out Kristen's pink scarf, and another in a fairly hideous baby blue, and straightened up again.

"Do I get to touch?" he asked, and he wasn't smiling anymore.

"No," she told him sternly. She reached for his arms, pulled them together, and wrapped the pink scarf around his wrists. "Scoot down to the end of the bed."

He looked at her, his eyes intense, mouth firm, and slowly obeyed. She pulled his hands overhead, fastened them with the trailing ends of the scarf to the slat of the headboard.

"And that's as much as you get to see," she told him when he was tied tight. She lifted the blue scarf and put it gently across his eyes. "Lift your head up." She slid the scarf around and fastened it at the side, so the knot wouldn't be uncomfortable. She was so considerate.

She looked down at him, there below her. Tied up and blindfolded, all that muscle and determination under her control, and wondered why he somehow looked all the more dangerous for it.

"Know what I'm going to do to you?" she asked.

"No, what?" His voice was a little rough now.

"I'm going to lick you everywhere," she told him. "I'm going to touch you all over. I'm going to rub myself against you. And then, when I'm ready, when I decide it's time, I'm going to work on you with my hands and my mouth until you're squirming. Until you're moaning. Until you're not anybody's captain anymore. Until you're all mine."

"And then," she put her mouth next to his ear and whispered, "I'm going to ride you hard. And I'm going to be touching myself while I do it. You're going to be wishing so much that you could watch me. That you could touch me, and kiss me. That you could be in charge of me. But you won't be, will you? All you'll be able to do is listen. And...feel."

And then she did it. And he thought, he really thought, that he was going to scream. He heard his own harsh breathing, the sounds he couldn't suppress as she continued, as she drew it out. Licked him, kissed him, ran her hands over him. Everywhere, for much too long. And then...focused. Gave him the best he'd ever had. Slow, and wet, and oh, so thorough. Proved that she'd been paying attention, every time he'd told her what he wanted, what he liked. And not being able to see it, not being able to touch her...that was torture, and it was blisteringly, scorchingly hot.

When he'd lost control, was writhing in exactly the way she'd promised, his groans loud in his ears, he felt her sit back. He let out an inarticulate sound of protest, his hips lifting off the bed toward her.

"I'm taking off my clothes now," she said softly. "The bra. And the G-string. But I'm leaving the stockings on. Don't you wish you could see how I look?"

Oh, he did. He really did.

"I'm so wet," she told him. "For you. And you wish you could touch me, don't you?"

"Yeh," he got out. "I want to touch you."

"Well, you can't," she reminded him. "So I'm just going to have to touch myself, aren't I? But I think," she sighed, "that I need something else while I do that."

He heard the nightstand drawer opening and closing again, the rip of the packet. Then felt her rolling the condom slowly onto him. And then, finally, finally, she was rubbing herself over him. And she was right, she was wet. He could feel the tops of the stockings, too, against his sides, and it was killing him.

"Ally," he groaned, unable to stop himself from begging. "Do it. Please. Do it."

"What?" she whispered. "This?" Then she was over him, wriggling, slowly impaling herself on him. And it was so good. She pressed her body to his, leaned down to kiss him, her breasts against his chest, her mouth sweet and soft against his. And then she started to move, and that was the best thing yet.

"Know what I'm doing now?" she asked a few minutes, or an hour, later. He couldn't tell. He'd lost all track of time. She was starting to pant, and he could feel the difference, the way her excitement was rising, the force of it. "I'm touching myself. I'm riding you, and I'm touching myself. And oh, Nate. Oh, God. I'm going to…I'm going to come."

And then she did. And the way it felt…She was contracting around him, and she was riding him hard, crying out her pleasure. And he'd lost control. He was shouting, unable to form words. His arms were pulled tight over his head, and he was on his heels, his hips leaving the bed, thrusting to meet her with every bit of force he had, and it was so intense, it was almost painful. And it was incredible.

♡

She untied his hands first. She had to work on the knot for awhile, he'd pulled it so tight, straining against his bonds. But she got it loose eventually, and he pulled his arms down, reached for the scarf over his eyes, and looked at her. Kneeling over him in the warm glow of the flickering candles, naked except for those stockings.

Bloody hell. Those stockings. Her dark hair was loose around her shoulders, her cheeks flushed, and if he'd been in charge, he knew what he'd be doing right now. It had been so hot, not being able to see her, not being able to touch her. But when he could… it was going to be so good. He was going to make the most of his time. He was going to wear her out.

She sat back, stretched a leg in the air, began to roll a stocking down her thigh.

"That looks like something your sex slave should be doing for you," he said.

She stopped what she was doing, looked at him, then smiled slowly. "You know, I think you're right. Why don't you come down here and do it?"

He knelt between her legs, put his hands around her thigh. Stroked it for a bit, and then carefully, slowly, began to pull the delicate material down. She was leaning back on her elbows, her dark eyes luminous in the candlelight, her gaze intent on him.

"Can I ask you a question?" he asked her, pulling the silky item off her foot and handing it to her, then moving to her other leg. Getting in a fair amount of touching in the process of taking hold of the second stocking. Doing some things that, he saw, were having their effect on her.

"What?" she asked, sounding a bit breathless.

"Just how flexible are you? I've always wondered."

"Very flexible," she assured him. "Maybe not quite ballet-dancer flexible, but I can do the splits."

"The splits, eh," he said speculatively. He had the second stocking off, and she'd set both of them carefully down next to the bed, rolling over to do that, showing him that backside again. Which was adding yet another item to his list for the next day.

"And you're getting a little ahead of yourself, aren't you?" she asked, back on her elbows again, shaking her hair back. Looking sexy, and wicked, and nine kinds of dangerous. "You're still on my time. I'm still in charge, or did you forget that?"

"Nah," he said, drinking her in. "I didn't forget that. D'you have some more orders for me, then?"

"Oh, yeah," she smiled. "I think I do. I think you've got another job to do before you're finished for the night."

He let her wear the stockings the next day, when it was his turn. But only the stockings. Made her cook him breakfast that way as her first job, which she found pretty distracting, especially with him sitting at the table watching her do it. And when she set their plates down, she was startled to find herself pulled into his lap, her plate moved next to his. Which made it just way too difficult to eat. She kept losing her focus on her eggs, especially when his hands began to roam and she was squirming in his lap, lying back against his chest as he fondled her. But by the time he laid her down and had her for dessert...she wasn't exactly hungry anymore.

By the end of the day, Kristen's poor silk scarves were never going to be the same again, because Nate had managed to be a whole lot more inventive with them than she had.

Oh, sure, he'd got around to using one of them to tie her wrists behind her back. But after that, he'd made her stand there while he used the other one on her, the smooth silk rubbing over her faster, then slower, harder, then softer, until her legs were shaking, until she was begging him. Until she would have done anything for him if only he'd finished it. By the time he'd let her drop to her knees, put a pillow down on the floor and gently pushed her forehead down onto it, she'd been nearly incoherent. And when he'd finally been inside her, one hand bracing himself against the floor, the other stroking her, allowing her to let go at last while she shuddered and moaned out her gratitude...at that moment, she really had been his.

At last, though, her hands were free, her body was her own again, and she was lying in bed, her head on his shoulder, stroking his chest.

"So how was your birthday?" she asked him.

"Sweet as," he said with a grin. "Best birthday present ever."

"Hmm," she agreed languidly. "I thought about giving you a sweater, but..."

He laughed. "Yeh. This was a much better choice. And I'd still like to pay for it. For this place, I mean. I think I may have got a bit more present than you intended."

"Well, maybe," she admitted. "You're very creative, aren't you? Especially without advance notice. I'm so impressed. But I enjoyed it, too. And no, you can't pay for it. It was *my* present, and I gave it to you."

"You certainly did," he agreed.

"But you can buy Kristen a couple new scarves. And you can buy me a new pair of stockings, too, since you destroyed those, making me wear them while I...while I did all that. And who knows? I might want to wear that outfit again sometime."

He bent and kissed her on the top of the head. "I'll do that," he promised. "Because I may want to see that outfit again myself."

wedding song

♡

"Is this all right?" Kristen asked as soon as she opened the door. "I looked it up, but I wasn't positive. Am I OK?"

Liam smiled. "You're more than OK." He leaned forward and gave her a kiss on the cheek. "You're beautiful."

"But for the marae. Are there any rules? And you look very handsome, by the way."

He glanced down at the black suit, custom-tailored to his broad frame. "Cheers. But for you...Just the same rules you'd have for any wedding. No different on the marae. Though come to think of it, you *are* breaking one rule. Reckon you're going to outshine the bride."

"I tried not to be too flashy." She ran her hands nervously down the pretty blue-and-green dress she was wearing over black tights and ankle boots in deference to the rain. "Is it still too much?"

"Nah." She'd really worried about it, he could tell, and as always, her vulnerability pierced his heart. "You can't help being beautiful. It's OK. And we should go."

♡

Despite his words, Kristen was definitely feeling some butterflies during the short drive. She'd be meeting Liam's parents today,

235

and some of his family as well. But just as a friend, she reminded herself. They didn't have to love her to accept her as his friend.

Liam held the door for her, held an umbrella over her head as she emerged from his car into a rain-soaked carpark behind Wellington University. She took his arm for the walk to the shelter of an overhang where a group of thirty or forty people waited, and was comforted, as always, by his solidity and strength.

"Liam. Darling."

This had to be his mother, a statuesque woman with Liam's eyes, the same warm smile, coming forward to hug and kiss him. And about half the rest of the group, she found, seemed to be related to him too, in one way or another. His father, an older and broader version of him, greeted his elder son with a fierce hug that communicated his love and pride.

Kristen met one of his sisters and her husband, the other sister and a brother, she knew, working across the Ditch in Australia. Then an aunt and uncle, and innumerable cousins. How could one person have so many cousins?

She tried to remember names at first, but soon gave up. Marika and Vernon, she could manage those. But between the size of the group and the many Maori given names and surnames, she was quickly lost.

"I'm sorry," she said with a laugh. "I hope you don't test me on names, because I'm afraid I'm already overwhelmed."

"That's all right, darling." Marika reached a broad arm around Kristen's waist, gave her an encouraging squeeze. "We'll take care of you, no worries. Is this your first time at a marae?"

"It is," Kristen said with a grateful smile. She should have known that Liam's parents would be warm and loving. He had to have got it from somewhere. "And I'm excited, but I'm not sure what to expect or what to do, so I hope you'll tell me. Are we waiting here for something?"

"Just for the whole group to come," Marika explained. "So they only have to karanga once. But I think we're good now."

Kristen moved forward with the group, grown to at least fifty by now, as they walked down the strip of pavement surrounded by green lawn toward the building, open at both front and back, its overhung, steeply pitched roof edged by two intricately carved beams painted a bright red. The wharenui, the ceremonial meeting house where the wedding would take place.

At least it had stopped raining, which was fortunate, because a group of women had come out from the sheltering roof to stand in front of the building, and the visitors had stopped some meters away.

One of the women facing them stepped slightly forward and began a...not a song, exactly, more of a call. She continued the call, or chant, or whatever it was, for some minutes, moving her hands in accompaniment to the Maori words. When she finished, Liam's mother stepped forward and performed her own call in return, then took a pace back into her group. Silence fell for a few moments, until the woman in front of the building performed one final brief call and motioned them inside.

"The karanga," Liam told Kristen quietly. "Greeting us, welcoming us. Mum thanking her in return. And both of them clearing a pathway for our ancestors to meet as well."

The group of visitors stopped beneath the overhang, and everyone bent down to remove their shoes before stepping inside, where rows of chairs with ribbons on the back were set up, looking like any wedding anywhere. But the surroundings, Kristen saw as she took her seat with the rest of the visitors on one side of the aisle, were unlike anything she'd ever seen.

The roof was supported by beams, a carved, stylized figure at the bottom of each. Jutting bellies and big heads, faces and thighs marked with traditional tattoos, long-fingered hands on bellies, oversized tongues displayed. Each beam painted above its supporting figure with curving designs in red, white, and black. The space between the beams paneled with flax woven into geometrical designs of white and brown, every panel boasting a different but harmonious pattern. Kristen's aesthetic sense was at once stimulated and soothed by the beauty of the woven designs, the contrast between their elegant simplicity and the elaborate carvings and paintings, the harmony of it all. Men carved, women wove, Liam had told her, and both skills were valued and proudly displayed.

She was diverted from her study of her surroundings by several men standing and moving forward from each side of the aisle, facing each other at the front of the room. Several rounds of speeches followed, host first, then guest, followed by a second man from each side, then a third.

Kristen let the melodious language wash over her. More welcoming, she guessed, part of the protocol Liam had told her was always followed at the marae. She was beginning to realize that Maori could *talk.*

And sing, because as soon as the speeches ended, the entire group burst into song, everyone on both sides of the aisle chiming in with full-throated enthusiasm and smiling faces. One song, then another, both seeming to be perfectly well known to all present, including young children. And sung so beautifully, even without accompaniment, Kristen got chills.

The second song ended, and Liam got up with the rest of the men on the guests' side and lined up before moving forward, one at a time, to greet the man Kristen guessed was the host. Each man placed his left hand on the host's shoulder, the host placing his own hand on his guest's left shoulder, touched foreheads and noses twice, then moved on. Marika pulled Kristen up by the hand with a smile and stood with the other female guests, where they got in line behind the men to greet the host in their turn.

Kristen couldn't help feeling a little shy and awkward doing her own hongi, wondering if it could really be all right for such an obvious outsider to participate, but was reassured when the host smiled at her in welcome.

"Just don't head-butt him, and you'll be right," Liam had laughed when he was explaining the process to her. And practicing with her, which had felt...good. His big hand on her shoulder, and having an excuse to put her hand on his shoulder at last herself, to feel all that solid muscle under her palm. And to touch her face to his, even if what she had wanted was to kiss him. To keep holding him, and to feel him holding her, too.

She pulled her mind back with an effort, took her seat again. And finally the welcoming was done, the tapu was removed, and the ceremony could begin.

There was none of the solemnity she'd expected. Instead, it was joyous, and fun, and warm, and...beautiful. A Christian service conducted by a minister, with a few songs thrown in just because, Liam had told her, Maori needed to sing.

Kristen found herself tearing up as the couple exchanged their vows, looking so happy to embark on their life together with their huge extended families around them. How would it feel, she wondered, to be surrounded by all that love and support?

She felt the familiar wrench of her heart at the memory of her own wedding, nobody but Hannah and Drew, her brother Matt there to represent her family. A winery wedding, the ceremony conducted beneath a rose arbor in a vineyard she'd never been to before, by a celebrant she'd never met before, in front of people who'd mostly meant nothing to her. A hundred or so of Marshall's business contacts, with a few of her own friends sprinkled in. Marshall's parents, his younger sister, too, none of them seeming all that enthusiastic about her entry into their family. They must have known, she'd thought later, that there would be no point in getting attached, because it wasn't going to last.

What she would have given, that day, to have been part of a family like this. To have had a father to walk her down the aisle, maybe cry a little at the thought of his baby girl growing up. A mother to help her get dressed, to reassure her. Parents and grandparents to tell her that they were proud of her, that they loved her. She'd had Hannah and Matt, and that was all. She'd thought she had Marshall too, but she'd been so wrong.

She reached for a tissue in her bag, wiped the tears away as the bride and groom walked down the aisle, husband and wife now, and the entire congregation began to sing a song she recognized. *Pokarekare Ana,* the most famous Maori love song, a song of the love of a man for a woman. A man who thought he could die if he wasn't allowed to marry his beloved. A man who would love her forever. A man who would die for her.

Liam's big hand, then, coming around hers as she continued to cry. Not demanding anything of her, just holding it. And it was as if all the strength and comfort she felt every time she was with him was passing from his hand into her own. As if he were holding her close, holding her tight, exactly the way he held her rope at the gym. Letting her know that he was there, that he had her. That he would never let her go. And that he would never, ever let her fall.

self-control: sadly overrated

♡

Ally awoke early on Sunday morning, stole quietly out of the bedroom. Nate was still sleeping, but she was feeling so energized, she had to move. It had rained on and off all throughout the previous day, and she'd woken at night to hear more of it, drumming hard on the roof of the bach. Perfect weather to stay indoors and be Nate's sex slave, she thought with a happy shiver of remembrance as she stepped off the porch and ran across the road to reach the break in the dunes that offered access to the beach on the other side.

Today, the clouds had parted, the sun was shining, even if not warmly, and she was on a kilometers-long, deserted stretch of beach, feeling like the only person in the world. She kicked off her jandals, chose a direction at random and began to walk. And when that wasn't enough to release her fizzing spirits, began to run. The sand was firm under her feet near the edge of the surf, and when a lone wave came up higher on the beach, she didn't run away from it. She embraced it, letting the cold water wash over her feet and ankles, glad she had worn her shorts so she was free to play.

She turned at last, began to run back the way she'd come. Still nobody else around, she saw with pleasure, none of the little town's few hundred residents fancying an early-morning beach walk. She ran past the spot where she'd entered, then gradually slowed. Put her head back, into the wind. Listened to the pounding of the surf, stretched her arms wide, and twirled. Around and around, feeling six years old again, able to surrender herself completely to the magic of the moment.

She took a final spin and saw Nate coming through the break in the dunes towards her. She waved at him, an extravagant gesture, her arm sweeping above her head, laughed out loud. Saw him start to jog towards her, the economy of motion, the controlled power, as always, impressing her. Thrilling her.

She wasn't quite ready to give up on her outdoor fun, though. She didn't want to talk. She wanted to move. She started to run. But not towards him. That would be too easy. No, she ran away from him.

Faster and faster, loving the feeling of stretching out, skimming along the sand. And of teasing him, she realized as she looked back over her shoulder, saw that he was chasing her, gaining fast. She began to sprint, putting all her effort into it. Cast another quick glance back, and saw that he was closer still. Her heart was pounding, her breath coming hard. And still she ran, until she could hear his footfalls behind her.

One moment she was running. The next, she was off her feet, his arm around her waist. A few more slowing steps, and they were falling to the sand. She felt him twisting in midair to take the impact, the breath leaving her lungs with a *whoosh* all the same as they landed, rolled until he was on top of her, his arms still around her.

She was gasping from the effort of her sprint, the shock of the fall. And then his hands were around her head, his mouth was on hers, and he was stealing her breath entirely. Kissing her fiercely, the hunger in him like a tangible thing. He was at her mouth, her throat, and he was popping the button on the waistband of her shorts, yanking the zip down. Reaching inside then, his hand hard against her, and it was as if all the effort, all the excitement of her run, of the chase were here, at her core, because she was gasping for a different reason now. The heat rising higher and higher as he rubbed her, kissed her, bit her. Nothing gentle about it. This was pure physical, animal excitement, and it had her caught in its grasp. She was almost there already. And then she was crying out, her back arching as the delicious spasms overtook her.

He didn't stop until the last shudder had left her. Then he rolled again so she was lying on his chest, breathing hard against his neck.

"That's what I do to girls who run away from me." His voice sounded uneven, his breathing harsh. She could feel him against her, how much he wanted her, how much he needed her, and knew that he wasn't going to do anything about it, not here. Because somebody might see them. Because he couldn't let himself lose that last bit of control, couldn't risk the exposure.

"That's all?" she asked, doing her best to control her breathing, to sound disappointed. "When you went to all that effort to run me down and catch me?"

"What?" he asked, his gaze arrested on her face. "You want more? That wasn't enough?"

"It was pretty good," she hastened to assure him. "It was fine. It just wasn't as much as…It wasn't completely…exciting, was it?"

"It wasn't exciting," he said slowly, brows coming down in his intense, intimidating frown.

"Well, not quite what…But good," she added hastily, trying to look reassuring. She put a hand on his arm. "It was very exciting. Forget I said anything."

"Right," he said grimly. He stood up, pulling her with him, grabbed her around the hips and, in one quick, smooth movement, shoved his shoulder into her waist and lifted her, his arm firm around the sandy backs of her thighs. Then started back along the beach, moving fast.

Oh, yeah. This was it. The blood was rushing to her head, and she was bracing her hands against his back, holding on, feeling the sand there, too. She could sense the purpose in every stride, and was shivering with it.

"Nate," she managed to get out through the bumps as she bounced against him. "I didn't mean anything. You don't..."

"Be quiet. You want exciting? I'll give you exciting." They'd reached the break in the dunes now, and she spared a thought for her jandals, at the mercy of the tide, then decided to sacrifice them to the cause. Because Nate was crossing the road, pushing through the door of the little house, and dropping her on the bed.

"Get those clothes off," he ordered, stripping off his own T-shirt, his shorts. She looked up at him, raised her hands hesitantly to her own sweater, then stopped and bit her lip.

"Now. Move," he told her. He was naked now, grabbing in the drawer for a condom, but still watching her as she scrambled to the other side of the bed, got to her feet.

"It's not your day anymore," she protested.

"Oh, it's my day," he assured her. "Take off your clothes."

She kept her eyes on him as she reached slowly for the hem of her sweater and shirt, pulled them over her head, tossed them aside.

"The rest of it," he said. "Now, Ally. You make me do it, you aren't going to like it."

Ooh. She was really scared now. She bit her lip again, looked up at him questioningly, then slowly unfastened her bra and let it drop, pulled her shorts and underwear all the way off.

He sat on the end of the bed. "Come here," he ordered. And when she wasn't moving fast enough for him, reached for her arm and pulled her the rest of the way. Pulled her down, all the way to her knees, grabbed her head in both hands. And at that moment, or long minutes later, when she was bent over the bed, her hands gripping the edge of the mattress, her arms shaking with the effort of holding herself up, hearing herself keening out the hard pleasure of it, she couldn't have said, even teasingly, that it wasn't exciting. Or that it wasn't enough.

♡

"Aw, geez," he said when they were lying together on their backs, catching their breath. "What did I do?"

"You got everything awfully sandy, is what you did," she said, brushing ineffectually at the duvet. "I'm going to have to take this outside and shake it out. And I need a shower."

"Ally. Don't change the subject. I need to tell you that I'm sorry."

She turned her head on the pillow to look at him. "Sorry? Why?"

"I shouldn't have...I pushed too hard. I tackled you, for a start. Can't believe I did that. And then, on the beach like that, where anybody could see. But the worst thing, when you said that bit about it not being exciting enough, I went too far. Something just...snapped."

"Hmm." She ran her hand over his chest, leaned over to kiss his shoulder. She did love his shoulders, the smooth, firm bulge of muscle there, the way it curved down and then back up again into the swell of bicep and tricep. She did love *him*. How fierce he was, and how sweet. How worried he was right now.

"You lost control," she suggested.

"I did," he admitted. "All the way. And I don't do that. I said I wouldn't force you."

"And you didn't, did you?" She sat up and looked down at him where he lay, his eyes troubled. "You might have *felt* out of control, but what did you actually do? Made sure we fell so

I wouldn't get hurt. OK, you touched me out in the open, on an empty beach, without either of us taking any clothes off. Big deal. If someone had come by, I guess you'd have had to do the perp walk, pull your T-shirt over your head on the way home. Which would probably have made me laugh, sorry to say. I kind of wish it had happened now."

He shuddered. "Don't even say it. But that wasn't all I did, and you know it."

"Yep," she agreed. "You carried me off, which was pretty hot, by the way. And then told me to take off my clothes, and did some things to me that I enjoyed too, thank you very much. Just a little more...forcefully than usual, that's all. Which isn't the same as forcing me. What would you have done if I'd said no, during any of that? If I'd told you to put me down? Asked you to stop?"

"I'd have stopped," he said immediately. "If you'd said to stop, I'd have stopped."

"That's right. You would have. I was never worried that you'd hurt me, or that you'd do anything I didn't want, if I told you I didn't want it. I know you won't do that. I trust you, Nate. I know who you are, and I trust you. So it's not so bad if you let me push your buttons a little. You don't have to be careful all the time. You can show me your wild side, because it seems I've got a pretty good one too. Just an adrenaline junkie through and through, I guess."

He was looking up at her, an arrested expression on his face, speculation beginning to dawn in those sharp eyes.

"Ally," he said slowly. "*Were* you pushing my buttons?"

"Well, yeah," she admitted. "Of course I was. What?" She started to laugh. "You really think you didn't excite me enough, catching me like that, giving me one heck of an orgasm, right there on the beach?"

She braced her hands on either side of him, bent to kiss him.

"You excite me," she told him, still leaning over him, smiling into his eyes. "You thrill me. The things you do, the things you say. And then thinking about them later gets me going all over again, even when you're not around. Even when you're in South Africa for two *very* long weeks. I'm pretty much in a perpetual state of arousal here, haven't you noticed?"

He laughed reluctantly, reached to push her hair behind her ear. "I can't believe I let you play me like that. That I let you get to me. You're a pretty naughty girl, aren't you?"

"I'm working on it," she assured him, getting up and brushing off a bit more sand. "Plus, I'm guessing not too many women can say they've been tackled by the captain of the All Blacks."

"Nobody but you," he agreed, rolling over and standing up himself. "Not *this* captain, anyway. And you'd better make some room in that shower, because I'm coming in with you."

some of us are more important than others

♡

" This is a lot of days off for you, too, isn't it?" Nate asked
her a few hours later. They'd cooked breakfast together,
both fully dressed this time, had gone to the Sunday market in
Foxton, bought fish and vegetables for dinner. Now, they were
going for a regular, suitable-for-public-viewing beach walk, since
it was miraculously still not raining. And walking barefoot on
the beach with Nate, his hand warm and strong around hers, was
just as good as all those online dating profiles suggested.

"It is. A three-day weekend."

"Mac gave it to you, then?"

"Huh. Not hardly. I earned it. Traded a bunch of hours with
Robbo and a couple of the other guys, the last few weeks. Ended
up working all the weekend days. It didn't really matter, since
you were gone and nobody else asked me out. Joke," she added
hastily as he swung around to frown at her.

"I know I'm not here all the time to take you out," he said,
beginning to walk again, still wearing that frown, she saw with
a quick peek at his face. "That I can't give you that much attention, and that I won't be here much at all, the next month or so.
But I don't care. I don't want you seeing anybody else."

"You're jealous," she realized.

"Too bloody right I'm jealous. I told you I would be."

"When?"

He gestured in exasperation. "When you asked me how I'd feel if you went off to live in another country without me."

"Back *then?* You still remember that? That was just a hypothetical question! If you'd *hypothetically* been with me for six years, remember?"

He was walking faster now, and she had to skip a little to keep up, as he still had a tight grip on her hand.

"I don't care if it's six years or six weeks," he said. "It's you and me, and that's it. You said no other people, and that's the way it is for me too. I don't share."

"I said no other people in *bed* with us," she said with a little laugh. Wow. He really *was* jealous. That should bother her, right? So why was it giving her a little glow of pleasure? And why was it kind of...hot? "I meant, I'm not having some threesome with you and one of your teammates."

She went on hastily when he glared at her again. "Come on, you know I'm teasing. I don't want to date anybody else. Are you kidding? When I have you? You're worth waiting for. I thought I already made that pretty clear."

"Good," he muttered, looking a bit embarrassed now. "Why do you always get me so bloody worked up?"

"I don't know," she said. "Why do I? And it goes both ways, you know. I don't care how famous you are, or how far away you are. Nobody else for you either, buddy. You're all mine."

"I am, am I?" he asked, beginning to grin.

"You are. And if you have any doubts about that, remember, I still have those scarves, and I'm not afraid to use them."

He laughed, swung her around by the hand, then up into his arms. Lifted her right off her feet for a kiss.

"Kissing me on the beach again," she said severely when he let her go. "Getting pretty far out there, Mr. Proper."

"Kissing's allowed. Geez. I need to go back to work just to get a rest. You turn my head all the way around. And you never answered my question, you know. Why was it so hard for you to get the days off? Why couldn't you just have asked Mac for them? Seems like he should be happy enough with you. I made it dead clear that you were the reason we did the team thing there, back in January. And the reason I've been coming back, and you can't tell me that hasn't helped. Gave him that signed jersey for the wall and all, too. He loved that."

"Wait a minute," she commanded. "Back up. *You* set up that team thing? The one in January?"

"Course I did. Why, what did you think?"

"I thought maybe Liam," she said slowly.

"It was the backs, remember? And I know rugby isn't your game, but you have sussed out by now that I'm a back and he isn't, right?"

She refused to be diverted. "You did that? Really? Why?"

"Why d'you think? Because I wanted to see you again. And because it was a good idea," he added honestly. "It really *was* a good team-building exercise."

"Wow. I'm reevaluating like crazy over here." She snuggled her hand a little further into his, felt her heart give a funny little skip. He'd done all that, just to be with her? "And to answer your question, no, I don't think any of that's helped me that much with Mac. But I'm awfully glad you did it anyway."

"Not as glad as I am," he said. "Got one hell of a birthday present out of it, for one thing. But let's back up again. So hard to stay on the topic when I talk to you. Why couldn't you ask Mac for the days? That's not going any better? Still not interested in your suggestions?"

She shrugged, but didn't say anything.

"Ally," he demanded. "Answer me. You're always talking about me, but you never tell me anything, d'you know that?"

"But it's not—" She stopped.

"Not what?" he prompted.

"My work problems are so...small," she tried to explain. She laughed, tried to make a joke of it. "Way below your pay grade."

He looked down at her, eyes troubled. "You don't trust me to be interested in you, is that it? Because you think I've got an important job, and you don't? I play footy, I'm not the bloody prime minister."

"But you're successful, that'd be the difference. About as successful as a person can get. And I'm not."

"Whether your work problems are important—that's got nothing to do with how much money you make. If I were playing club rugby, I'd still be taking it seriously. Because it's what I want to do. Because I love it. So why don't you take yourself, what you want, seriously?"

"It's complicated," she said weakly.

"So explain it to me."

Those eyes weren't letting her get away with anything. This was the bull again. And he wasn't going to let up, she knew, until he got his answer.

"Mac doesn't think I'm anything special, that's all," she said at last. "I show up on time. He likes that. I show *up*, period. I don't call in sick. I'm reliable. Go, me."

"Still not listening to you, eh."

She shrugged. "Oh, well. Maybe someday."

"Maybe someday what?" he pressed. "What is it you want to do? And why don't you think it matters?"

"Because the only dream I have is impossible, and kind of ridiculous. Not serious. And other than that, I still don't know what I want to be when I grow up." She shrugged again, gave him a rueful smile.

"Know what my dream was, growing up?" he asked. "Being an All Black. Which was only the dream of about a million other

Kiwi boys. You want to talk about impossible, I'm it. So come on, tell me. What's your dream?"

"OK," she sighed, "it'd be doing what I'm doing, but being in charge. Getting to do it my way. That's what I want to do, have my own gym or climbing guide company or kayaking company, something like that," she finished in a rush. "You can laugh now."

"Why would I laugh?"

"Well, it's not a real prospect, is it? My parents sure don't think so. They're still waiting for me to do something with a 'career track.' They keep reminding me that they'll pay for grad school. I might not know what I want to do, but I'm pretty sure I don't want to do that. Not with no plan, at least."

"Grad school in what? I know you went to Uni, but you didn't tell me what you did there." He grinned at her. "Physical education? Basket weaving?"

She laughed reluctantly. "My degree's about as incongruous as yours. Math, with a minor in Business. Marketing statistics, that was what I was really interested in. Go figure. I still like it. If I were Mac, I'd..."

"You'd what?"

"I'd have a Facebook page, a better website, be running polls, contests, all sorts of things. Finding out what people wanted, and doing those things. Collecting data on my membership, crunching those numbers. You know, the basic stuff."

"So what happened, between that and this? Between studying all that maths, and spending your valuable time teaching boofheads to climb?"

"I guess it was that my real minor was in 'things I can do outdoors,'" she said. "I learned to kayak and climb in college, then I taught people to kayak and climb, then I just kept doing it, because I liked it so much. And I still do, and I think it's great for other people to do it too, and I want to help them do it. Especially women. Climbing's great for women, because you just have to lift your own weight. You get strong, you get flexible, you conquer your fears, all those important things."

"So what's wrong with that?"

"Well, you can't make a real living at what I've been doing, for one thing. I've never wanted to be rich, but I don't want to be renting a room in a house forever, either. I've never bought a car, not even a secondhand one. I'm going to have to get a real job sometime here. My dad keeps pointing out that statistical analysis is a hot area right now, and he's right. I keep dragging my feet, though, because I really don't want to work in an office. So there you go. That's where I'm stuck. Can't make a living doing what I like, can't stomach doing anything else."

"That's a problem," he admitted.

"Yep," she sighed. "And Mac won't even let me *help*. At least back home, I was the assistant manager. Which doesn't mean all that much, just that you have the keys, but at least I got to share my ideas a little. At least I got to do *something*. So I don't know." She shrugged. "My family said I was just spinning my wheels coming to New Zealand, and even though I love it here, I know they were right. I'm not going to get anywhere doing this."

"Not if you give up, you're not. That's one thing I'm dead sure of."

This was why she hadn't wanted to tell him. Because she'd known it would make her feel inadequate, and that's exactly what it had done. She could manage to feel inadequate all by herself, during her down moments. All she had to do was compare herself to her college friends. Comparing herself to Nate, though…that was just depressing.

"Come on," she said instead, dropping his hand. "Let's run." And did what she always did to get out of a funk. Moved.

all good things must end

♡

"OK," Ally said the next morning, pushing "Send" on her mobile. "I've told Joanne we're out of here, and we're good to go. I don't even have to hide you in the car again."

They'd cooked another big, leisurely breakfast, packed up the food and loaded it into the car like some kind of...real couple. And it had felt great.

Nate smiled. "I appreciate the anonymous weekend, but it's not really necessary."

"It is, though. I wanted to give you a few days where it was just you and me. Where you wouldn't have to think about anything else, or about being anything else." Except for the market the day before, but that had been fairly low-key. There was no way for him to escape notice entirely, not in New Zealand, but she'd done her very best.

He pulled her to him for a kiss that had her hanging on and kissing him back. She just never got tired of that.

"And you did," he assured her. "You gave me just exactly that. Maybe I could pack you in my suitcase tomorrow, take you with me to the Mount, on to Aussie. Keep me relaxed all week."

"Your roommate might notice something a little funny," she said, reluctantly going to the door and reaching for her bag.

"I'll do that." He grabbed the handle with one hand, hefted his own duffel with the other. "And I'm afraid you're right," he sighed, waiting while she cast a last look around and pulled the door to the little house closed behind them. "Pity."

"Are you driving?" he asked with surprise when he'd stowed the luggage and she was opening the driver's side door. "I'll do it if you like."

"My car," she pointed out, waiting while he got into the passenger side and fastened his seatbelt. "Does it really bother you to be driven by a woman? I thought we got over that with the climbing lessons."

"Well, not a *woman*," he said slowly.

"What?" She shot him a startled glance before pulling out onto the road. "You don't like how I drive?"

"Bit fast, isn't it?"

"Oh, man. I *scare* you." She started to laugh, got to the edge of town, and put her foot down. "This OK with you?" she asked solicitously. "I'm going the limit. Too frightening? Want me to slow down to ninety?"

"Oi," he protested. "I may have been blindfolded on the way up here, but I wasn't deaf. And those tires squealed round the corners a fair bit. It's a Yaris, not a Porsche. And the limit's there for a reason, you know."

"Well, excuse me. I'll try to take account of your tender sensibilities and not frighten you, how's that?" She took another look at the speedometer. A hundred and eight. Well, that was reasonable, surely.

"Cheers," he said with a reluctant smile. "But I was serious, earlier. It was a good weekend. Wish it wasn't over. What d'you think about staying with me tonight? You don't have to work till tomorrow, do you?"

She glanced quickly across at him, then concentrated on taking another sharp corner. The tires only squealed a little bit.

Well, she wasn't going to drive like an old lady, no matter how proper he wanted to be.

"Not till the afternoon," she said. "I could give you a lift to the airport in the morning, maybe?"

"Sounds good."

"I'd have to see about my schedule, whether I can pick you up, though," she realized. "Whether I have to work. Because that'll be Sunday, right?"

"Right. If not, I'll get a lift from one of the boys, no worries. Wish I could know you'd be off when I am, though, at least on the Sundays. At least at *night*. I want to be with you when I'm home."

Well, wasn't that just the thing to give her a happy glow? Even though, however badly he wanted to be with her, she was pretty sure she wanted to be with him more.

"I'm not sure, though," she had to add after a brief consultation with her nether regions, which were letting her know in no uncertain terms that they were closing up shop for a while, "how much I'll be up for tonight. I'm a little sore, tell you the truth. There might not be too much entertainment value in it for you."

"Aw, geez," he groaned. "I knew I was too rough yesterday. Why didn't you say something?"

"Because I still wanted to do it, that's why." Because he'd still been jealous, she'd been able to tell. Had been a little possessive. A little demanding. And because that had been so damn hot.

"It's not a *bad* sore," she tried to explain, shooting him a quick grin, seeing his reluctant smile in response. "Just a little... overused. I need a rest, that's all. Give my poor overworked lady-bits a chance to recover. So what do you think? Still want me?" She waited a little nervously for his answer. He wouldn't say "no." Surely he wouldn't.

"Yeh," he said with decision. "I still want you. I liked that we had some time yesterday to do normal things, too. Walk on the beach, go to the market, cook dinner, read, all that. I'd like another day like that, even though I've got some work to do today. And I'd like to sleep with you. I mean, *fall* asleep with you. Holding you. As it's going to be a while."

"That's nice," she said softly. "I'd like that too." She felt so mushy inside that she actually took her foot off the accelerator around the next corner. And didn't make the tires squeal one little bit.

♡

She was past Porirua when she saw the lights in her rear-view mirror. And, a moment later, heard the siren.

"Aw, hell," Nate groaned.

"He probably just needs to pass," she reassured him as the white car with the familiar blue checks came up fast. She edged to the left, towards the verge, and, with a sinking heart, saw the car slowing behind her. Heard the *blip* of the siren, pulled over with a sigh that Nate echoed, leaning his head back against the headrest.

"Morning," the officer said when she'd lowered the window. "Going a bit fast there, weren't you?"

"Sorry," she said with a winning smile. Tears didn't usually work, she'd found long ago. Smiling and apologizing sometimes did, though, and looking as cute as possible. Well, occasionally. Worth a try, anyway.

"May I see your license, please?" he asked.

"Sure." She reached for her purse in the back seat, pulled out her wallet. But the officer wasn't looking at her anymore, his gaze arrested by her passenger.

"You're Nate Torrance, eh," he said.

"I am."

The officer seemed less certain. "Sorry. Have to ask for her license, all the same."

"No worries," Nate said. "Do what you need to do. You're right, she was speeding."

Ally turned and stared at him. "That's helpful," she muttered. "Thanks."

"Miss?" The officer asked. "Your license?"

And that, she found, was that.

♡

When they were pulling away again, the ticket tucked into Ally's purse, she was finally able to explode. "Oh, that's just great. That's just what I needed. Thanks a lot."

"What?" Nate asked in surprise.

"You're right, she was speeding," she mimicked. "Why didn't you just write the ticket for him?"

"What the hell did you expect me to do?" he asked, not a single bit of sympathy evident in those hard eyes, she saw with a glance across at him. If anything, he looked mad at *her*. "You heard him. You were doing one-twenty. The limit's a hundred every single bloody place in En Zed, if you haven't noticed. I offered to drive, said you were going too fast. You didn't want to listen, and you got pulled over. What was I meant to do about that?"

"Maybe, I don't know, smile at him and talk about rugby or something? Tell him that you're late for training? However you do it. I mean, all I've got is being cute. But you're a *celebrity*. So you must know how."

"Nah, I don't," he said shortly. "Just how many tickets have you got? And how many have you got out of?"

"What, ever?"

"Yeh. Ever. How many?"

"Well...*ever*...Four, that they've actually written. But two of those were when I was a teenager," she said hastily. "And I haven't had one for a couple years at least. So OK, this was number five.

Still not that many, on average. And a hundred's, what? Sixty miles an hour? Ridiculous. I was barely doing..." She did the calculation. "OK, I was going just over seventy. That isn't that fast. That'd barely keep me up with traffic in California. And everyone gets tickets sometimes. How many have you had?"

"None," he answered, still looking upset.

"Really? None? But then," she realized, "nobody's going to write *you* a ticket. Not here, they aren't."

"Nah, they aren't, because I'm not going to put anybody in a position where they have to make that decision. Which is why I don't do one-twenty. I'm meant to be a solid citizen, you know. It matters."

"You can't even get a speeding ticket? That's too racy?" She was still annoyed, but a little fascinated now, too. "You're kidding."

"No," he said grimly. "I'm not kidding."

"Wow. I guess touching me on the beach *was* a really big deal," she said wonderingly. "Not to mention hauling me off like some kind of Viking raider."

He groaned. "Don't remind me. Can't believe I did that."

She found her spirits rising again despite herself. "I sure did pull you out of your comfort zone this weekend, then, didn't I?"

He smiled reluctantly. "Yeh. You did. I'd like to avoid actually getting arrested, if it's all the same to you. But I'm beginning to think that you're going to take me straight over to the dark side. Who knows where the bloody hell I'm going to end up."

too much honesty

♡

A lly slowly rose from a deliciously deep sleep the next morning to the comforting solidity of Nate's arm across her body. And the awareness of the rest of him, even more solid, pressed against her from behind.

"Mmm." She wriggled backwards a little just to feel him respond.

"Still sore, I know," he murmured in her ear. "Just sleep with me a minute more. Let me hold you."

"Not that sore anymore," she breathed, and wriggled a bit more. "Not if you're gentle."

He groaned softly. And then started being gentle.

She sighed with sleepy pleasure as his hand moved over her, brought her body slowly to life. And when she was ready, he slid into her from behind. Still slow, still gentle, touching her the whole time, all sighs and slow, smooth movement.

No rocketing descent down the hill this time, just the best, the easiest, most delicious glide. And the knowledge that this was Nate. Holding her. Touching her. Kissing her. Loving her all the way there, until she was breathing hard, until slow and gentle weren't enough anymore. Until he shifted their position, and she felt the pleasure of the change in angle, the increased friction, sharp and sudden, and was gasping with it.

"When I'm gone," he told her, his breath coming hard now, "I wake up in the night, roll over, wish I had you underneath me. I want to be inside you. Want to hear you. See you. I want you so much."

His words were all she needed. "Nate," she got out as the delicious contractions overtook her. "Oh, I love you. I love you."

She felt his entire body still for a moment. But only for a moment, because he was too close. And then he was joining her, shuddering with it.

♡

"I'm sorry I said that," she said quietly when they were in her car again. She pulled to a stop at a red light and glanced across at him. They'd had a quiet morning, cooked breakfast together, and she'd watched him pack for the week with an economy that spoke of the hundreds of times he'd done exactly that. He hadn't said anything, but she'd felt the weight of her declaration hanging in the air between them, and she didn't want him to leave this way.

"I didn't mean to," she went on, feeling a little forlorn when she saw the look on his face, the guarded expression that had been missing lately, when he was with her. "It just slipped out, that's all. Heat of the moment, you know how it is. You don't have to worry. No obligation."

The light changed, and she moved with the traffic again, waited to hear what he'd have to say. She really had no idea what it would be, except that she was pretty sure she wasn't going to like it.

"I care about you," he said after a minute. "I want to be with you. I just...I don't want to say that if I'm not sure. It's not right."

"Yeah," she said, trying not to let the bitterness show. "Like telling her you're not ready for a relationship right now. Not fair to raise her expectations, have her...what did you say? Hoping."

"It's a relationship," he assured her, sounding so uncomfortable that, despite herself, she felt sorry for him. "But I'm not ready to commit to anything. I've got something too important to do just now. That's where my focus is. That's where it has to be."

"Ah," she said. "I see."

"But I want you," he went on hastily. "I don't mean that. I just...I don't know, all right? I keep thinking that we should slow down, that we're going too fast. But then I'm away from you, and I want to see you again. And then I *do* see you again, and I like being with you so much, and I tell myself it's just a couple days, that we're both enjoying it, so why not? But it's only been a few months. And I have the test matches coming up, too."

"Yeah," she said. "I've got it. The All Blacks."

"That's where my focus has to be," he said again. "I need to keep it there."

I never have been, he'd told her when she'd asked him if he wanted to be passionately in love. *Too focused on the footy.*

She should have listened then, but it seemed like she never learned, even when the guy could hardly have spelled it out better if he'd been using semaphore flags. Nate wanted sex, and fun, and maybe even some closeness. He didn't want love, or the complications it would bring. She'd come all the way around the world just to find another guy who wasn't ready for a commitment. Well, not to a person. Not to her, anyway.

"I've got it," she repeated. "I just have one question."

"What's that?" he asked warily.

"How the hell," she asked, her speed creeping up along with her voice despite her best intentions, "do you feel entitled to be all possessive and jealous like that? Acting like you want me so much that you can't stand to think of anybody else being with me? Why'd you work so hard to get me if you don't really want me after all?"

"I *do* want you, though," he said with obvious exasperation. "I just said so! And you're right, I *can't* stand that. Nobody else, Ally. I mean it."

"So we're exclusive," she said slowly, "except that rugby comes first."

"I have a commitment," he repeated. "This is my focus. This is my life. Can't we just go on like this for now? Aren't we having a good time together?"

"Yeah. We're having a good time." Except for this particular moment. This particular moment sucked.

"Then can't that be enough, right now?" he asked. "Can't we just spend time together, enjoy each other? Does it have to be all or nothing? Does it all have to happen so fast?"

"When you put it like that," she said, slowing as she neared the terminal, "I feel ridiculous. But I don't think I *am* ridiculous. I don't know. I'll have to think about it."

"I'll phone you," he said when she'd pulled into the curb in front of Air New Zealand Departures. He was out of the car, his duffel slung over his shoulder. "Tonight."

"I'm working till nine," she reminded him. "It'll be ten by the time I walk home."

"Right," he said with a frown. "Wish you didn't do that. Walk home, I mean, so late."

She shrugged. Not much she could really say about that. The car was Kristen's, not hers. So it was walking or taking the bus, and he knew it. Anyway, her danger in Wellington seemed a lot more likely to come from her wayward heart than anything else.

"I'll just text you later, then, tell you we got in. And phone you tomorrow," he said when she didn't answer. "Not working late then, are you?"

"No. Tomorrow's good."

"I'll phone you," he repeated. "And Ally. This weekend... Thanks."

She nodded, fought the tears that wanted to rise as he bent to kiss her through her open window. Not how she'd expected to be saying goodbye to him. It wasn't supposed to feel like this, not after what they'd shared. But you couldn't make somebody love you, could you? Not if he didn't. Not if he couldn't.

♡

"So," Kristen said that evening from her spot on the couch. "Long weekend, huh?"

The two of them were drinking herbal tea together before Kristen went to bed. Ally knew she ought to eat something, but she didn't have the energy to think about it.

She'd spent the day at work trying not to think about what Nate had said, what she had said. Had found herself blinking back tears, fighting an uncharacteristic sadness that kept threatening to overwhelm her, and now she was exhausted.

"Can I just say," Kristen offered tentatively when Ally didn't immediately respond, "that you don't look as happy as I thought you'd be? Is it saying goodbye again? Or did it not go well?"

Ally hadn't told her the details of what she'd planned, just that she'd wanted to take Nate away, give him a break. And Kristen had been excited for her, had urged her to take the car despite the inconvenience of being without it for three days. Now, Ally's eyes filled with tears again as she looked across at her friend. So loving. So concerned.

"It's just that..." She shrugged helplessly, found that the tears, held back so long, refused to be denied any longer. "He doesn't *love* me."

She choked on the words and began crying in earnest, which had Kristen running for the box of tissues, then coming to sit next to her and wrap a comforting arm around her shoulders.

Ally sobbed until she didn't have anything left, even as she felt the ridiculousness of it. What had she lost? Nothing but the product of her imagination. Nothing but a stupid dream. And cried harder at the realization.

She tried to stop, made a couple attempts to talk, but lost the battle every time. Leaned into the comfort of Kristen's supporting arm, and cried because it wasn't Nate there, holding her. Because Nate didn't love her like that, and she was pretty sure he never would.

"How come I can't find a man who loves me the way you do?" she asked at last with a watery laugh, a few more gulps, and a vigorous blow of her nose.

"Is that it?" Kristen asked. "Did you break up?"

Ally shook her head, gave her eyes one final wipe, and reached for her cup of tea. Tried to pull herself back under control. "No. I don't know. I don't think so. It was all going so well, and then I told him, this morning, that I loved him. While we were... When I was...It just slipped out, that's all. And you'd have thought I was telling him I had herpes," she said with another choked laugh. "It wasn't exactly welcome information."

"Wow. You said it first?" Kristen asked. "You're so brave. I've never done that."

"Yeah. Well. I don't advise it," Ally sighed. "It didn't work out too well."

"So what did he say, exactly?" Kristen pressed. "Did he say he didn't?"

Ally shook her head, reached for another tissue as the tears showed up again. "No. He just said he wasn't sure. And that his commitment is to *rugby*," she added with disgust. "To his team, and the frigging *All Blacks*. He made it totally clear that it wasn't to me. But why can't it be both? How can a man be in love with a team? It's like it's his wife! Drew fell in love with Hannah, didn't he? So is it just me? That I'm not lovable?"

"Of course it's not you," Kristen said firmly. "You're great. You're *totally* lovable. But Drew had been captain for a long time when he met Hannah. He was comfortable in it, I think. Sure of himself. And Nate's..."

"Scared," Ally finished for her. "Consumed. I know he is. But I could *help* him. I already did, I think. I think I *do*. But probably," she sighed, "it's me. I'm not the type of woman men fall madly in love with, and I never have been. I'm not mysterious or exciting. I'm like some kind of Girl Scout, the happy pal the boys let into the tree house because she doesn't count. Because she's not a real girl."

"I'm pretty sure Nate sees you as a girl," Kristen said with a smile. "I don't think that's it."

"Then *why?*" Ally demanded. "How many men have told you they loved you?"

"Lots," Kristen admitted. "But that doesn't mean they meant it. Maybe they thought they did, but it wasn't really me. It was the idea of me. Or just that they wanted something, and thought they could get it that way. And for a long time, they were right. But Nate isn't one of those guys. He's a decent man, a grown-up man who won't say something he doesn't mean. He doesn't want to lead you on."

Ally nodded glumly. "That's what he said. And here I am with my grand total of one man who's ever said that to me, and didn't really mean it anyway, not in the way I want. So what do I do now?"

"I think," Kristen said slowly, "that you decide whether what he has to give is enough for you."

"Yeah," Ally sighed. "You're right. Let's face it, I'm only here another six months anyway. I got all carried away, that's all. But I don't know if it *is* enough. I'm not sure I can be happy with just a piece of him."

"Another thing," Kristen said. "If you do stay with him, you probably guard your heart a little more, don't you think? See if you can do it for...for fun, maybe?"

"I finally figure out what I want out of life." Ally slumped back against the cushions with a sigh. "What I want to do, and who I want to be with. I finally get the guts to say it, to wish for it. And turns out none of it's realistic. None of it's even possible. Wouldn't you know it? Just my luck."

we try harder

♡

Nate rang off with a frown. No answer again. He hadn't left a message this time. He was starting to feel like some kind of stalker. It was just that Ally'd always been around to talk to him before the game. He'd got used to it, that was all. Somehow, it had become his pregame ritual. And not being able to reach her...it was throwing him off. She'd said she didn't have to work today, so it wasn't that, unless the schedule had been changed.

Was she avoiding him? She hadn't sounded the same when he'd phoned her a couple nights ago, even though he'd remembered to text her when he'd got to the Mount, and to Canberra as well. He wanted to make it right between them again, but how was he meant to do it? What more could he do?

"Something wrong?" Mako asked from the other bed, where he was lying reading a book. Nate had already sneaked a peek. Some literary thing.

"Nah. Want to go for a bit of a walk, something like that?"

"I need to do this," Mako said apologetically. "You know I do."

"You need to read some boring, depressing book before the game. I've never understood that. What kind of a footy player are you? Give us all a bad name."

Mako smiled a bit at that. "Takes me out of myself. Can't play good footy if you're strung up."

He marked his place carefully, set the heavy hardback down, and sat up a bit straighter. "Come on. What is it? Something about tonight? Or the ABs? Or something personal? Because, mate, something's on your mind, and it's been there all week, since we were at the Mount. Better get it off your chest now if you're going to be right to run out there tonight."

Nate sighed, stood up and grabbed the hand exerciser Ally had lent him, which he'd somehow never bothered to give back. It actually *had* been good for his ball-handling skills, given him just that bit more control. He began to pace the extent of the room, squeezing the thing rhythmically, one finger at a time.

"How d'you send a woman flowers?" he asked abruptly.

"You're telling me you've never sent a woman flowers," Mako said slowly. "Never *ever?*"

"Nah. Never. And I think I need to. So how d'you do it?"

Mako looked at him for a long moment, then picked up his mobile, clicked around a bit, and handed it over.

"You ring this number," he instructed. "Tell them what you want, how much you want to spend. What colors they should use. What you want on the card, where to send them. Sending them to her work's best, so everyone else can see them too."

"I don't care if everyone else sees them," Nate said irritably. "Just want her to."

Mako sighed. "Doesn't matter what *you* care about, mate. That's the point. When you send them to her work, she gets to show everyone else there that somebody sent her flowers, make them a bit jealous, eh. Makes her feel special, eh."

"It's all blokes there. I don't think anybody's going to envy her getting flowers."

"And that wouldn't be a good thing? Show all those blokes she works with, who're there when you're here, that she's got

269

somebody sending her flowers? That she's got *you* sending them? Letting them know that you'll rip their fu—their frigging heads off if they even think about it?"

Nate looked at him. "Trying not to swear," Mako explained. "Self-improvement program, eh. Somebody I'm trying to impress myself, and I've got the flowers bit down. Going for the advanced level now."

"Huh. You're right," Nate said with decision. "Definitely sending them to work. You said colors, though," he remembered. "What d'you mean, colors? Don't you just do roses?"

"Ally doesn't strike me as the red roses type," Mako said. "What's her favorite color? Start there."

"Her favorite *color?* No idea. How'm I meant to know that?"

His friend heaved another sigh, looked at him pityingly. "Right. OK, then. Tip for you: that'd be a good thing to find out. What color does she wear most?"

"Uh...When I first met her, she was wearing a yellow shirt. I remember that."

"Yellow's good," Mako said with decision. "She's the yellow type. Sunny. Happy. Tell them that. Happy colors."

"Not too happy just now, I don't think," Nate said glumly. "Not with me, anyway. Maybe not at all. I made her feel pretty bad."

"Ah," Mako said. "Then do the flowers. Definitely do the flowers. Tell them, best they've got, doesn't matter what it costs. And think hard about the message you have them put on the card. Something that'll mean something to her. Something personal."

♡

"Sure you need to get back?" Robbo asked Ally. "Because we could go have dinner. Get a hamburger, maybe. I'm hungry, after all that."

"I want to watch the Hurricanes game," she said.

He glanced across at her, pulled out of the Adrenaline Park carpark and onto the motorway. "We could do a pub. They'd have the footy on. Bound to."

"No, I'd better get home." She shifted restlessly in her seat. She'd looked at her mobile when they'd got back to the car, and seen four missed calls. And now it was too late. Nate would already be getting taped up, preparing to go out there. If she didn't hurry, she wasn't even going to be in time to watch him, and then she'd *really* feel like she was cheating on him.

Which was ridiculous, she reminded herself. Nate didn't love her, and he'd all but told her he didn't need her, either, that this was just for fun. She didn't owe him a damn thing. Feeling this way was counterproductive, and wimpy, and *ridiculous.*

"I got a speeding ticket here recently," she told Robbo now. "So be careful."

With Nate, she thought with a pang. Just last week, though it seemed like a lot longer ago than that. And when she'd been going through the treetop ropes courses of the adventure park today, all she'd been able to think about was how much she'd like to take him there. Tease him about it, make him go on the highest, toughest routes. And then see what he'd figure out later, how he'd manage to even the scales. She shivered a little, thinking about it. If only he weren't so great, this would be a whole lot easier.

Well, she had a life to live, too. So here she was, having a good time without him. Having a *great* time.

"I had a really good time," she told Robbo now. "Thanks a lot for asking me to come along today. I enjoyed it."

"We could do more things like this," he suggested. "Next time we have a day off together. Or, I don't know. Go out after work sometime, have a beer, next time we close."

She cleared her throat. "Probably not a good idea. I meant what I said. Friends, that's all. I'm actually dating somebody."

Robbo shot a glance across at her. "Bloody Captain Fantastic," he said with resignation. "I should have known."

"Well, yeah," she admitted. "That is who it is."

"And he doesn't mind you going out with me for the day?" Robbo asked. Looking a little nervous, she realized.

"I don't think he's going to come around and beat you up, if that's what you're worried about," she said with a smile. "I'm allowed to have friends. If you still want to be friends, that is."

♡

"I'm allowed to have friends," she told Nate the next day, feeling a whole lot less loving towards him than she'd been when the huge vase of tulips—at least three dozen of them, in shades of red, orange, and yellow that just made her happy—had been delivered to the gym that morning. Which had been completely over the top, and she'd had to take the bus home, sit with the gigantic bouquet in her lap, barely able to see around it. And had felt like maybe he really did care after all. That maybe this thing could work. Especially when she'd read the note.

> *To my s.s.*
> *From your s.s.*
> *I miss you every day and every night.*
> *Please let me try harder.*

She'd thought she would melt right there, right in the middle of the noisy gym, surrounded by sweating men, wishing one of them was the *right* sweating man.

But now, standing in her flat with him, the flowers overwhelming the little coffee table, she wasn't even sure she wanted to go to dinner with him, let alone anywhere else.

"I said no other people, and I meant it," he said, looking furious, and dangerous, and much too sexy. And totally and completely exasperating.

She sighed. "Robbo's a *friend*. I've told you about him. You're *gone*, Nate. I wasn't working, and I wanted to do something fun. So I went out with a friend and did it. Something I was *thinking*, at the time, I'd like to take you to do. But you weren't there, were you? I'm sorry I wasn't available when you called me, but I can't just hang around all the time and wait for you, you know. As you've gone to some trouble to remind me, I'm not exactly central to your life. I can't put my own life on hold for you, and I won't."

"Not asking you to put your life on hold for me," he muttered. "Just...can't you make some girlfriends? Do...girl things?"

"I don't like to do girl things! What, am I supposed to go get my hair highlighted or something? Have a...a pedicure? Go shopping? I do outdoors things. They're what I do, you know that. And the people I do them with often happen to be men. You can either accept that, or you can forget it. This isn't Saudi Arabia, and I'm not some weak flower who's going to be overwhelmed by whatever male is in my vicinity. I'm allowed to speak to men, I'm allowed to spend time with my friends, and you're being ridiculous!"

This was a whole lot easier, she realized, when she could be mad instead of sad. Maybe she should thank him for being so damn unreasonable.

"Bloody hell." He ran both hands over his hair, held his head for a moment. Blew out a deep breath. "Right. Start again."

He looked up, wearing his most determined expression. "I felt bad," he said. "Because talking to you before the match means a lot to me, and you weren't there. I worried that you'd given up on me. And then finding out you were with somebody else, that made it worse. Because I meant what I said on that card. I want to try harder. I want to be a better boyfriend. Try to put you higher up the list, do the right things, make you feel... cared for."

He still couldn't say "loved." She didn't miss that. But what he had managed to say...it was pretty good.

"I'm sorry I wasn't there for you," she said through the lump in her throat. "I felt like a fool after you left, after what you said. Hanging around waiting for you to call me like I'm sixteen years old, sitting in my room looking at the phone, wishing it would ring. If you'd told me it mattered, if we'd worked out a time..."

"That's me," he said immediately. "That's me taking it for granted you'd be there, not thinking about you enough. I won't do that anymore, I promise."

"Then," she said, feeling the tears rising again, "I promise that I'll be there to talk to you. Even if I have to take a break from swinging through the treetops to do it. With my friend."

"Right," he said with a sigh of relief. "But I want to meet this Robbo again. I'm going to pop by tomorrow, get Mako to come in with me and do a bit of climbing."

And stare the other man down, he promised himself. Make sure he got the message. But just now, he had a girlfriend to hold, and kiss, and somehow persuade to give him another chance. Because he needed to be with her tonight, and tomorrow night. And every day and night afterwards that she'd have him.

all black attack

♡

"Wow," Ally said when she'd followed Kristen and Hannah down the row of seats in cavernous Eden Park, a sea of black tonight, except for the occasional tricolored flag.

"It's pretty overwhelming, isn't it?" Hannah said. "And the stadium isn't even full yet. But an All Blacks game is always special. The French are tough opponents, too, and everyone knows it."

Kristen and Ally had flown to Auckland for the game. Not even that big a hit to her extremely modest budget, Ally thought happily, since Hannah was chauffeuring them, and putting them up as well. Not for the first time, Ally blessed the day she'd given a nervous, shaky Kristen her first climbing lesson, because just about everything good in her life right now had come out of that day.

Hannah had urged them both to stay, since Drew was in the Bay of Plenty, talking about coaching opportunities for the next season. "Come hold my hand," she had pleaded. "It's going to be so strange to watch a game and know that Drew's not part of it." And Kristen and Ally hadn't been a bit hard to convince.

Now, Hannah gave warm hugs to the two women who stood to greet her. Well, she gave one a warm hug. With the other one, they were basically reaching around each others' bellies.

Hannah made the introductions, then said, "Kristen, you know Kate, of course, but I don't think you've ever met Emma."

"No," Kristen said with a smile. "And Kate looks a little different from the last time I saw her. When are you due, Kate?"

"The same day as Hannah," the petite brunette told her. "And before you say anything, I know, she barely looks pregnant, and I look like the delivery room's on standby. But believe it or not, I still have three and a half long months to go. Koti's going to have to push me around in a wheelbarrow before long."

"But you're looking great," Kristen hastened to assure her as the women took their seats, the two sisters sitting together and immediately becoming engrossed in conversation.

Ally couldn't help casting a surprised look at Kristen, and Kate saw it and laughed. "Kristen and Hannah both got the tact gene," she told Ally. "I don't look great. I look huge."

"It's just because you're so small," Emma assured her. She scooted around Ally to sit at the end of the group of women. "I want to keep an eye on my son," she explained to Ally. "He thinks he's too old now to sit next to me. I was big too, though," she told Kate, "and I'm not nearly as small as you."

"Plus Koti being so much taller," Kate sighed with a hand on her belly. "They say that doesn't mean you'll have a bigger baby, but I have to say I'm doubting it."

Ally was still a few steps behind. "You and Hannah have the same due date?" she asked in surprise. "That's quite the coincidence."

Kate and Emma looked at each other and exchanged a wry glance.

"Both due nine months after my wedding day," Emma said. "I guess it was inspirational."

"Hey," Kate objected. "It was *romantic*."

"Clearly," Emma agreed with another smile. "It was for me, anyway."

"Do you know what you're having?" Ally asked.

"Well, a human being, hopefully," Kate said tartly, then smiled. "Sorry. Couldn't resist. That's what I always want to say when people ask that question. But the answer is, a girl. Just like Hannah there, too. Pretty fun, huh? I like to think that they'll grow up to be friends. Of course," she went on, "both Emma's and my lives are pretty well entwined with Hannah's anyway, aren't they, Em?"

"It's true," the pretty blonde laughed. "Seeing as how she helped me get my job, for which I'll be forever grateful. We work together," she explained to Ally. "At 2nd Hemisphere, the merino company."

"Ooh," Ally said. "Lucky you."

"I know," Emma said happily. "I tell myself that every single day, for all kinds of wonderful reasons."

"And Hannah didn't just get me a job, though she did that too," Kate told Ally. "She also introduced me to my husband. And I'm guessing, from what I hear about you and Kristen, that she's been at it again, huh? Or is it just a coincidence that the pair of you are dating a couple of hot rugby boys?"

Ally laughed. "No, you're right. Hannah introduced us. Well, sort of. I'd seen Nate before, but he didn't exactly make a good impression. And then he kept on not making one, but somehow, he's won me over pretty well by now."

"They have a way of doing that," Kate said. "But here they come," she broke off, and Ally saw the members of both teams beginning to trickle onto the field to start warming up.

Nate was first out, as usual, and Ally's heart did the same funny somersault it always performed when she saw him play. She wondered if you ever got used to that. Especially tonight, being here to see his first start as the new captain of the All Blacks.

She'd spoken to him briefly on the phone earlier in the day, and he'd been his usual controlled self, or even more so. Between his journeys away for the several days of All Blacks training during each of the past few weeks, then his regular games with the Hurricanes, she hadn't had much time with him, and when they had been together, he'd definitely been a little preoccupied. He had to be keyed up now, achieving his dream at last, and she was so glad she could be here to watch him do it.

"Who's that with Nate?" she couldn't help asking as another player in black trotted out and began running back and forth with Nate, passing the ball. Even from here, she could tell that he was put together just a little bit better than anybody else.

"That would be Koti," Kate said proudly.

"Oh," Ally said abstractedly. That was some serious eye candy. "I think you could get pregnant just by *looking* at him." Then realized she was sitting next to his wife, and hastened to apologize.

Kate just laughed. "It's OK. It's true. He can't help it. He and Kristen, they're in the Pretty People Club. And if it's your first All Blacks game," she added, "you still have the big treat. The one that I swear *could* get you pregnant. The haka."

"I've heard of it," Ally said. "I've never seen it, though."

"Well, watch and learn," Kate said. "And then tell me you aren't glad that you get to go to bed with one of them."

Ally was so surprised, she let out a little snort, and threw a hand over her mouth. "You're as bad as me," she told Kate with a grin. "How cool is that? I love Kristen to death, but she's always so careful. Always so nice, you know? I'm shocking her all the time. Oh, whoops," she hastened to say. "I don't mean you're not nice."

Kate was already laughing. "No worries. I know. Same with Hannah. And Kiwis are awfully polite too, aren't they?"

"They are!" Ally said with delight. "Isn't anybody nasty here?"

"Nobody but us, I guess," Kate said with a gusty sigh. "Somebody's got to inject a little snark, and I guess we're the last resort."

♡

Ally had been excited all day, especially once they'd arrived here. But nothing could have prepared her for the sight of Nate leading his team out of the tunnel at last, warmups pulled off now to reveal the black jersey that, she knew, had been made especially for this game, embroidered with his name, the date, and the venue. And, above all else, with the silver fern he wore over his heart.

She stood with the rest of the crowd for the singing of the anthems, that much more emotion rising inside at the intensity on the players' faces while the singer performed the New Zealand anthem first in Maori, then in English, and most of them sang along. She'd known that it mattered. She hadn't realized how much.

She started to sit down again once the applause died down, and then stopped. Because nobody else was. Instead, the stadium was humming, then erupting in a low roar as the All Blacks formed up in rows, the French making a line of their own to face them, hands around each others' shoulders.

But Ally wasn't watching the French team, because one figure in black was pacing behind the front row now, beginning to shout out instructions in Maori. Liam, she registered as the rest of the men dropped into a crouch, began to slap their thighs. And to chant.

This was the haka. The black-clad figures were slapping and stomping, faces stretched into grimaces, chanting the challenge, every movement, every expression on the big screen overhead telegraphing their intensity, their purpose, and Ally actually had goosebumps. She had a flash of what the first Europeans must have felt, leaving their ships to be met with this. Because if the ferocity of the group performing the ritual tonight was any indication, it must have been terrifying. She hoped it was terrifying the French, anyway.

"Well, that was fun," she sighed after the last stare had been delivered, the last "Hei!" shouted, and the answering roar of the crowd had died away, everyone finally taking their seats again. "I've been entertained. I'm ready to leave."

"I know," Kate said happily. "That's my favorite, too."

"Only because you're always too busy looking at Koti to understand the game," Emma teased gently.

Ally knew what Emma meant. She didn't need a tutor tonight, though, to see what was going on. Or to have her question answered about whether the French had been intimidated, because they so clearly hadn't been. Nate had told her that you never knew which French team would turn up on the night, that their play was notoriously uneven, but this group had clearly come to play. Which was unfortunate, because the All Blacks definitely looked a little rusty.

It wasn't hard at all to see that the French were pushing hard at the breakdown, and that the All Blacks weren't getting into any kind of smooth rhythm. The whole thing, in fact, was the kind of messy rugby that usually put her to sleep, but tonight was only making her anxious. Scrums and scrum resets, short runs followed by tackles. So few of the long sequences of precise passing that, she had heard, normally marked an All Blacks game. Instead, control of the ball shifting again and again. And then a pair of penalties within ten minutes in the wrong half of the field, first for a knock-on, then for not releasing the ball after a tackle, and France was suddenly up 6-0.

"What's happening?" Ally asked Kate in frustration after the second French kick sailed between the uprights.

"France has been playing together in the Six Nations, the European championship," Kate explained, not laughing anymore. "Whereas the All Blacks have only had those few mini training periods together. The first test of the year is always rough. It sure is tonight."

At last, a New Zealand try before halftime to energize the crowd again, the conversion made, and the All Blacks were up 7-6 when the teams trotted back into the tunnel. The exhilaration before the game was replaced by a more subdued mood during the break, and on into the second half. Ally did her best to hold onto her faith as the score shifted back and forth. The crowd, which had started the evening out in full voice, were still quiet, the French performance taking them out of the game.

And then there were three minutes to play, and the All Blacks were ahead by two, the French pressing on attack. No joking even from Kate now as the All Blacks tackled again and again, fought for a ball that the French refused to turn over. The French were patiently moving the ball down the field, inside the New Zealand 22 now, and the clock was ticking down.

"Come on," Kate muttered beside Ally. "Come *on.*"

They were going to do it, Ally thought, her heart in her throat. The defense was going to hold. The French attacked the line over and over, the seconds relentlessly disappearing on the clock. A gain of a meter, another for three. It wasn't going to be enough. The All Blacks were going to win.

And then the hooter sounding, time running out. But, Ally knew by now, the game didn't end until the team in possession lost the ball, and the French still had it. One run after another, one tackle after another. And, finally, a long pass back to the French Number 10. The man lifting the ball, sending the drop-kick cleanly through the posts, a long groan from the crowd. And the French had won it by a single damning point.

♡

It was a quiet crowd that filed from the stands, and the five women who had started the evening so happily were no exception. Hugs all around, promises to call, and Kristen and Ally were headed back to St. Heliers with Hannah.

"The first test match is always tough," Hannah said, breaking the silence with an echo of Kate's earlier words. "It's lucky that it's a three-game series, isn't it?"

But when Ally said as much to Nate the following evening, he brushed the comment aside.

"It was ugly," he said briefly over dinner. "Leave it at that. We'll be putting those things right this week."

Ally took another look at his shuttered expression and considered trying again. But he turned the conversation, and she went along with him. The loss was still too recent, she guessed, and too raw. Well, he'd have a chance to relax tomorrow, and that had to help.

She was wrong, though.

"I know we talked about doing something today," he said over breakfast the next morning. "But I should really watch the game, make some notes, get ready for the week. D'you mind if I take you home after we're done here?"

"Well," she hesitated. "Well, yes. I mean, don't you think it might be better if you took a break? I know it's raining, but we could still take a walk, maybe. Or just stay in and watch a movie. At least for the morning."

"I need to do this," he said again, gave a sigh, and went on. "I'm going to need to focus for the test window, the last bit of the Super 15 season too. You and I'll have a bit of time before the third test, though, as we're playing it here, and that's just a week away. We can do a couple nights then. And once the season's over, before the Rugby Championship starts, we'll have more time.

Maybe you can make some plans for us. Another month or so, that's all. Can you give me a bit of a pass until then?"

For a *month?* But what choice did she have? None, she realized. And it was a little pathetic to beg somebody to spend time with you, wasn't it? Even though she really *did* think that he needed a break. All right, he didn't want to share his disappointment at the loss. But still...Wouldn't it help to be with her? Didn't he *want* to be with her?

"So..." she said when he was dropping her at the flat an hour later. "See you next week, when you're back from New Plymouth?"

"Yeh," he said. "I'll text you, and talk to you Saturday afternoon. And I'll see you Sunday night."

And would send her flowers, too, she thought as she stood in the lobby and watched him drive away. He wasn't ignoring her, not exactly. Just not letting her in.

Anyway, she had the day off. Too bad she didn't have anything to do with it. Kristen was with Liam, and she'd bet *he* wasn't watching game film today.

a new world

♡

" I have news," Kristen said almost two weeks later. Liam had collected her from home as usual, and they were in New World now, pushing a trolley through the veg aisle. Which suited him down to the ground.

"What's that?" he asked, tossing a bag of spinach into the trolley and beginning to sort through the kumara. They'd fallen into the habit of cooking dinner together at his house, then watching a movie on the night before a home game, and sometimes the day after a game too, when he was too knackered to go out. A routine that was more than welcome, on this evening before the final All Blacks match against the French, the one that would decide the series. New Zealand had won the previous week's game, but it had been too close, and tomorrow's match was by no means a foregone conclusion.

So, yeh. He needed the distraction, and Kristen was nothing if not distracting. In fact, sitting on the couch with her could fairly be described as torture. After their one experiment with a rom-com, they'd agreed to stick with old stuff, and some of the milder action films. Because if sitting on the couch with her was hard, watching a love scene with her...well, he was only human, and there were some things that were just too much to ask.

"Remember how we were talking about how my store, how we hardly have any shoe selection?" she asked.

"Yeh," he said, moving on to the meat department. "I remember. Venison OK?"

"Sure," she said, sounding distracted. "Anyway. While you've been gone, big news! I asked if I could present a proposal for expanding the shoe department, and Simone said yes!"

He turned to her in surprise, saw her eyes sparkling. She was all but bouncing. "That's awesome! When are you doing it?"

"Three weeks from now. July fifth. I've been working on it all week, doing the research, but there's still so much to do. All my boards to prepare, and my regular job too, of course. But it's worth it."

"Boards?"

"Oh. My presentation boards," she explained. "Theme board, color board, line board. To show what we'd do, how it would coordinate with our clothing line."

"I'll take your word for it," he decided. "Though if you want to practice with me before you do it, I'd be happy. We'll be playing here that week, so I'll be around. You could run through it a few times. That'd help, on the day."

"It would," she said. "But really? You'd be willing to do that?"

"Course. Can't promise to ask intelligent questions, but I'll do my best. It's probably not too different from a footy match. The more you practice every scenario, the more effortless you can make it look. And the more likely you are to win."

"I'm going to take you up on that," she said. "I'll be using you mercilessly."

And that was another flash of imagination that didn't do him any favors at all. Of her on top of him, using him mercilessly. Oh, yeh. He'd let her use him.

Geez, this celibacy thing was hard. And getting harder all the time, in more ways than one. Some days, he thought he would actually explode.

"Heaps of work, then?" He forced his mind back with a herculean effort.

"Yes, it is," she said, "and I have to do projections, too. That's harder, but Hannah's been advising me some. I'm really nervous, but it's exciting. Even if they don't agree to it, I'm showing that I have ideas, you know? It feels like a big step."

"It *is* a big step. It's awesome," he said again. He reached out and gave her a cuddle, just because she looked like a little girl looking forward to a birthday party, and at the same time, like a woman who was rightfully proud of what she'd done. Because she was Kristen, and she was trying so hard, and she was getting somewhere. And because he loved her, and he wanted to touch her.

"I'm really proud of you," he said, giving her a kiss on the cheek, smoothing a hand over the golden hair. And that was just about enough of that, or he was going to be in real trouble. He stepped back again, cleared his throat. *Bread,* he thought with relief, and set out for the next aisle.

"Are you OK with all that?" Kristen asked when they'd checked out and he'd gathered all the bags, turned for the door. "Do you want me to carry something?"

"Think I can just about manage it," he said seriously, then smiled at her. "I like carrying things for you, don't you know that? Makes me feel good."

"I think I *have* figured that out," she said with a laugh. "You're a pretty handy guy to have around. Somebody who wants to buy me shoes and send me flowers and carry my groceries? I think you're pretty much my Dream Man."

"Good," he said. "Let me know if I slip, because that's exactly where I want to stay."

"Sorry." He turned at the voice. A boy, six or seven, messy brown hair sticking up a bit. Standing there, shifting from foot to foot, looking anxious and excited. Liam glanced beyond him, saw the mum with her trolley at another checkout, giving him an apologetic smile.

"Sorry," the boy said again, earnest face raised to Liam's. "But I wanted to tell you, you're my favorite. Mum said I mustn't disturb, but I wanted to say."

"Well, if I'm your favorite, I want to hear that, don't I?" Liam answered. "Cheers, mate. Are you a forward, then, yourself?"

"A hooker," the boy said proudly. "Just like you. But it's dead hard sometimes, isn't it?"

"It can be," Liam agreed. "Something troubling you in particular?"

"Yeh," the boy said. "The lineout. I got two penalties last week for not throwing in straight. So I wanted to ask you, how d'you make sure?"

"Do it over and over, till you get it right," Liam said promptly. "Stay after if you have to, after practice. That's what I do."

"You do?"

"Course. I was having a bit of trouble with that myself, couple years ago. Spent extra time on it before every game. You practice hard enough, you're bound to get better, eh."

"Thanks!" the boy said. "I'll practice more."

"Cheers," Liam said. "Go on back to your mum, now. Help her carry those bags."

♡

"You were nice," Kristen said as they walked out of the supermarket together. "You really like kids, I've noticed that. I think that's great."

"Doesn't exactly make me unique," he said, "specially amongst Maori. We do tend to have some kids. Another of our many talents."

They were at the car now. "But you didn't, eh," he said. He glanced at her, then opened the boot and began to set bags carefully inside. "When you were married. Was that your choice?"

He waited for the answer, knowing how much it mattered to him. He thought he knew, but it was better to be sure.

"I didn't at first," she said soberly, leaning against the boot after he'd closed it. "When I was younger. I didn't know that much about being a mother. Not about doing it right, anyway. But then, thinking about Hannah, I realized I *did* know. I knew how she loved me, how she tried to help me, growing up. And I saw how good a job she did with Jack, and I thought, maybe I could do that, too. Maybe I could, if I tried hard. And I *would* try hard. I'd try so hard. I'd know how to love my child, anyway," she said, suddenly sounding fierce, totally unlike Kristen. "I'd know how to put my kids' needs above my own. I'd know how to protect my kids. I'd know how to do that, and I would. I *would.*"

"Course you would," he said. "I'd say you know how to love pretty well, from what I've seen. *Real* love, where you care more about the other person than yourself. I'd say you know all about that."

She remained silent, looking off into the distance, not moving from her spot, leaning against the boot.

"So it wasn't you," he prompted gently. Hell of a place for this, but he'd take it. "But still, no kids."

"No," she sighed, looking back at him again. "That was him. Marshall."

"What kind of man doesn't want kids?" he wondered.

"That kind, I guess," she shrugged. "He said…" She stopped. "You don't want to know this. It's embarrassing." She pushed herself off the car, turned away. "We should go."

"Kristen. Wait," he said, feeling the urgency of it. "You don't have to tell me if you don't want to, but I'd like to know."

She turned back again, looked down, ran the strap of her purse nervously through her hands as she spoke, still not meeting his eyes.

"It was that..." she began. "That, you know, that pregnant women were...gross. And afterwards, stretch marks. What happens to your...your breasts. And breastfeeding. He said," and she was crimson now, but plowed on regardless, "that those were his, and he wasn't sharing."

Liam could feel his body tightening with anger on her behalf, with outrage that any man could feel that way. That a man would say something like that to his wife, to the woman he'd promised to love and cherish, the woman he was meant to protect.

He forced himself to relax. Took a breath, so this wouldn't come out wrong. This was his chance, and he was taking it.

"Can't imagine that," he told her after a moment, when he was sure he could say it calmly. "Because a pregnant woman is beautiful. And a woman feeding a baby...all that. There's nothing a man should want to see more than that. I don't want to get too graphic here, but when a man's with his pregnant partner, what's he seeing? What's he showing everyone else? That that's *his* baby. That he did that. And same when she's feeding that baby. Not saying that's sexual," he went on hurriedly at her quick glance, "but, yeh, it is, a bit, all of it. Her belly, her breasts. If it's the woman you love, it is. Because all of that, it's the ultimate connection. It's a man's immortality, the only kind there really is, and a woman's the way you achieve it. The mother of your children...She's special, eh. She's beautiful."

He stopped, feeling frustrated with himself. "I can't say this the way I'd like to," he apologized. "Wish I could be more poetic about it. All I can tell you is, I know that's how I'd feel. And I can't speak for Pakeha, but that's how most Maori men would feel, too."

He tried a smile on her, wanting to see her smile back at him, wanting her to know this one thing for sure. "So it could be," he said, "that you've just been in the wrong country. And with the wrong man."

"Well, I know that," she said, and she *was* smiling, and she was beautiful. Shining for him, and his heart turned over. "The wrong man, I've known that for a long time. And the wrong country...I've been thinking that too, lately."

He shifted a little, cleared his throat. "How much longer on the celibacy, again?" he asked a bit plaintively, surprising a laugh from her.

"Five weeks," she said. "But I think we could...start. What do you think? Start slow? Would you be willing to do that?"

"Yeh." He could feel himself smiling back at her. "I think we could start slow. Slow as you like. Because I've been thinking," he said, even as he felt the desire, so long controlled, rising within him, a swift tide, "that slow is how I want to be with you anyway. I'm going to be taking my time every step of the way. Starting right now."

He reached for her, right there in the New World carpark. Put one hand on the side of her face, his other at her side, and gently brushed his lips over hers. Felt her mouth opening under his, her body swaying towards him, her own hands coming up to hold his shoulders as if they belonged there.

And he knew, as he continued to kiss her, to hold her, that he'd been right all along. She was his treasure. And he was her man.

reaching new heights

♡

" Ally. Look."

She heard Robbo's exclamation and looked up fast from the front desk, where she was checking in two new customers. She stared with surprise herself, and then found herself ridiculously pleased.

The couple opposite her turned to see what she was looking at. "That's Koti James," the woman said, her voice a little dreamy. "And Nic Wilkinson."

"And Liam Mahaka," the man added. "Wonder what they're doing here, with the game tonight. Don't they have training or something?"

"I don't care what they're doing here," the woman declared. "All I know is, if they're climbing, I'm going to take care to be next to them. Pity they brought their partners. I'll just have to ignore them."

Her own partner looked a little affronted, and Ally couldn't help smiling. Although her own photo had been in the paper with Nate more than once now, few of the gym's clientele had made the connection, and she'd been glad to be anonymous.

Not quite so anonymous anymore, though, because the couple were stepping aside as the group made their way across rosalind james

the busy gym to the desk, creating a stir amongst the Saturday-morning climbers.

"Hi," Kristen told her happily. "Liam thought the guys needed an outing."

"Bit of stretching," Liam said easily. "And I want to show these lazy buggers what a forward can do. Watch and learn, boys," he announced to some good-natured scoffing. "Watch and learn from the master."

Kristen hastened to make introductions, and Ally got the group checked in.

"Zack wants to climb, too," Emma told her. "Do you have kids' harnesses, though?" She looked around. No other kids here, as usual. Ally had made no headway at all there, no surprise.

"We do," Ally assured her. "Climbing's super fun," she told the seven-year-old, who bore a startling resemblance to his handsome father. "And sometimes," she added with a special smile, "kids are better than their parents at it. What do you think?"

"Sweet as," he said happily, making her laugh.

"Guess I'm watching," Kate sighed as Ally began to get the group set up with harnesses.

"I've got a maternity harness," Ally told her, "if you want to try. One of our regulars donated it after she had her baby." She'd tried to get Mac to buy more, with no luck at all.

"Is it safe?" her husband asked. "For her, and the baby?"

He was even better-looking up close, Ally couldn't help but notice. She sneaked a quick peek at the famous Maori tattoo, at least the part that was visible beneath the T-shirt sleeve he'd revealed when he pulled off his hoodie, and decided that Koti's might look even better than Liam's. Although Liam's had to be bigger to cover all that muscle. She wouldn't mind a bit of up-close comparison shopping. Maybe she could suggest that the guys climb with their shirts off. No, probably not. Sadly.

"As long as you pay attention while you belay her," she said, recalling herself. "There's no impact, and the harness goes around her belly, actually supports it. And you'll be holding the rope tight, right?"

"No worries," he said. "I'll be holding the rope tight."

One thing about teaching rugby players to climb, Ally thought, working with Robbo to take each pair through the usual routine on the training wall, they caught on fast. And Zack was a natural, scrambling up like a monkey. He'd clearly inherited some athletic ability too.

"Sorry we couldn't get Toro here," Liam told Ally when the group had finished their practice climbs and dispersed around the gym.

Ally glanced at him, then turned back to check on Kate. Koti *was* keeping the rope taut, she saw, and Kate was doing a good job, too.

"He probably had things to do," she said, trying her best to overcome her disappointment.

"What he said," Liam agreed. "A good distraction, we thought, but I've never succeeded yet in convincing Toro of the value of being distracted." He smiled at her again, then went over to join Kristen at the wall.

They were both doing really well, Ally thought, watching as Liam clipped in and began to belay Kristen. She might have taught Kristen initially, but her friend had gained confidence, the only thing she'd really lacked, in leaps and bounds since starting to climb with Liam.

By the time the group had been there half an hour, Mac was hurrying through the door, much earlier than usual for a Saturday.

"Is that a coincidence?" Ally asked Robbo.

"No," he said with a grin. "I rang him. Picture the scene if I hadn't. I'd have got the sack. Not you, of course, because it's pretty clear why they're all in here."

They didn't stay much longer, though. The gym had started filling up fast after their arrival, which Ally could easily trace to the many thumbs flying over cell phone keys. After an hour, they were wrapping it up.

"Well, that was fun," Kate told Ally happily when they were shedding harnesses again. "Not that hauling my belly up a wall is any easier than hauling it around in general, but it was a good challenge."

"I've had a lot of pregnant clients say that," Ally said. "A good stretch for you guys, too?" she asked Koti.

"Yeh," he said, flashing a fairly potent smile. "Though I got a bit nervous, worrying that Kate was going to drop me. Or leave me up there."

"You did not," Kate protested as the others laughed. "I'd only do that if you made me mad, and you haven't done that for at *least* a week. And even if you had, I want to watch you play tonight, so I had to let you down, didn't I?"

She gave Ally a smile and asked, "Are you coming? See you tonight?"

"Yes," Ally said, feeling unusually shy, but pleased to be included. "Kristen and I'll both be there."

"Great," Kate said with satisfaction. "We can have a snark-fest." Which made Ally laugh again.

"Did you see me?" Zack asked Ally, bouncing on his toes, brown eyes alight. "Did you see me on the big wall? I did more than Mum!"

"I did," she smiled at him. "You did awesome. High five." She put her palm up, and he smacked it happily.

"Got to get back to the hotel now, though," Liam said. "Lunch with the squad, and then another wee item to take care of today. But this was good. Thanks."

Mac had been low-key, to Ally's relief, but now he inserted himself to ask, "Could we do a quick photo before you go? That'd be one for the notice board."

"Course, long as you don't use it in any adverts," Nic said. "Unless you want Koti's shark of a manager let loose on you, and trust me, nobody wants that. Bloody nightmare."

When the little group had bunched up against a climbing wall for the photo, though, Liam called to Ally.

"Toro may not be here," he said, "but you ought to be. Come on over."

He slung a big arm around her, pulled her next to Kristen. "Good to go," he told Mac, and the photo was taken.

"Tell him he missed out," Ally said to Liam.

"I will," he promised. "I tell him all the time, though he never listens."

"The bull," she said.

"Yeh. The original bull."

♡

"So there you go," Ally told Nate two days later. "Mac's got a big, wonderful picture for his notice board, the All Blacks at the climbing gym. He about wet himself, he was so excited. And you know what's really aggravating?"

"No, what?" Nate asked, trying to hide a smile. He did like Ally a bit stirred up. Eyes snapping, head tossing. All that fire and passion, all for him.

"He took my picture climbing too," Ally said with disgust. "And put it on the board with the other one. Women climbers aren't interesting. But women climbers who are sleeping with the All Blacks? Now *that's* advertising."

"Mmm," Nate agreed. "Though I have to say, those are my favorite women climbers too. Specially the ones who sleep with the skipper."

"Huh," she snorted.

"Text me that photo, though," he went on more seriously. "I want that for my phone."

"What, the one of the guys?"

"Nah. I don't need to see Koti's ugly face. The one of you. I want that one." Ally climbing. Yeh, he'd like to look at that. Right along with the photo of her smiling face, the one he'd taken in the café that first weekend. The one he looked at every night he was away from her, before he went to sleep. The one of her looking so happy, so alive. Looking like Ally.

"And I'm sorry I couldn't be there myself," he went on, "but I have to focus, the day of a game." He'd felt bad about it, especially after he'd got her text, breezy as always, but sounding a bit hurt, too. And had got Mako's blunt assessment of the situation as well, back in the room. But it was the truth all the same. He'd focused, and the focus had paid off, hadn't it? This was his job. This was his *life*.

"No worries," she said saucily, getting up from the table with what he could only describe as a flounce. "I've decided I don't want you anymore. I'm going for Koti James."

He laughed, pulled her into his lap, and focused on today's job. Giving all his attention, as always, to the task at hand.

"Think Kate might have a word or two to say about that," he said when he'd come up for air, had her lying back against his arm, looking well and truly kissed.

"Mmm," she agreed dreamily. "I don't think she shares. Just like me."

She wasn't happy, though, a half hour later.

"What does he know?" she exploded, startling him from the editorial in the *Listener* that had captured his attention.

"What?" he asked. She was sitting bolt upright on the couch, smoke all but coming out of her ears.

"This guy," she said with an angry gesture at the computer in her lap. "John Farrell. He's used his whole column today to talk about you!"

"Ah. Not impressed, I take it."

"Questioning your leadership," she spluttered. "Saying you guys can't win. What does he know? And anyway, you *did* win the series, so how can he say this stuff? You lost *one game!*"

He reached out and took his laptop from her, snapped it firmly shut and set it on the table next to him. "Thought you were checking your email. You just lost your computer privileges."

"I can't help it," she muttered. "Sue me. I looked."

"Well, take my advice. Don't. Goes with the territory. The skipper gets too much credit for what goes right, too much blame for what goes wrong. Always the way of it, and you won't change it. Only thing to do is not to look."

"But why isn't it enough to win?" she asked. Still angry, he saw.

He shrugged. "Because that's how it is. Winning's expected. Not just winning, winning well. And any loss is one too many, because the ABs are meant to be the best."

He stood up, pulled her to her feet. "And that's over, and we've got a day. Let's get out of here, take that walk. And then come back and get in the sauna, because I'm still pretty ginger, and I need some anesthetic. And you're just the one to give it to me."

kristen breaks a vow

♡

"So in summary," Kristen said, clicking the mouse on the final slide, "I propose that we double or even triple our shoe line, and coordinate it with our sportswear. As you can see by my projections, I believe that we'll capture more sales not only from women buying shoes to match a clothing purchase, but also from those who buy shoes, and then want clothing to go with it. And, of course," she finished, "the more cross-training we do between departments, the more detailed our look books are, the more we'll be able to encourage that kind of cross-selling. And, ultimately, increase our revenues even more significantly."

She left the slide there, on the projections she'd worked out, reminded herself for the twentieth time during this short presentation not to look at the screen, at her boards, to keep her eyes on the group around the conference table instead. And that she'd run these numbers again and again, that she was confident in them, and in her proposal.

She looked at the group, lifted her chin, and smiled. "Questions?"

She was grateful once again to Hannah for going over this with her so many times, as she fielded the questions she'd expected with the answers they'd rehearsed. To Liam, and Ally, too, for listening to her presentation again and again this past week.

Finally, though, the last question had been asked and answered, the group of buyers and merchandisers was filing out of the room, and it was over.

"Good work," Anna told her, staying behind as the others left and Kristen gathered her boards, packed up her laptop. "We'll have to discuss it more, of course, but I was impressed."

"Thank you," Kristen said, and this time, the smile was genuine. "Thank you so much."

"I have to tell you," Anna confessed, "I wasn't sure about you at first. I thought Simone had been swayed too much by who your sister is, even how you look. And honestly, I thought you were in over your head at the start. But you've surprised me. I think you've surprised everyone."

Kristen put the words away to remember later, because she could hardly focus anymore. "Thank you," she said again. "I'm really excited to be here, and I want to learn as much as I can. So if you have any suggestions for me, if you don't mind my asking you questions, I'd love it."

Anna smiled. "Let's have lunch next week, then, shall we?"

"I'd love that," Kristen said. "Thank you." She had to stop thanking her. But she couldn't.

♡

She needed to tell Liam, she thought when she'd left the store at last, still riding high. They hadn't scheduled their usual dinner and movie date tonight. Had stopped doing them altogether after that evening in the carpark. Because despite what he'd said about going slowly...

"Kristen," he'd groaned that night, pulling himself away from her with a visible effort and leaning back against the cushions. "We have to stop. I need to take you home."

"What?" she asked in confusion, still lying against the arm of the couch. She looked down at herself and hastily pulled her sweater into place, then shoved herself up. The arousal was pulsing in her, and it was as if she could still feel his hand on her breast, his mouth at her throat. And she wanted him to go on. Right now.

"D'you want to do this tonight?" he demanded. "All of it?"

She had to stop and think. Her body was shouting "yes," but her mind said "no." That she'd set goals for herself, and she hadn't achieved any of them yet, and she needed to be sure that she wasn't looking to a man—even a man as wonderful as Liam—to fill the empty spaces inside her.

"No," she sighed. "Not...not yet. Because it's not fair to you."

He put his head back and groaned. "Because it's not fair to me to let me make love to you. You're going to have to explain that one, because at this particular moment, it's feeling pretty bloody unfair *not* to do it."

"You're too important to me," she tried to explain. She could see how aroused he still was. She hadn't been able to miss that anyway, not when he was lying over her. And she wanted him just as badly. They'd started out holding hands during the movie. His thumb had begun caressing her hand, and just that contact had made her weak. And when she'd shifted closer...things had got out of control fast.

"I want to know that it's right, between us." She did her best to pull her insistent body back under control and went on, because she needed him to understand. "That you'd be getting a real woman who was with you for the right reasons, not because you're strong and brave and you can protect me."

"But, not to have a big head about it," he said, still sounding pained, "I *am* strong and brave, and I *can* protect you, and I want to do it."

"I have to know," she pleaded. "It has to be right. It has to be fair."

"Right." He stood up with a sigh. "No more time on my couch, though. I'll take you home, and I reckon I'll kiss you in the car. I'll take you out to dinner next time, and kiss you in the car afterwards then, too, I'm sure. But don't come back to my house until you're ready for more. Because there's a limit, and I've just reached it."

♡

And that had been the end of their cozy evenings. She hadn't been sure how she'd be feeling after the presentation anyway, so she'd made a date with him for Sunday, after his game. A date to go out to dinner, but she'd been thinking it might be more. Because kissing in the car wasn't enough for her either, not anymore.

A few butterflies made their fluttering appearance when she was standing outside his front door. Maybe she should have texted instead of just showing up on his doorstep. Maybe this was a bad idea anyway. Maybe she should wait until Sunday.

But either he was home, or he was out. And if he were home, he'd want to see her. Surely he would. And anyway, she wanted to see *him.* She'd done what she'd come to New Zealand to do, what she'd needed to do. It was time, and she wanted this. She wanted *him*, and she was going to take him. The first step was to ring the doorbell. She took a deep breath and did it.

The door was opened, not by Liam, but by a young Maori woman. A *beautiful* young Maori woman. Nearly as tall as Kristen, but built on more statuesque lines, with the glossy black hair, the luminous brown skin and big brown eyes that Kristen had always admired so much. And she was barefoot, her hair tousled. As if... as if she'd just got out of bed. Or was just about to go there.

"Yes?" the woman asked.

"Uh…" Kristen said, trying to maintain. Because it couldn't be true. It *couldn't.* "I'd like to see Liam, please."

"Is he expecting you?" the woman asked.

"No," Kristen admitted, "but he'll want to see me, I think."

"Sorry," the woman said, her eyes hardening. "He's busy."

"Wait—" Kristen began.

But it was too late. The door was already closing. And it was true.

♡

"Who was it?" Liam asked, reaching for the remote to mute the replay of the game.

"Some fan, I guess," Kura shrugged. "Some girl, looking for you. Dunno how she got your address. Are you giving that out to random girls now?"

"Better be more careful, cuz," Amiri laughed, taking another swig of his beer. "That's a dangerous road. Get yourself a stalker or two, eh."

"She was a looker, though," Kura said. "Maybe I should've let her in after all. You may not've minded *her* stalking you."

Liam sat up straighter. "What did she look like?"

"Pretty," Kura said. "Nah. More beautiful, I'd say. Blonde, tall."

Liam shot off the couch and ran for the door, not even stopping to put his shoes on. He pounded down the steps to the pavement, looked wildly up and down the street, and saw her, just getting into her car, there by the corner.

He came level with her just as she was pulling out. She hadn't seen him. Not looking, he thought. Lucky nobody'd been coming, or she'd have crashed bang into them. He leaned forward, stretched out, brought his palm down hard on the boot and saw her head jerk to the mirror, her eyes meeting his. And then she'd braked, stopped the car where it was, half in, half out of the spot.

He was around to the driver's side in an instant, pulling the door open. No wonder she hadn't been looking, because she was crying.

"Kristen. Sweetheart," he said urgently, still breathing hard from his sprint. "Come on. Come back. What's wrong? Did something happen?"

She shook her head, the tears still falling, raised a hand in a futile attempt to wipe them away. "It doesn't matter. It's fine. You don't owe me anything. I need to go."

He stared at her in confusion. "Sorry. I must be slow. What don't I owe you? What's fine?"

"I mean..." she faltered. "I didn't think you'd do it, the celibacy thing. I mean, I hoped you would. But you..." The tears were coming again.

"I'll just go," she said again, reaching for the handle of the door he still held in his hand, giving it a tug that moved it not a bit. "I'm going."

He began to laugh, the relief overtaking him. Overwhelming him.

"Sweetheart," he said again. "No. That was my cousin. My *misguided* cousin. Come back, and I'll introduce you. Just before I turf her out of my house, along with her husband."

♡

"So," he said, turning from the door that he'd just shut behind his visitors. Turning to Kristen, standing in the entryway with him. "Time to start again. Time for me to promise you that I've done the celibacy thing right along with you, and that I'll keep doing it just as long as you do, until we're done. I haven't cheated on you, and I won't. Not now, and not ever."

"Not cheating," she protested. "You can't cheat if you don't have a commitment."

"Cheating," he said firmly. "I have a commitment. I have it to myself, and I have it to you."

"Oh."

That was all she said, but then she smiled. A smile that started slowly, spread across her beautiful face, and it was as if all the goodness and sweetness of her, every bit of her generous, loving spirit was there in that smile. And then she stepped close, closer than she ever had, put one graceful, long-fingered hand on each of his biceps, underneath his T-shirt sleeves, and ran her hands over his skin, up to his shoulders, then back down again, all the way to his wrists. Held him gently as she touched her mouth to his in a soft, sweet kiss before she put her hands to his face, stroked her palms down his cheeks, held him there, and kissed him harder.

For a moment, he was so shocked, he couldn't move. But only for a moment. And then he had his arms around her and was kissing her back, even as he felt her hands reaching down for the hem of his T-shirt.

She broke the kiss, stepped back to pull the shirt over his head, tossed it to the floor, and her hands were on him again, greedy for him. Running from his forearms to his shoulders, palms and fingers stroking down his chest, back up again.

"Liam." She looked into his eyes. "I love you so much. And I want you so much, I feel like I'm going to die. I need to feel all of you. Please. Please take me to bed."

He didn't need to be asked twice. He grabbed her hand, took her up the stairs and into his bedroom, meaning to pull her down onto the wide bed with him. But she was there first, pushing him down, coming over him, shifting herself further down the bed, bending her head to his chest, running her hands over him, starting to kiss him there. In a circular pattern around, he realized dazedly, the whorls of his tattoo. Coming closer and closer. And, finally, licking over a nipple, her teeth grazing it.

He felt the electricity of it jolt through him. His hands fisted in her hair at the sensation of her mouth against him, her hand caressing his other arm, his shoulder, his chest. And then that hand was moving further down, stroking the length, feeling the breadth of him. Taking him up fast. Much too fast.

"Kristen," he groaned, reaching for her hand. "Slow down."

She pulled swiftly back. "I'm sorry. I was too...You don't want me to."

He laughed, heard the unevenness of it. "I don't think I've ever wanted anything more. But if you keep going, it's going to be too fast. And I need to please you first."

He rolled with her so she was underneath him, propped himself on an elbow and reached for her blouse, began to flick open each little button, his fingers tracing a path down the valley of her breasts, over the sensitive skin of her midriff.

"Please, baby," he murmured between kisses at the corners of her mouth, trailing a path to her ear, feeling her shuddering beneath him. "Wait. Let me love you first. Let me take you all the way there. I need to do it."

He took his time, just as he'd promised her he would. Just as he'd promised himself. His hands and his mouth learning the secrets of her, navigating every curve and hollow, using her sighs, her moans as his guide. Discovering what she liked, and what she loved. What made her arch against him, and what made her grab his hair and call out loud.

And at last, she was lying there, looking like the most beautiful fallen angel there could ever be, gloriously naked, limp and shuddering, eyes closed, breath still coming hard from the last time, what he could tell had been the best one yet, and he was finally, finally sliding into her. Still slowly, because he wanted to feel every bit of this, and he wanted her to feel it, too. Their last first time. He needed to see her eyes fluttering open, feel her arms wrapping around him, hear her sighing his name as her hands reached for him again. Feel her running those hands over his shoulders, his arms, down his back, as if she couldn't get enough of him.

And still he kept it slow, loving every moment of watching her, listening to her, feeling her around him. He was inside her, but somehow, he was taking her inside himself, too. Taking her up again as patiently as he'd ever done anything in his life, staying with her every step of the way.

And if holding on to his self-control had been hard, losing it was the sweetest, sharpest pleasure he'd ever felt. When she was lost in him, convulsing around him, crying out. When he was, at long last, losing himself in her. Saying her name again and again. Coming with her. Coming home.

"We broke our vow," she said dreamily when they were under the covers and he was holding her against him, stroking his hand over her hair, down her back, just for the pleasure of touching her.

"We did," he agreed. "Even though we're still thirteen days away."

She raised her head in surprise to look at him. "Are we really? Have you been counting?"

"Well, yeh," he admitted. "But I can do a quick recalculation. And oh, yeh. I miscounted. What d'you reckon, it ends today after all."

"Good," she said, and her smile was all the way there now, and he had to kiss her again. "Just in time."

"But I would like to know," he said slowly, "why your first reaction when you saw Kura was to assume that I'd been cheating on you. Why you thought I'd do that, with everything you know about me."

He didn't want anything to spoil this, but he needed to know that she knew him, that she trusted him, that she believed in him. Needed it, he realized, as much as he'd ever needed anything.

"I guess," she said with a sigh, "that it was the shoe-dropping thing. Hannah and I talked about that once. That when something really good happens, we think—" She stopped, then started again. "Well, she doesn't, not anymore. But *I* still think, when that happens, that this can't be for me. That this isn't how my life works. And I wait for the other shoe to drop, for something to go wrong. I'm waiting for it. I'm *looking* for it."

"Well, stop looking for it with me," he told her firmly. "Because my shoes are staying exactly where they are."

"I'm trying to have faith." Her smile was wobbling a bit now. "I'm a work in progress, I guess. Do you think you can live with that?"

"I reckon I can." He smiled at her, held her to him, and thought that he could hold her forever. "Since I'm a work in progress too."

crusaders and their maidens

♡

" It's flat," Ally said, looking out of the little jet's window at the landscape below as they descended towards the Christchurch Airport in the dim light of a winter evening. "This is about the first flat place I've seen in New Zealand."

"The Canterbury Plain," Nate said with a smile for her eagerness, glad now that he'd made this choice. He'd been thinking about using this weekend to work on his kicking, but Mako had urged him to reconsider.

"You need to lighten up, mate," his friend had told him bluntly. "It's all good to be intense when you're here. That's you. But you're fit, and we've got the entire Championship ahead of us. You're going to burn yourself out, you go on like this. Take advantage of being out of it for a bit. I know I'm planning to. I just wish Kristen had been able to get more than a few days off, or I'd be taking her someplace farther away than Aussie myself. Pity about the short notice, but that's footy. So take a break, enjoy yourself with Ally, pay some attention to her. My advice. You've got a bit of work to do there, you don't mind my saying. Besides," he'd added practically, "you need to get fresh mentally before we go again, and there's no better distraction, eh."

Nate hadn't liked hearing it, and he still thought he could use the extra training time. He'd been gutted by the loss in the quarterfinal that had ended the Hurricanes' Super 15 season, and he didn't intend anything like that to happen during the upcoming Rugby Championship, not if he could help it.

But Mako was right, he *did* have two weeks off before he had to report back to the All Blacks, and not too many other obligations in there. He'd spend a few days of them with Ally, go see his family for a few more. And *then* practice his kicking, and do all the rest of it, too.

Ally had been so excited at the prospect of seeing a bit of the South Island, he was grateful that he'd decided, in the end, to bring her down here. Doing anything with Ally made him see it through fresh eyes, she was so full of enthusiasm. And enthusiasm was something you could never get enough of.

"I guess I always think of earthquakes happening in hilly places," she was saying now. "Alaska, Turkey. And San Francisco, of course. Did they know how much risk there was here?"

"Nah." He stood up once the plane had come to a stop and pulled their bags out of the overhead bin. "Nobody knew. They didn't even know the fault was here until the first big one happened."

Ally followed him out the door of the plane, down the steps to the tarmac. She'd been impressed by his being last on, first off, by the valet parking at the airport. Things he'd taken for granted for a long time now, things that were a necessary part of a sportsman's life, especially one with as many commitments as he had.

No need to pick up a car here, anyway, because his mate George was there to meet them, and had promised Nate the use of his Land Rover for the weekend as well.

George might be retired now, but he was still looking fit. The big lock grabbed Nate's hand with one of the giant paws that had manhandled him so often on the paddock, then took Ally's in a gentler grip and completely swallowed it up.

"You ready to see how real men play footy?" George challenged him with a hard stare when the greetings were over.

"Nah," Nate said with a grin. "Have to wait a few weeks for that, won't I."

Since they were going to be down here anyway, he'd decided they might as well watch the Crusaders play in the semifinal.

Ally had liked that idea, too. "Maybe I'll actually get an idea of what's going on, if I watch with you," she'd said hopefully.

He'd laughed a bit at that. "I may not be the best company," he'd tried to explain. "I'll want to watch how the Reds go, as I'll be seeing some of those boys again on the Wallabies squad in a few weeks."

"Oh," she'd said, looking a bit disappointed. "Oh, well. I still want to go."

So here they were, climbing into George's car for the journey to the stadium. Well, to a spot on a side street a fifteen-minute walk away, actually.

"We got a stadium of sorts, in the end, but no parking," George apologized to Ally as they began the trek together with a steady stream of humanity. Young and old, men and women and children. Going to a Crusaders game, now more than ever, was a family affair, the mood festive, and Nate was reminded once again that what had been his livelihood and his life for so many years was a night of recreation and relaxation to everybody else.

"What would you like to eat?" he asked Ally when they were inside the funky little building that had been upgraded and pressed into service a couple years earlier to replace the rugby stadium that had been damaged beyond repair. Portaloos instead of toilets, just a few food stalls here and there, and metal scaffolding everywhere.

"What are my choices?" she asked.

"Well..." he admitted, "sausage and chips, or nachos. And beer. Or...beer."

She laughed. "Sausage and chips, please. And beer. This is the high-end experience, I see."

"Nah. But definitely an experience," he assured her.

He cast an appraising eye over the players as they warmed up. The Crusaders would be playing a pacey game tonight, trying to tire the Reds, coming off a tough win in the quarterfinals against the Stormers the week before, then having to make the journey all the way from Safa immediately afterwards. He said as much to George, talked a bit of rugby.

They were interrupted, in the end, by the swell of music, the voice booming over the PA system. "Ladies and gentlemen. The Crusaders...*Maidens!*"

He saw Ally sitting up a bit straighter as the group of twenty or so young women strutted onto the field. And then she started to laugh, and just kept on, until she was helpless with it, and he had to smile himself. Not the reaction he'd been expecting.

"You're kidding," she got out. "The boots! And the swords!"

"What?" he asked plaintively. "Good clean fun, that's what that is." He gestured to the women as they danced and posed in their ultra-short "leather" tunics, flung their long hair about. All right, the thigh-high boots might be a bit much. Not to mention the swords. Hmm. He'd better study this a bit more closely, since he could tell that Ally was going to be teasing him about it. The poses were probably a little suggestive. And the huge silver swords...

"Phallic symbol much?" Ally gasped, burying her head in his shoulder. "Oh, man. The boots. I need some of those boots."

George was grinning now as well. "Think you've got your work cut out for you with this one, Toro. She doesn't seem impressed."

"Oi," Nate protested, trying, and miserably failing, to keep a smile from escaping. "You're meant to be jealous, Ally."

"Want me to get some?" she asked, laying a hand on his arm and looking up at him with patently false sincerity. "Some boots like that? I could have used those a couple months ago," she murmured in his ear. "Bet you'd have liked that."

"Sounds good to me," he agreed. Ally in a pair of those boots and nothing else? Yeh, he'd take that.

"No, but seriously," she said, "how come you guys don't have cheerleaders? Do the other teams have them?"

"Nah. Well," he corrected himself, "the Highlanders have bagpipers, and the Chiefs have some Maori fellas who do a haka. But the Crusaders are the only ones who have girls."

"What would Hurricanes cheerleaders dress up as anyway?" she wondered. "They could have their skirts be blown off by the wind, maybe. How about that?"

"Hmm," he said. "I may just have to pass that one on. Because that would work. What d'you reckon, George?"

"Yeh," he said with another grin. "That'd do me."

"Guys are pretty hard to please, it's true," Ally agreed. And then she was jumping and laughing again as a half-dozen horses burst onto the field, each draped in true medieval style with cross-bedecked trappings and carrying a rider costumed as a knight. The well-trained animals did several circuits, their riders pulling them up in impressive formation in front of each stand, drawing their own swords to thunderous background music over the speakers.

"No Muslim population here?" Ally wondered aloud. "I mean, the Crusaders weren't exactly good citizens, you know. Why Crusaders, anyway?"

"Because of the Cathedral," Nate said. "Which was destroyed, you know, in the quake. But that's the symbol of Christchurch. And luckily," he added, "these Crusaders *are* good citizens. I've never heard any objection to the name, have you, George?"

"Nah," George said. "Not so far."

"It's like a high school football game, or a hockey game in Canada, with all this energy," Ally decided. "Like you hear about Friday night football in Texas. All the families, all the kids. Like the only game in town."

"Because it is," Nate said, serious now. "The only game in town. One of the only things Christchurch still has in the way of entertainment, and the boys know it. And I'm sorry," he said as the horses galloped off the field again, the Maidens making their hair-tossing exit, the crowd stirring in anticipation of the players taking the field. "But now I do need to watch. I'll see the film, of course, but I'll learn more here tonight. Which means I won't be very good company for you."

"You do what you need to do," she told him. "I'm good."

♡

"So what did you think, Ally? Pretty boring? I know scrummaging isn't your favorite, and I counted five resets in that second half. A bit sloppy there, the Reds, eh, George," Nate said from his spot behind Ally's seat a couple hours later.

"I thought that I enjoy watching more when you're playing, scrummaging or not," Ally answered promptly. "At least then I get to admire you. Though it was exciting watching the Crusaders win. I was supposed to be going for them, right? Guess I should've checked."

"Yeh," Nate agreed. "You were meant to be supporting them."

"At least if you wanted a lift home," George put in.

"Sorry I couldn't explain more to you," Nate apologized again. "Footy players aren't actually the best blokes to watch a match with, I'm afraid. Just another day at the office, eh."

"No worries," she said saucily. "The guy on my other side was super helpful. Explained all the penalties to me and everything. I think," she said, turning around in her seat and opening her eyes wide at Nate, "he might have liked me. What do you think?"

"I have just two words for you," he said. "Crusaders Maidens."

"And I have just two words for *you*," she threw right back at him, and Nate saw George shaking his head, beginning to chuckle. "Dead Meat."

♡

She wasn't laughing the next morning, though, when George took them out after breakfast for a tour of the city. Skirting the

Red Zone, the city's cordoned-off central business district, where most of the lives had been lost, was bad enough. Blocks and blocks, the heart of a once-vibrant city, deserted now. The cheerful signs still in the windows, advertising sales that would never happen. The symbols scrawled in red paint on the outsides of buildings that still looked normal, but would never be open for business again.

"What do those mean?" she asked George. "Those red marks?"

"That the building was searched for bodies," he explained. "That it's clear."

"Oh." She swallowed. "Oh."

He took them, then, to the eastern neighborhoods, once tidy and prosperous, bordering the Avon River. Across rebuilt bridges, highways still under construction, into the worst of it.

"It's like one of those movies," she said in a small voice as they turned a corner, no other cars in sight on a street that stretched for blocks. "After the zombie apocalypse or something. It looks like all the people got swept away."

She looked out at front gardens that had clearly once been cherished, lovingly tended in true Kiwi style. At rosebushes and camellias growing wild now, overtaking grass that stood high around front porches where nobody would ever sit.

"Lots of these houses look OK, though," she said. "Like the people just stepped out, and never came back. Are they really so unsafe that the whole neighborhood had to be abandoned?"

"If you look more closely, George told her, "you'll see that they're all sitting too low. That they've sunk right down into the ground."

Once he'd pointed it out, she could see it. "How could that happen?" she asked. "How could they just sink?"

"You see the dirt there, in the front garden?" George pointed. "That's liquefaction. That's what everyone thought was good soil. Turned liquid, bubbled to the surface. Nothing for a house to stand on, eh. Just a sea of mud to sink into. And that's what they did. Sink. And crack straight through, some of them."

"You know a lot about it," Ally said.

"Oh, we've all become geology experts round here," George assured her.

He turned off the residential street onto a main road, to Ally's relief. The sight of all that loss weighed her down like the liquefied soil of Christchurch, once the solid ground on which so many had built their lives. All those couples, saving and planning, signing their mortgage papers with so much optimism, excited that their dream of homeownership had come true. The chance to own their own piece of the pie, taking such care with it, keeping it so neat, tending their gardens so lovingly. She felt her heart break just a little for every one of those lost dreams.

She said something of that to George, and he nodded soberly. "Nobody realized how bad it was going to be, at first," he said. "They were out in their gardens, out in the road, shoveling away the mud by hand. Using the portaloos for months on end, thinking it would stop. That it would all go back to normal. But the mud just kept coming, and so did the shakes. And the houses got inspected, eventually, condemned. Some of them thought they could fight it, that they could fix the damage or build again. Holding on, the last ones for streets around. No neighbors, living in a ghost town. The kids playing in the front garden, nobody to kick the footy with, all alone. But eventually, they had to give up, too. And now they're all gone from here."

He pulled off another main road and stopped in front of a school that, as far as Ally could tell, was open for business. "Look here," he said. "This is something to think about, eh."

Ally looked at the grassy playing field, featureless except for a large boulder, twice the height of a man, in its center. "What?"

"That wasn't there before," George said. "Nobody saw it come down, but there it was, next day. Didn't take down the fence round the school or anything. Which means it hit above, on the hill there, where you see the empty spot, see?"

He pointed, and Ally saw what he meant, a scar on the cliff face behind the school. "And then," he said, "it bounced high enough to clear the fence, landed twenty meters away, in the center of the field. More than two meters high, that fence is. Gives you an idea of the power of it, how the cliffs and houses came down."

"But your house is OK, right?" Ally asked. "And it's on the cliffs."

"Different geology, Sumner," George said. "And a bit away from the worst of it. Which caused me some sleepless nights, too, not suffering as much as some. Survivor's guilt, they call that. Reckon there are enough people in Christchurch who can tell you something about that."

He pulled to a stop on the street outside a pub, clearly doing a thriving trade although the businesses around it were shuttered, the rest of the block deserted.

"I'm surprised they still have customers," Ally said when they were inside, tucking into their meat pies and salad.

"Yeh, yellow zoned round here," George agreed. "Some buildings OK, some not. But we're not exactly spoilt for choice in Christchurch these days. Any good spot that's still open gets a fair bit of custom. Because it's not all doom and gloom," he hastened to assure her. "Not a bit of it. Life goes on, and so does the city. We're rebuilding now. Pulling up our socks and starting over."

quite a nice walk

♡

"I'm guessing you're not planning a move to Christchurch," Nate said the next day.

Ally had to wait a moment to answer him, because she didn't have any breath to do it with. She'd been surprised by how quickly the landscape had changed when they'd left the city yesterday, though she shouldn't have been. She'd been in New Zealand long enough to know that an hour or two could take the visitor from the heart of a sophisticated metropolis, to a fern-filled forest where the only sound was the call of bellbirds and tui, to the most pristine, deserted beach, or to a rugged mountain landscape, an alpine lake.

And rugged mountains were what she was looking at right now. Arthur's Pass in the middle of the Southern Alps, to be exact. Not much snow right now, but the peaks were impressive for all that, forested in the lower elevations, their rocky summits appearing and disappearing in the mist.

"Quite a nice walk," Nate had called it this morning when she'd been pulling on her boots in the comfortable room in the Arthur's Pass guest house. She hoped it got a little easier as they got further up, because so far, it was one of the steepest trails she'd ever hiked. The fact that their hostess had looked a bit surprised when Nate had told her where they were going, though, made her wonder.

"Good on ya," she'd told Ally. "You'll have lovely views if it fines up. Gets a bit steep, though, Avalanche Peak," she'd cautioned.

Now, Ally realized that had been typical Kiwi understatement. Because this wasn't "a bit steep." This was grabbing-onto-roots climbing. This was the world's biggest stairway.

"What?" she asked Nate, heaving herself up yet another step, determined not to have to ask him to slow down. They'd been at this nearly an hour. Once they got over this beginning part, it would surely get easier. It was a popular track, Nate had said. "What did you say?"

"Christchurch," he said, sounding not in the least out of breath, to her annoyance. "Thinking that you won't be shifting house."

"Oh. No," she agreed. "I was glad to leave." She pretended she was thinking instead of catching her breath, then gave it up. Talking would take her mind off how hard this was, maybe. And if the sentences came out in gasps, too bad.

"I know George said that people had adjusted," she said, "and I guess you do that, if you have to. And I know that New Zealanders are tough. But I don't think I could live there, and I guess I'm surprised anybody stays. That more people haven't moved out. That the guys on the Crusaders, especially, are still playing here. Surely they have opportunities elsewhere."

"Loyalty," Nate said simply. "Christchurch has been through the wars, it's true. Bit of a siege mentality, sticking together and that. Rugby's been one of the things that's helped people get back to normal there. You saw that the other night, how strong the support is. Stronger than ever now, and the team feels the same way. Hell of a side, the Crusaders. They always have been, but there's something more there now. Playing for the city, for everybody there."

He went on, and she let him talk, glad to listen, to focus on climbing. "You know, that first season, before they got the old stadium fixed up so they could play there, those boys played every game on the road. Away from home nearly every night, all year long, while their partners and kids, their parents and grand-parents rode it out, sometimes more than one quake a day. Not able to be there when one hit, when their kids were crying. Not knowing whether the next one would be the really big one that'd do the whole place in. That was rough."

"Tough season," Ally got out, clambering up and over a big boulder that surely had no place in the middle of a marked trail.

"Yeh," he agreed. "How'd you imagine they finished on the ladder, that year?"

"Not too well, I'm thinking," she said.

"You'd be wrong, though. Lost in the final. Barely. All that, and they nearly won the whole thing."

"Wow. What do you think it was? That they were, what you said? Playing for everybody at home? Or do you think other teams, maybe, didn't play them quite as hard?"

He laughed. "Not bloody likely. That's not the way it works. You're always busting a gut for the win. After the match, you can be mates. While it's happening, you're bashing the hell out of each other, no matter what. That's footy."

He stopped a moment, turned around. "Doing all right?"

So he had noticed her breathlessness. "I'm good," she said. "As long as you keep your elbows to yourself."

"Have a bit of compassion on my tender male ego," he com-plained. "We're putting the 'Epic Fail' tag on that one and shov-ing it to the back of the cupboard."

"What about you?" she asked as they began climbing again. "Planning to change teams? Going back to the land of your childhood? The Mainland?"

"Nah. I'm the loyal sheepdog type, I guess. Make a decision, stay with it."

"Toro," she said. "The bull. No going sideways, no going back. Damn the torpedoes, full speed ahead."

"You've got a bit of a metaphor problem there," he pointed out. "But that's the idea."

"You know," she couldn't help mentioning, "in some places, when people build a trail up a mountain, they put in switchbacks. They don't just go straight up it."

"Those places wouldn't be in En Zed, then," he decided.

She laughed in spite of herself. "Probably not."

Another half hour, and they were done with the roots, to her relief, were coming out above the treeline into an alpine environment of yellow-green grasses, blowing in the chilly breeze. The clouds were still heavy around them, obscuring any view. Ally looked ahead, could see the track winding up, and another two ridges rising, one behind the other, above the one they were crossing, whatever lay ahead disappearing into the mist again, but surely they were near the top now.

And still the track stretched up, and up some more. Always another ridge or two appearing through the mist, no matter how many they crossed. She wasn't trying for conversation anymore, was just concentrating on putting one foot in front of the other. On following Nate's back, climbing steadily.

Nate slowed as they approached a young couple, the first people they'd seen on the track, who were sitting in the shelter of a large boulder, screened from the wind blowing across the open ridge. Great. A break. Because no Kiwi seemed able to run into anyone without stopping for a chat.

"How're you going?" Nate asked. "Been to the top already, or just having a bit of a rest?"

"Deciding what to do," the young man said in what Ally's untrained ear thought might be an English accent. "How much farther is it to the top, do you know?"

"You've got a fair bit left," Nate admitted, and Ally suppressed a groan. She hadn't dared ask, because she'd been afraid to hear the answer. And "a fair bit" definitely sounded ominous.

The man looked at his girlfriend.

"Go back," she said instantly. "They told us at the I-Site," she complained to Ally, "that this was a nice walk. This isn't a nice walk. This is a death march."

"Oh, not that bad," Nate protested. "And if we get the mist clearing, you'll get a view to make it all worthwhile."

"I'll look online and pretend I was there," the woman said firmly, making Ally laugh.

Ally's attention was diverted by a large, drab-colored bird that had flown up behind the couple and landed on an open day pack. "Look, Nate," she said, pointing. "What *is* that? It looks like some kind of parrot!"

"It *is* a parrot," Nate said. "You'll want to watch your—"

Too late. The big bird had reached into the pack with a formidable beak and one taloned foot, and was now half in and half out, dragging out the contents. The young woman gave a little shriek, and the man grabbed for the pack, dislodging the bird, but not before it had stolen a packet of sandwiches, with which it flew a little distance off, proceeding to rip open the cling film and starting to work on the couple's lunch.

"What *was* that?" the young man asked in frustration, stuffing the contents of his pack inside again and closing it up.

"That would be your kea," Nate said, keeping a straight face. "Got to watch yourself up here in the mountains. They're bad enough with your lunch. What they really want, though, are the bits of rubber round your car windows. They'll take those straight out, strip the whole thing. Thieving little buggers."

He turned to look assessingly at the track ahead. "Ready to go?" he asked Ally.

"Sure," she sighed. "What the heck."

♡

Nate had been right, she thought when they were finally at the bottom again, several grueling hours later. Near the top, when they'd been carefully traversing a razor-backed ridge of shale that dropped steeply off on either side into slabs and chunks of black rubble, the mists had cleared in patches, revealing a vista of steep, forbidding peaks, lonely mountains rising out of the fog, even more spectacular for being so briefly glimpsed.

But when they had turned to make their way down the slightly less vertical descending track, she had wished that, instead of parrots, there were some giant eagles up here to take them off what looked exactly like the slopes of Mount Doom, and felt like it too. Because she'd been *tired*. And that was before her knees and ankles had taken the brunt of kilometers of down-climbing.

"We'll go for lunch," Nate said when they were back in the little village again, a few buildings scattered amongst the trees, the mountains rising sharply on either side. "Have a beer."

She groaned. "I'm so grubby, I'd like a shower first. But once I have one, I'm not going to want to move again. So I guess we should do lunch."

♡

"What?" he asked when they were in the little café. "Why are you looking at me like that?"

"Here's the question," she said, pinching one of his chips, as usual, and fixing him with what he could only describe as a glare. "Why did we just do that?"

"If you want chips," he couldn't resist pointing out, "I'll get you some."

"I don't want chips," she said. "I just want a few of yours." Which made him roll his eyes.

"Why?" she insisted again.

"What, the walk? Because I thought you'd like it," he protested. "That it'd be a challenge for you."

"Uh-huh," she said skeptically. "It wouldn't be that you wanted to do something where you'd be so obviously better than me, would it? Because that was the hardest damn hike I've ever been on. That was *ridiculous.* And it looked to me like you could have run the whole thing."

"There *is* a race every year," he pointed out helpfully.

She groaned. "I so did not need to know that. New Zealanders are crazy. But come on. Was that why?"

He started to laugh. He couldn't help it. "I hope not. Because that would be pretty low of me, wouldn't it?"

"Yeah, it would," she scowled.

"Never mind," he consoled her, reaching for her hand. She looked so cute with that frown drawing her dark brows together. So severe, like the world's sexiest librarian, about to shush him. "I'll take you somewhere else tomorrow, and you can outperform me. And Susan there, back at the guest house," he added with another smile. "She does massage. A shower and an hour or so with her, and you'll be a new woman."

♡

And both of those things *did* help. But when he reached for her that evening, she looked at him in astonishment.

"You have got to be kidding," she told him. "You have no idea how sore and tired this body is."

""Oh, I have a pretty fair idea," he smiled, leaning over to kiss her. "And sex is a pretty good anesthetic. Come on. Let me make you feel better."

"You'd better be prepared to do all the work," she sighed. But her protest was pitifully weak, because his fingers were running softly over the sensitive skin between her breasts in the low-cut undershirt she had worn to bed.

"It could be like having sex with a blow-up doll," she got out, "because I'm not moving. But if you want a sex toy to play with…" She squirmed a little. He was using one finger to trace the outline of her shirt now, and that felt *good*.

"I'll play with you," he promised. "I'll do it all. You just lie there and be my toy."

So she did. He went slowly, his hands, then his mouth gentle against her sensitive skin until she could swear she was aware of every separate nerve ending. He was pulling the edge of the shirt a bit further down, still concentrating on the tops of her breasts, the valley between them, his touch so light it nearly tickled. And then, when she was moving a little underneath him despite herself, he transferred his attention to her inner thighs, finding erogenous zones she hadn't even realized she had.

By the time he was slowly pulling up the undershirt, caressing and kissing every centimeter he uncovered along the way, she was moaning. And when he had finally finished playing with her and was sliding inside, beginning his long, slow ride, she really was as limp and boneless as any sex doll. And feeling a whole lot better.

"Goodnight, toy," he murmured at last with a gentle kiss, pulling the duvet over her.

But she barely heard him, because she was already sinking into sleep.

ally gets her card back

♡

"And here we are," Nate said. They had come down out of the high pass into wide-open expanses of hill shading into river valley, a few sheep the only living things visible for kilometers around.

He pulled into a large carpark, populated with only a few cars on this Monday morning. "Get your climbing shoes and come on," he told Ally. But she was ahead of him, had already reached back and rummaged them out, was yanking off her shoes and socks.

"Slow down," he grinned. "The rocks aren't going anywhere."

"So many boulders, so little time," she said happily. "That's limestone. Oh, wow."

"Thought you'd like it," he said modestly, getting himself into his own shoes. "Course, I've never stopped here before, but I did a bit of checking around. This was actually the point of the whole journey. Saving the best for last."

And, he thought an hour later, as she tackled yet another of the weirdly shaped monoliths that studded Castle Hill, the huge gray knobs and pinnacles standing sentinel over the rugged terrain, he might have taken her up Avalanche Peak the day before to soothe his own ego after all, just as she'd suspected. Because he couldn't believe what she was doing now, how she made those microscopic shifts in balance that enabled her to somehow smear her way up a seemingly sheer boulder with none of the obvious handholds of the climbing gym.

"How did you do that?" he complained when she'd reached the top, a good three meters above him, and then, even more incredibly, had made her way back down again.

"Here," she pointed out. "Get your toe on this. And your hands here."

He looked, and could barely see the protrusion. Tried a few more times, and couldn't even get off the ground.

"Never mind," she laughed. "I'll find you something easier."

"Bit different from the gym," he admitted as they climbed the hill together. No mist today, not down here, just white clouds scudding across the blue sky in the cool breeze. Gray stones, green grasses, the mountains rising steeply to the west, the sheep grazing in the paddock beyond.

The Mainland, and his heart felt easy, as it always did down here. He liked Wellington, had built a good life there. But this was something else. The peace, the vistas, the endless space of mountain, plain, valley, and sea. This was home, and someday, he knew, he'd be coming back.

"It is," Ally said, and he had to work to remember what they had been talking about. "It's so much better, isn't it? Being here? Outdoors?" She gave a spin, arms flung wide, ponytail flying, her broad smile reaching all the way to those sparkling dark eyes, and his heart filled just a little bit more at the sight of her, the way she fit here.

"Come on," she urged. "Race you. First one to the top of that big one that's shaped like an M, there." She pointed to a stone near the apex of the slope. "First one there wins. Ready, set, *go!*" And before he could say anything, she was running.

He made it there first, of course, by a fair margin. And that was as far as he got. Because while he was still struggling to get off the ground, she had caught up, wriggled and stretched her way to the top, following a path he couldn't even begin to pick out, and was lying on her stomach, peering over the edge at him.

"I win," she pointed out unnecessarily. "And, yes, I now forgive you for the horrible hike yesterday, which goes down in history as another one of Nate's Bad Ideas. Do you want some help finding your way up here?"

"Yes," he was forced to admit. "I do."

"I even feel better about being your sex toy now," she said when she'd climbed back down and coached him up the thing, which, thankfully, actually did have a few places where a normal person could put his hands and feet. "I was worried last night that they were going to take away my Feminist Card for all the things I've done with you."

"Nah." He was looking down at her now. "Help me get down off this, and I'll personally give you your card back. And as far as the other thing, tell you what. You can be on top tonight, show me who's boss. I'm putting my hand up here and now to be your sex toy. It's a hell of a tough job," he sighed, "but somebody's got to do it."

Her eyes were full of mischief as she looked up at him. "I won't say your idea doesn't have potential," she said. "Quite a relief, actually. I was half expecting that I was going to have to pretend to be a maiden while you dressed up as a Crusader. I was thinking that I could get a sword, too, so I could dance around the house for you. Or maybe you'd like to have a sword battle. I'm sure I'd be supposed to lose, right? Would that be some good sexytimes for you? Unfortunately, I'm afraid I'd just laugh."

He laughed out loud at that himself. "One thing you can be dead sure of," he promised her, "I'll never be dressing up as a Crusader. Boots or no."

knee-deep in it

♡

Nate swore as he shoved a recalcitrant cow off the slow-moving rotary milking stand, got spattered with manure again in the process.

"She got you there, mate," Ned laughed. "She's a clever one. Knows if she stays on, she gets more treats." He moved the next batch of Jerseys up, each animal moving obediently into her slot, as familiar with the twice-daily routine as the man supervising them.

"Missing the glamorous life of a farmer yet?" he asked Nate with a grin an hour later, hopping off the ATV in the cold light of a Southland winter morning, opening the back of the trailer to let the dogs out, their morning's work done after moving the cows to fresh pasture.

Nate pulled his beanie down a bit against the chill, looked wryly down at his manure-bedecked gumboots. "Remembering why I play footy. Allergic to hard work, I guess."

His older brother shot him a glance. "Nobody thinks that, bro," he said gruffly. "We all know."

Nate looked at him with surprised gratitude, but didn't reply, just nodded.

"Dad's thinking of selling up," Ned said abruptly when they were in the house again, showered and changed, and finished with their mother's hearty breakfast of eggs on toast, ham, and bacon. She'd fed them, then headed out with their dad to pick up a load of hay, and the brothers were sitting over a second cup of tea, relaxing after the morning's chores.

Nate looked up from his mobile, his attention pulled abruptly from the text he'd been reading.

Haven't been this deep in bullshit since you read me that Farrell column, he'd texted. *Can't wait to stop working hard and come home. Get the sword and boots ready.*

To which Ally had just replied, *Dream on big shot,* which had made him laugh.

Now, though, he set the phone down, stared at his brother. "He is? Why?"

Ned shrugged. "Sixty now, says he's done it long enough, and so has Mum. Thinking of moving into town. And you know he can get a fair bit for the herd, and the place. We've got nearly four hundred, and there's a good market for Jerseys just now."

Nate was still reeling. His dad and mum off the land that had been his grandfather's, and his own father's before him... it was too big a change to contemplate. "What about you?" he asked. "You own a good bit of it yourself. Have you thought of buying Dad out? Because if you wanted to, you know, I could help out with a loan."

He held his breath a little after saying it. He'd never offered money to his brother before, and wasn't sure it would be welcome. But he needed to do it all the same.

Ned waved a hand. "Nah. Bad enough that you don't have more of a share."

"Doesn't matter," Nate said brusquely. In fact, he'd long since told their dad to leave him out entirely. That he hadn't worked the farm since he was fifteen, that he was investing a fair bit of the money he was earning, looking ahead to the days when he wouldn't be playing. And that he wasn't entitled to anything, and wasn't expecting it either.

"Still my son, aren't you," Frank Torrance had said. "You're due your share." And that had been that. There was no arguing with his dad.

"I'm happy to do it," he told Ned now. He'd press a little more. He knew that his brother, like their father, was a proud man, that he wouldn't want Nate's money. "It wouldn't be a gift. Just a loan. Business. You're a pretty good investment."

"I've got plans, tell you the truth," Ned said. "Time to settle down, you know."

"Settle *down?*" Nate asked blankly. "How could there be any way you could be any more settled?"

Ned looked at him with some exasperation. "Well, let's see. I could be married and have some kids, couldn't I. You may not've noticed that I'm still single. I was thirty last year, and Mel's going to get tired of hanging about, if she isn't already. And she doesn't want to be married to a cow-cocky. She'll do it if that's what I want, but I know she doesn't want the life."

"You'd do that for her?"

"Not much I wouldn't do for her," Ned said, then cleared his throat, looked down at his cup, and took another swallow. "Besides, I'm a bit tired of it myself, tell you the truth. Tired of smelling like shit all the time, of getting up so early. Doing something else would feel like a holiday, I'm thinking. And I'll get a fair bit, too, when Dad sells. Enough to set up in something new, something in town. I've got an idea, truth be told, wanted to talk to you about it."

Ned wanting his advice. That was a role reversal, and one Nate wasn't sure he was comfortable with.

"Course," he said. "What's the idea, then?"

"Ian McGregor," Ned said. "He wants to sell the feed business, retire himself. None of his kids want to take it on. They're all in Dunedin, you know."

Nate nodded. He knew. Southlanders were a hardy breed, but not everyone wanted the rural life. He knew he hadn't.

"And I thought," Ned went on, "as I've done the business end of this ever since I came down from Uni, that I could manage. And Mel's a bookkeeper, you know," he added with a smile. "Dead clever of me, wasn't it?"

"Sounds like a plan," Nate agreed.

"So I was thinking," Ned said, "maybe you'd go round there with Mel and me tomorrow. Have a chat, look at the books. Just a preliminary meeting, but you may think of questions we wouldn't. Ian's a good bloke," he hastened to add, "and he wouldn't cheat me, but it never hurts to ask the hard questions, eh."

"Course," Nate said automatically. "Though what I know about the feed business would fit on the head of a pin, with room left over."

"Never mind," Ned said with a quick grin. "Just give him that stare you do, and you'll have him babbling everything he'd meant to leave out."

"I'm the intimidation factor, am I," Nate grinned back.

"That'd be you," his brother agreed.

♡

Nate thought it over again on the quick flight back to Wellington three days later. His parents and Ned off the farm. He still couldn't get used to it. Time moved on, he knew that. They were moving with it, that was all.

"What about you?" Ned had asked during the ninety-minute drive that morning to the airport in Dunedin. "Any plans for settling down? You aren't getting any younger yourself, you know."

"Twenty-eight," Nate protested. "Not quite tottering towards the grave yet. Just getting started."

"Not serious about that girl you're seeing?" Ned pressed. "It's been a while now."

"Haven't thought about it," Nate admitted. "I'm focused on the footy just now, you know that."

Ned nodded. "I can see that. But she's, what, American?"

"Canadian."

"Working holiday visa, then?"

"Yeh, I s'pose. Never thought about it. Why?"

"Because," and his brother sounded a bit exasperated now, "that's only good for a year. We get a fair number of kids through on their OE, helping out. It's one year, mate. How long has she been here?"

"Uh..." Nate tried to think. "Came at the beginning of December, I guess."

Ned nodded. "August now. So, what? You go off on the European tour, end of October, wave goodbye to her, she goes merrily on her way? That the plan?"

"I don't know what the plan is," Nate said in exasperation. "How'm I meant to know that? Got enough to think about with the Championship coming up. I can't be worrying about Ally as well. I'll think about her, about us, when that's done."

"And that's all right with her? Quite happy to fit herself into those wee spaces in your life, is she? Because, mate, Mel wouldn't go for that. Not in a pig's eye, she wouldn't."

"I'm lucky that Ally's good with it, then, aren't I," Nate said shortly.

"Casual, is it?" Ned asked, still not letting go. "You seeing other people? Have some kind of agreement? That's why you didn't bring her down here with you, eh. I wondered, seeing how often you've texted. She's just for now, is she?"

"Course we're not seeing other people," Nate said irritably. "And she wouldn't have wanted to come. The delights of the dairy farm? I don't think so."

"Huh." Ned didn't sound convinced, and Nate had a quick flash of Ally's face when she'd dropped him at the airport, the day after they'd returned from Christchurch, then thought about Liam taking Kristen to the Gold Coast in Aussie for a beach holiday last week. And taking her to stay with his parents this weekend, his friend had told him. *Had* Ally wanted to come with him? Would he have wanted her here? Yeh, he thought. Probably. Definitely. But that would be serious, and he wasn't ready for serious.

"I'm not ready for that much complication," he told Ned now. "Got enough to think about," he repeated. "I'll sort it out once the Championship's over."

"One thing at a time, eh."

"Yeh. One thing at a time," Nate said with relief. "That's how I work."

"Pity it isn't how women work, then," Ned said. "But I'm guessing you may find that out for yourself."

♡

Nate remembered Ned's words two weeks later, lying in bed with Ally the night after the first game of the Championship. Which the All Blacks had lost to the Wallabies at Eden Park, to Nate's frustration. It had been close, but close didn't count, did it? Because they still weren't firing on all cylinders. Too many mistakes, not enough grunt from the forward pack, not enough impact from their new loosies. And the kicking, which had been shocking. That had been the killer.

"Sorry," he told Ally again. "I'd like to spend the time with you, you know I would, but I need to spend a fair bit of time tomorrow thinking about Sydney. We don't have the boot we need at first-five. Nobody we can rely on like we did Hemi, or a game manager as good, either. Which means I'm likely to be playing 10 next week, and either Nico or I'll be doing the goal-kicking. And I need to work on both those things, specially as we'll be without Koti as well, which is piling it on."

"Kate told me," Ally agreed quietly, pulling away from his side. "That Koti would be out for most of the next month. I thought it was really sweet that he was taking paternity leave. I didn't realize that was an option."

Nate snorted. "Because nobody else has done it, not for that long. And not while the squad's in transition like this. Losing one of our impact players when we don't have to, when he isn't injured...I don't know how he can do it."

Ally sat up, reached for her nightdress on the floor where Nate had dropped it. Looking narked with him again, Nate thought with an inward sigh.

"I guess he has other priorities," she said stiffly, pulling the thing over her head and settling it into place. "That he thinks being with his wife while she has their first baby is important."

"I'm not saying it isn't important," Nate argued. "Just that it's part of this job to go with the team. Every time, no matter what. It's what he signed up for."

"So he loses his spot on the team?" she challenged him. "If he does this?"

"Nah," he said impatiently. "Course not. We need him there. That's the point, eh."

"Well," she said, "if it doesn't cost him his place on the team, and considering that he's played so hard for you guys, and for the Blues too, all these years, maybe it doesn't have to be part of the job to give up absolutely everything. To give up the chance to be there to support Kate, to give up being there with his baby. I have a feeling he thinks that's the most important thing in his life right now."

Nate was losing this argument. He could tell that he wasn't going to make her understand. And he didn't, he really didn't need another loss this weekend.

"Well," he said, "he's doing it. Nothing I can say to change it, so all we can do is try to make up the difference. Which means that I need the time tomorrow. So let's get some sleep." He rolled over and gave her a kiss and a cuddle that, to his relief, she returned. "So we can make the most of the time we do have. I have an idea about how I want to wake you up, and I'm planning to try it."

liam sings a song

♡

The buzzer sounded, and Kristen flew to the box on the wall, pushed the button. "Hello?"

"Got time in your life for a lonely hooker?" she heard over the intercom.

She laughed happily. "I sure do. I'm buzzing you up now."

"That's my cue to go to my room," Ally said, getting up from the couch.

"Oh, don't go," Kristen protested. "Stay and say hi to Liam."

Ally smiled. "Maybe another day."

A quick flash of concern marred Kristen's mood for a moment. She wished Nate were here too. If only Ally could be as happy as she was, that would make everything perfect. If only Nate were focusing the kind of attention on Ally that Liam had given her. Instead, it seemed like he'd been spending less and less time with her in the weeks since the Championship had begun, and that it was only getting worse.

But then she heard the knock, and her attention was all for the man on the other side of the door.

"Got a surprise for you today," Liam told her once he'd finished kissing her hello. "You ready for a surprise? Willing to come along with me for it?"

"I'm ready to go anyplace you take me." She reached out to hold him again, just to feel those big arms go around her.

"I missed you so much," she sighed against his cheek, loving the solidity of his back under her palms, his broad chest like a stone wall. "Did you miss me?"

"Is this a trick question?" he asked, giving her another gentle kiss. "Been almost a week, eh. I've missed you for, oh, I'd say maybe five days and twelve hours. Somewhere in there."

She ran her hands under his T-shirt sleeves, stretching her fingers to reach around the heavy muscle, and thought about the tattoo she'd be kissing later. Going slowly, all the way from his forearm up to his shoulder, then moving to his chest. About how she'd be loving every bit of him. And how good it would feel to have her hands on those arms when the muscles were flexed, supporting his weight. When he was lying over her, murmuring the words she loved to hear, moving so slowly, taking exactly as long as she needed, until she was dissolving with the bliss of it.

She couldn't wait, but she wanted to wait. Wanted to see him smile at her, wanted to tell him how proud she'd been to watch him last night. Wanted to hear him tell her about the game. And *then* feel his arms, and every other part of him, too.

"If I'd known how good you were going to make me feel," she said, wishing she didn't have to let go of him, "our celibacy wouldn't have lasted nearly so long. This has been a really, really great couple of months. You should have told me how good you are at it."

"Yeh," he agreed. "Because that would've worked so well with you, I'm sure."

She pulled back with a smile for him. "You're right. Why do you have to be right so often? And OK. I'm ready for my surprise."

♡

"This is the surprise?" she asked when he parked in the CBD, helped her out of the car, then went to the boot and pulled out a guitar case. "You going to play for me? Or are you in some kind of band?"

"Just wait," he promised.

He held her hand for the few blocks' walk to Espressoholic and took her inside, where he propped the guitar case carefully against the window, next to a table at the front. A table with a *Reserved* sign on it.

He pulled out her chair, held it for her with the courtesy he always showed her. "Trim flat white?" he asked. "Or tea?"

"Tea, please."

"Anything to eat?"

She laughed. "No. I'm good."

He came back to the table after placing their order. "I thought about doing this the first place I saw you," he told her. He was standing opposite her, legs braced, arms relaxed. Strong and broad, solid as a totara tree. Her Liam.

"The climbing gym," he went on to explain. "Didn't seem quite right, though. So I decided, maybe use that day when I was walking down the street with Toro. Looked in the window, saw you in here, and couldn't believe my luck. Still can't, every single day when I wake up knowing how much I love you, and that you love me, too."

She could feel her eyes misting over already, reached for his hand. He squeezed hers in return, then let it go. And instead of sitting down, reached for the guitar case, opened it and pulled out the wooden instrument, then set the case back down, moved his chair away from the table, and seated himself with the guitar on his lap, pulling the strap around his neck.

"Now?" she asked, brows raised.

"Now," he confirmed.

"Wow. Singing in public," she said happily.

The warmth in his eyes, as always, went straight to her heart. "Listening to Maori sing is the other New Zealand national sport, didn't you know? On every tourist's list. Reckon I'll make it into somebody's travel diary today."

Whatever she would have answered was cut off as he began to strum the instrument, the tune soothing, sweet and slow. And then he started to sing, his deep voice filling every corner of the café, his gaze steady on her. The conversations around them ceasing, all action stilling as everybody stopped to listen.

She didn't know what most of the words meant, of course, though the poetry of them, the meaning she saw in his eyes was making her melt. And then he began the English verses, and he was calling her his angel, telling her he would love her forever. Singing words she'd never thought she'd hear again, not from somebody who meant them. Somebody she could trust to mean them. "Through sickness and health. Till death do us part."

And then it was Maori again, and this time, she knew what it meant.

"E ipo," he finished, drawing it out, with one last strum across the strings. And she knew what that meant too, because she'd heard it before, murmured in the night. "My darling."

The last note died away, but he just sat. Sat and looked at her.

She couldn't say anything, couldn't answer him, because she was crying. Her hands were at her mouth, her eyes streaming as everyone in the café began to applaud.

He set the guitar carefully against the window, handed her his napkin with a smile, reached for her other hand across the triangular table.

"I'm a pretty imperfect fella," he began. "Made heaps of mistakes in my life, as I may have mentioned. But I've tried my best to learn from every one of them. And one thing I know for sure," he went on, the deep voice losing a little of its firmness, his eyes beginning to glisten with unshed tears, "is that when you find something that's right, you hold onto it with everything you have, and you never let it go. You're my right thing, Kristen. And I want to be yours."

She nodded, not trusting herself to speak. His face was serious now. Letting her know that she could trust him. Letting her know that it was safe to love him.

"I'll never make you a promise I can't keep," he told her. "So you know I mean it when I promise you this. Wherever we go, whatever happens in our lives, I'll never leave you. However long God gives me on this earth, that's how long I'll be loving you. I'll give you everything I have. I'll give you everything I am. That's my promise."

A smile broke out at last on his broad face. "And maybe you should stop crying now," he said gently, "or everybody's going to think you're saying no."

That surprised a choked laugh from her. "I can't, though," she got out. "Oh, Liam. I love you so much."

"Then we'd better do this next thing," he decided. He got out of his chair, put one big knee on the floor. Reached into his pocket for a box, opened it to reveal a ring made of...bone?

"Not the real thing," he assured her. "Because I want you to choose exactly what you want. But this is my big moment, so here I go."

He looked into her eyes, took a deep breath, and said it. "I love you, Kristen. Will you marry me?"

She knew she was still crying. And she wanted to answer him, wanted to say "yes" with every fiber of her being. But she had to ask first. "Can I...Can *we*. Can we have a baby?"

He laughed. "We can have as many babies as you like. I'm Maori. But they'll have me for a dad, you know. Won't be as pretty as you, eh."

"They'll be the luckiest babies in the world," she said, and she'd never meant anything more. "Because they *will* have you for a dad. Besides," and she was laughing herself now, "I'm pretty enough for both of us."

"Yes, you are. And is that a yes?" he prompted.

"Yes." She couldn't seem to stop laughing. "Yes. Yes. That's a yes."

He slid the ring onto her finger, then stood, took her in his arms, and kissed her.

Kristen heard the clapping, the whistling around her. She knew, in one part of her brain, that this whole thing was going to be on YouTube before the day was over, and that she might even watch it herself. Because she'd never get enough of this moment. Or this man.

the end

♡

Kristen hadn't come back after leaving in mid-afternoon with Liam, which wasn't much of a surprise. But that left Ally to get dressed to see Nate by herself. She raided Kristen's closet, as always, stood daunted by the array of choice, wishing she'd asked Kristen to pick out an outfit for her earlier. Pants? Skirt? Dress? And what kind of shoes?

Well, skirt or dress, she decided. Nate liked looking at her legs, she'd figured that much out. And if she wanted his attention tonight, the shorter and tighter the better.

She was a little nervous about the evening, she thought, fingering a flirty little deep blue skirt with a star-spangled chiffon overlay. More nervous than seemed normal, all these months into a relationship.

It might be better tonight, though, she thought hopefully. The win over the Springboks in Auckland last night should help, surely. The team was playing better, even she could see it, and that must mean that Nate could let up a bit, allow himself more than a night or two a week with her. He'd said he wanted more, and maybe now they could do it. Because she hadn't seen him really relaxed since the day at the Adrenaline Park a month earlier, before the Championship had begun. Even when he was with her, he'd be spending time with his notebook, preparing for the next game, or watching film. The only time she really felt like she had his full attention lately was in bed.

When he'd gone to visit his family without her, she'd wiped away tears all the way home from the airport. No matter how desperately she tried to school her wayward heart, it insisted on being his. And she was becoming increasingly afraid that he didn't want it.

She'd start out by seeing how thoroughly she could distract him tonight, she decided. And maybe then, maybe now there could be more. With that in mind—and with no Kristen to give her any other outfit advice—she went back to the leather skirt and lace top. An oldie but a goodie.

And when Nate arrived, the look in his eyes told her it still worked. He focused on her over dinner, too. Answered her questions about the game, talked about the upcoming trip to South Africa and Argentina with more attention than he'd been showing her lately. Although his attentive-boyfriend manner could, she conceded, have more to do with wanting to unzip her skirt than anything else, because she could tell that he definitely wanted to do that too.

He did do that, after dinner. And he seemed to enjoy it just as much as the first time.

♡

"I'm glad we finally had some time together," she said softly, running her hand over his chest afterwards. He'd made love to her with his usual thoroughness, and even more than his usual inventiveness—the leather skirt, probably—but she could almost feel his mind drifting away from her now. Away from this moment.

"Yeh," he sighed, his arm draped around her, his hand absently stroking her shoulder. "But this is going to have to be it for a while."

She felt the cold, held at bay during the past few hours, begin to seep back in. "I thought..." She paused, then decided to say it.

"Since you don't have to leave for four more days, and you'll be gone for more than two weeks afterwards, that maybe we could take a little more time. Have another night, maybe even two, before you go. I'd like to spend more time with you."

He could think that was demanding, if he wanted. Too bad. Forget being a low-maintenance girlfriend. This was just being taken for granted, and she hated it.

"That's what I'm talking about." He let go of her, pulled himself up to sit against the pillows. "I think we should take a break for a bit. I have too much to focus on just now, too much on my mind, to be involved. The team's finally getting a bit of traction, and I need to keep that going. I can't do the boyfriend thing right, and it's not fair to you."

"In other words," she said slowly, sitting up herself, pulling the sheet and duvet over a body that had suddenly grown cold, "you're not ready for a serious relationship right now."

"That's it," he said with relief. "I'm not."

The cold was being replaced by fire now, little flames of anger licking up from her chest. She threw the covers back and got out of bed, bent down to find her discarded clothes.

"Ally," he said urgently. "I don't mean break up. I mean take a break, for both our sakes. See where we are after the Championship. It's just another month or so."

She ignored that. If he didn't know that that wasn't how it worked, this was hopeless. She pulled on her underwear with a jerk, took three tries to fasten her bra, her hands were shaking so badly.

"Kristen told me," she got out, hearing her voice tremble and hating it, "that when the guy says that, about not being ready, that's when you get up and put your clothes back on. Because what he's really saying is, this is a one-night stand. That it's going to be short, like you said, remember? But you didn't even give me the chance, did you?" She'd found her skirt now, was yanking it around her hips, fastening the zip. "No, you made sure you got off first. *Then* you told me."

"Because I wanted to see you," he protested. "And because, when I *do* see you, I want to be with you."

"You see me, and you want to go to bed. Too bad we wasted time having dinner, then, isn't it? Sure you don't want to reconsider?" She pulled her top over her head, settling it into place with a few quick tugs. "Maybe we should just redefine our terms, huh? How about if we kept it to the occasional booty call? Would that work for you?"

"I wouldn't do that to you." He was getting up himself now, reaching for his own clothes. Starting to look mad, like he had some right to be. "I'm trying to do the right thing here. I'm trying to be fair. Not to disappoint you, have you expect something I don't have to give right now."

"Like love," she shot back. "Because that would be so *distracting,* wouldn't it? Do you really think you're going to do better, that the team's going to win every game if you just focus on rugby 24/7? If you don't give yourself anything else at all, even the chance to relax with somebody who loves you?"

She saw him flinch. "That's right," she told him. "I'm going to say the big, scary L-word again. I love you. And I want to help you, and I think I can. I think I *do.* You need to lighten up, Nate. You don't need to work harder, you need to work—easier. You need to take a break with somebody who loves you whether you win or lose, whether you're the captain or not. You can't be this... this lonely hero, doing everything by yourself, never sharing any of the load with anybody. You can't keep pushing, and pushing, and pushing yourself, or *you're* the one who's going to break."

She could see the controlled anger in every movement as he pulled on his pants with a jerk, yanked the zip up, fastened his belt with a final shove, then faced her across the big bed. Straight on, jaw set.

"You don't have a clue what it's like to be in my position," he told her, and there was none of the warmth he'd showed her in the past. Nothing at all there for her. "You have no idea how much focus it takes every week, how much effort it takes every *day* to do this job. What's it like to never be allowed to have a down day, an off day. To be so bloody tired and sore you can hardly put one foot in front of the other, and then to have to lift again, get your passion back, put your body back out there to do it all again. Every single bloody week, over and over again, ten months a year."

"Yes, I *do,*" she began to insist, but he interrupted her.

"You don't," he said. "You can't. And maybe," he added, his eyes as hard and cold as ice, "if you spent more time thinking about succeeding in your own life and less time worrying about mine, you might actually get somewhere yourself, wouldn't have to do it all through me."

"Oh, that's it, is it?" She knew that would hurt later, when she remembered it. She had to force herself to go on, to hurry and say this, because any moment now, she was going to start crying. "That I'm a loser who's never accomplished anything? I'm not good enough for the captain of the All Blacks? All right, I might not have much of a career, but at least I have relationships. I know how to love somebody, and be there for them. I know how to love *you.* And you can't even accept it. You can't even let me love you."

The tears were there, then, and not even her anger could quell them or the hurt that swamped her. Because what he was really saying was that he couldn't love her. That he didn't love her, and he was tired of pretending. She tried to wipe them away, tried to stop them falling, but she couldn't.

She sobbed once, twice. Tried to get herself back under control one more time, and failed again. Grabbed for her shoes, shoved them on.

"Ally," he said, and he looked so wretched that, despite herself, she felt sorry for him. Because she loved him, and even now, his pain was her own. "I'm sorry. I didn't want to hurt you. Let me take you home, and we'll talk tomorrow."

She shook her head blindly. She'd dropped her purse when they'd come in, she remembered. She took off fast down the stairs, heard his bare feet hitting the steps behind her. Found her purse in the entryway and reached for the door handle.

"I'll take you home," he said again. "It's late."

"No," she got out through her tears. "No." And she was out the door, down the steep flights of concrete stairs, swinging herself around the landings. Stopping to pull off the stupid high heels that she'd worn, trying to be a girl. Trying to be the kind of woman he'd want, the kind that would keep him interested. The kind he could fall in love with.

She held the shoes in one hand, ran barefoot down the concrete path, down onto the road, trying to move fast enough to leave the tears behind.

"Ally!" she heard Nate shout behind her, sounding furious. Another two blocks, and she could hear his car approaching, slowing to keep pace with her as he buzzed down the window.

"Get in the car," he said. "Right now."

"Go *away*," she got out, swiping a hand under her nose, not even caring that he saw her do it. "Leave me alone!"

"You can't run all the way home," he said, still pacing her. "You're not even wearing shoes, and it's too late. I'm only going to tell you once more. Get in the bloody car, or I'll put you there."

She'd reached the path through the park now, though. Was ducking onto it, picking up speed again as she raced down the hill. Running home. Running away.

And this time, he didn't come after her.

ups and downs

♡

Ally had slept at last, tears and emotion finally exhausting her, was still lying in bed when she was awakened by the sound of Liam and Kristen's voices in the bedroom next door. She thought about getting up, but quickly changed her mind as she heard the sound of dresser drawers opening and shutting, hangers clattering. Kristen packing, because Liam wanted her there with him as long as possible before he had to leave. Was bringing her here to change and pack a bag, probably taking her to work so he could pick her up again afterwards. So he could spend time with her.

The thought made the tears rise again, and she buried her face under the pillow so the two of them wouldn't hear her sobs. If Kristen saw her, she'd know. And Liam would know too, and they'd both feel sorry for her. When Kristen came home again, when they were alone, she'd tell her then.

A few minutes later, she heard the flat door closing. She got up, unable to sleep any longer. Pulled a dressing gown over the underwear that was all she had worn to bed, when she'd been too tired and dispirited to shower and change, even to wash her dirty feet, which felt truly disgusting by now. That was going to be her first job this morning, she vowed. Take a shower, and scrub her feet. Right after she got a cup of tea to help her wake up.

She went into the neat little kitchen, found a note on the table, penned in Kristen's loopy handwriting.

Hi Ally
I'll be at Liam's till they go.
Don't need the car, use it.
See you Thurs.—hope you had fun with N.
XXX Kristen

Oh, yeah. Fun.

♡

"Hey, roomie," Ally said when she came home from work Thursday night, grateful to find Kristen, at last, ensconced in her evening spot, curled up on the couch under a throw, watching an old movie on TV.

"Hi!" Kristen said, hastily getting up and coming over to give Ally a hug.

"Somebody's in a good mood," Ally smiled.

"Want to know why?"

"Why?" Ally played along. "Because you finally got rid of Liam?"

Kristen giggled. Actually giggled. She stood back from Ally and held out her left hand. "I'm engaged!"

"Wow," Ally said blankly. Then looked at Kristen's shining face, and laughed. "Wow! That's great! And wow again," she said, taking another look at the ring. "That thing's a pretty big reason to be happy all by itself. You could put somebody's eye out with that. Or come out way ahead in a street fight."

"Isn't it gorgeous?" Kristen demanded.

"Not a diamond, huh? I'm kind of surprised. Liam seems like a traditional guy. But that's, what, a sapphire?"

"Uh-huh," Kristen agreed, taking another peek at the ring herself, twisting it so the big stone reflected the light. Which

349

was also getting picked up pretty well, Ally noticed, in the many pavé diamonds winking brilliantly from the graduated ovals that made up the platinum band on either side. It really *was* beautiful.

"We both wanted something different," Kristen went on. "Something special for us, different from anything from…before. And he said," she sighed, "something that matched my eyes."

"He's a pretty romantic guy," Ally smiled, going over to sit on the couch with her friend, swiping a sip from her cup of herbal tea.

"He is," Kristen said happily. "Can I show you how he proposed? Would you want to see?"

"What?" Ally asked, startled. "He recorded it?"

"No," Kristen laughed. "But lots of other people did." She bounced up again, went for her laptop, and clicked on a link that, to Ally's amusement, she'd bookmarked.

"Just how many times have you watched this?" Ally teased.

"Well, not too many times before today," Kristen said. "Not when I had him right there with me. But today, since they left? Ummm, I'd call it…" She smiled. "Lots."

When Ally had watched it all the way through, then had Kristen start it over so she could watch it again, she could see why.

"Wow." She wiped the tears away with the back of her hand with a laugh, reached for Kristen and gave her a hug. "You do realize, of course, that men all over the world are cursing Liam's name right now. Because he's just reset the bar. "

"He's so wonderful, isn't he?" Kristen sighed. "I'm so lucky, I can't believe it. And I know I sound so sappy," she added with a little laugh. "But I can't help it. I just love him so much."

"That's great." Ally found that she really meant it. "That's wonderful. Have you talked about the wedding?"

"This summer, we thought, since we don't have to schedule too far ahead for people in the U.S. Hannah and Drew are already here, and my brother Matt never needs too much notice, He's always ready to quit a job to go someplace new. We're thinking December, after the All Blacks get back from the European Tour. And at Liam's marae, though Hannah and Drew offered their place, of course. But Liam says his mother would never forgive him if it wasn't at the marae, And a Maori wedding—won't that be terrific?"

"Hannah must be thrilled for you," Ally said.

"She is," Kristen assured her, and Ally thought that Kristen's smile, when she was truly happy, could light up a room. Liam was a lucky man.

"And it's so good," Kristen said earnestly, "to know that I'm making her happy too, after all the years she's worried about me. To know that she doesn't have to worry about me any more. Now we can be better friends than ever, I hope, now that we'll be... the same."

"That's great," Ally said again, wishing she had something better to offer.

"But I'm being so selfish," Kristen said, clearly recalling herself. "I haven't asked anything about you. I was hoping I'd see you at the airport today, dropping Nate off. You couldn't get the time off?"

"No. Well, yeah. I mean, I couldn't. But that wasn't why." Ally swallowed. This would be the first time she'd said it, and it was going to be hard, she could tell. "Nate and I broke up."

"Broke *up?*" Kristen asked, her hand going to her mouth. Kristen was the only woman Ally knew who actually gasped. Kristen was the total girl.

The thought crossed Ally's mind that if Nate had met Kristen first, maybe things would have been different. Liam had certainly fallen for her hook, line, and sinker. *Liam* wasn't conflicted about mixing rugby and love. Liam could even say the word. She'd just heard him do it.

"What happened?" Kristen went on, her eyes full of concern.

Ally shrugged helplessly. "Just the same old thing. That he needs to focus on rugby. Well, really," she forced herself to say, and felt her throat closing around the words, "that he just doesn't...he doesn't l-l-love me."

It was such a relief to have Kristen there this time to hold her, to soothe her while she cried. She hadn't done it—well, much—since that miserable Monday, but it seemed that she'd been storing up the tears until she had somebody to share them with.

When she'd got home Sunday night, the empty flat had seemed to mock her in her loneliness. And Nate, texting her to make sure she'd made it home all right—that had just been another mockery, another pale, watered-down imitation. She didn't want him to feel responsible, to do what was right. She wanted him to love her, and he didn't, and that was all there was to it.

"I couldn't even afford to go out and drink too much, like a normal person," she said with a watery laugh after she'd cried herself out, told Kristen the story. She blew her nose again. "I thought about going to New World for some cheap wine, but getting drunk here alone—that would just be too pathetic. Anyway, I need to start saving. I only just got Nate's birthday weekend paid off, and I'm not going to have anybody buying groceries any more, or taking me out."

"And here I've been," Kristen said in distress, "going on and on about how happy I am. I wish I'd known, so I could have been more sensitive. I'm so sorry."

"Don't be," Ally assured her. "Hearing about you and Liam doesn't make me sad. Thinking about Nate and me, that makes me sad, but hearing about you? That makes me feel better."

♡

Being angry at Nate, and sad about what had happened, Ally found, didn't make watching the All Blacks lose to the Springboks in South Africa any easier. She hadn't wanted to get up in the wee hours with Kristen to watch the game, hadn't wanted to care so much. But, in the end, she had, because she hadn't been able to sleep. And then had wished she hadn't.

"That's going to make it awfully hard for them to win the Championship, isn't it?" Kristen asked when the referee finally blew his whistle to end a game in which the huge Springboks forwards had simply out-muscled the All Blacks. The kicking had been a bright spot, though, Nic Wilkinson, the fullback, making all but one of his attempts. And, again, it had been close, although Ally knew what Nate would have said. That close was nice, but a loss was a loss.

"They can still do it," Ally said. "But with two losses now… it's sure going to make it harder."

defending nate

♡

A lly stood back to check a newbie's belay technique, stepped
forward with a word, an adjustment of the hand, the rope,
then swept the gym with her eyes, making one of the constant
checks that were such an important part of her job. Until the
conversation of the two men next to her, putting their harnesses
on, distracted her. Because they were talking, she realized, about
the game.

"Don't know what the selectors were thinking, choosing
him," one of them, a burly guy she recognized all too well from
his past visits, was saying loudly. "All right, he's a pretty good
second-five, but he's rubbish as a skipper. Rubbish on the Canes,
rubbish on the ABs."

"To be fair on him, though," the other man answered more
mildly, "losing the blokes they have this year hasn't helped. And
a downturn the year after a team wins the World Cup, that's happened before, eh. Look at the Boks themselves, last time they won
it. Lost the Tri-Nations pretty comprehensively the next year."

"Didn't happen to the ABs last time," Burly Boy insisted.
"Won every game but one the next season. It's all down to the
skipper. He pulls the squad up, or he drags them down. Truth
is, there've been weak spots on the ABs for years now, and we're
finally seeing the results. Having Callahan there has masked it,

though he was past his sell-by date the last year or two. Still a bloody good skipper, though, kept them punching above their weight. Now he's gone, and they're not. Simple as that."

"Really?" Ally couldn't help herself. Her hands were shaking, and she could feel the hot rage rising inside, impossible to quell. She took a step towards the men as they turned to her in surprise. "You really think that's the reason, that it's his fault? It's his first season as captain! How do you think Drew did his first season? Did he win every game? And who do you imagine would be able to do a better job than Nate? Seeing as they've lost their best loose forwards, and the best first five-eighths in the game too? How's one man supposed to make up for all that?"

"That's the skipper's job, to make up for it," the big man said impatiently, "and everyone knows it. If you'd read John Farrell's column today, you'd know it too. The stats don't lie. Have you looked at the ladder, by any chance? Are you blind, that you haven't seen how out of form they are? All those handling errors? How shocking the set piece is looking?"

"I don't care what some columnist says," Ally flared back. She'd read it too, and her resentment had been simmering ever since. "Farrell's always down on the All Blacks. I don't think he believes half of what he says anyway. He's just trying to stir up controversy. I'd like to see him, or you for that matter, go out there and do anything close to what those guys do every single day. I'd like to see *you* put your body on the line for New Zealand, week in and week out, the way Nate does. Then you might have some room to talk."

"Gets paid a bloody fortune for it too," the big man scoffed. "It's not a charity. You pay me close to a million a year, you'll see how much I'm willing to do for New Zealand. And what d'you imagine you know about it anyway? Some Yank girl thinking she's going to set Kiwis right about the All Blacks? Blow that for a joke."

"I know a whole lot more about it than you!" Ally was trembling now. She felt her hands fisting at her sides, itched to smash the smirk right off this jerk's face. His friend was looking a little worried, she saw, as he gave a yank to the other man's arm.

"Pull your head in, mate," he cautioned. "Don't want to have a stoush with a girl. Let's climb, eh."

Robbo was at Ally's side now, alerted by the rising voices. "What's going on?" he asked her.

"Your little friend here reckons she knows more about rugby than Kiwis do, that's what," Ally's opponent said. "Bloody arrogant Americans. Stick to gridiron," he told Ally contemptuously. "Maybe you know something about that, though I doubt it. You probably just like how the boys look in their tight jerseys."

"Well, she does know a bit about it, for all that," Robbo said, putting himself between Ally and the two men. "Seeing as she's Nate Torrance's partner."

That brought the other man up short, but he wasn't one to stay down for long. "What I said," he insisted after a moment. "Tight jerseys. Or tight something else, maybe," he added with a smirk.

He would have said more, but his friend was there again, speaking quietly and urgently, herding him off.

Meanwhile, Robbo had Ally by the arm, was pulling her away, towards the entrance.

"Ally. Stop," he hissed as she twisted against him. "Mac's looking. Go to the toilet. Go. I'll take care of it."

She came back to herself, looked up to see Mac's hard gaze on her, and cast a quick, horrified glance at Robbo, who gave her a push in the direction of the toilets.

"Go," he said again. "Right now."

She took a few steps, looked back to see Robbo approaching the two men, his hands spread wide in a gesture of conciliation. She turned and walked blindly to the toilet, hit the swinging door with a violent burst that wasn't enough for her, so she smashed the side of her fist into the wall.

"*Ow!*" It was a strangled wail. Because that hurt like *hell.* Why did guys *do* that? It was just *stupid.* She stomped a circular path in the tiny space, shaking out her hand and muttering every swear word she knew.

And was brought up short by the sound of the toilet flushing, the stall door opening.

"All right?"

Ally stood holding her hand, staring blankly at the vaguely familiar fortyish woman, an occasional lunchtime climber, who was looking at her with concern, edging toward the sink a bit cautiously, as though Ally might be dangerous.

"Oh! Uh...yeah," Ally said. "Yeah. Sorry. Just...just rehearsing," she improvised wildly. "Practicing." She tried a smile. "Sorry."

The woman finished washing her hands, reached for a paper towel. "I'd say you've got it," she said with a smile of her own. "I'd say you're good."

Well, no, she wasn't. But she was better.

♡

She came out again a few minutes later, after a soak of her sore hand in cold water and a stern internal talking-to. *Without* swear words. The two guys were climbing in a distant corner, she saw with relief. She saw Robbo over by the training wall, went to join him.

"All right?" he asked.

"Yeah. Thanks. Sorry."

"No worries. He's a bloody idiot, always has been. But you need to watch yourself. Can't attack the customers, you know, or you'll get the sack."

"Did Mac say something?" she asked nervously.

"I took care of it. Gave them a card for a free session, told them you had PMT. Sorry," he went on hastily at her outraged glance. "It was the only thing I could think of at the moment. It worked, anyway. And I gave Mac some nonsense about them not wanting to take advice from a girl."

"Thanks," she said again.

"No dramas. But you can't fight Nate's battles, you know. He wouldn't want you to, I'm sure. Part of the job, getting rubbished in the press. Don't tell him you did that, is my advice. He's a pretty proud bloke. He won't like it."

"He won't know. Or care. We broke up," she admitted at Robbo's sharp look.

"So why are you defending him, exactly?"

She sighed. "Because I can't help it."

"Ah." He nodded, and Ally could tell that he knew what that meant. That Nate had broken up with her, and that she still loved him anyway. But all he said was, "Bugger. Breaking up's the shits."

She had to laugh a little in spite of herself. "Yep. It sure is."

the internet is forever

♡

Was she showing something she shouldn't? Ally wondered a few days later. Or did she look better than she felt? Because it seemed like half the guys who'd walked into the gym this morning had taken an extra look at her, or downright stared. At first she'd been flattered, but now she was just confused.

She finally murmured a word to Robbo and ducked into the toilet to check. She looked carefully in the mirror. No food on her face, no sudden acne eruption, and she wasn't wearing anything with a zipper that could have been undone. Sports bra, tank top, climbing pants, check. She bared her teeth. Nothing on them, either.

She didn't look fabulous, but she didn't look all *that* bad, so that couldn't be it. A little tired, maybe, a little shadowed around the eye area. Which was no wonder, because once again, she hadn't slept well the night before. She'd thought it had been hard having Nate away on a road trip when they'd been together. That was nothing to how hard it felt now, knowing he wasn't coming back to her. Her chest tightened at the thought. At least she wasn't crying anymore, but maybe it still showed. Maybe those guys had never seen a woman suffering from unrequited love before. Nobody in love with *them*, anyway. Ha. That was probably it.

She had to smile a little at the idea, grimaced at herself in the mirror, splashed a little water on her face, dried her hands, and went back out into the gym. And found Robbo standing with a couple of their regulars.

The men broke off their conversation abruptly at the sight of her, moved apart. The climbers headed over to one of the walls, and Robbo went to the box of returned climbing shoes, began to sort through them.

"What's going on?" Ally asked, coming over to join him, picking up a pair of shoes and the can of disinfectant, giving each one a spray.

"What do you mean?" Robbo continued to sort shoes, not meeting her eyes.

"Why is everyone looking at me?" Ally pressed. "Because they are, aren't they?"

"You haven't heard, then." He glanced up at her, then back down again, looking truly uncomfortable now. "What's been happening online."

"Somebody reported that Nate and I broke up," Ally said with resignation. "Is that it?"

"No. Don't think anyone knows that. That was the point of it, wasn't it?"

"The point of *what?*" she asked in exasperation. "What the heck is going on?"

"Bloody hell," he said. "I don't want to be the one to tell you, I really don't."

"Tell me what?" she demanded. "Do it now. Whatever it is."

Robbo sighed. "There are some…photos of you, and they've got your name on. On Facebook, Twitter, like that. Don't know where they got started."

"Photos of me," she repeated with puzzlement. "With Nate, you mean? Why would that be a big deal?"

"No. Not with Nate. With some other bloke. And, Ally. You're naked in them. And…having sex."

"I'm *naked?*" She felt the blood drain from her head, found herself wrapping her arms around her suddenly chilled body as her fuzzy brain tried to process the information. "How can that be? Who is it? The guy?"

"Don't know." Robbo was looking more uncomfortable than ever. "Dark hair, they said. That's why it's obvious it's not Nate."

"It can't be me either, then, whatever it says online," she said with relief. She and Brian had never taken naked pictures, and anyway, his hair was light brown, like Nate's.

"Somebody's put my name on some porno pictures and shared them," she realized. "Trying to cause trouble for Nate and me, not realizing they didn't need to bother. Because it's too late anyway."

Although knowing it wasn't her in the photos wouldn't help that much with the embarrassment, actually. Not if it was big enough news that every guy at the gym seemed to know about it. But only because they knew her personally, and how many people did? Hardly anyone.

"They're pretty sure, Ally," Robbo said gently.

"Well, it can't be," she repeated firmly. "Because I haven't posed for any naked pictures. Ever. Unless they photoshopped my face in." The thought sent a shaft of anxiety through her. "That would be an awful lot of work, though," she decided, "and they'd still need a picture of me to do it. Who would bother?"

"Never sexted?" Robbo pressed. "Never sent some bloke a snap?"

"Of course not," she said impatiently. "What, do you think I'm stupid? The Internet is forever. Every woman with two functioning brain cells to rub together knows that by now."

"Hope you're right," he said with relief. "Course, I haven't looked, and I won't."

"Thanks," she said with real gratitude. "You're a good friend, and a good man."

He looked a bit embarrassed at that. But they didn't manage any more conversation, because Mac had walked over to join them.

"What d'you think this is, bloody happy hour?" he barked. "Not paying you to chat. Ally, didn't you notice those new blokes, waiting for a training session? Get over there and get to it."

"Sure," she said distractedly, walking across the gym toward the two guys standing near the low wall. Who were both looking at her with interest, then exchanging a glance. Just like the guys she was passing now, the ones who'd inspired her little meltdown on Monday. The big one smirking openly, the other looking a little embarrassed.

This was either somebody's idea of a sick joke, or maybe a former girlfriend out to cause trouble. But as soon as people knew she wasn't dating Nate anymore, she reminded herself, trying her very best not to cringe, there'd be no story, and this would all be over.

♡

"Naked pictures?" Kristen asked in horror when Ally's shift had ended and she'd climbed the hill to the flat.

"Yeah," Ally said with a sigh, going for her laptop and setting it on the kitchen table. "So I guess we'd better check, see how much they actually do look like me. And figure out what to do. Not that I can imagine there's much I *can* do."

She waited the several minutes it always took for her computer to boot up, her heart beating harder despite the reassurances she'd been giving herself all day. She needed a new laptop, she thought irrelevantly. Ha. Like that was happening. Her parents had bought her this one when she'd graduated from college six years ago, making it an antique, and with performance to match.

Finally, though, it was up and she was online. She took a deep breath, typed "Allison Villiers" into the search bar, and hit the return key.

More seconds, and then the results. At least a page of them, she saw at a glance, and probably a lot more. An exclamation of distress from Kristen, and Ally clicked on the first, a blog post referencing a tweet. She clicked on that, came up with "Allison Villiers Nate Torrance gf #AllyNudiePix." Well, that was clear enough.

And then the link came up, and it was clearer than that. Ally scrolled down the group of three pictures. And if she'd been cold before, she was frozen now.

Because it was her. On her back, taken from overhead, her face clearly visible. In one of the pictures, the man's head was at her breast, and she couldn't have said who it was, but she knew all the same, even before she looked at the second one, where his face was in profile. Devon. And there was absolutely no doubt what the two of them were doing.

"Oh, my God," Kristen breathed. "Oh, Ally."

Ally heard herself making a sound that didn't even sound human, a whimper like a wounded animal. And then she was running for the bathroom, reaching the toilet just in time. Dropping to her knees and dry-heaving. No lunch to come up, she realized as she continued to retch. She hadn't been able to eat, and she hadn't even known it was true.

She stayed where she was for long minutes, her stomach continuing to contract in painful spasms, her eyes filling with tears that dripped into the porcelain bowl. Kristen was there, holding her hair, murmuring something soothing. But Ally barely heard her.

♡

She had the early shift the next morning. Well, she thought, climbing out of bed on legs that felt like lead, she'd get it over with fast. And today would be the worst day. After that, she'd be used to it. You could get used to anything, she'd heard. Besides, the public attention span was short. In another week or two, this would be old news, some new scandal arising to take its place. She'd just have to suck it up and tough it out. She could do that.

So much for starting over in New Zealand. Kristen seemed to have done it, but all Ally had managed recently was a whole lot of crying into her pillow, which wasn't like her at all. She was going to change that, she vowed. Starting today.

She was surprised to find Mac at the gym when she showed up. He usually didn't come in until ten or so. She murmured a hello, went to stash her gear behind the counter where he was standing.

"Need to have a chat with you," he said. "My office."

Oh, boy. Ally followed him into the tiny space, moved a few file folders off the straight chair, and sat down as he seated himself at the metal desk opposite. Maybe he was giving her a raise. Yeah, right. He wasn't giving her a raise.

Mac cleared his throat, reached for an envelope sitting next to his computer. "I wanted to tell you that I'm letting you go. You know," he hurried on at her look of shock, "it's winter, and there just isn't enough work to go round."

"I've been here the longest, though," she got out. "And I'm the most reliable. I've never missed a shift. I've never even been late. And you need a woman on staff."

"Think I know what I need better than you do," he said curtly. He handed the envelope across, and she found herself taking it. "Here's your final statement. Your pay's already been transferred into your account."

"This has to do with those photos," she realized. "Doesn't it?"

"Nah," he said, shifting a little in his seat. "Like I said. Staffing."

"It does," she insisted. "It totally does. Those pictures were taken without my consent. I haven't done anything wrong. I'm the *victim* here. I know who posted them, and he did it either to embarrass me, or more likely, to embarrass Nate. But it doesn't matter anyway," she went on, and hated the pleading tone in her voice, "because Nate and I broke up. So this is a nine days' wonder, that's all."

"This isn't open for discussion," Mac said. He stood, gestured for her to stand as well. Ally obeyed, found herself moving to the door. Mac reached for her bag under the counter, handed it to her. And in another minute, she was standing outside the gym. Fired.

♡

Darkness had filled her bedroom by the time she heard Kristen's key in the lock. She thought for a fleeting moment about getting out of bed, then abandoned the idea. It just seemed way too hard. She registered the sound of Kristen moving around the flat, managed to turn her head when she heard the tentative "Ally?" from the doorway.

"You OK?" Kristen asked with concern, coming across the room to perch on the edge of the bed beside her. Laying the back of her hand across Ally's forehead. "Are you sick? No wonder, you poor thing."

Ally closed her eyes and swallowed against the lump in her throat. She'd thought she'd done all the crying a human possibly could, but it seemed she was wrong. She felt the ticklish tears inching into her hair, dripping into her ears. "I got fired," she got out.

"*Fired?*" Kristen asked incredulously. "When? Today? Because of the...the thing?"

Ally nodded, tried to stop the tears. "As soon as I got in. I've never been...I've never been fired. And it hurts so *much*."

"Oh, Ally," Kristen said, and the sympathy in her voice just made Ally cry harder. Kristen reached for her, pulled her up against her, and Ally let it all go yet again.

She'd walked back home, still numb, and booted up her laptop. Had spent hours unable to keep herself from endlessly refreshing, morbidly fascinated as the hits increased. Reading the blog posts and comments, many of them vindictively pleased and downright vicious. "Skanky" was particularly favored, she'd found. She hadn't realized how unpopular the new All Black captain's association with yet another North American would be in certain quarters, but she sure knew now.

The pain of knowing that she was adding to Nate's burdens made her feel even worse. The posts that talked about his poor judgment, blamed the team's losses on his lack of focus. She'd longed with an overwhelming ferocity to respond, to defend Nate, to defend herself, to explain. Had had to force her fingers away from the keys to keep herself from doing it, because she was pretty sure that would only make things worse.

And then there was the rage at Devon, boiling over at intervals throughout the day like lava, red-hot and corrosive. And, to a lesser extent, at Mac. So much anger, and nothing to do with it, no place for it to go. She'd found herself wanting to call her mother, to crawl into the security of her love and concern, but the thought of her parents seeing those pictures, how horrified and disappointed they would be…No, that hadn't been an option.

"How could Devon do that?" she asked Kristen when she could speak again, taking the handful of Kleenex she offered and doing her best to mop up. "What did I ever do to him?"

"Some people are just angry," Kristen said, stroking Ally's hair, smoothing it back from her tear-streaked face. "Everything's somebody else's fault. And I think Devon's one of them. But it'll be OK," she soothed. "This'll blow over, and you'll get another job. Everything will be OK."

"Oh," she remembered. "I need to show you something." She left the room, came back with her purse, pulled out her mobile. "A text for you from Liam."

Ally took the phone from her, did her best to focus on the tiny characters.

Tell Ally: Kia kaha.

"It means, be strong," Kristen said.

"I know. That was sweet of him. But, Kristen, if he sent you that…It means Nate probably knows too." Which was the thought that had hurt most of all today, even more than being fired. Even more than the prospect of looking for another job, knowing that anywhere she applied, they'd know about this. If not as soon as they saw her name, at least as soon as they did a computer search for it.

But none of that was the worst. The worst was envisioning Nate going online and seeing her like that. Her mind shied away yet again from the thought. "Have you talked to Liam?" she asked Kristen instead.

"Not yet. We have a call scheduled for late tonight. So hard with the time difference."

"I heard from Robbo." Ally pulled herself up against the pillows and battled to shake off some of the cloud of misery that had enshrouded her all day. "He texted me, wants to meet me for lunch tomorrow. I probably shouldn't, though," she realized. "I need to save my money."

She'd turned her phone off, she remembered. Reached under the pillow for it and checked. A string of voicemail messages that she wouldn't be answering, the reason she'd turned the phone off in the first place. Journalists from both New Zealand and Australia, wanting her reaction. A text from Lachlan saying how upset everyone at the gym had been at the news, which was nice of him. And one from Nate.

I heard. Phone you as soon as I can.

Well, that was one conversation she definitely wasn't having. Call her a coward, but she just couldn't do it. She texted quickly back.

Sorry about it. Don't call me. Good luck on Sat.

"Don't tell Liam I lost my job," she begged Kristen. "I don't want Nate to know."

"Ally…"

"Please. Promise me. It would upset him, I know, and what's the point? All this is going to be hard enough on him, and it's not like there's anything he can do about it. At least don't tell Liam until they're back here. I mean, obviously it won't be a secret at that point. Please? Wait till then?"

"OK," Kristen said reluctantly.

"Thanks," Ally sighed. "And that's all the nobility I've got. Maybe by tomorrow," she said, the tears closing her throat again, "I'll be able to think of some alternative to just lying down and dying, you think?"

"Oh, sweetie," Kristen said. "I know you will."

finding ally

♡

Nate tried ringing Ally again as soon as the plane landed. No voicemail greeting this time. Instead, a recording telling him that her number was no longer in service. Had she changed it, then? He shuddered to think of her humiliation, the harassment she must have undergone. He had a publicist who could say "no comment"—and had—but Ally didn't have anybody. She certainly hadn't had him.

He drove from the airport, and realized as he pulled into the garage that he couldn't remember a moment of the journey. He walked in his door, dropped his duffel, carried his pack into the kitchen and pulled out his laptop, waited impatiently for it to connect. Still no answer to the first email he'd sent, and the second had bounced. She'd changed her email too, then.

At first, when Mako had broken the news, Nate hadn't believed it. He'd been pretty gutted anyway, he'd had to admit, the entire time he'd been gone. Well, to be honest, before then too. Ever since Ally had left. Ever since she'd run away from him.

He'd thought about chasing her, that night. Had actually pulled over, got out of the car. Then stopped himself. What was he going to do when he caught her? Carry her back, fighting all the way, force her into the car? Kidnap her? She'd broken up with him. It was killing him to think about her running all the way home, barefoot and cold, this late at night. But it was his own bloody fault. He'd stuffed up with her about as badly as it was possible to do. Again.

And then there'd been all the time since. Each long evening stretching ahead of him, nothing but work to fill it. That's what he'd thought he wanted, so why did it feel so...empty?

He'd never been lonely before this year, but it was different now. Now he kept finding himself wishing he could text Ally, could see the cheerful, saucy replies that always made him smile, gave him a little lift. That he had her funny, sweet emails to read at night, before he went to sleep. That he could phone her, no matter how inconvenient the time differences were, hear her voice, just have a chat. He hadn't realized how much he'd come to count on that simple contact, but he had. He definitely had, and it had made him begin to wonder if he'd made a mistake after all. Especially when he remembered her face. How devastated she'd been. How she'd cried. How she'd run. Every time he thought about it—and he thought about it much too often—he ached.

He'd tried to set it aside as something to think about later, once the two tough matches were behind him. Had gone through the motions of the various outings and PR moments, called on his considerable willpower to focus on the training sessions, the game plan. But when Mako had showed him those photos on Thursday night in the hotel, forced at last to do it when nothing less would convince him...there was no amount of discipline in the world that could've helped him, those next few hours.

"Sorry, mate," Mako had apologized. "I wouldn't have told you at all, not till after the match, but I was afraid somebody else would mention it, specially some journo, and you wouldn't be prepared. And the other boys...some of them will've heard. Well, to be honest, probably all of them. Thought it was better to let you know now, give you some time to process."

Nate had texted Ally that night, seen her text in return the next morning. Had tried to phone all the same, and got her voicemail. Had left a message that she hadn't answered. Mako had told him she wasn't doing too badly, and that had helped a little, but not much. Going out for the Captain's Run on Friday, preparing for the game the next day had been the greatest test of his self-discipline he'd ever faced.

He'd done it, in the end. Had compartmentalized with everything he had, channeled all his anger into his performance, tackled with a ferocity to match the Pumas' own, and somehow, probably through his teammates' efforts rather than his own, come out with the win. And afterwards, had been so shattered that he'd barely managed the postgame interviews, the journey back to the hotel.

It hadn't been until he was on the plane again that it had all really hit him. When there was no game to prepare for, no distraction from the anger and the pain. And the concern for Ally, so strong now that he could barely hold still, let alone sleep off the post-match aches and fatigue as most of his teammates were doing.

He'd slept, finally, hadn't been able to deny his body the rest it needed. But his dreams had been chaotic and troubled, and he'd woken still heavy-eyed and unrefreshed, had gone through VIP Customs in Auckland like a zombie, operating on remote, his responses automatic. Had sat in the Koru Lounge in the Auckland Airport drinking one coffee after another, trying to wake himself up. By the time the attendant had told the four of them that the rest of the aircraft to Wellington was loaded and they could board, he'd been some kind of bizarre mixture of fatigue and jitters.

And now he was home. He still hadn't showered, hadn't changed out of the clothes he'd been wearing now for—what?— nearly twenty-four hours. His body was heavy, aching with fatigue from the restless flights, the residue of the match. But he couldn't waste any more time. He needed to find Ally. So he trotted down the steps, back into the garage. Climbed into his car, and headed to her flat.

He stood for minutes in front of the building, ringing the bell. At first he'd thought she was ignoring it. But after the tenth or twelfth time, he had to concede that she must not be home.

At work, he realized, could have smacked his forehead at the dullness of his thought processes. Of course. It was the middle of the afternoon, and she was at work.

Back in the car, down to the CBD. The frustrating circling to find a spot in a carpark, then jogging to the waterfront, along to the familiar door. Ally's photo wasn't on the notice board anymore, he realized. Why was that? Mac taking it down because of all the publicity? He was just as glad. He hated to think of blokes coming in here to have a squiz at her, after seeing...that.

He stepped inside, looked around. Couldn't see her, but maybe she was in the back. He noticed Mac at the front desk, saw the smile of recognition, and went to meet him.

"Good to see you, mate," Mac said. "Didn't realize you were back. Congrats on the win. Pretty convincing. Good to see the squad fizzing again. You had a good game, too."

Nate brushed the greeting aside. "Ally here?" he asked, not caring if he sounded abrupt. And saw the shift in the other man's eyes, the way he looked down at the papers on the desk, lifted a binder and put it down again.

"Nah," Mac said. "Not working here anymore, mate."

"Since when?" Nate demanded.

"Been a few days now."

"Where did she go, then?" Nate pressed. "Another job? What?"

Mac shrugged. "Can't help you, I'm afraid." And, Nate saw, he really couldn't. He turned in frustration, headed for the door again.

"Nate." He heard the low voice, turned to see Robbo, sorting out harnesses.

"Looking for Ally?" Robbo asked, not looking up, his hands still busy.

"Yeh. Know where she is?"

The young Australian shook his head. "Got the sack," he said economically. "Himself," he said with a jerk of his head toward the counter, "thought she was hurting the gym's image. And since he knew you'd broken up with her..." He shrugged. "Said she was a liability."

Nate felt sick. Everything seemed to catch up to him. His part in all this, his responsibility for it weighed him down like a 115-kilo prop lying on top of him in the breakdown, and he couldn't shove it off again.

"Cheers," he said blankly to Robbo, and headed for his car again.

Kristen, he thought. Kristen would know where she was. Bound to. Ally might have taken refuge with Hannah and Drew, he thought suddenly. That would have been like them, to offer her a place. Yeh, that could be it. He just had to find Kristen and ask her. And then go after Ally.

♡

"What d'you mean, you don't know?" he asked in frustration half an hour later.

He'd leaned on Mako's doorbell till he had finally answered, wearing nothing but a pair of pajama bottoms and appearing as menacing as only an enraged Maori could, short on sleep and interrupted in the middle of making up for lost time with his fiancée. If Mako hadn't been his best mate, Nate would actually have been a bit scared. As it was, Mako had finally taken pity on him, allowed him in as far as the lounge, then disappeared to get Kristen, who was sitting on the couch now beside Mako in her dressing gown, hair disheveled and looking a bit worried herself.

"I mean I don't know," she repeated. "I'm sorry, Nate. She got fired from her job, and she was in pretty bad shape. I tried to get her to stay here, in the flat I mean, in Wellington, because I didn't like the way she looked, but she said no. Then I suggested that she go up and stay at Hannah and Drew's bach for a week or two, give her some time to decide what to do. Hannah offered," she explained, giving Nate another stab of guilt to go with the arrows that were piercing him everywhere now. "But she said she had to go. That there was nothing left for her here. That it was just too hard."

"So she flew back home," Nate said. "Home where? To Calgary?"

"No," Kristen said. "To San Francisco. The Bay Area, where she was living before. She thought she could get a job there."

"But where's she staying?" Nate pressed.

"I don't *know,*" Kristen insisted.

"Don't know?" Nate barked. "Or won't tell me? I need to know. Tell me."

"I—" Kristen started to say, but Mako was there first.

"She doesn't know." He had risen to stand in front of Kristen, was glaring down at Nate. "Talk to her like that again and you're out of my house." His voice wasn't any louder than usual, but the look on his face couldn't have been clearer.

"Sorry," Nate said, raising his palms. "Sorry. I'm just—I don't know where I am. I don't know what to think."

And that's when it hit him, like the hardest blow to the chest he'd ever received. It literally took his breath away.

He was in love with Ally. He wasn't just concerned about her, or feeling guilty that this had happened to her, or even feeling empty and forlorn, as he had before, because he'd had an awesome girlfriend and now he didn't. No, he felt like shit because he loved her, and he needed her, and he'd thrown her away. And she was hurting now, paying the price for being involved with him, and he couldn't see how to fix it. And he was afraid he'd never get her back.

Mako looked at him soberly, nodded once, sat down again.

Nate tried to focus. "If you don't know, you don't know," he said to Kristen. "But sooner or later, she'll tell you, won't she?"

"I think so," Kristen said slowly. "It's hard for me to say, because I've never seen Ally like this. She's always so cheerful, so optimistic. She always...bounces. But all that was knocked out of her, I think. Just too many things, one after the other."

"Life can do that," Mako said. "One blow too many."

"Yeah," Kristen sighed. "I think that was it. But she has to get me her new email address eventually, and her physical address too, or I won't be able to forward anything. Mail, you know. Tax stuff."

One blow too many. Bloody hell, it hurt to hear that. "When she does," Nate said, "will you tell me? Please?"

"I don't want to see her hurt any more," Kristen said hesitantly.

"I won't be trying to hurt her. I made a mistake, and I need to tell her that. If I talk to her, and she doesn't want me any-more," he said, swallowing against the thought of it, "I'll leave her alone, I promise. I won't harass her. But I do need to talk to her. To find out how she feels. To tell her how I feel."

Kristen hesitated, looked quickly at Mako.

"Your choice," he said gently. "Toro means it, but you're the one who knows her best. Your choice."

Thanks, mate, Nate thought bitterly. No question where Mako's loyalties lay. Kristen would never be in any doubt of that.

Kristen nodded with decision. "When I hear from her," she promised Nate, "I'll let you know. Everyone makes mistakes, I know that. Sometimes you just need a second chance. I'll help you get yours, if I can."

on international boulevard

♡

Nate turned the corner at the prompting of the GPS, muttering, "Right, keep right," as he had been ever since he'd exited the freeway in Oakland. He could have concentrated better if he hadn't been distracted by the group of young men loitering outside the corner liquor store, the graffiti marking every available bit of wall. He was glad the fella at the hire car place had insisted on the GPS, when Nate had told him where he was going.

"You don't want to risk getting lost," the man had cautioned. "The motels there are cheap, I know," he said, giving Nate a quick inspection, clearly unimpressed by the rumpled, unshaven bloke standing before him in a T-shirt and jeans. "But you get what you pay for. You really don't want to be staying on International Boulevard. It's not, like, *International,* classy or something, like you might be thinking. Spend a little more, stay someplace else. My advice."

"I can take care of myself," Nate said.

"You look like you can," the man agreed. "But we're not talkin' fistfight here. We're talkin' guns."

"I promise not to get shot," Nate said impatiently. "Or to let the car get shot either. Just give me the bloody thing, would you?"

Now, he saw what the man had meant. And this was where Ally was living? His gut clenched at the thought.

He hoped she was home. It was just after two in the afternoon. Kristen had said that Ally had found a job, so who knew. If Nate had lived in this neighborhood, he wouldn't have spent a minute more here than he had to. But then again, if Ally was living in this neighborhood, it was because she couldn't afford anything else, so her entertainment options during her time off might be limited.

"Destination is on the right," the GPS prompted, and Nate eased to the curb, shifted into Park. A wooden-framed house, its stark lines unadorned by any trim or embellishment, painted white much too long ago and divided into flats. Iron bars on the narrow windows, front garden concreted over like most on the street to allow more parking. None of the trees he'd seen on other streets, some of their leaves changing now. Just a bit of rubbish blowing down the road in the crisp autumn breeze.

Nate shoved the GPS unit into the glove box and got out, taking care to lock the doors behind him, walked up the uneven pavement, the four cracked concrete steps. Two doors, one to the downstairs flat, the other to the upstairs, he guessed. She was A. Downstairs, then. Worse and worse. He pressed the button. And waited.

♡

Ally heard the doorbell, got up off her narrow bed with a sigh. She'd been doing some online research, dismayed by the cost of every program she'd found. But this was her future, she reminded herself as she walked past the kitchen that her new roommates never seemed to clean, through the depressingly messy living room—the reason she spent most of her free time in her bedroom—toward the insistent bell, ringing again now. She was going to be investing in herself. Anything worth having was worth working for. And, she hoped, worth going into debt for. Because she needed to do this, and she needed to do it herself.

She bent cautiously to the peephole drilled into the cheap, hollow wooden door. She wasn't expecting anybody, and the last occupants of the flat had apparently not been any too savory. Some of their former associates—or customers—hadn't got the news that their pals had been evicted, and continued to show up from time to time. She'd started being careful on Day One, and had only grown more so. Man, she hated being poor.

She focused on the peephole, took a look. Stood up fast, then bent to look again, jumped at the sound of the doorbell as he pressed it yet again. Out there looking impatient, and big, and furious, and like...Nate. Her heart was pounding at the sight of him. At how good he looked. At how *mad* he looked.

She jumped again as his fist hit the door. All right, then. Stop staring at him and open it. See what he wanted. Why he was here. Why he was *here.*

She twisted the locks, her fingers fumbling a little, swung the door wide, and there he was. Unshaven, eyes like two chips of ice, square jaw set, mouth hard.

"Nate," she said, then remembered to take a breath. "What are you doing here?"

He stepped inside, forcing her to take a couple rapid steps back, and slammed the door behind him. "What I want to know," he said grimly, "is what the bloody hell *you're* doing here."

"What?" she asked in confusion. "I live here."

"Why?" he demanded.

"Why? What do you mean, why?"

"Why here?" he asked, still looking much too big and angry. "Is this the best you could do?"

"On my budget? Well, yes. It is."

"Kristen said you were working, though."

"And saving," she agreed. "And this is cheap."

"I'll bet," he muttered. "Where are you working?"

"Emeryville. Next town up," she elaborated. "The climbing gym there."

He nodded again, a quick jerk of the head. "Can we sit down?"

"Uh..." She looked around. She didn't want to take him into her bedroom, so it was going to be here. "Sure." She sat on the couch, its duct-taped upholstery covered by a sheet, and indicated the chair, which was actually a little better. No duct tape, anyway.

He moved the stack of newspapers from the seat to the floor, then sat down, rested his forearms on his knees, hands clasped, and treated her to another hard stare. "Do your parents know you live here?"

"Of course they do," she said in surprise. "Of course they have my address."

"No," he insisted. "Do they know you live *here.*"

"Oh. Well, not exactly. But it really isn't that bad."

"It isn't, eh. So you feel safe, driving home from work at night."

"Uh...I don't exactly drive. I don't have a car." She gestured to the bike propped against the wall under the front window. "But I ride really fast," she said, trying a little laugh.

He swiveled to look at it, then stared back at her. "You weren't living like this in En Zed," he pointed out. "And that isn't cheap. So why?"

Because there was no Kristen here, that was why. And because she needed to save. But why was she answering him?

"First of all," she said, struggling to gain some semblance of power in this conversation, "what gives you the right to come here and judge how I'm living?"

"Loving you," he said immediately, taking her breath away in a rush. "That's what gives me the bloody right. Loving you."

"Oh," she said weakly. "That isn't...the answer I was expecting."

"Why d'you think I'm here?" he demanded. "I've been trying to find you since I got back from Argentina, and that was four weeks ago. Why didn't you let Kristen know where you were sooner?"

"Because I wanted to wait till I got a job and a place. I didn't want to worry her."

"Where were you staying before, then?"

"Couch-surfing," she admitted. "Staying with friends, friends of friends. Moving around a little. Don't want to wear out your welcome, you know."

He closed his eyes for a moment as if he were in pain. "People you didn't even know."

"Well, yeah. Sometimes. It was fine. I was lucky to find people willing to do it. I was pretty broke when I got back here, after the plane ticket."

"Your parents, though," he suggested.

"My parents what?" she challenged, starting to get annoyed now.

"Why didn't you ask them for help? Why didn't you ask Kristen? Why didn't you ask *me?*"

"That'd be pretty adult of me, wouldn't it, asking my parents to bail me out? Never mind my ex-boyfriend, who dumped me, whom I've just *humiliated* in front of the whole country. I was supposed to come begging to you? Don't you think I have any pride at all?"

"I think you have too bloody much pride," he muttered. "And that—" He waved a hand. "That online thing, those photos. I've already checked into that. One reason I wanted to find you. You need to come back so you can file a report."

"What? What are you talking about?"

"You didn't pose for those photos," he said with certainty. "I know you didn't."

She hadn't thought she could be any more mortified, thought she'd been to the bottom and had put the whole painful episode behind her. But looking at Nate, knowing he'd seen those pictures, knowing he'd seen the visual proof that Devon had taken them, that Devon had seen her like that...it was the worst.

"No," she said quietly. "I didn't. He must have had a camera somewhere."

Nate nodded. "He probably did it to everybody he slept with, because that's the kind of scungy bastard he is. And then, when he knew we were involved, he realized he could use them. Waited for his chance until I was down already, until he could sink the boot in, embarrass me as much as possible. Because that's why he did it. You were just the means. That's what makes me so bloody furious. He didn't have the balls to come after me, so he used you. But you need to come back," he repeated. "Because what he did, it was a violation, and it's a crime. You need to tell the police that he took those photos without your knowledge, without your consent. You need to file a complaint. I'd rather do him over myself," he said, and the look on his face gave Ally no doubt at all that he meant it, "but he's gone to the U.K., is working there. He'd gone by the time I got back from Argentina. That was his last shot, his farewell fuck-you to me, and you got caught in the crossfire."

"But if he's in the U.K.," she said, "they can't prosecute anyway."

"You can file a complaint," he insisted. "At least we'd both have the satisfaction of knowing that if he ever did come back, he wouldn't just be getting the beating of his life, he'd be facing prosecution as well. I've already put the word in to some fellas I know in the U.K., and he's not going to be getting too far over there, either. And once you report it, we can arrange for that to be leaked to the media so they know what he did. Give him a taste of humiliation himself, let him see what it feels like."

"I don't know..." She hesitated. Revenge sounded so good, but..."I'm not sure if I could stand to bring it up all over again. It's bad enough to know those pictures will never go away. But, Nate." Hard as it was to do it, she looked him in the eye. She hated talking about this, but she had to. It was there between them, and it always would be. "If I came back to New Zealand, especially if you had anything to do with me, it would all flare back up again and embarrass you even more. And you don't want that in your life. I know you don't."

"D'you think that's the last thing that'll come up in our lives to test us?" he demanded. "Because it isn't. It's the first thing. We start with this, and we find out we can do it. We find out that what matters is us, the two of us. And then, when the next bad time comes along, we can face it together and know that we're going to come out on the other side."

He went on more gently, his eyes intent on hers. "If this keeps you from coming back to me, he's won. I know you don't want to let him win, and I sure as hell don't, either. I want *us* to win, and the way we do that is to be together. That's what I want, and I came here to see if it's what you want. Or to see if I could talk you into giving it another go," he said, with a smile that she could tell he was forcing. "Come back with me, Ally. Pack your things right now and come back with me."

She'd begun shaking her head halfway through his speech. "It wouldn't work. I can't do it."

"Why not?" The smile was gone. "Are you telling me you don't care about me anymore? Because I don't believe it."

He was interrupted by the sound of the door opening behind him. And a man's voice.

"Hi, honey! I'm home!"

She saw Nate whirl, stand up fast as Jim stepped inside, juggling a couple of grocery bags while he shot the deadbolt into place.

"You didn't lock the door, Ally," he said. "You need to be more careful."

He turned and noticed Nate for the first time, faltered to a stop. And Ally could guess, from the look that crossed Jim's face, what he was reading on Nate's.

"Hey," Jim faltered.

Ally was on her feet now too, her hand on Nate's arm. "This is my friend from New Zealand," she told Jim. "This is Nate. And this," she said to Nate, emphasizing every word, "is my *roommate.* Jim."

"Yeah," Jim said. "I'll just dump these," he said, lifting the bags with a nervous laugh. "In the kitchen."

"Stop it," Ally hissed to Nate. "Stop it right now and sit down."

"What?" he asked. Well, really, it was more of a growl. But he sat, to her relief.

"I'll be in my room," Jim said, popping his head back around the corner. "If you, you know. If you need me." He shot one more look at Nate and was gone.

"Not my boyfriend," Ally said firmly as she heard Jim's door closing. "My roommate. And no business of yours if he was. Because you didn't *want* me, Nate. I didn't leave you. You let me go."

"I know," he said, looking down at his hands. "I know I did. And I was wrong. I hurt you over and over again. I know I did. And that *is* my business," he said fiercely, his eyes meeting hers again. They weren't ice anymore. They were fire. "Because we belong together. I know we do. I know that now, too. And I don't believe that you don't care about me anymore. You can't sit there and tell me you don't."

"I care about you." She wished so much that she could believe him, that she could accept what he was saying, that she didn't know better. But she'd done too much thinking in the past month for that. She forced herself to keep looking him in the eye, determined to be honest with him, and with herself, if it killed her. Which, right now, it felt like it just might do.

"I care about you too much to come back with you, knowing it wouldn't work," she tried to explain. "I went to New Zealand in the first place because I was running away. Trying to escape from my unsatisfactory job, my unsatisfactory relationship. Thinking that if I ran that far, I'd be able to hide from the fact that I still hadn't figured out what I wanted to be when I grew up. Because women can be Peter Pan too," she said with a choked laugh. "Hey, I just realized something. I was Peter Pan, and you were Wendy."

"I was *Wendy?*" he protested. "Ally…"

"No, wait. Let me finish. So I ran away. Into, guess what? Another unsatisfactory job, another unsatisfactory relationship. Because it's what they say, isn't it? Wherever you go, there you are."

"It wasn't unsatisfactory, though," he argued. "It was good. It was right. I know that now. Ever since I let you go, I've missed you so much, and I need you back. I need to make up for everything I did wrong. Please, Ally. Please give me another chance to get it right."

"I can't," she said sadly. "I can't fit into the spaces that are left after rugby. Because that's always going to come first for you. First, last, and always. You belong to rugby body and soul, I've realized that. It's the one best thing in your life. You were my one best thing, and I needed to be yours, and I never will be. And I can't live with that. I'm not saying that to make you feel bad," she hurried to explain. "I'm saying, that's how it is. That's how it has to be. You can't get distracted, and I can't either, not anymore. I need to *do* something with my life, Nate. I've got a goal now. You helped me see that I needed to do that. I've got it now, and I need to accomplish it."

She reached for one of her brochures on the end table, handed it across to him. "Look. Graduate school in sports management. That's me, next fall. I'm saving. I'm working on my applications. I'm checking out student loans. And someday, somehow, I'm opening my own gym. I'm doing it. I'm going for it. And I'm growing up."

"That's awesome," he said slowly, turning the brightly colored brochure in his hand, looking at the image of a smiling young man standing amongst an array of weight machines. "But what about me?"

"What *about* you? You'll be good. You'll be *great*. You'll do what you do, lead your team. Your teams. Win rugby games. Because you're a great player, Nate." She could feel herself beginning to choke up, and went on regardless. "A great captain. A great leader. The way you kept them all going, kept them fighting, came so close to winning the Championship after all. The way you played in Argentina, especially, because that was the turning point, wasn't it? I finally watched it on YouTube last week, and what I saw was a captain who lifted his entire team. I saw them rising to match you, playing for you. They're going to walk through fire for you, you'll see. Because you're going to be walking right in front of them, leading the way."

He looked down at the piece of paper in his hands again, seemed to be having some kind of conversation with himself, then shifted onto the couch next to her, set the brochure carefully back onto the stack, and, finally, turned to face her.

"I've learnt heaps this year," he said, taking her hand. "It's been the hardest, and the best, and the worst year of my life. And one of the things I've learnt is that I need something beyond rugby in my life. You're right that I love it. I always have. It's been my dream and my passion since I can remember, and as long as that fire burns, as long as the body holds up, I'll be out there every week, giving it everything I've got. But body and soul..." he went on. "That's not the way I belong to rugby. That's the way I want to belong to you, and the way I want you to belong to me, too. Because the best things this year... so many of them were the times I spent with you. And because it's been so bloody hard to do this, these past weeks, without you with me. I finally realized that even when you weren't *with* me, you were still...with me, before. When you were with me, I mean."

He stopped in confusion. "I'm not making any sense, am I?"

"I think I'm getting it," she said, feeling like she'd been running too fast, because she was having trouble getting her breath. "But keep going."

He clutched her hand tighter, turned his gaze on her with that focus, that intensity that was all Nate. "I should've practiced this," he muttered. "Right. Start again."

He took a deep breath, and began. "In my heart, I mean." He laid one big palm across his chest. "I realized that I had you with me here, inside, even when I was gone. And knowing I was in your heart too, knowing that you were there, loving me—that mattered. Reckon that mattered most of all."

His quick, sweet smile appeared for just a moment. "And besides, I need to lighten up, remember? I need to work easier. I need somebody to love me enough to make me take a break. Somebody to kidnap me and take me on a sex slave weekend. Somebody to make me laugh, and make me jealous, and make me send her flowers just because I love her, and I miss her, and I want to be with her. I need you to come back to me, because I need you to come home to."

"But it doesn't work, because we're not on the same level," she forced herself to say. Her heart was beating so hard that she was sure it must be visible, pumping in her chest. But they had to get this right. They had to work it out, because if they tried again and the same thing happened, she thought it just might destroy her. "We're not...even. I can't be just your fun. I can't be your recreation. I can't be your toy."

"And I don't want you to be," he promised, his hand firm around her own, those pale eyes locked on hers, everything in his face telegraphing how much he meant this. "Not my toy. That's not what I want. I want you to be my partner, and I want you to be everything you want to be. If that means going back to Uni for another course, then that's what you should do. But they have sport management courses in En Zed too, you know, and gyms as well. And that's where you—" He broke off, then went on again. "That's where I think you belong. Where I hope *you* think you belong. With me."

"I don't have a visa, though," she faltered. "Or the money."

"They have student visas," he insisted. "And you have somebody to help you get one, and to help you with the rest as well. Me. You have me. That's the whole idea, that we're helping each other. Supporting each other. Loving each other."

He shifted a little closer on the shabby couch. "I know I'm rubbish at relationships," he said. "I know it. But I'm trainable. I'm coachable. I can do most things if I try, and I'd be trying, I promise you that. Don't give up on me, Ally. Please don't, because I need you."

"If you really think..." She couldn't think how to say it, how to be sure. But he seemed to know, because his next words answered her. And the emotion was bubbling up from deep inside now, because what he was saying was exactly what she needed to hear.

"You don't have anything to prove to me," he insisted, and she could feel the tears welling, spilling over as he went on. "You don't have to be anything more than what you are, because what you are is awesome. You don't have to accomplish anything else for me to love you, because I already do. But if you need to do another course to get where you want to go, I'll do everything I can to help you do it. All I'm asking is, do it with me."

She brushed the tears away with one shaking hand, smiled back at him, although she could tell the smile was a little wobbly. "Even if I ruin your perfect image? Even if I get a speeding ticket? Even if I make you carry me off the beach?"

"Specially if you do that." His arms were around her at last, his eyes full of warmth. Full of love. "I want my Ally. I want *you*. I need you, and I love you, and I'm not leaving this...this absolutely disgusting flat without you."

She laughed, even as the tears continued to fall. "I want you too," she whispered, and felt the lightness of it, the rightness of it. Felt a burden she hadn't even realized she was carrying dropping from her. The burden of being alone, of living in the world without him.

And then she was moving closer, wrapping her arms around his neck, laying her head against his chest. Feeling him pulling her into him, where she fit. Where she belonged.

"I want you," she said again, louder this time. Wanting him to hear it, and to know it. "And I need you. And oh, Nate. I love you."

mr. most improved

♡

Fourteen months later

Ally broke off in mid-sentence as Nate stood beside her and raised his glass. Conversation at the big table gradually ceased, until all nine pairs of eyes were turned to him in expectation.

"Should know how to give a speech by now," he said with a little laugh, "but I'm a bit nervous, tell you the truth. I'm not really used to talking about anything but footy. But I'll give it a go. So—here's to Ally," he said, looking around the restaurant table. Seeing, Ally thought, everyone he'd brought together to celebrate this milestone with them, to make sure her day was as special as it could possibly be. His parents, her parents, Liam and Kristen, Ned and Mel.

"To Ally," he went on, "because she's awesome, and as of today, she's awesome with a certificate in Sport Management as well. Because she's worked so hard," he said, giving her his special smile, "and because she's made all that hard work pay off, and because I know this is just the beginning."

He raised his glass. "To Ally," he finished, and she heard the others echo his words.

He leaned down and gave her a kiss. "So proud of you," he murmured in her ear, and she thought her heart would actually melt.

"OK." She stood up in her turn as Nate sat again. "I don't have any experience at all making speeches, but if there's one thing I've learned from Nate, it's that if you never start, you'll never get anywhere. So I guess I'd better start."

She cleared her throat, tried to think how to begin. She wished she'd prepared something, but she'd been so focused on getting through to today for so many months now, she hadn't dared to look beyond it. And now the day was here, and she had made it and it felt even better than the day when Nate had told her that Devon had lost his job with his English soccer club, and that he wouldn't be getting another. She liked to think of him working in a paper hat somewhere, asking people if they wanted fries with that. Well, really, she didn't bother to think of him much at all anymore. Because Nate was right. She had won. *They* had won.

"I guess I should just say thanks," she said now. "Because I have so much to be thankful for. First of all, to Kristen."

She looked across the table at her friend, looking more beautiful than ever, shining with happiness and hugely pregnant with the baby girl due at the beginning of the new year. "For keeping me company while the guys were gone," she continued. "For listening to all my ideas for my business plan, and reading my final paper so many times. For showing me that it's possible to change your life. For bringing me to New Zealand, and for being such a good friend to me. I love you, Kristen. Almost as much as Liam does. You're the best."

She went on as best she could over the lump in her throat. "And to my parents. Thanks, Mom and Dad, for not giving up on me even when I disappointed you. I know it took a long time for me to grow up, and you must have wondered if it would ever happen. I hope I can make you proud."

"Oh, sweetheart." Her mother was choking up too, Ally could tell. "You've always made us proud. Although," she added with a watery laugh, reaching in her purse for a tissue, "I could wish that you hadn't chosen to change your life from quite so far away."

"You'll just have to come visit more often," Ally said firmly. "After two beach Christmases, you're going to be too spoiled to stay in the snow anyway."

She looked at Nate's parents next. "And to Georgia and Frank, of course, for doing such a good job being my surrogate parents this year, and making me feel so welcome. Thank you."

"You know that's been nothing but a pleasure, darling," Georgia said.

"She's just happy to see Nate settled at last, that's the truth of it," Frank added gruffly.

Retirement suited them, Ally thought. Nate's dad had seemed a bit lost at first, but he'd found a new calling in helping to coach one of the local rugby teams, and it was only a matter of time, she suspected, before he was elected president of the Gore Rugby Club. Some people just ended up in charge, no matter what, and Frank was one of them. And so was his son.

She looked down at Nate, sitting back, looking so proud, letting her have her moment, and lost a little more of her composure.

"I guess I'd better say the most important thing," she decided. "Though I don't even know how to start. Thanks for believing in me. Thanks for supporting me through this. Thanks," and the tears were there now, refusing to be denied, "thanks for loving me."

"Nah," he said, and he was looking a bit rocky now, too. "It's the other way round, isn't it. Though I do think I deserve one thing. I reckon I win 'Most Improved' in this relationship. Which means, as we all know, that I was rubbish at the start, and yet I'm still here, still giving it a go, and maybe not quite such rubbish anymore."

"Congratulations, then." She pulled him up with her, unable to resist giving him a quick kiss, just because she loved him so much, and it had been such a long five weeks without him. "Mr. Most Improved. And before I forget," she added, "because it's such a tiny little thing, we'll just say congratulations on another successful European Tour. And what was that other thing? Oh, yeah. The Rugby Championship."

"Think we both know which one was the real achievement. Because I wasn't sure I'd make it." His arms were around her now. "A couple times there, admit, you were ready to give up on me."

"Never." She put everything she had into it, because he needed to know this one thing for sure. "I'll never give up on you. I may get mad at you from time to time, but I'll never give up on you."

She laughed a little, raised a hand to swipe at her eyes. "And, shoot. You've got me crying again, and this is the world's longest speech. So," she announced, lifting her glass from the shelter of Nate's arms, "everybody, I'll just say, thanks."

♡

"Am I done?" she begged him as everyone at the table raised their glasses in return. Everyone who mattered most to both of them, everyone who needed to hear what he had to say next. "I don't know how you do that. That's *hard.*"

"You're almost done," he promised. "Just got a bit of listening to do now, because I've got one more thing to say." He took her glass from her, set it down with his own. "This is going to be a tough one for me too," he told her. "Hoping you'll give me a pass if I stuff up. But you've done that so many times now, what's one more?"

His heart began to pound as he took both her hands in his, turned her to face him. Beating harder than it had during the most important rugby game he'd ever played, because it was beating for her now, and she mattered more than anything ever had.

"Two years ago today," he began, "I met you. And I made a pretty bad impression, and then I made a worse one. And after that," he said with a smile for her that she returned, though her eyes had widened, and she didn't seem to be breathing any too easily herself, "I *really* notched up a couple of Epic Fails. And even though that day didn't go too well," he went on, trying to tell her with his eyes everything he held in his heart, "I'm glad for every single minute of it. Because meeting you was the best thing that's ever happened to me."

He saw the stillness that had settled over everyone at the table, and hoped he could get this right. "Can't do this quite like Mako," he said with a laugh that didn't sound any too convincing. "If I tried to sing, you'd be sure to say no. I'm going to do my best to say what I'm feeling, and hope that it's enough. And it's this. You've frustrated me like nobody ever has. You've got under my skin, and you've turned my head all the way around, and you've made me lose control. And you've made me happier than anybody ever has too. You've been the best thing in my life, and I need you so much. And I'm going to keep on needing you forever."

His voice wasn't one bit steady anymore, and the hands holding hers were shaking. "So," he finished, "what I'm trying to say is, I love you, and I'm asking you to marry me. I'm asking you to walk out of here with me and go find a ring that's big enough and beautiful enough to say everything I can't. Because two years with you isn't nearly enough. Because I need it to be forever, and I need it to start here and now."

"Oh, Nate." She'd lost it entirely, the tears spilling down her cheeks, and he could see that his mum, and her mum, and Kristen, and Mel had all joined her, and that Mako wasn't looking too steady, either. And he hoped, he really hoped, that nobody was filming this, because he had a bad feeling that he might be crying, too.

"Yes," she managed to say at last. "Yes, I'll marry you. Of course I will. But I have to ask." She was laughing up at him through her tears, her brown eyes sparkling. His sweetheart. His one best thing. His Ally. "Two years? Exactly? How do you know?"

"How d'you think?" He laughed back at her, and he was holding her in his arms now. Holding her tight. Holding her in his heart, the way he would be every day. Every single day, until the day he died. "I calendared it."

The End

Sign up for my New Release mailing list at www.rosalindjames.com/mail-list to be notified of special pricing on new books, sales, and more.

Turn the page for a Kiwi glossary and a preview of the next book in the series.

a kiwi glossary

A few notes about Maori pronunciation:
- The accent is normally on the first syllable.
- All vowels are pronounced separately.
- All vowels except u have a short vowel sound.
- "wh" is pronounced "f."
- "ng" is pronounced as in "singer," not as in "anger."

ABs: All Blacks

across the Ditch: in Australia (across the Tasman Sea). Or, if you're in Australia, in New Zealand!

advert: commercial

agro: aggravation

air con: air conditioning

All Blacks: National rugby team. Members are selected for every series from amongst the five NZ Super 15 teams. The All Blacks play similarly selected teams from other nations.

ambo: paramedic

Aotearoa: New Zealand (the other official name, meaning "The Land of the Long White Cloud" in Maori)

arvo, this arvo: afternoon

Aussie, Oz: Australia. (An Australian is also an Aussie. Pronounced "Ozzie.")

bach: holiday home (pronounced like "bachelor")

backs: rugby players who aren't in the scrum and do more running, kicking, and ball-carrying—though all players do all jobs and play both offense and defense. Backs tend to be faster and leaner than forwards.

bangers and mash: sausages and potatoes

barrack for: cheer for

bench: counter (kitchen bench)

berko: berserk

Big Smoke: the big city (usually Auckland)

bikkies: cookies

billy-o, like billy-o: like crazy. "I paddled like billy-o and just barely made it through that rapid."

bin, rubbish bin: trash can

bit of a dag: a comedian, a funny guy

bits and bobs: stuff ("be sure you get all your bits and bobs")

blood bin: players leaving field for injury

Blues: Auckland's Super 15 team

bollocks: rubbish, nonsense

boofhead: fool, jerk

booking: reservation

boots and all: full tilt, no holding back

bot, the bot: flu, a bug

Boxing Day: December 26—a holiday

brekkie: breakfast

brilliant: fantastic

bub: baby, small child

buggered: messed up, exhausted

bull's roar: close. "They never came within a bull's roar of winning."

bunk off: duck out, skip (bunk off school)

bust a gut: do your utmost, make a supreme effort

Cake Tin: Wellington's rugby stadium (not the official name, but it looks exactly like a springform pan)

caravan: travel trailer

cardie: a cardigan sweater

chat up: flirt with

chilly bin: ice chest

chips: French fries. (potato chips are "crisps")

chocolate bits: chocolate chips

chocolate fish: pink or white marshmallow coated with milk chocolate, in the shape of a fish. A common treat/reward for kids (and for adults. You often get a chocolate fish on the saucer when you order a mochaccino—a mocha).

choice: fantastic

chokka: full

chooks: chickens

Chrissy: Christmas

chuck out: throw away

chuffed: pleased

collywobbles: nervous tummy, upset stomach

come a greaser: take a bad fall

costume, cossie: swimsuit (female only)

cot: crib (for a baby)

crook: ill

cuddle: hug (give a cuddle)

cuppa: a cup of tea (the universal remedy)

CV: resumé

cyclone: hurricane (Southern Hemisphere)

dairy: corner shop (not just for milk!)

dead: very; e.g., "dead sexy."

dill: fool

do your block: lose your temper

dob in: turn in; report to authorities. Frowned upon.

doco: documentary

doddle: easy. "That'll be a doddle."

dodgy: suspect, low-quality

dogbox: The doghouse—in trouble

dole: unemployment.

dole bludger: somebody who doesn't try to get work and lives off unemployment (which doesn't have a time limit in NZ)

Domain: a good-sized park; often the "official" park of the town.

dressing gown: bathrobe

drongo: fool (Australian, but used sometimes in NZ as well)

drop your gear: take off your clothes

duvet: comforter

earbashing: talking-to, one-sided chat

electric jug: electric teakettle to heat water. Every Kiwi kitchen has one.

En Zed: Pronunciation of NZ. ("Z" is pronounced "Zed.")

ensuite: master bath (a bath in the bedroom).

eye fillet: premium steak (filet mignon)

fair go: a fair chance. Kiwi ideology: everyone deserves a fair go.

fair wound me up: Got me very upset

fantail: small, friendly native bird

farewelled, he'll be farewelled: funeral; he'll have his funeral.

feed, have a feed: meal

first five, first five-eighth: rugby back—does most of the big kicking jobs and is the main director of the backs. Also called the No. 10.

fixtures: playing schedule

fizz, fizzie: soft drink

fizzing: fired up

flaked out: tired

flash: fancy

flat to the boards: at top speed

flat white: most popular NZ coffee. An espresso with milk but no foam.

flattie: roommate

flicks: movies

flying fox: zipline

footpath: sidewalk

footy, football: rugby

forwards: rugby players who make up the scrum and do the most physical battling for position. Tend to be bigger and more heavily muscled than backs.

fossick about: hunt around for something

front up: face the music, show your mettle

garden: yard

get on the piss: get drunk

get stuck in: commit to something

give way: yield

giving him stick, give him some stick about it: teasing, needling

glowworms: larvae of a fly found only in NZ. They shine a light to attract insects. Found in caves or other dark, moist places.

go crook, be crook: go wrong, be ill

go on the turps: get drunk

gobsmacked: astounded

good hiding: beating ("They gave us a good hiding in Dunedin.")

grotty: grungy, badly done up

ground floor: what we call the first floor. The "first floor" is one floor up.

gumboots, gummies: knee-high rubber boots. It rains a lot in New Zealand.

gutted: thoroughly upset

Haast's Eagle: (extinct). Huge native NZ eagle. Ate moa.

haere mai: Maori greeting

haka: ceremonial Maori challenge—done before every All Blacks game

hang on a tick: wait a minute

hard man: the tough guy, the enforcer

hard yakka: hard work (from Australian)

harden up: toughen up. Standard NZ (male) response to (male) complaints: "Harden the f*** up!"

have a bit on: I have placed a bet on [whatever]. Sports gambling and prostitution are both legal in New Zealand.

have a go: try

Have a nosy for…: look around for

head: principal (headmaster)

head down: or head down, bum up. Put your head down. Work hard.

heaps: lots. "Give it heaps."

hei toki: pendant (Maori)

holiday: vacation

honesty box: a small stand put up just off the road with bags of fruit and vegetables and a cash box. Very common in New Zealand.

hooker: rugby position (forward)

hooning around: driving fast, wannabe tough-guy behavior (typically young men)

hoovering: vacuuming (after the brand of vacuum cleaner)

ice block: popsicle

I'll see you right: I'll help you out

in form: performing well (athletically)

it's not on: It's not all right

iwi: tribe (Maori)

jabs: immunizations, shots

jandals: flip-flops. (This word is only used in New Zealand. Jandals and gumboots are the iconic Kiwi footwear.)

jersey: a rugby shirt, or a pullover sweater

joker: a guy. "A good Kiwi joker": a regular guy; a good guy.

journo: journalist

jumper: a heavy pullover sweater

ka pai: going smoothly (Maori).

kapa haka: school singing group (Maori songs/performances. Any student can join, not just Maori.)

karanga: Maori song of welcome (done by a woman)

keeping his/your head down: working hard

kia ora: welcome (Maori, but used commonly)

kilojoules: like calories—measure of food energy

kindy: kindergarten (this is 3- and 4-year-olds)

kit, get your kit off: clothes, take off your clothes

Kiwi: New Zealander OR the bird. If the person, it's capitalized. Not the fruit.

kiwifruit: the fruit. (Never called simply a "kiwi.")

knackered: exhausted

knockout rounds: playoff rounds (quarterfinals, semifinals, final)

koru: ubiquitous spiral Maori symbol of new beginnings, hope

kumara: Maori sweet potato.

ladder: standings (rugby)

littlies: young kids

lock: rugby position (forward)

lollies: candy

lolly: candy or money

lounge: living room

mad as a meat axe: crazy

maintenance: child support

major: "a major." A big deal, a big event

mana: prestige, earned respect, spiritual power

Maori: native people of NZ—though even they arrived relatively recently from elsewhere in Polynesia

marae: Maori meeting house

Marmite: Savory Kiwi yeast-based spread for toast. An acquired taste. (Kiwis swear it tastes different from Vegemite, the Aussie version.)

mate: friend. And yes, fathers call their sons "mate."

metal road: gravel road

Milo: cocoa substitute; hot drink mix

mind: take care of, babysit

moa: (extinct) Any of several species of huge flightless NZ birds. All eaten by the Maori before Europeans arrived.

moko: Maori tattoo

mokopuna: grandchildren

motorway: freeway

mozzie: mosquito; OR a Maori Australian (Maori + Aussie = Mozzie)

muesli: like granola, but unbaked

munted: broken

naff: stupid, unsuitable. "Did you get any naff Chrissy pressies this year?"

nappy: diaper

narked, narky: annoyed

netball: Down-Under version of basketball for women. Played like basketball, but the hoop is a bit narrower, the players wear skirts, and they don't dribble and can't contact each other. It can look fairly tame to an American eye. There are professional netball teams, and it's televised and taken quite seriously.

new caps: new All Blacks—those named to the side for the first time

New World: One of the two major NZ supermarket chains

nibbles: snacks

nick, in good nick: doing well

niggle, niggly: small injury, ache or soreness

no worries: no problem. The Kiwi mantra.

No. 8: rugby position. A forward

not very flash: not feeling well

Nurofen: brand of ibuprofen

nutted out: worked out

OE: Overseas Experience—young people taking a year or two overseas, before or after University.

offload: pass (rugby)

oldies: older people. (or for the elderly, "wrinklies!")

on the front foot: Having the advantage. Vs. on the back foot—at a disadvantage. From rugby.

Op Shop: charity shop, secondhand shop

out on the razzle: out drinking too much, getting crazy

paddock: field (often used for rugby—"out on the paddock")

Pakeha: European-ancestry people (as opposed to Polynesians)

Panadol: over-the-counter painkiller

partner: romantic partner, married or not

patu: Maori club

paua, paua shell: NZ abalone

pavlova (pav): Classic Kiwi Christmas (summer) dessert. Meringue, fresh fruit (often kiwifruit and strawberries) and whipped cream.

pavement: sidewalk (generally on wider city streets)

pear-shaped, going pear-shaped: messed up, when it all goes to Hell

penny dropped: light dawned (figured it out)

people mover: minivan

perve: stare sexually

phone's engaged: phone's busy

piece of piss: easy

pike out: give up, wimp out

piss awful: very bad

piss up: drinking (noun) a piss-up

pissed: drunk

pissed as a fart: very drunk. And yes, this is an actual expression.

play up: act up

playing out of his skin: playing very well

plunger: French Press coffeemaker

PMT: PMS

pohutukawa: native tree; called the "New Zealand Christmas Tree" for its beautiful red blossoms at Christmastime (high summer)

poi: balls of flax on strings that are swung around the head, often to the accompaniment of singing and/or dancing by women. They make rhythmic patterns in the air, and it's very beautiful.

Pom, Pommie: English person

pop: pop over, pop back, pop into the oven, pop out, pop in

possie: position (rugby)

postie: mail carrier

pot plants: potted plants (not what you thought, huh?)

poumanu: greenstone (jade)

prang: accident (with the car)

pressie: present

puckaroo: broken (from Maori)

pudding: dessert

pull your head in: calm down, quit being rowdy

Pumas: Argentina's national rugby team

pushchair: baby stroller

put your hand up: volunteer

put your head down: work hard

rapt: thrilled

rattle your dags: hurry up. From the sound that dried excrement on a sheep's backside makes, when the sheep is running!

red card: penalty for highly dangerous play. The player is sent off for the rest of the game, and the team plays with 14 men.

rellies: relatives

riding the pine: sitting on the bench (as a substitute in a match)

rimu: a New Zealand tree. The wood used to be used for building and flooring, but like all native NZ trees, it was overlogged. Older houses, though, often have rimu floors, and they're beautiful.

Rippa: junior rugby

root: have sex (you DON'T root for a team!)

ropeable: very angry

ropey: off, damaged ("a bit ropey")

rort: ripoff

rough as guts: uncouth

rubbish bin: garbage can

rugby boots: rugby shoes with spikes (sprigs)

Rugby Championship: Contest played each year in the Southern Hemisphere by the national teams of NZ, Australia, South Africa, and Argentina

Rugby World Cup, RWC: World championship, played every four years amongst the top 20 teams in the world

rugged up: dressed warmly

ruru: native owl

Safa: South Africa. Abbreviation only used in NZ.

sammie: sandwich

scoff, scoffing: eating, like "snarfing"

second-five, second five-eighth: rugby back (No. 9). With the first-five, directs the game. Also feeds the scrum and generally collects the ball from the ball carrier at the breakdown and distributes it.

selectors: team of 3 (the head coach is one) who choose players for the All Blacks squad, for every series

serviette: napkin

shag: have sex with. A little rude, but not too bad.

shattered: exhausted

sheds: locker room (rugby)

she'll be right: See "no worries." Everything will work out. The other Kiwi mantra.

shift house: move (house)

shonky: shady (person). "a bit shonky"

shout, your shout, my shout, shout somebody a coffee: buy a round, treat somebody

sickie, throw a sickie: call in sick

sin bin: players sitting out 10-minute penalty in rugby (or, in the case of a red card, the rest of the game)

sink the boot in: kick you when you're down

skint: broke (poor)

skipper: (team) captain. Also called "the Skip."

slag off: speak disparagingly of; disrespect

smack: spank. Smacking kids is illegal in NZ.

smoko: coffee break

snog: kiss; make out with

sorted: taken care of

spa, spa pool: hot tub

sparrow fart: the crack of dawn

speedo: Not the swimsuit! Speedometer. (the swimsuit is called a budgie smuggler—a budgie is a parakeet, LOL.)

spew: vomit

spit the dummy: have a tantrum. (A dummy is a pacifier)

sportsman: athlete

sporty: liking sports

spot on: absolutely correct. "That's spot on. You're spot on."

Springboks, Boks: South African national rugby team

squiz: look. "I was just having a squiz round." "Giz a squiz": Give me a look at that.

stickybeak: nosy person, busybody

stonkered: drunk—a bit stonkered—or exhausted

stoush: bar fight, fight

straight away: right away

strength of it: the truth, the facts. "What's the strength of that?" = "What's the true story on that?"

stroppy: prickly, taking offense easily

stuffed up: messed up

Super 15: Top rugby competition: five teams each from NZ, Australia, South Africa. The New Zealand Super 15 teams are, from north to south: Blues (Auckland), Chiefs (Waikato/

Hamilton), Hurricanes (Wellington), Crusaders (Canterbury/Christchurch), Highlanders (Otago/Dunedin).

supporter: fan (Do NOT say "root for." "To root" is to have (rude) sex!)

suss out: figure out

sweet: dessert

sweet as: great. (also: choice as, angry as, lame as...Meaning "very" whatever. "Mum was angry as that we ate up all the pudding before tea with Nana.")

takahe: ground-dwelling native bird. Like a giant parrot.

takeaway: takeout (food)

tall poppy: arrogant person who puts himself forward or sets himself above others. It is every Kiwi's duty to cut down tall poppies, a job they undertake enthusiastically.

Tangata Whenua: Maori (people of the land)

tapu: sacred (Maori)

Te Papa: the National Museum, in Wellington

tea: dinner (casual meal at home)

tea towel: dishtowel

test match: international rugby match (e.g., an All Blacks game)

throw a wobbly: have a tantrum

tick off: cross off (tick off a list)

ticker: heart. "The boys showed a lot of ticker out there today."

togs: swimsuit (male or female)

torch: flashlight

touch wood: knock on wood (for luck)

track: trail

trainers: athletic shoes

tramping: hiking

transtasman: Australia/New Zealand (the Bledisloe Cup is a transtasman rivalry)

trolley: shopping cart

tucker: food

tui: Native bird

turn to custard: go south, deteriorate

turps, go on the turps: get drunk

Uni: University—or school uniform

up the duff: pregnant. A bit vulgar (like "knocked up")

ute: pickup or SUV

vet: check out

waiata: Maori song

wairua: spirit, soul (Maori). Very important concept.

waka: canoe (Maori)

Wallabies: Australian national rugby team

Warrant of Fitness: certificate of a car's fitness to drive

wedding tackle: the family jewels; a man's genitals

Weet-Bix: ubiquitous breakfast cereal

whaddarya?: I am dubious about your masculinity (meaning "Whaddarya…pussy?")

whakapapa: genealogy (Maori). A critical concept.

whanau: family (Maori). Big whanau: extended family. Small whanau: nuclear family.

wheelie bin: rubbish bin (garbage can) with wheels.

whinge: whine. Contemptuous! Kiwis dislike whingeing. Harden up!

White Ribbon: campaign against domestic violence

wind up: upset (perhaps purposefully). "Their comments were bound to wind him up."

wing: rugby position (back)

Yank: American. Not pejorative.

yellow card: A penalty for dangerous play that sends a player off for 10 minutes to the sin bin. The team plays with 14 men during that time—or even 13, if two are sinbinned.

yonks: ages. "It's been going on for yonks."

Find out what's new at the **ROSALIND JAMES WEBSITE.**
http://www.rosalindjames.com/

"Like" my <u>Facebook</u> page at facebook.com/rosalindjamesbooks
or follow me on <u>Twitter</u> at twitter.com/RosalindJames5
to learn about giveaways, events, and more.
Want to tell me what you liked, or what I got wrong? I'd love
to hear! You can email me at Rosalind@rosalindjames.com

by rosalind james

Cover design by Robin Ludwig Design Inc.,
http://www.gobookcoverdesign.com/

Read on for an excerpt from
Just Not Mine
(Escape to New Zealand, Book Six)

the combat zone

♡

Hugh Latimer had his eye on the ball.

Fifteen minutes left in the deciding game of the Rugby Championship, the score, despite every desperate effort, stuck at 14 to 6 in favor of the Springboks, and the capacity crowd of fifty thousand South Africans at Loftus Verfeld was sniffing victory, baying for All Black blood.

The noise was a physical thing, an assault, but it didn't matter. There was no pain, no sweat, no fear. Only one thing mattered. Where was the ball, and how could he get to it and take it back.

The Boks were moving fast. Jan Strauss, the blazing winger, took the pass and was off with a burst of acceleration. Hugh read the tiny movement of his head that signaled one of his deceptive jukes, saw the line he was aiming for, and was into space in that fraction of a second to cut him off. He brought him down in a bone-jarring tackle a bare five meters from the tryline, sprang to his feet and went for the ball, keeping his balance to avoid the penalty that would put the chance of victory beyond reach. He planted both feet hard and solid, kept his body weight low, and used every bit of strength in his hands, arms, and shoulders to wrest the ball loose from Jan's grasp.

He was aware of Liam Mahaka barreling in in support, his ferocity, as always, undiminished by the gash to his head that had sent him to the blood bin for stapling minutes earlier. But Hugh wasn't thinking about that either. He kept his focus on the ball. That was his target. That was his only goal.

He felt the moment when he won, began to pull the ball to his side of the line even as he saw all hundred-twenty kilos of Flip van der Jongh bearing down on him in a desperate attempt to wrest it back. Flip's right eye was nearly closed, the area around it angry, red, and swollen, the injury only increasing his determination. Flip dove, his elbow cracked into Hugh's left hand where he had the ball in a death grip, and Hugh didn't let go, because that wasn't an option.

He barely felt the impact at all, because the ref was blowing his whistle, and the ball belonged to the All Blacks, and he had won. He sent the ball fast to Nate Torrance for distribution, and saw, as he got himself back into position, that Toro had immediately offloaded it himself to Nic Wilkinson behind the tryline, who got it off his left foot and safely to midfield. The try was saved, the disaster averted. For now.

Hugh wasn't celebrating. He was sprinting the moment the ball left Nico's foot, calculating angles, assessing the Boks' positions. Jean le Vieux, the centre, was running straight at Kevin McNicholl as Hugh had expected, testing the buggered foot that had been obvious from twenty minutes into the match. Kevin threw himself in for the tackle with undiminished courage, and Hugh was there in support, going for the ball again.

Except that he couldn't, because his left hand was crocked. He'd hardly noticed the pain, but he couldn't move his thumb, couldn't grab at all, couldn't tackle. He was useless.

No hope. No choice. He was jogging off the field, his replacement running on. His game was over, and he was on the sideline with an ice pack strapped to his hand, ten minutes left in the match and the big screen still showing 14 to 6, two scores away from a win, and nothing left to do but watch.

He had something cheering to watch, for a while. Four minutes out, and the All Blacks were driving. Koti James had the ball, was breaking the line, throwing a head-fake one way, making a couple seemingly impossible changes of direction, drawing three tacklers and offloading the ball at the last possible half-second out the back door, a quick flip from his left hand to Nate. The ball in and out of the skipper's hands in a flash, and before the Springboks could react, Kevin again, somehow still managing to run on that foot, crashing his big frame over the tryline in the corner, miraculously keeping his left foot off the chalk that marked the touchline, and Hugh was rising with the rest of the men on the bench in exultation, because that was surely a try, and they were in with a chance.

But both men had paid the price. Koti had been hit so hard his mouthpiece had gone flying, he'd crashed to the turf in a heap and hadn't risen again, and Kevin had pounded that foot once too often and was hobbling up now, trying to get back to midfield, but he wasn't going to make it. The medic was bent over a still-prone Koti even as Nico was nailing the kick and making the score 14 to 13, which was so close, but Koti and Kevin were gone too, and the chances had just got even slimmer.

Every man on the field was digging deep, giving everything he had, but there wasn't enough time, and nothing the All Blacks could do to knock the ball loose from the Springboks' grip as they held on, this match as important to them as to their New Zealand counterparts, because if New Zealand's blood ran black, South Africa's ran green.

Three minutes. Two minutes. Sixty seconds. The clock ticked down, and still the Springboks held the ball. The hooter sounded, a Bok kicked the ball into touch, and the game was lost, and so was the Championship.

You played the match you got on the night, played what was in front of you with all your heart and all your passion and every last bit of drive and determination and strength you could screw out of your body and your soul. You played for your teammates, and for the jersey, and for your country, and for mana.

And sometimes, it wasn't enough.

a trained professional

♡

D r. Eva Parker opened her white lab coat to reveal what she was
wearing beneath it, smiled in slow satisfaction at the reaction
in the shocked eyes that were definitely *not* staring into her own.

Her outfit matched the coat, if sheer white lace could ever be
said to match starched white cotton. A hard-working, low-cut
demibra offered up her full, round breasts like treats on a shelf,
while the tiniest thong curved over the perfectly smooth, perfectly moisturized skin of her rigorously-dieted hips, highlighted
her absolutely, positively flat stomach. A diamond winked from
the concave slit that was her navel, and a suspender belt kept her
stockings clinging to the endless legs that tapered to the exclamation point of the killer black heels she always wore at work.
Unless she was in the operating room, of course.

"Eva." Bruce Dixon, the hospital's administrative officer,
groaned out the word. "I'm a married man."

"My favorite kind," she purred. Her fingers worked through
his neatly combed blond hair, lingered on his smoothly shaved
cheek, then traveled downward to splay against his chest. But
not for long, because her hand was on a mission now, a heat-
seeking missile homing in on its target, stroking down and down
as she watched his eyes glaze, as she touched his abdomen with
the lightest of caresses, landing at last on his belt buckle, her

long, slim fingers with their red-polished nails playing with the leather strip, letting him know that she was more than ready to take it off, that he was well and truly hers.

"Ah, yes. My *very* favorite kind." Her voice was low, sensuous, full of promise. "The *talented* kind. Because I can tell you've got a major talent right here. Talents are meant to be used, you know. I can't wait to see how you'll use yours. I plan to use it myself, too, be warned. And be afraid." She smiled, a red-lipsticked thing that was pure predator. "Because I plan to use it, to use you, until you're begging for mercy."

"I can't just make ethics charges go away," he protested, sounding weaker by the moment.

"Of course you can." She took hold of his necktie, leaned against his desk, and pulled him into her. She gave him a long, slow kiss, saw his eyes closing, felt every lingering bit of his reserve weakening, and smiled again. She was seductive, oh, yes, she was. She was deadly. She was a man-eater, a Black Widow, and she loved it.

"A man as powerful as you," she told him, sweeping an arm behind her to send his pile of files tumbling to the floor, "can do anything. Anything you like."

"And…cut!" Mike said with satisfaction. "That one's in the can."

Josie sat up, let go of Clive's tie, and grinned at him. "Got you going there, didn't I?"

"I am a trained professional," he said, grinning back at her. "Just like you."

♡

acknowledgments

My sincere thanks to those who aided
in the research for this book:
Christchurch earthquakes and geology: Joel
Bensing; Marlene Villeneuve, Ph.D., Lecturer in
Engineering Geology, University of Canterbury
Fashion, merchandising, and the beauty burden: Erika Iiams
Rock climbing: James Nolting, Rick Nolting

As always, my heartfelt thanks to my awesome critique group:
Barbara Buchanan, Carol Chappell, Anne Forell, and Bob Pryor.

Cover design by Robin Ludwig Design Inc.,
http://www.gobookcoverdesign.com/

Made in the USA
San Bernardino, CA
15 February 2019